COVEN

Kana is a rare male witch ostracized by his coven. When he claims two familiars, rather than the standard one, he knows he has to run away to keep his coven from taking advantage of his power. After years of constantly looking over his shoulder, Kana realizes he should have been paying better attention to what's right in front of him. He's drawn the interest of a different sort of coven: vampires.

Vampires, and the werewolves who protect them, want power, and Kana has a lot of that. Even with the support of his familiars, Kana isn't sure if he'll survive the attentions of the vampires. Except, perhaps it's the werewolves, and one handsome wolf in particular, that Kana ought to be afraid of.

HUNTER

Kana never dreamed he would be affiliated with a werewolf pack, but when Alpha Ember asks Kana for a favor, Kana agrees. However, helping Ember and his wolves means exposing Kana's existence to the larger magical community. Breaking his safety net is something Kana doesn't take lightly, but if it means Ember might finally notice him, Kana is willing to try.

Unfortunately, actions have consequences. A magic hunter is on the way to the city, and Kana is worried he's the target. Laying low in the company of werewolves isn't as easy as Kana hoped, and when the hunter turns his focus on Kana, Kana quickly realizes the pack and Ember might be the ones who suffer as a result.

WITCH

Kana spent his life hiding from those who might take advantage of his power. Now that he's living with his lover, werewolf Alpha Ember, hiding is impossible. However, living in the open means accepting the inherent risks. Kana hopes he and Ember together are strong enough to survive whatever might come. Then a new witch moves to town.

Dealing with the witch should be the most important thing for Kana, the pack, and their allies, but something else is lurking in the shadows—something dark, and evil, whose only goal is to destroy everything Kana holds dear.

WITCH'S CIRCLE

The Complete Series

Mell Eight

COVEN

Prologue

THE CIRCLE WAS ready. Though only white chalk lines on a black, chalkboard-painted floor, the circle had taken an hour to draw. Each line was perfect, from the arc of the circle to the straight lines and exact angles of the points of the pentagram. Even the runes, drawn between the lines of the star, were as impeccable as any Kana had ever drawn.

Kana studied the circle, then let out a relieved breath when he didn't see a single flaw. The room in the special building for advanced spells was empty; no one had come to watch his initiation into adulthood, nor his moment of calling a familiar. No one was there to give him a second set of eyes to check the circle either. He wasn't at all surprised they hadn't come to help him. He was a male witch. While not unheard of, male witches were extremely rare.

Most men affiliated with the witches' coven couldn't kindle any magic; his own father hadn't been able to cast any magic, but his mother had been a full member of the Seattle coven's circle of power. They had died five years ago when Kana was thirteen, and the coven had since undertaken his rearing. At least, they had until they realized he was gay.

A man with power was expected to pass on that power to his daughters so they might become contributing members of the coven's circle. According to the coven, that was literally Kana's only purpose in life, and he had failed them when he had come out.

Well, whatever. His suitcase was already packed and the bus ticket purchased. No one would look for him if he simply vanished—no one would even care he had gone—but before he left, he had to complete the last rites that signified his ascendance to adulthood. Kana was determined to leave this place with everything he was due as a proper witch.

Kana stepped into the circle, careful not to smudge any lines, and settled with his legs crossed into the empty space at the very center. He placed his palms flat on the floor on either side of his thighs and called up his magic.

The lines of the circle started to glow a soft white, lighting the dark room and growing brighter and brighter until it seemed Kana was completely enclosed in a white, shining disk. Somehow, a large spot in the circle right in front of where Kana was sitting remained dark and then got blacker even as the chalk's glow continued to grow in intensity.

In the darkness, something moved. A soft brushing sound whispered through the space as a massive paw touched the ground, and then another barely audible susurrus as whatever was approaching drew closer and closer to Kana within the black hole in the middle of Kana's spell. Kana poured more magic into the circle until he was squinting through the light to see what was approaching in the dark.

Whatever it was, it was huge. A brief glimpse showed a furred creature at least six feet long, with a tail equal in length. White, shot through with jagged black stripes.

The creature was studying him, watching from the pit of blackness as Kana pushed more and more magic into the circle to keep the portal open. He was being judged, and suddenly the description in his school-books of how this spell worked—a feeling of being scanned both inside and out as if subjected to X-ray vision—made sense. Kana was sweating and panting for breath, his fingers cramping where they were pressed to the ground, and yet he couldn't stop funneling magic to keep the circle going.

The creature must have come to a decision because the sense of being scanned suddenly stopped. The creature turned around and Kana caught a glimpse of the massive, furred face of what might loosely be called a cat, but then a small, white with black stripes, furred ball of kit-ten dropped from the larger cat's mouth onto the slate floor on Kana's side of the circle. The gigantic cat turned away, and Kana was about to lift his hands and end the spell, when it suddenly turned back. A second ball of fluff dropped onto the slate floor, this one black with white stripes.

This time when the cat turned away, it ripped what was left of the spell circle from Kana's hands. The magic vanished with the circle, and the room immediately went dark. Kana blinked, trying to see through the bright spots covering his vision. The two kittens moved at his feet, a rustle echoing in the otherwise empty room, and Kana carefully reached out until his fingers touched soft fur. He blinked again, trying to see, and let out a shocked breath when a soft mew answered his stroking.

A cat was the highest form of familiar, but this wasn't a mere house cat. No, the massive creature who had delivered the kittens to Kana was a primordial, magical tiger, and the kittens were likely the same. And he had two! Multiple familiars did happen on rare occasion, and sometimes a witch even received multiple cats, but cats like these? Never.

If the coven knew... Kana's breath caught in his throat. No, they couldn't know. They would lock him up, force him to breed, all in the hopes of creating a female witch who might be granted the same powers as his in the calling circle. Any freedom his packed bags and bus ticket represented would vanish.

Kana needed to disappear much more thoroughly than he had originally planned. It would be easy enough to change his last name from his mother's to his father's, which had been abandoned when his parents married. The coven likely didn't remember. He would have to take multiple bus trips, paying in cash and going in opposite directions, to a destination they would never expect. He could do it, but first he had to get out of the building.

His eyes had finally adjusted to the dark room, so he could see clearly, but his breath was still caught in his throat as his fingers gently brushed down the backs of first one kitten and then the other. They were his familiars. They would have to bond over the next few months as they learned about one another and about how to meld their magics so he could use the powers held inside them to augment his own. He wouldn't get those months if he were caught here.

"I need you to hide and stay very, very quiet," Kana said, his voice a soft whisper just on the off chance someone was actually waiting by the door. Both kittens unrolled. The white and black one had blue eyes, the black and white had green, but both looked at him with total comprehension. "The coven can't know you exist."

Kana carefully picked them both up, cradling them in the crook of his elbow, and walked to the door where he had left his jacket. Rather than putting the jacket on, he draped it over his arm, covering the kittens. His skin felt sticky with sweat, which luckily meant anyone who saw him would understand why he wasn't wearing the jacket when he walked outside into the cool spring afternoon. Kana called on his magic, which responded sluggishly after using so much of it on the circle. He smoothed his fingers over the bumps of his kittens' bodies, and where his fingers passed, the bumps disappeared until the jacket looked like it only hung over his arm.

Kana set the spell and released the magic, then studied his arm to make sure he hadn't missed a single spot.

"Don't move," he hissed in reminder and then reached out with his free hand to pull open the door.

The sunlight outside had him blinking again, but he strode forward onto the gravel path connecting all the central buildings in the coven village. His house was on the outskirts, a one-room bungalow granted him by the village council, who granted housing to all witches, usually the women, but he had grudgingly been given this one small boon. He couldn't wait to leave the key on the kitchen counter for them to find the next time someone decided to be nosy and go into his place to look through his stuff.

"Wasn't today your coming of age?" his neighbor, an elderly woman named Jane, who he suspected was the one chiefly responsible for those searches, called from her front porch.

"The spell circle collapsed," Kana responded, trying to sound despondent.

Jane tsked and shook her head. "Such a shame, but you are male. I hope you weren't too disappointed, child."

Kana let out a heavy sigh, trying not to overplay his act. "I'm hoping to petition the circle council to let me try again."

"Perhaps they might," she said, her voice noncommittal. "Well, have a good evening." Jane walked into her house and shut the door.

Kana hurried into his own house, and once he was out of sight of any of the windows, he pulled the jacket off his arm.

Home? one of the kittens asked. His voice sounded inside Kana's head. Kana didn't know them well enough to differentiate their voices just yet, but he would. He would have to work at it, but at least in this case the darker cat with the green eyes was looking at him, so Kana assumed it was that kitten.

"This is where I live now, but if I stay here bad things will happen to us. We need to run away and find a new home."

We will run fast, a second, marginally higher voice said. *What do we need to do?*

Kana let the kittens drop to the floor as he went over to his closet. His suitcase was right where he left it, and a backpack from his school days sat nearby. If he took out the top layer of the backpack and stuffed those few things into the outer pocket of his suitcase, the kittens should fit.

First, though, he had to wait to be certain he wasn't being watched.

Kana walked across the room and into his kitchen, where he started putting dishes away. He was going to leave the house spotless, as if he had never actually lived here, and cleaning was also a good way to kill time. The kitchen had a view out the front windows, which allowed him to surreptitiously watch the comings and goings of his neighbors.

At first, all Kana could see was his own reflection in the glass. His features were a fairly even mix of both his parents, although he was basing that judgement on his memories as he didn't have any photographs of them. Still, his hair was the same light-brown shade that brightened under the summer sun to a honey gold as his mother. His eyes were hazel like his father's, and they changed color based on what he was wearing or even on how blue the sky might be on a given day. His button nose was his mother's, fuller bottom lip his father's, and he was middling tall at five foot eight like his father.

Would they be proud of him? Kana wondered. What would they

think of their son, who had fought to learn magic against all the odds stacked against him and had somehow managed to earn two wonderful cat familiars? Kana hoped the answer was yes, but in the five years since their death he had hoped many things about them. He no longer knew what might be true when it came to his parents, but he liked to think they would still support him in what he was about to do.

Reminded of his task, Kana shifted so he stopped seeing his reflection and could instead look outside. The flowers of early spring were turning brown and falling to the ground as the first buds of green leaves slowly began to overtake them. The sight was beautiful even in the fading light of the afternoon sun, but Kana wasn't looking at the beauty. He was watching his neighbors, waiting for the moment he knew he wouldn't be seen to make his escape.

He didn't have to watch long before Jane bustled out of her house, wrapped in a thick jacket and scarf despite the fact spring had already thrown off the claws of winter. She was no doubt off to tell whoever she reported his activities to about his plan to request a second attempt at the circle.

Kana waited, putting the last of the dishes into their cabinets, until he was certain she was gone. He turned off all the lights, dug the key out of his pocket and placed it on the kitchen counter, and then went over to his suitcase.

"If you climb in here," he said to his kittens while holding open the top of his backpack, "I can carry you without needing to conceal you with magic."

The kittens hopped inside and curled up around each other. Kana zipped the bag almost closed, leaving just enough space for an air hole, and carefully slid it onto his back. He picked up the suitcase and went to his back door.

Magic came at his call, thankfully less sluggish after a bit of time to recover, and he cast it out behind the house. The magic swept into the woods surrounding the village but didn't impact a concealment or alarm spell. Nothing in the woods was currently watching him, though that might not be true in a few hours. It was now or never.

Kana opened the door, walked outside, closed the door firmly behind him, used a touch of magic to turn the lock, and then strode off directly into the woods toward what he hoped would be a better, new life.

Chapter One

"WE NEED TO do an exclusive, and we need to do it before anyone else jumps on it."

With that one sentence, Kana knew he should have cast some sort of forgetting spell on the speaker. He wasn't at all surprised the assignment had fallen in his lap. The newest hire always got the crappy jobs, and his undergraduate degree in journalism was still warm from the printer.

After years of fighting to get hired for this job, Kana wasn't exactly in a position to say no. He had stayed on the run from his old coven for two years, covering his tracks and making fake trajectories all over the country. He had felt safe enough after that to try settling down, but four years had flown by while he tried to get his feet back under him. Over those years, he had worked hard to go from homeless, to living in a crappy apartment, where he was just thankful to have a roof over his head, to slowly saving every penny so he could go to college. Four more years in college, studying full time while working two jobs to pay for everything, and finally, finally, Kana could say he had made it.

Except, a vampire coven had just moved in, and the cities of Albany and Schenectady were collectively losing their minds.

Humans couldn't look at Kana and immediately pinpoint him as a witch. To his coworkers, he was a human with emotional support cats. Which meant his supervisors had chosen to send a young, untried, and unprotected human into the den of monsters, all in the hopes he could somehow convince said monsters to agree to an interview.

Kana couldn't turn down the assignment, not as new as he was. At least he was only visiting the vampires once to conduct the initial reconnaissance. He would gauge the vampires' willingness to be interviewed, ask some basic questions to get all the baseline facts solidified, and hand over his notes to the big guns. The guys who wrote the story for the website and the newspaper, and who put together the interview plan for the TV reporters would do the rest, but only after Kana had already paved the road for them.

And with vampires, his coworkers were very, very happy someone else got to be the guinea pig first.

The bus slowed to a stop and the doors popped open. Kana hurried outside and looked around to get oriented. He was on Route 7, a four-lane thoroughfare connecting Albany and Schenectady, the two neighboring cities that made up the Capital Region of New York State. On either side of this section of Route 7—which was closer to Schenectady—were residential neighborhoods, each one fancier than the last. The largest and most majestic house in those neighborhoods had remained empty for the last seven years. According to Kana's research, the previous owner's deteriorating health had forced him to move to assisted living, but he had refused to sell the house he had lived in for fifty years.

Only after his death had his children been able to put the house on the market, and the vampires had bought it.

After moving in, the vampires had solidified the house's fortifications, building a ten-foot stone wall around the perimeter of the six-acre property, a huge gatehouse, and who knew how many other improvements inside. Kana knew the defenses were necessary for their protection; humans weren't exactly welcoming to creatures above them on the food chain, and humans were often the least of a vampire's worries. Yet, vampires had to live in urban areas if they wanted to eat. They didn't have a choice about where to live, in the same way as Kana didn't have a choice about this assignment.

Kana glanced at the setting sun, glad to see he had enough daylight left to get to the house, but he wouldn't arrive so early as to be insulting. He settled the straps of his small backpack into place on his shoulders—just big enough to hold a notebook, some pens, and one cat—and headed into the neighborhood in the direction where the vampires were waiting.

The sidewalks petered out after fifteen minutes of walking, and Kana had to, instead, walk on the road next to carefully mown lawns. Old growth trees blocked any view of the house as Kana approached the driveway with a massive ironwork gate. As he approached, a door opened in the wall next to the gate, and a man stepped outside.

"Can we help you?" he asked, and while he sounded cordial enough, something in his voice had Kana hesitating to take those last few steps forward to be within comfortable talking distance.

Wolf, Mika said.

Werewolves? There were only supposed to be vampires here, not werewolves too. Kana let some magic drift from his fingers to surround his bag and felt the spell circle he had meticulously stitched into the side of the bag take hold. Mika's scent was now masked, so he would be protected, at least. Kana, on the other hand, still had a job to do.

"I called ahead," Kana replied. He reached into his pocket and pulled out his work ID to show the wolf. "I'm here to interview the household."

The wolf studied the ID, then glared at Kana's face as if memorizing the placement of every pore.

"This way," he finally said. He didn't quite turn his back to Kana as he led the way to the door and inside the guard building. They walked through a dozen twisting hallways, and Kana suspected he was being taken in circles. There weren't any decorations on the walls. Everything was painted beige, the floor was tiled white, and it all looked pristine, so he didn't even have a smudge of dirt to let him know he had passed this way before. Eventually, they walked through a doorway to a staircase that led downward. The werewolf jumped down the stairs, skipping every other step, and Kana continued to follow. The hallway below was the same beige and white, but there weren't any more turns or side halls. Kana guessed they were finally heading to the house.

The long hallway ended in a wide room. A fireplace was burning merrily to the left, two long couches were centered around a wooden coffee table, and two overstuffed armchairs filled the rest of the space. The right-hand wall held one closed door.

"Sit. They'll come soon." The wolf pointed at the couches briefly before spinning on one heel and walking back the way they had come.

Kana swung his backpack around and sat in one of the armchairs with the bag in his lap. He opened an outer pocket and pulled out a small notebook with a pen jammed down the metal spiral spine, then carefully placed his bag on the floor between his feet.

Only a minute passed before the door swung open and another werewolf walked into the room. This wolf was tall, at least six foot five, and his light blond hair was cut tight to the sides of his head and an inch long at the top in a very military style. His eyes were deep brown as they studied Kana, and his shoulders were...yum. Kana had to look away before his eyes betrayed his thoughts.

How yum? I wanna see! Mika demanded. Kana bumped his heel against his bag to tell Mika to be quiet.

"Can I get you some coffee or tea?" the werewolf asked, and his voice was low and rumbling in a way that sent a happy shiver up Kana's spine.

"No thank you," Kana replied, glad when his voice didn't waver and betray the gutter his thoughts kept falling into. "I'm just here to conduct the preliminary interview."

The wolf's nostrils flared as he took in a deep breath, and Kana hoped his spell hiding Mika held, but all the wolf did was nod.

"They'll be here in a moment. Let me go see how much longer." He left, but the door didn't latch firmly behind him, and Kana could hear him talking to someone on the other side. "Tell them to eat first. This one's no good."

Damn. Kana let out a breath and forced his fingers to relax from where they were clutching at his notebook. He didn't know if the werewolf had already figured out he was a witch, but he knew something. At least Kana wouldn't have to prove he had power by fighting off a vampire looking to turn him into dinner.

However, that wouldn't save his coworkers if the vampires decided to snack on them when it came time for the big interview.

Five more minutes passed before the door was pushed open again. The wolf led the way, followed by a man and a woman. Both were pale white, their skin almost translucent. The man had a beaked nose like a hawk and wore a vest, jacket, and cravat over embroidered pants. The woman's black hair was pulled up high on the top of her head in some sort of updo that matched the wide skirts and corseted bodice of her equally embroidered dress. Kana didn't need magic to know they were vampires. Despite the fancy clothes, a heavy air seemed to emanate from them.

"You requested to speak with us," the man said. "My advisor informed me it would be in our best interest to agree. So speak."

Kana swallowed but obeyed. "I'm from the Herald. We're a local news agency, but we're also part of a larger media conglomerate. There has been some concern that vampires have moved into the neighborhood, so we're looking to do a piece to help alleviate those fears."

"They fear we will kill them to harvest their blood," the man said. "They need not fear such. A dead human can no longer produce fresh blood, so it is of no use to us to kill our prey."

Kana, nodded, focusing on the content of their words rather than the phrasing. "The people need to know they have nothing to worry about, which is why the Herald and Channel 7 are looking to produce a piece."

"A number of humans would come to our territory to interview us?" he asked. It seemed like a rhetorical question, but Kana couldn't help noticing the pointed look the two vampires shared: hunger and eager anticipation.

Territory, Mika hissed. *It's always about territory.*

Of course. The vampires were forced to behave outside of their castle. Vampire hunters and other supernatural species forced them to obey society's rules. However, there was no one to stop them from misbehaving inside their own territory.

"I accept this proposition. It will be interesting to learn whether the new technology allows our visage to appear on film. Set it up,

Ember," the male vampire added to the wolf.

Ember nodded. "It will be done."

The vampires stood and walked from the room without so much as a glance at Kana, let alone a goodbye.

"What else do you need today to be prepared for the interview?" Ember asked.

Kana looked away from the closed door and over to Ember, who had finally sat in the other armchair. His deep brown eyes were looking at Kana as if he were trying to read Kana's innermost thoughts. Given one glance at Ember sent Kana's innermost thoughts into the gutter, Kana really hoped Ember couldn't actually read them. Kana forced himself to look down at his notebook where he had some questions scrawled.

"I need to know their names," he began and then recklessly added, "and I need some assurance my coworkers won't become lunch."

Ember's lips quirked slightly, as if he found Kana funny, but he didn't actually smile. All of a sudden, Kana wanted to see that smile, to see what Ember's face looked like if he lost his seriousness.

"You met Master Octavius and Mistress Penelope. They will likely be the only vampires you will encounter while you are here. As for your coworkers, I make no promises. Perhaps knowing they might get fed on while they're here will convince them not to come. Any other questions?"

Kana looked at his notes again to double-check, but his duties as the initial contact were simple: find out who was being interviewed, any interesting tidbits the interviewee should ask, and set up the date and time for the formal interview.

"When would it be best for us to come?"

Ember stood and pulled a card out of his pants pocket. He held it out for Kana to take. The card read, *Ember Maxwell, Security Chief,* and included a phone number.

"Talk with your people and call this number with a couple of days and times. I'll let you know which one is best, but I still recommend them not coming at all."

Kana tucked the card into his notebook, slid the pen back down the spiral spine, and put it all back into the outer pocket of his backpack. He stood and carefully swung his bag onto his back.

"I will mention it to them," Kana replied, wishing he could sound convinced he would be able dissuade his supervisors. They wanted the next, best, newest scoop, and they wanted it before anyone else had a chance to swoop in and snatch it from them. The vampires in town were the hot topic, and Kana wasn't sure even a threat to their lives would stop his coworkers from moving forward with the story. Well, he would have to try anyway.

"I'll show you out." Ember led the way back to the long hallway, then up the stairs and into the maze.

Kana was pretty certain by the time they reached the door that he had been taken in circles again, but that wasn't a question worth asking. He was just glad to step outside again.

The door closed with a thud that made Kana jump, and he hurried onto the street and back through the neighborhoods so he could find the bus to take him home.

They might be trailing us, Kana pushed down the bond he shared with Mika and Sora.

Mika grumbled at having to stay hidden in the bag for longer. Sora just snorted in amusement from where he was following, hidden in the grass of the front yards Kana was walking past.

You wanted to go inside, Mika, Sora teased. *That's what you get for your curiosity.*

You're just disappointed you didn't speak up first, Mika replied, his voice cutting, yet still teasing.

Kana was happy to listen to their playful banter for the rest of the walk through the neighborhood and back to the main road to catch the bus. A touch of magic kept people from noticing Sora took the bus too, and it wasn't long before they were getting off at the stop a few blocks from Kana's apartment.

He didn't live in the best part of town, but it also wasn't the worst. The building was old, but the brick facade was well maintained and the front door locked firmly behind him when Kana let himself inside. Sora scampered up the inside stairs ahead of them and Kana felt the pull on his magic when Sora changed from his house cat sized form to his human one. He was waiting, completely naked and not caring, when Kana caught up outside the door to his apartment.

Kana opened the door quickly, hoping his neighbors didn't come out and see Sora naked…again…and then locked it behind him once they were all inside.

Mika squirmed his way out of the bag before Kana had a chance to take it off. He leapt from Kana's shoulder as a house cat, but when he reached the ground, he had also assumed human form.

Mika and Sora were completely identical in basic features—the shape of their nose, eyes, chin—but their coloring was opposite. Sora's skin was beautifully dark, but all the hair on his head, arms, legs, and groin was white. The contrast made him look ethereal. Mika had pale white skin, but all his hair was the deepest black, so he seemed to glow from within.

Despite their similar looks, they weren't related by blood. Familiars were formed in the ether, in the power beyond which Kana tapped into with his spells, and when Mika and Sora had chosen their human forms, they had decided to choose similar features.

They were gorgeous, and they were all Kana's.

Sora padded over and hugged Kana from behind.

"I don't think they know you're a witch, but they definitely know you're something," Sora said into Kana's neck where his nose was pressed. "Otherwise, they definitely would have tried to take your blood."

"Which means my secret is still safe," Kana replied. He bent his head to give Sora better access, and Sora obligingly nipped gently at the exposed skin. Kana let out a groan that was halted when Mika took his mouth, tongue rubbing deep and swallowing any noises Kana made.

"I'm more interested in your handsome wolf," Mika said, pulling away briefly to start on the buttons of Kana's shirt. "I didn't get a good look at him. Is he really that pretty?"

"I liked his eyes," Kana admitted, his voice gasping and airy as Sora's hands pressed and rubbed against his skin as Mika revealed it to the room with every unhooked button.

"And his shoulders," Mika added, his voice and his grin cheeky. He sank to his knees in front of Kana, his fingers fumbling with the button and zipper on Kana's pants.

Sora's strong arms held Kana up, his rumbling purrs echoing in Kana's ears even as his length pressed against Kana's butt, while Mika worked with his mouth.

Kana sank into the dual sensations, letting the magic of their bond and their love draw him away into oblivion.

Chapter Two

THE ALARM WENT off in a series of loud beeps arranged to form a song melody but were so annoying he'd downloaded the tune to use as his alarm tone. Mika let out a soft yowl, and Sora answered with a grumble, but neither moved from where they were twined around Kana.

Kana laughed and started the laborious process of extricating himself. Once he was finally free, Mika and Sora simply rolled into the warm spot he had left, curling around each other to contentedly sleep for another half hour. Kana eyed them with envy, wishing he could crawl back in with them, but a glance at the clock forced him to keep moving.

He showered quickly and got dressed in a pair of slacks and a button-down. Mika, finally awake, pushed a plate of buttered toast and a cup of tea in front of Kana's seat at the kitchen table when Kana headed over, and he and Sora took their own chairs to eat their preferred marshmallow bomb cereal drowned in milk. Toast was more than enough for Kana this early, but he had snacks in his desk at work to tide him over until lunch if he got hungry early.

They left their dirty dishes in the sink to deal with later that night. Kana found his backpack where it had been abandoned by the front door, while Mika and Sora shifted to their house cat form. Neither wanted to climb into the bag, which was fine. A touch of magic—the same spell Kana used on a slightly larger scale at work—kept anyone from noticing them.

"How was the meeting last night?" Beth asked the second Kana arrived in their shared cubicle space.

Mika and Sora crawled underneath Kana's desk where he had left them an overstuffed pillow. Kana retrieved his notebook from his bag, stuffed the bag in a drawer, and then turned to Beth.

"About as well as a meeting with vampires can go. When are we gathering so I can give my report?"

Beth clicked on her computer for a few seconds. "Calendar invite we got says ten."

"Just enough time to check my email and have another cup of tea," Kana joked, even though they were both buried beneath work over-assigned to the new employees. Every time Kana started to catch up, someone dumped another assignment on his desk, much like what had happened with the vampires last night. He would barely have time to get his notes in order before the meeting.

Kana logged in and got to work.

*

"SO YOU'RE SAYING they're willing to be interviewed," Stephen said. He sounded excited, and like Kana feared, he ignored everything else Kana said.

"I'm saying they might have an ulterior motive to being

interviewed," Kana repeated, hoping this time Stephen and the rest of the room might listen. "If you walk into their house, they consider you easy prey. You might not walk out again."

Beth, at least, seemed to understand his worry. "They also weren't certain they would even show up on camera, right?" she asked Kana. "Won't be much of a story if it looks like we're interviewing air."

Stephen waved his hand as if he were physically brushing Beth's words aside. "We've worked with less before; we can certainly work around that."

Kana wanted to ask *Can you work if they've stolen all your blood?* but Stephen was past listening.

Except, Stephen seemed to have a moment of clarity as he looked around the room. "Now, I don't want to offend our hosts by wearing a garlic necklace, but can anyone think of something slightly less gauche to encourage them to continue being good hosts?" No one answered, and Kana saw what was coming his way even before Stephen turned to look at him. "Kana, please research this." Stephen picked up Ember's business card. "I'll give them a call and let them know we're free all next week. They can pick the best date and time for them."

Kana let out a breath as the meeting ended. The interview was still happening, but at least everyone was warned. And Kana had the opportunity to provide some protection. His coworkers didn't need to know he was using magic to protect them, so if he could spell up an oil or perfume for them to wear, he could hopefully keep the vampires away.

Kana didn't know what herbs would work best, though. Garlic, certainly, and he could get his hands on some holy water for the base, but even the humans, let alone the vampires, would be able to tell they were wearing vampire repellent just from the smell. No, Kana needed to come up with something smelling lightly flowery or of citrus, but still incorporated the protective parts of garlic.

Everyone started to stand and gather papers, so Kana did the same. His seat was at the far end of the room, so he had to wait for everyone else to leave first. Eventually, Kana was able to walk with Beth back to their desks.

"Kinda crazy, interviewing vampires like this," Beth said. She sat and fluffed her pixie-cut hair for a moment while she thought. "I still can't believe you went to the preinterview alone like that."

Which was actually part of Kana's problem. Because he had emerged from the interview unscathed, his coworkers, and Stephen in particular, probably thought they could do the same. Kana needed to keep his powers a secret for his own protection, but hiding them, unfortunately, caused his coworkers to dismiss the potential threat. Well, Kana would simply have to put together a good spell to protect them and they could remain blissfully ignorant.

"It's going to be so exciting though," Beth continued. "I've never met a vampire before, let alone talked to one!"

"Does the Herald interview a lot of supernatural creatures?" Kana logged into his computer, but instead of loading his next work project, he pulled up his favorite online herbalist. There had to be a combination of herbs he could use to help mask the smell of garlic.

"Stephen says he interviewed a guy possessed by a demon once, but I think he got played. The guy was probably a wannabe."

Or he was a warlock, whose magic derived from summoning all kinds of creatures, demons included, to power their spells. Stephen probably didn't know the difference, though, which meant it could have been any sort of magical whatsit, or just a regular human wannabe like Beth said.

"That's why Stephen is so excited about this. None of the other local news agencies have ever even thought to try something so ambitious." Beth leaned closer and lowered her voice, so Kana obligingly leaned close too. "I think," she paused and glanced side to side to check whether anyone was nearby to overhear. "I think Stephen wants to pad his resume with this. If he has interviewing vampires on his resume, I bet he thinks the bigwigs at the national headquarters will pluck him out of our local station and give him a big-time job."

"It might look good on a resume, but all the big stations have to do is talk to Stephen to learn better. We're not getting rid of him so easily," Kana joked, although at the back of his mind a twinge of worry that a vampire might actually "get rid of him" slipped through.

Chatter sounded from around the corner, and Beth and Kana sprang apart, swiveling their chairs around to return to their desks. Kana got back to work.

About four that afternoon, just when Kana was starting to save his work so he could head home, Kana and Beth's emails simultaneously pinged.

"Monday at seven thirty," Beth read. "Damn, that's soon!"

Kana had all of Friday and the weekend to concoct his spell. Not much time, but he would have to make it be enough.

Kana shut down his computer and dug his backpack out of the drawer. He helped Mika and Sora inside and swung the bag onto his back.

"See you tomorrow?" he asked Beth.

Beth grinned at him. "Yep. Have a good night!"

They waved at each other and then Kana headed for the elevator and the bus home.

*

KANA AND MIKA carefully lifted the coffee table and walked it over to an empty space in the kitchen. Sora rolled up the rug and then leaned it against the TV stand where it would be out of the way.

The first thing Kana had done after moving into his apartment was rip out a large square of the wooden floor. He had replaced it with a chunk of seamless, smooth slate—one of his first big purchases after he had settled down for college. If he ended the lease on his apartment, he would remove the slate and use magic to replace the floorboards, which he was currently storing in the hall closet, but for now he had the perfect space to write his spells.

Mika handed him a piece of chalk. Kana crouched and gently placed the tip of the chalk down on the slate. He kept his arm steady and spun on the balls of his feet to draw a large, perfect circle. Drawing the pentagram required a steady elbow and stiff wrist to ensure he drew five straight lines. Kana was pleased with how the completed circle looked when he stood to study it.

A simple circle without any amplifying runes allowed the spell to focus on his potion, which was the important part of the magic today. Mika took the chalk back and Sora brought over the candles—white, for protection. Kana placed a candle at all five points where the pentagram met the circle's edge.

Sora and Mika carefully stepped over the chalk lines. Sora put Kana's smudge bowl down, Mika placed a large vial full of water and floating bits of plant next to it, and then both shifted into their house cat form. Kana draped his spell robe—also white because this was a spell of protection—over the back of the couch and, naked, stepped into the circle. He sat directly in the center and Mika and Sora arranged themselves on either side.

"Ready?" Kana asked, his voice soft. The rising moon shone through the kitchen window. It was waxing, which was a lucky coincidence. Any phase of the moon would have worked for the spell, but a growing moon meant growing power.

Ready, Mika and Sora both said.

Kana placed his hands on their backs and let out a breath. He called on his magic, opening the channels between him and his familiars. Power flowed through their bond, melding the three together into one. He delved downward, rooting his power into the ground, then soared upward to spread his magic through the circle like a tree spreading its branches. When he opened his eyes, the chalk circle had become a glowing sphere, surrounding them with gentle white light. The pentagram was glowing softly as well, its lines pulsing as power flowed through. Kana shot magic down the lines, and the candles burst into flame. Their light melded seamlessly with his circle, but also gentled the power so instead of pulsing, the light began to flow evenly.

Kana lifted his right hand from Sora's back and reached out to stir his fingers through the contents of the smudge bowl. Fire followed his fingers, and a gentle smoke quickly rose and began to fill the sphere. Mistletoe did not have a scent, but the ashy smell of burning wood enveloped Kana.

Mistletoe warded off evil and brought good luck, both of which would be needed for this spell. Kana waited until the sphere was completely full of smoke and then uncapped the vial.

He had previously ground garlic to a paste, then squeezed it through cheesecloth to extract the oil. His apartment still smelled of it and it had taken multiple scrubbings to get it off his hands, but he had gotten enough for an extract. Boiling the garlic oil with fennel, mugwort, and chamomile, with a base of holy water, had reduced the scent considerably. Fennel and mugwort helped to repel evil spirits and chamomile was...chamomile. There wasn't much chamomile couldn't be used for. At its base, chamomile was simply a plant of good, and goodness was exactly what Kana's spell needed.

Kana passed the open vial through the smoke, slowly drawing a pentagram. The second he connected the last line of the smoke-drawn pentagram with the first, magic throbbed through the circle, making Kana's bones ring like a tuning fork. The sphere flared with light, forcing Kana to shut his eyes, and then, suddenly, the light vanished.

The sphere, pentagrams, smoke, and candles were all gone when Kana opened his eyes again, but the contents of the vial glowed softly in the unlit room.

Kana hoped his spell worked, but unfortunately there was only one way to test it: have a vampire try to bite someone anointed in the oil. He hoped it didn't come to that tomorrow, but even if it didn't keep the vampires away completely, Kana was pretty certain the spell would do something to stop them.

Bedtime? Sora asked, his voice hopeful even as he planted his front paws on the ground and stretched out his back with his tail high in the air.

"Let's put the room back together first, and then yes. I'm ready for bed," Kana answered, then paused to let out a yawn as the late hour and the magic expenditure hit him.

The exhaustion was worth it, though, Kana reminded himself as he corked the vial and carefully set it aside for the morning. The vampires wouldn't be hurting anyone tomorrow night—he was going to make certain of that.

Chapter Three

TWO VANS AWAITED them in the parking lot outside the office at six thirty Monday night. The camera crew loaded equipment into the back while everyone else milled around waiting. Stephen was getting his makeup touched up, but otherwise no one else was doing anything.

Kana pulled the potion vial out of his bag and walked over to Stephen.

"I found a good vampire repellent. It would be best if everyone put some on now," Kana explained.

Stephen didn't move because he was getting mascara applied, but his lips tightened in a small, disbelieving sneer.

"Fine," he said, much to Kana's relief. "What do you need to do?"

Kana held up the vial for Stephen to see. "I need to dab a drop of this on both sides of your neck and the inside of both wrists, to protect your exposed pulse points."

Stephen snorted, but he waved the makeup artist away and tilted his neck for easier access. Kana dipped an applewood toothpick into the potion, coating just the tip, and quickly drew a small circle and pentagram with the oil onto Stephen. Both sides of the neck, both wrists, and Kana quickly moved on to the next person.

He made sure every single person climbing into one of the vans was treated with the oil, and then Kana took his seat and buckled up for the drive to the vampire's castle.

It's my turn to go inside, Sora insisted. *I want to see the pretty wolf with the shoulders.*

It's not like I got to see him last time, Mika argued back. *I had to stay inside the bag the whole time.*

It's my turn, Sora repeated, and as if that ended the argument, he climbed into Kana's lap and tapped the bag with a paw in a demand to be let inside.

Kana obeyed, but he reached down to give Mika's ears a scritch in consolation.

They reached the compound a little after seven. Two wolves wearing identical green polo shirts and black pants—possibly their official guard uniform, though no one had been wearing the outfit last time—were standing outside the gate, waiting for them.

"You'll walk from here," one of the wolves said. He waved toward the open door leading into the guard house and Kana winced. He remembered the long walk from before, as he was taken in circles, and didn't envy the camera crew's job lugging all the equipment inside.

Luckily Stephen didn't try to argue that the driveway continued past the ornate black iron gates, and it would be easier to drive the vans to the front door. He didn't look pleased, though.

Kana carefully put on his backpack, and then went to help the camera crew with some of their extra bags. Mika used the confusion of unloading to conceal himself as he snuck out of the van and went to find somewhere to hide so he could be close in case Kana needed him.

The walk through the hallways was just as long, and Kana's arms and back were already aching by the time they reached the staircase. Going down the flight of steps while carrying heavy bags was tiring, as was the last, long hallway. The werewolf guides waved the group into the sitting room at the end, and Kana and the others let out a relieved sigh at finally reaching their destination.

Ember waited for them alone. He had a curly earbud in one ear and wore the same green polo shirt, except he had an extra patch on the sleeve that Kana assumed denoted his rank. The green against his brown eyes had Kana reflexively swallowing, so he looked away before Ember noticed.

"Get set up," Ember told them once everyone was inside. "When you're ready, the master and mistress will come speak with you." Ember stepped back until he stood directly in front of the door Kana assumed led into the rest of the house.

Kana gave his bags to the camera crew and then went to help Beth organize the cue cards and scripts Stephen and his co-star Marilyn would need during the interview.

Every once in a while, Kana caught a scent of chamomile, or of campfire smoke, but he didn't smell garlic. He could only hope the vampires wouldn't notice and be offended, but the oil appeared to be unobtrusive enough.

What if I just poke my nose out? It's so busy; there's no way anyone would notice. Sora's voice was hopeful and plaintive, but Kana knew better than to give in. Sora would ask for the world if he could, whereas Mika was much more practical.

Don't even think about it, Kana replied through their bond.

There's no telling what those werewolves are capable of noticing.

Ugh. That's not fun. Sora thankfully subsided and Kana was able to focus on his work.

Everything was set up by eight. Marilyn walked over to Ember, tossed her blonde hair over her shoulder—Kana didn't want to know how much hairspray she had used, because it moved as one solid mass—and smiled her best reporter-on-camera smile.

"We're ready," she said.

Ember nodded. He reached behind himself and knocked three times on the door.

Nothing happened for a few long minutes. Marilyn shifted her weight in her spike heels and Stephen huffed from where he was waiting by the long couch where the lights and microphones had been set up, but Ember's stern face didn't even twitch in response.

Suddenly, Ember took two steps forward and shifted to the side so he could turn the doorknob and hold the door open. Master Octavius and Mistress Penelope swept into the room. Octavius's cravat and Penelope's dress were both two sizes larger than when Kana had last seen them. The cravat spilled lace and puff down his neck and chest, emphasizing the straight lines of the tooled and embroidered jacket. He was carrying a black cane with an engraved silver head, and she was carrying a lacy fan with some sort of red-and-black pattern on it. Penelope's skirts were so wide they brushed either side of the doorway as she walked, and Stephen had to stumble out of her way to keep from getting hit. Kana wouldn't have thought it possible, but her skirts had more embroidery than Octavius's jacket.

Ember closed the door and resumed his post in front of it. The vampires sat on one couch and Stephen and Marilyn took the other, and Kana had to pull his focus from Ember and back to his job.

"Thank you so much for speaking with us today," Stephen began, his smile and his voice his perfect reporter level of smarmy.

"We are most intrigued as to whether we are visible on the new technology," Master Octavius said. He looked straight at the camera, his face a perfect mask of gentle curiosity.

Kana suddenly hoped they were completely and perfectly visible. Something about the dark depth in Octavius's eyes said this was more than idle curiosity, and Kana had a sinking suspicion as to why. If they didn't show up in modern cameras, then if they attacked someone in public, no human could record them in the act. If confronted afterward, they would say it was another vampire, and no one could disprove them.

Kana let out a relieved breath when Joe, the guy behind the camera, grinned. He turned the view screen around to show the vampires. From Kana's vantage off to the side where he wouldn't get in the way of the shot, he was able to see both Octavius and Penelope in the frame. Their outlines were blurred, but the basic features were easy to make out.

"How intriguing. It is amazing how technology had changed so significantly in so short a time. Please, ask your questions."

Beth passed Kana the first cue card to hold up. Stephen glanced his way, then turned back to the vampires.

"We have never had vampires living in our city," Stephen began. "Tell us a bit about yourself and your kind?"

Octavius smiled with his lips closed, but Kana couldn't help noticing the corners of his eyes didn't move. Despite hiding his teeth, somehow that smile still sent a cold, apprehensive shiver down Kana's spine.

"We are very similar to humans because we were once human ourselves. Humans have far less to fear from us than from creatures who have never known humanity. Yes, we drink blood, but we have grown practiced at surrounding ourselves with willing donors, so the general populace need not fear our presence here."

A slight movement visible out of the corner of his eye caught Kana's attention, and when he turned his head to look, he saw Ember slowly straightening his fingers. Had something Octavius said made Ember clench his fist? Kana held up the next cue card on autopilot, trying to mentally parse through Octavius's words.

Less to fear from vampires because they were once human was a canned, bullshit phrase. Anyone who knew their basic history lessons knew vampires, werewolves, and other magical creatures who had lost their humanity were what caused the most trouble for humans. That was why hunter groups specific to both creatures existed, but there weren't hunters targeting sylphs, for example. Of course, there were all sorts of hunter groups out there, including ones who hunted what they perceived as bad witches, which was yet another reason Kana had to keep his powers secret. Some hunters targeted what were referred to as monsters, like lamias who ate children, but those were the most extreme cases. Vampire hunters were the most common type because vampires were the most common problem for humans.

Ember couldn't have been reacting to that, then, which meant it was either what Octavius had said about the willing donors, or that the local community didn't need to worry about the vampires. The latter half of the statement was more bullshit, although Stephen and Marilyn seemed to be buying it as their shoulders were loosening and their plastic smiles had gained a touch of genuine warmth. Which meant the former part of the statement was where the problem lay. If Octavius and Penelope had willing donors, Kana wondered who they were, and just how willing were they?

Why would werewolves choose to play guard to vampires? Sora asked, apparently following Kana's thoughts. *Plus, they live in packs. Why are there only one or two around?*

More than one or two, Mika cut in. *But they're all squeezed into the small house in front. I don't smell any wolves on the lawn or around the doors of the big house.*

Kana automatically took another cue card from Beth to hold up. *Don't wolves need space to run?* Kana asked. *Everything I've read says they have to run and hunt, especially on a full moon. Also, Mika, why are you sniffing around the grounds? I thought you were staying outside?*

These wolves are definitely not hunting, Mika replied, blithely ignoring the second part of Kana's question.

Kana glanced at Ember again, as if the answers would be as blatantly visible as on Kana's cue cards, but Ember's face and body were back to a completely stoic mien.

Something wasn't right here, and Kana had a sinking feeling it had to do with the two vampires sitting on the couch, blithely answering Stephen and Marilyn's questions.

Beth passed Kana the last cue card and Kana held it up.

"Thank you so much for taking the time to meet with us," Stephen said after a quick glance in Kana's direction to read the card. "We appreciate your being candid, and I know the residents of our great city will be much more welcoming now they know how wonderful you'll be as our neighbors!"

"I anticipate a lovely relationship with everyone," Octavius replied, and his odd, closed-mouth smile returned.

The interview ended and Stephen and Marilyn stood to shake hands with Octavius and Penelope. Kana turned away to help Beth gather the scattered cue cards and to start packing up. The sooner all the humans got out of the vampire's territory, the better.

Kana was just zipping up the bag full of his and Beth's supplies when a sharp, bright light flashed through the room. A woman screamed and Kana spun around.

Mistress Penelope was writhing on the ground, both hands pressed to her mouth. Stephen was standing next to her, his eyes wide with shock. One shaking hand touched the side of his neck, right where Kana had applied his potion, but when he pulled it away to look at his fingers, they were clean.

"She tried to bite me," Stephen said, his voice breathy as if he couldn't find the oxygen to get the words out.

Penelope screamed again, a bestial sound of defiance. She stood, staggered, and then fell back to her knees, catching herself on the hard floor with one hand.

Her mouth and most of her lower jaw were black and the skin was flaking off like ashes from a cold firepit blowing in the wind. The black was spreading too, crawling up the sides of her face until her cheeks were covered. The air smelled faintly of chamomile and charred flesh.

Kana's spell had done that? Kana fought to keep his face blank, to prevent his shock and pleased surprise from alerting anyone he was the genesis of the magic. A spell he had made up on the fly had managed to keep Penelope from making Stephen her lunch. Kana couldn't help being happy at his success, even as Penelope let out another terrible shriek.

The black was creeping down her neck too. Kana half-expected to feel some sort of remorse or stomach-churning despair at having hurt another living being, but he didn't feel bad at all about what his spell was doing to Penelope. Had she left everyone alone, had she treated the humans like welcome visitors instead of prey, everyone would have walked out of the room completely unharmed. Instead, she proved everything she and Octavius had said during the interview about being harmless to humans was a lie, and she was paying the price. Kana's spell being the reason generated nothing but satisfaction in Kana.

Octavius walked past Penelope. She held out a shaking hand toward him as if beseeching him for help, but he didn't even look in her direction. He did glance briefly at Ember as he reached the door.

"Find the culprit," Octavius said, his voice cold and emotionless.

Ember bowed and pulled the door open.

"Yes, Master Octavius," Ember replied, and his voice was as blank as his face. Kana had missed his initial reaction to what was happening to Penelope. Ember had complete control over his body now, which was showing as little emotion as Octavius's.

Octavius swept through the open door and Ember shut it firmly behind him.

Chapter Four

ONCE OCTAVIUS WAS gone, Ember turned back to the room. His gaze swept over every human, the beautiful deep brown color hard and calculating as he studied each person for a few long seconds. When he reached Kana, his glare increased and Kana couldn't help swallowing hard.

Ember must know Kana wasn't a normal human, otherwise he wouldn't have warned the vampires off the evening Kana had come for the preinterview. Kana had no idea how Ember knew—perhaps Kana's magic had some type of smell Ember had detected—but he did know and now that knowledge was going to bite Kana on the butt.

Except, when Ember finally stepped forward, he walked to Stephen.

"Pardon me," Ember said. Then he bent down to sniff Stephen's neck. When he straightened, he reached out and ran his fingers directly over the tiny pentagram Kana had drawn. He brought his fingers to his nose and inhaled again.

"Chamomile...and a faint hint of garlic," Ember said, his voice soft as if he was thinking out loud. "Where did you get Hunter's Bane?"

Stephen didn't move his body, but his eyes slid to the right, in Kana's direction.

Ember's lips thinned and Stephen took a quick step back as if he thought Ember was pissed. Kana didn't agree—there was the slightest upturn at the corners of his lips as if Ember were suppressing a smile. Although, Kana couldn't say whether it was a smile of triumph or of amusement.

"I thought so," Ember said. He turned away from Stephen to face the rest of the room. "Finish packing," he said loudly so the entire room could hear him. "I'll have someone escort you out." He strode to Kana and stopped right in front of him. "I think you and I need to have a chat."

"He's a valuable member of our team!" Stephen said. "We can't leave here without him."

Ember cut his eyes to Stephen and Stephen's momentary bravado shriveled. He scuttled back to stand within the crowd, all of whom had returned to packing as quickly as possible. Ember touched his earbud and murmured something too low for Kana to catch, but a few seconds later two wolves walked up the staircase. One was carrying a sheet, which he draped over Penelope's body. She had stopped screaming, although Kana could still hear a sort of wheezing whimper every once in a while. She wasn't dead yet, but Kana didn't think she would heal. After she was covered, the wolf returned to his partner waiting by the stairs.

"They'll escort you outside," Ember said to the room. He turned to look pointedly at Kana, one hand outstretched to indicate Kana should start walking. Kana obeyed. Ember held open the door to the main house for Kana too, and he shut it firmly behind them.

The hallways of the guardhouse had been spartan, the sitting room had been simple and functional, but the main house... Kana stopped just on the other side of the door to gape.

Opulence didn't even begin to describe the ostentatious glitter filling the entire hallway. The walls were covered in what appeared to be hand-printed paper with a pink-and-red rose pattern. A small side table was off to one side, the edges of the dark-stained wood carved into ornate swirls and fanciful leaves. A table runner lay down the middle, every inch of it covered in embroidery, and in the middle of the runner a three-branch candelabra stood. The candelabra was made of gold and gilt, the metal artfully twisted and as carved as the table. Shimmering crystals hung on thin gold chains from each branch.

"This way," Ember said.

They walked down the hallway. Every step brought more grandiose, overly decorated opulence into view. Kana wasn't sure if it was better to squint to save his eyes or stare because he would never get to see something so utterly ridiculous again. Ember led the way through another door. The contrast between the hallway and the new room was stark: the small space had white walls, a small, completely ordinary wooden table, and two wooden chairs on each side. It almost looked like a stereotypical interrogation room. Which was exactly what it was, Kana realized when Ember waved for Kana to take one of the chairs.

Kana sat where he was told, and Ember took the chair on the other side of the table. Ember just stared at Kana for a few moments, and Kana tried not to squirm. He hadn't done anything wrong.

You want to run, we can take him, Sora said, his voice fierce. *One wolf against you doesn't stand a chance.*

We don't know anything about him, Kana replied. *For all we know, he could be a superwolf, or spell resistant, or something.*

Plus, Mika cut in, *we don't want to reveal ourselves if we don't have to. Something's not right here, and I'm going to sniff out what before we make any moves.*

Be careful, Kana replied, his mental voice as firm as possible. Mika scoffed and then his attention faded away.

"Hunter's Bane was a good choice," Ember said, suddenly cutting into the silence of the room. "Except, Master Octavius was very careful when he chose this city to relocate to. There are no hunter groups close enough to take any notice of his activities, which means no one capable of selling it to you is in the area." He paused to look at Kana again, as if evaluating what he was going to say next. Kana hoped he was successful at keeping his face blank; there was no need to advertise the jittery feeling growing in his stomach as Ember continued to talk. "I can tell you're something more than the rest of those humans. You smell like a cool night breeze with a touch of ozone after a gentle rain. Most humans smell like whatever they last ate, or like sweat and their deodorant flavor. Each one has a unique scent, but they don't smell like you." He paused again, this time as if waiting for Kana to fill the silence.

Kana didn't dare answer. He couldn't let anyone know what he was. Ember wouldn't be able to keep it secret, not if he had to report to Octavius. The story would spread through the magical community, and if his old coven found out he had created a potion powerful enough to kill a vampire on contact, they would have all the confirmation they needed to force him back into their fold.

"I did some research to find out if you might be a threat to my pack, but your scent wasn't listed in our records. I did find a very similar scent, but they're all supposed to be women."

Uh-oh, Mika said, and at first Kana thought it was in reaction to Ember's words, but Mika continued. *They saw me. Turns out these wolves do know how to hunt. They're pretty good at chasing.* Even Mika's mental voice sounded out of breath.

So run faster, Sora taunted, except his voice sounded a bit worried.

They've got big teeth. I'm running as fast as I can.

Saving Mika was more important than not confirming Ember's guess. *I'm going to grab you,* Kana told Mika.

Ready, Mika answered immediately.

Kana's fingers twitched as he organized his magic and pulled a touch of power from Sora. Ember tensed, but before he could do anything more, Kana yanked with his magic.

The channel between Mika and Kana was wide open and clean. Mika slid through without any resistance and popped into view on Kana's lap, where he sprawled, panting for breath. Kana ran his fingers through Mika's fur as he tightened the channel again so their magic wouldn't spill.

"It's not nice to chase harmless kittens," Kana said, his voice soft but stern.

Ember's lips twitched in that barely there smile, and he touched a finger to the earbud he was still wearing.

"Stop the search. The cat is with me." He turned his attention back to Kana. "If that's a harmless kitten, then I'm a shih tzu. You're a male witch, and you brewed the Hunter's Bane."

"What are you going to do with me?" Kana asked. There was no sense in verbally confirming what Ember already knew.

Ember tilted his head as he studied Kana. "I'm going to tell Master Octavius the truth. The culprit has been punished." He sighed. "As far as I'm concerned Mistress Penelope is the one at fault for her own demise, so I won't be lying."

Mika stretched in Kana's lap, flexing his claws, although he didn't puncture the skin of Kana's thighs. He straightened and then hopped onto the table. He looked at Ember, who looked back, neither of them blinking for a long moment in some sort of dominance fight.

I like him, Mika finally said. *He is definitely yummy.*

No fair! I want to see too, Sora whined, although Kana's bag didn't even twitch to give him away.

He doesn't need to know I have two familiars, Kana replied as sternly as he could.

Ask him about why the werewolves don't get to roam the grounds, Mika said. *I think if we know the answer to that, we'll know why he's willing to stretch the truth for you.*

"Thank you," Kana said to Ember. At the same time, he thought to Mika, *I'm not going to ask him that! He's doing us a favor, and I don't want to antagonize him.*

Ask him! Mika insisted. He meowed and stomped one paw on the table. *Ask him or I'll shift forms and ask him myself.*

You can't do that! Kana begged.

Then you ask him!

"Sounds like he wants something," Ember said.

Kana jumped, looking up from where he had been glaring at Mika and hoping he didn't look guilty.

"He wants me to ask you something." Kana trailed off, trying to figure out a polite way to word Mika's question.

Ember gave Kana another of his barely there smiles. "Ask. I won't be offended by a question from a cat."

Mika hissed at him and stomped his foot again. *Rude!*

"He, er. Well, he wants me to ask why the wolves don't run around the grounds. Mika says there's a lot of land out there, but no scent of the wolves using it."

Ember's face completely shut down, all traces of humor from a second ago gone in a flash. Mika recoiled, dashing off the table and back into Kana's lap.

"I'll take you back to your coworkers now," Ember said. He stood and waited pointedly for Kana, who lifted Mika onto his shoulder before standing and joining Ember at the door.

They walked down the overly decorated hallway and back into the now empty sitting room. Penelope's body was gone and the floor where her ashes had flaked was clean. No sign that anyone had used the room recently remained. Ember seemed to reverse the route they'd taken to get here. By the time they reached the front door again, Kana was thoroughly lost. Finally, they reached the door outside, and Kana stepped out first into the cool air of the evening.

"Kana!" Beth called, sounding relieved. "We were so worried!"

One of the vans was gone, but the second was full of members of the crew Kana was friendly with. Only Beth was outside, and she jogged over toward him.

Suddenly, a sound like a bat screeching echoed around them, and a shadowed body dove from the top of the iron gate, heading straight for Beth, fangs first.

Kana didn't have time to think. Even if his oil protected her neck, it wouldn't save her from claws or the violent impact. He threw open his channels, drawing power from Mika and Sora, and stomped one foot on the ground.

Four circles of light erupted. The ones that manifested under Kana, Beth, and Ember were simple protection circles: the pentagram with the circle connecting all five points. They glowed softly.

The fourth circle bloomed under the vampire, moving along the pavement as he flew through the air. It started as the same basic circle, but between the pentagram's lines runes blazed into existence. Big runes for earth and sun nestled on either side of the top point of the star. Below the earth rune in the next open slot Kana wrote the combined runes for apple and mistletoe. Below sun he added the rune for growth. In the final open space at the bottom of the pentagram Kana added the rune for power. He closed the circle and a jet of magic blasted from him.

Light shone within the circle, and the vampire shrieked again. A tree thick with strangling mistletoe erupted upward, shaking the ground and splitting the pavement, and thrusting through the center of the vampire's chest. The shriek abruptly stopped.

Flakes of ash floated down to the pavement as the light from the circles faded away. Beth peeked out from between upraised arms and then gaped at the tree.

"What happened?" she asked, her voice shaking.

The rush of magic faded away, and Kana's butt hit the ground when his knees refused to hold him. Mika meowed and climbed into Kana's lap.

Nice work, Mika said, sounding as tired as Kana felt.

"That," Ember said, his voice slow as he likely fought to find the right words, "was Master Xavier. I believe he went mad, and the house defenses reacted to stop him. I'm sorry for the fright, but you were never in any danger." Ember strode forward and held out a hand to Kana, who took it and allowed Ember to help him back to his feet. "I suggest you all get in your van and head home," he finished.

Beth nodded. "Amen. I am ready for a drink. Coming Kana?"

Kana nodded, but when he tried to pull his hand free from Ember's, Ember didn't let go.

"We are going to have a talk about tonight," Ember said in a soft, growling voice that pleasantly renewed the weakness in Kana's knees. "Whether you like it or not."

Kana nodded. He cradled Mika in his arms and followed Beth into the van, hoping Ember would be too busy with the death of two of the vampires he was supposed to protect to remember Kana.

Chapter Five

SUNLIGHT POURED THROUGH the windows of Kana's apartment. He groaned and rolled over, smushing his face into his pillow where the light couldn't bother him. He was just drifting back to sleep when the morning alarm on his phone blared. Kana stuck one hand out from under the covers, tapping his fingers over his nightstand and not finding his phone.

"It's over here, still in your pants pocket from last night," Sora said.

The alarm stopped, and the bed sank as Sora sat on the edge of the mattress at Kana's side.

"Can't you skip work today? We're all still exhausted from yesterday," Sora asked, his voice hopeful.

Kana rolled so he could look up at Sora. "I can't. They'll be worried at work if I don't come in, or they might think something happened to me. Besides, I'll likely have to do some damage control after all the magic they saw. It's probably a good bet they're going to change their write-up for the interview after Stephen almost got bitten, but I want to make sure they don't have anything about my potion in there."

Sora sighed. "You're right. I'll brew some tea and start breakfast. You go kick Mika out of the shower."

Kana crawled out from under the covers, but instead of going to the bathroom, he reached out and wrapped his arms over Sora's shoulders. Sora tilted his head just right and bent, Kana pushed up onto his toes, and their lips met.

"Good morning," Kana said when he pulled away, his lips feathering over Sora's as he spoke.

Sora laughed. "It is now. Go tell Mika good morning too so we can get today started."

Kana obeyed, heading to the bathroom where the shower was still going strong.

Mika liked water, particularly when he was in his human shape. Sora tolerated it as a necessity to stay clean, but Mika was standing, unmoving under the warm spray, letting the water completely soak him. Kana stared at him for a long moment, taking in the beauty of his sleek human body and the water droplets rolling down over taut muscle and smooth skin. Kana let out a heavy breath and tried to refocus. He had to get to work, which didn't leave time for all the filthy, wonderful things the sight of Mika was inspiring. Especially when his lips were still tingling from Sora's kiss. He shook his head to clear those thoughts away. He had to get to work today.

"Did you at least bother with the soap?" Kana asked, his voice almost steady. He shucked his pajamas and tossed them into the corner, and then climbed into the tub with Mika.

Mika rumbled out a purring laugh and opened his eyes. "Yes. I did that first, but I'm sore from all the running yesterday and was trying to use the hot water to ease my muscles."

He stepped out of the way so Kana could get under the water and handed him the shampoo bottle once Kana was wet enough. Five minutes later, Kana rinsed off the last of the soap. He reached for the handle to turn off the water, but Mika's hands landed on Kana's hips. He yanked Kana backward until Kana's back was pressed to Mika's chest.

Mika purred in Kana's ear. "You never told me good morning." His hands drifted forward and down, one taking Kana's quickly growing length in hand, the other reaching past to caress Kana's balls. Mika's fingers were skilled, his fist strong, and his purring breaths an aphrodisiac in Kana's ears. Mika thrust his own length against Kana, using the pressure between their bodies to pleasure himself as he pleasured Kana. It didn't take long before Kana was moaning out his release. Mika's length pulsed as he let out his own moan.

Kana leaned against Mika's body, waiting for his knees to remember they were supposed to hold him up. Mika chuckled and then manhandled Kana so he was back under the spray where the evidence of their fun would be washed away. By the time Mika was done cleaning him, Kana's brain was back online. He shut the water off and grabbed towels for them both off the rack.

"You're going to be late!" Sora yelled, his voice easily penetrating through the bathroom door.

"Crap," Kana muttered. If he missed his usual bus, the next one wasn't for twenty minutes and then he'd be really late. He rushed to get dried and into clothing and ran out the door with a piece of toast in his mouth, a travel mug of tea in one hand, his bag in the other, and two cats trailing behind. It wasn't until he was on the bus—which pulled up just as he got to the stop—that he was able to straighten the strap on his bag and open the top so Mika and Sora could climb inside.

He made it to work on time and trudged inside. Beth was sitting at her desk. She glanced up at Kana and grimaced.

"You have a hangover too?" she grumbled. "I'm gonna be dragging all day." She thumped her head down on her desk, then groaned. "One of these days I'm going to remember I'm not twenty anymore, and I can't drink like I used to," she said through the arms she had crossed over her head.

Kana placed his bag on the ground and turned on his computer while Mika and Sora squirmed out the top and went to curl up on their pillow.

"Do you need any painkillers?" Kana asked.

"Waaay ahead of you, but thanks," she replied, still with her head hidden.

Kana shrugged and sipped tea from his mug while he waited for the computer to load. Once it was running, he opened his email to see if anything had landed about the interview.

There was one email. Kana opened it and sighed. "We have a meeting in a half hour about yesterday," he told Beth.

"You're joking. Don't they realize some of us need a bit more time than that to recover from yesterday?"

"Well, they did decide to still go through with the interview even after I told them it was dangerous," Kana answered. "Hopefully the meeting is to apologize?"

Beth lifted one of her elbows so she could side-eye him. "Have you met Stephen? He doesn't apologize. This is probably a meeting for how to spin this so he comes out looking good."

Kana rolled his eyes. "You're probably right. Think I can get the notes for the Kreller Op-Ed done before the meeting?"

Beth snorted and dropped her elbow back into place. Kana left her to it and got to work.

*

EVERYONE IN TODAY'S meeting had also been present in the previous one. Kana and Beth took the same seats at the far end of the table and settled in to wait until Stephen was ready to start.

Five minutes later, Stephen strolled into the room. He took the chair at the head of the table and waved his hand to get everyone's attention. Once everyone's eyes were on him, he leaned forward.

"For anyone who wasn't present at the interview yesterday, we had a bit of excitement."

"Understatement of the year," Beth muttered under her breath. Kana elbowed her to get her to shut up.

Stephen luckily hadn't heard because he was still talking. "We had what appeared to be a solid interview, but in reality, the vampires were working their wiles to placate us. The second they believed the cameras were stopped, I was viciously attacked. Thankfully for us, we always keep the cameras rolling until after our subjects have left the room." He beamed at the room as if waiting for someone to drop accolades on him. Since that was company policy rather than Stephen's brilliant idea, no one said anything. "I, and our editing team," he added belatedly with a nod to two men sitting in a corner, "have pieced together a video that I'm proposing we use when we air this segment."

Stephen tapped the audio/visual controls on the touchscreen panel sitting in front of his seat. The lights dimmed and the overhead projector turned on.

Master Octavius and Mistress Penelope sitting together on the couch in the sitting room came into focus. Octavius was giving the creepy closed mouth smile that kept his fangs hidden.

"Yes, we drink blood, but we have grown practiced at surrounding ourselves with willing donors, so the general populace need not fear our presence here," Octavius said.

"You will not touch any humans in this city to feed from?" Stephen's voice asked through the speakers, although he didn't appear on camera.

Octavius shook his head. "As I said, we have no need to touch the unwilling. No human need fear us."

The video paused and the lights came up. "Here seems like a good spot to add some commentary," Stephen said. "I was thinking we could say something along the lines of how we believed them, and they seemed genuine, then start adding some foreshadowing."

"Drama hooks viewers," Marilyn added. "Maybe say something like: we should have listened to our history books instead."

Stephen frowned at her for interrupting but jumped right back in when she was done speaking. "We don't want to overdo the foreshadowing, of course, but I think adding a warning that the content might not be suitable for all viewers here would be good."

Stephen hit the play button and the lights dimmed again.

This time, the camera angle wasn't perfect. Kana could make out Stephen's back because of his hair color, and Penelope because of the size of her wide skirts. However, Stephen was still wearing his mike clipped to his lapel.

"Do you want a tour of the house?" Penelope asked, her voice completely clear. In the video, Kana could see her lean toward Stephen. The camera zoomed in, which made it go a bit blurry, but Kana could definitely see her mouth open wide as she bent toward Stephen's neck.

And then a flash of bright yellow light obscured the scene, and a screech filled the air. The camera cleared just in time to catch a glimpse of Stephen's shocked face as he said, "She tried to bite me."

The video ended, and the lights came back up.

"What do you think?" Stephen asked the room.

"We need to fill in some of the details," Amanda, Kana and Beth's boss said. "You had assurances before the interview that you would be safe? We don't want anyone thinking we provoked the vampires into attacking."

"We didn't provoke them! We were invited," Stephen replied.

Kana couldn't help wondering whether Stephen had forgotten all of Kana's warnings, or if he just didn't care.

Amanda shook her head. "That doesn't answer my question, but if we stick with the story about being invited we should be fine. What about the flash of light at the end? Did you add some sort of special effect?"

"Of course not!" Stephen replied, sounding affronted as his back stiffened. "That was some sort of goo Kana slapped on us. He said it would help protect us."

"Kana?" Amanda asked, and suddenly the entire room was looking at him.

He should have expected this. Kana wracked his brain, trying to come up with a plausible story.

"Well," he said, trying to stall for time to think. He didn't bother trying to hide his nervousness or the shaking in his voice. "It's probably not something you'll want to share. I went to a bunch of different shops, but no one had anything that would repel vampires. But I stopped at a little pop-up tent in the square—you know where they hold the flea market every Friday? The old lady running it promised the oil would keep vampires and mosquitoes away, so I bought it. I figured it was better than nothing?"

"You bought snake oil?" Stephen gasped. "You put some sort of unknown grease on me?"

"It worked, though," Amanda cut in sharply. "Snake oil or no, you still have all your blood thanks to it."

"Well, I can't talk about some unknown old lady and her creepy goop," Stephen said, his voice firm as his outrage vanished.

Amanda shrugged. "So, we spin it. Despite being invited, you weren't certain of their intentions. You were smart enough to take some precautions just in case, and they paid off. It makes the network look good for doing something to protect our employees."

And it wouldn't hurt Stephen's image either, Kana thought when Stephen immediately jumped on board.

"All we have to do is iron out what we want to say on air, and what we want to write for the newspaper and website columns," Amanda said when Stephen stopped preening.

Kana let out a breath, relieved attention had been diverted from him, then focused on taking notes for the meeting. He and Beth were likely going to write the first drafts of the columns—which would then be completed by the writers with bigger names so they would get the author credit and drum up interest—so he needed to know what was hashed out.

Two very long hours later, Kana and Beth staggered back to their desks. Beth immediately went to her desk in search of more painkillers while Kana collapsed into his chair.

"I need a nap," he said aloud.

Told you we should have skipped work, Sora said, sounding smug. He yawned and stretched on the pillow, then curled up again and pressed his nose to Mika's side. A second later Sora was as asleep as Mika, and all Kana wanted to do was crawl under his desk and join them.

"If only," Beth groaned. "But I don't think we'll be allowed to leave today until we submit an acceptable draft."

Beth's words proved to be prophetic. She and Kana wrote four drafts. The first three were returned heavily edited. The first was edited by Amanda, the second by Stephen and Marilyn—mostly Stephen—and the third by the writing staff who would be putting their name on the final product. Each draft had to be approved by every single person on the list, so they had to wait for Amanda, then Stephen, and finally the writing staff to approve the fourth and, thankfully final, draft before they could finish work that day.

Kana was just short of staggering and was yawning heavily when he and Beth were finally allowed to leave. The sun was setting, its blinding glare making Kana squint as he stepped outside the building.

"You sure you don't want me to drive you home?" Beth asked, concern in her voice.

Kana yawned and waved his hand at her. "Thanks for the offer, but I live in the opposite direction. No sense in you going out of your way. I'll just take the bus."

"If you're sure..." Beth trailed off, but when Kana didn't change his mind, she sighed. "Don't fall asleep on the bus and end up two towns over."

Kana laughed. "Don't worry. I'm not that tired. My brain is fried, that's all."

Beth smiled at him. "Mine too. Okay. See you tomorrow."

"See you." Kana walked to the bus station while Beth went in the other direction to the parking garage across the street. He had about five minutes before the bus was scheduled to arrive, which was more than enough time to mosey his tired body across the street and down one block to the stop.

The crosswalk light changed quickly, and Kana walked to the other side of the road. He turned to walk to the bus stop when a black SUV suddenly stopped at the curb right next to him. Both passenger-side doors flew open, and two werewolves jumped directly into his path.

"Get in the car," the closer one growled.

Kana shook his head. "No thanks." Either Mika or Sora were growling from inside Kana's backpack. Kana widened the channel between them, letting more magic flow. His circle to repel werewolves would need aconite, but Kana would combine that rune with the rune for flower so it would only stun them. The roots and seeds of aconite were deadlier than the flower. Werewolves called aconite wolfsbane, and it was extra potent against them.

Kana couldn't go with the werewolves, but he still had to stay hidden, so he would also need a secrecy spell. A second rune layered beneath and around the wolfsbane one would keep any passersby from noticing.

The closer wolf reached out and the second one put a piece of paper into his hand. The wolf held up the paper for Kana to see.

"What would happen if this photo were put online in a blog post reading: witch with two familiars!"

The photo was of Kana, toast in his mouth and two cats running after him as he sprinted for the bus that morning.

Kana's gathered magic froze, and his breathing stuttered into a gasp. The circle faded from his mind, replaced by the photo. Kana's face was clear; anyone who saw it would recognize him, even all these years later. He would definitely be found if that were posted.

"Our Alpha said if you didn't get in the car, this would be all over the internet by tonight. He wondered who besides him might come knocking on your door?"

"What..." Kana's voice came out as a croak and he swallowed to try to get some moisture back into his mouth. "What does your Alpha want from me?"

The wolf shrugged. "Just to talk."

Kana very much doubted that, but what choice did he have?

What do I do? he asked Mika and Sora.

Go with him, I guess, Mika replied.

We can always blast them all later, Sora added.

Kana looked at the photo again, then up at the wolf whose face was stern and unbending. Kana didn't think he was lying.

"Just to talk," Kana said as firmly as his shaking voice could. He turned and climbed into the back seat of the SUV. Two more wolves were inside, one driving and the other across the seat from Kana behind the driver.

The spokes-wolf took the front passenger seat and the second wolf waited until Kana moved over to take the middle seat before he climbed in and shut the door. Kana buckled up and closed his eyes, hugging his backpack tightly to his chest and hoping this adventure really would be "just to talk."

Chapter Six

THIS IS DEFINITELY not the way to the vampire's house, Kana told Mika and Sora after they were driven for ten minutes in the opposite direction, heading north toward Saratoga Springs rather than west to Schenectady.

Maybe there's more than one pack living in this city? Mika guessed. *They might not be happy the vampire's pack moved in and want your help?*

Which means they were watching the vampire house and saw your spell, Sora added with a grumble.

And they followed me home and had someone surveil me this morning, otherwise how else did they get that picture? Kana said.

How did they avoid your detection spells? Sora asked. *We put warning circles all around the neighborhood.*

Did we calibrate them for werewolves? Mika asked.

Kana mentally sighed at them. *Of course not. I didn't think werewolves would be a problem. Those circles are meant to detect witches and other witches' circles. It would be far too complicated to make a circle to detect every single magical being.*

The car left the city entirely, now heading out into the rural areas where land was cheap and mostly used for farms. Werewolves would much prefer having space rather than being squeezed into a house in the city, even one with as much land as the vampires' house.

Twenty more minutes found them at the foot of a long, paved driveway. The car turned in, and after another minute, they rounded a curve and stopped at a large iron gate set between ten-foot stone walls that appeared to surround the entire property. The driver rolled down his window and pressed some buttons into a keypad and the gate rolled to the side. The car drove through the gate, and a glance behind showed the gate slowly rolling shut again.

Kana didn't think the driveway would ever end. The car continued to drive along an endless sea of neatly mown lawn. Neither shrubbery nor even a dandelion was visible as a potential landmark. He guessed they traveled at least a mile before a house suddenly appeared on the horizon. From what Kana could tell at first glance, the house appeared massive, sprawling across the lawn with wings in all directions. It was at least four stories and Kana noticed casements so there likely was at least one basement level.

The driver stopped the car in a wide parking area in front of the house, although the driveway continued to the left to where Kana guessed a garage of some sort must be located.

"Out," the spokes-wolf growled—the first thing he had said since getting Kana into the car—before opening his own door and climbing out.

The wolf sitting next to Kana on the passenger's side got out and held the door for Kana, who obeyed and stepped outside. The car drove away the second the doors were closed again.

"Follow me," the spokes-wolf said. He climbed the front steps and opened the door, holding it until Kana and the other wolf had walked inside. He closed it and started walking farther into the house.

If the vampires' house had been overstated opulence, this house was its exact opposite. Everything was elegant and simple, from the smooth, wide-plank wood floors to the simple paint on the walls. The occasional picture or side table filled the space, but they fit with the overall theme. The place felt light and airy to Kana, who couldn't help breathing in the calm the building exuded.

They didn't walk in circles. After only two hallways, the spokes-wolf stopped and knocked on a closed door. He didn't wait for a response, simply opening it immediately after. He held the door for Kana, but didn't go inside. Once Kana had walked through, he closed the door, leaving Kana in a sitting room.

A man was standing next to one of the windows, looking outside with his back to Kana. He turned and Kana blinked, surprised.

"Ember?" he asked.

Ember nodded and walked over to one of the long couches in the center of the room. "I told you we'd be speaking again soon."

Sora snorted. *Typical controlling alpha wolf,* he said in a scathing voice.

"Come and sit." Ember sat down and waved to the other couch. Kana walked over, set his bag on the seat next to him, and sat.

"I want to know what's in the bag," Ember said. He leaned forward and his eyes were intense as he stared, unblinking, at Kana.

Kana tried not to squirm. Ember's eyes were beautiful and fiery, and rather than scaring Kana into answering, they were igniting a completely different emotion.

"Why do you need to know that?" Kana finally answered after the moment of silence dragged on a bit too long.

Ember opened a manila folder sitting on the coffee table between them, pulled out a photograph, and pushed it across the table for Kana to see.

"Because I think you have a couple of cats hiding in there, and I want to see them both."

Kana looked down at the familiar surveillance photo, Mika and Sora completely visible where they trailed behind him.

"Why were you watching me?" Kana asked, rather than answering Ember's demand.

"To find useful leverage. I didn't expect to find it so quickly, though," he added, his voice almost admonishing.

"I overslept," Kana replied, then paused when he realized it sounded like he was pouting.

Except, Ember's lips tilted in that amazing half smile, and he let out a short chuckle.

I wanna see! Sora demanded. A paw slid out the side of the bag, where Kana hadn't fully zipped it closed, and then pushed the zipper open farther.

Don't! Kana gasped. *I want to keep you a secret!*

Sora's head popped out of the hole, and he looked at Kana with a reproachful frown. *He already knows about us. No sense in prolonging the inevitable. And I want to see this pretty wolf!* Sora squirmed all the way out of the bag and hopped up onto the table.

Mika's head popped out of the bag a second later. *I agree with Sora. Your pretty wolf already knows we exist, so there's no point in my suffocating in that bag any longer. But, I think he wants more from *you than just confirmation of two familiars.* He hopped up onto the table next to Sora.

The cats were studying Ember just as Ember was looking at them. Kana had no idea what any of them were thinking, but Ember seemed to make some sort of decision because he leaned back into the couch cushions and returned his attention to Kana.

"Male witches are supposed to be incredibly rare," Ember began, and his voice was light, almost as if he was musing his internal thoughts out loud. "When they do occur, they're allegedly fairly weak. In the history of witches, has there ever been a male with two familiars? Two cat familiars, even?" He leaned forward, placing his elbows on his knees as if the closer proximity to Kana would force Kana to answer. His eyes were piercing in their intensity, and Kana didn't want to look away. "I am an alpha wolf, the alpha of my pack, and I know fellow predators when I see them. There is no way those are regular house cats."

Neither Mika nor Sora twitched, but Kana let out a soft gasp.

Ember's half smile returned. "I thought so. You really have no talent for lying, you know that?"

Sora and Mika both laughed. *He's got you there!* Mika said in a jovial voice as he continued to laugh.

Kana just sighed. "That's why we're hiding."

"Let me guess. Your witches' coven put up with you because you had a bit of power, but the second they realized you had actual, real power, they tried to take advantage of you?"

Kana nodded, then shook his head. "I ran before they found out I matched with two familiar cats. I'm hoping they never bothered to look for me, but just in case, we're trying not to be conspicuous."

Ember snorted. "And then those dumbasses in your office decided it would be a great idea to go interview a couple of vampires." He paused, as if he were deciding something. "You brewed the Hunter's Bane," he said, his voice firm as if he was stating fact instead of guessing. "Without the benefit of the hunter's recipes too, which means you made it up on your own. Plus, you drew four circles out of thin air when Master Xavier decided to attack. Most witches I've encountered need a smooth surface, chalk, candles, and incense just to get their magic to work. How powerful are you?"

Ember didn't need to know about Kana's childhood: getting the dregs of the magic schoolbooks after the girls had chosen the best. Studying alone because no one wanted to bother teaching him and haunting the library so the matron didn't know what spell books he was reading. Then, after running away, practicing in secret so he wouldn't be discovered, with only Sora and Mika to help him figure out how to work his spells in the ways he wanted.

"I've never had the chance to compare my powers to another witch," Kana answered instead. Although, given he had two familiars, and Mika and Sora were each able to assume three forms, Kana was fairly certain he was pretty strong.

"If you say so," Ember replied with a shrug. "But that brings me to why you're here."

Finally, Sora said with a groan. *I'm hungry. The sooner we finish this talk, the sooner we can get dinner!* Sora flopped down into a sprawl on the table. Mika hopped over to curl up in Kana's lap.

"What do you know about werewolf and vampire relations?" Ember asked.

"Not much," Kana answered with a shake of his head.

Ember chuckled. "Then I apologize in advance for the history lesson. I'm sure you know vampires and werewolves are both creatures who were born human and turned into something else. Vampires' dominion is the night because they cannot tolerate the sun, and they are immortal because of it. Werewolves can exist both in day and night and have a normal human lifespan but are subject to the whims of the full moon, which usually became visible after dark.

"Since vampires are helpless during the day, and werewolves are impacted by the moon at night, a very long time ago they created a symbiotic relationship. Werewolves help protect the vampires when they are most helpless, and vampires do the same for the wolves."

"But something isn't right between you and the vampires," Kana guessed.

Ember nodded and his face turned stony and dark, his cheekbones emphasized as he gritted his teeth.

"There is an imbalance of power. You have to understand vampire biology to really understand what happened. Basically, there is no way to tell how powerful a human might be as a vampire until after they are turned. The meekest, weakest human in existence could become the most powerful vampire, and vice versa. I believe Master Octavius was a very weak human when he lived about six hundred years ago. He may have been a servant, but certainly he was abused. He craved power and found it when he was bought by a rich vampire merchant and became a blood slave. Somehow, he convinced the merchant to turn him and over the next six hundred years consolidated power. Then, twenty years ago, he showed up at my pack house. He killed my father, who was alpha at the time, killed the alpha council, and killed any alpha candidates he could find. I survived because I was so young my mother was able to hide me."

Ember's voice was completely flat, without a single emotion escaping to color his words, but Kana was pretty sure that wasn't because Ember didn't feel anything. Rather, it was because Ember felt too much and had to lock down every emotion about the story he was telling or succumb to it.

"He said in the interview that humans didn't need to worry about the vampires because he already had willing donors," Ember continued. "But that isn't true at all. He controls us by taking the weakest among us, the ones I'm supposed to protect. He keeps them locked away and feeds from them to ensure they stay weak. If anyone tries to disobey him, he hurts them."

This time, Ember's voice did break. As alpha, it was his duty to protect his entire pack, particularly the most vulnerable, and he was failing. Kana wanted to stand, walk around the coffee table, and join Ember on the other couch where he could then pull Ember into a hug the wolf definitely needed. Except, Kana didn't think Ember would appreciate it. Aside from the fact that Kana was basically a complete stranger, Ember wasn't in a position to allow even the barest moment of weakness to escape. He had to be strong in order to keep his pack going. A hug wouldn't erase that, and it also wouldn't help him at this moment.

Maybe—after this was all over and Ember's pack freed—then Ember would be willing to entertain the idea of a hug.

Still, Kana wasn't completely blinded by his infatuation. "You want my magic."

Ember nodded. "I admit the two vampires you killed were not nearly as powerful as Master Octavius, but with your help, I think my wolves might have a chance."

He looked at Kana as if he expected an immediate answer, and a very large part of Kana wanted to say yes. But could Kana really help them? He was untried, self-trained, and in hiding. The only positive on his side was he had two familiars and therefore access to double the magical reserves. However, without the proper training, could he really use those reserves in an actual battle?

And it also begged the question of whether he wanted to get involved with someone else's problem. He could walk away; forget about Ember and his poor wolves and continue living his quiet life. Except, Kana's conscience was screaming no. He wanted to help the wolves being held captive; he wanted to bring more than that small half smile to Ember's lips. If he ran away, neither would ever happen.

Before Kana could come up with some sort of answer, Ember's watch started beeping an alarm. Ember pressed the button to stop it and stood.

"I have to leave now to get back to the vampire house in time. Can we meet again tomorrow?"

Kana nodded. "I need some time to think, but tomorrow should be fine. Around the same time?"

"I'll send a car, but no threats this time," Ember added with a joking quirk of his eyebrow.

They walked to the door together. Ember opened it and courteously held it for Kana, and then Kana followed Ember down the hallways and back to the front door where two wolves were waiting for them.

"Drive him back home," Ember told one of the wolves. The wolf nodded and loped off, probably to go get the car, Kana assumed. Ember and the other wolf walked outside where a car was already waiting. The wolf got into the driver's seat, but Ember waited until a second car pulled up behind the first. Kana got into the back seat of that car, Mika and Sora hopping in after him, and only once Kana's door was closed did Ember get into the back seat of his own car. The cars pulled away, and Kana couldn't help being relieved that he was heading home.

Stars were starting to appear overhead when the car dropped them off in front of Kana's apartment. Kana hurried inside and let out a sigh of relief when his apartment door was firmly closed and locked behind him.

"That wasn't how I expected my afternoon to go," Kana said.

Mika and Sora shimmered for a moment as they shifted into their human forms.

"Now dinner's late, and I'm soooo huuunnnngry!" Sora moaned.

Kana was too hyped to feel hungry, but he knew as soon as he calmed he would probably fall asleep, so he ought to eat too. This wasn't an evening for cooking. Kana opened the freezer and pulled out three meals he had previously cooked and then frozen. The first one went into the microwave while the others waited their turn on the counter.

Kana also went to his pantry and pulled out his cardboard container of salt.

"Let me do that," Mika said. He pulled the salt from Kana's hand, turned Kana around, and gently pushed him back in the direction of the microwave. "You focus on the food."

Mika drew an unbroken line of salt across the threshold by the front door, then moved to the closest window. Sora was busy pulling cups out of the cabinet so he could set the table. Kana turned back to the microwave and watched the plastic Tupperware spin in circles.

Innocent werewolves held captive by a power-mad vampire. Just that thought read like a tabloid news headline, yet Kana absolutely believed everything Ember had told him. Ember's stoic face, the lack of emotion, and even his desperation in turning to Kana for help all said he was telling the truth. And, quite frankly, Kana was much more apt to believe in Ember than in Octavius, who had invited a bunch of humans to his house on a pretense in order to have a fresh snack. Kana absolutely believed that had his spell not sucker-punched Penelope, more of his coworkers would have been attacked and some of them might not have walked out of there alive.

He shuffled meals to microwave and plate three times. By the time he was done heating their dinners, Mika had put the salt away and Sora was sitting at the set table, waiting impatiently for his food. Kana placed one meal in front of each seat and happily dug in. Only after Mika and Sora had finished most of their dinner—and Kana had discovered he was hungry too after a few bites—did he broach the subject.

"What do you think we should do?" he asked them.

Sora finished chewing and swallowed before answering. "You want to help them."

"I won't make a decision without asking you both first," Kana insisted.

"Yes," Mika said softly, "but we're your familiars. We want what you want."

Kana frowned at him. "You both are perfectly capable of voicing your dissent if you don't like something I'm doing. Don't pretend otherwise."

"We are abstract magic given solid form thanks to your intent," Sora cut in. "When it comes to emotional needs, physical needs, we are independent. When it comes to magic, you are our master. This is a matter for magic."

"But I'm making my decision based on an emotional response," Kana said. "You can't tell me you felt nothing after hearing Ember's story."

"I could hear his pain and feel yours in response through our bond," Mika said. "I know saving those wolves would be the right thing to do, so I suppose I have no objection to our getting involved."

"Sora?" Kana asked.

"I know bad witches have done similar terrible things to their familiars as what is happening to those wolves. I wouldn't want to wish that on anyone, so yes, I agree we should save them."

"So, tomorrow we tell Ember we'll help him however we can," Kana finished for them and then glanced between Mika and Sora just in case they might have any sort of objection. When none came, Kana finished eating.

He was yawning by the time he dropped his dishes into the sink.

"We'll do them in the morning," Mika insisted. "Bedtime."

Sora turned out the lights behind them as they headed into the bedroom, and Kana was thankful the bed was nearby because he was asleep within minutes.

Chapter Seven

THE CHOICE OF car wasn't subtle—big and black, and parked right in front of Kana's office. The second Kana stepped outside, a wolf hopped out the front passenger side and pulled open the back door for Kana.

Good thing Beth got held up, Kana said to Mika and Sora. She would have all sorts of comments and questions about the five-star treatment and would definitely not have let up until she had pried the story from him.

He got into the car quickly, before anyone from work saw, and they pulled into traffic a moment later. Kana expected to have a long drive all the way out to the gigantic house, but the car parked in a small lot only ten minutes later.

"Where are we?" Kana asked the wolf who had opened his door again. They weren't in the worst part of the city, but the building was similar to a place where Kana had lived when he was still getting back on his feet.

"City safe house," the wolf grunted.

Kana followed him inside the apartment building, up a flight of stairs, and to an innocuous door among a row of identical ones. The wolf knocked twice, then turned and walked away, leaving Kana alone in the hall with just Mika and Sora in their bag for company.

Only a few seconds passed before he heard the lock click, and the door swung open to reveal Ember.

"Sorry we had to come here," he said as he held the door wide for Kana to walk inside. "I don't have that long before I need to be at the vampire's house, so I had to stay close."

"This is fine," Kana replied with a shrug. "I'll get home faster tonight, at least."

His backpack rustled and Mika stuck his head out of the opening.

Hurry up! Sora whined.

Oh hush, Mika whined back, but he clambered up onto Kana's shoulder. Sora pushed his head through the opening next, but he stayed in the bag.

The apartment was simple and old. The carpet was worn in a path from the door to the living room and the blinds over the windows were bent and cracked. Still, it was clean.

Two wolves stood by the windows in the living room, and they turned to look at Kana when he stepped inside.

"These are two of my betas, Ralph and George," Ember said. "They're going to work with us. That is..." he paused and turned to Kana. "Are you going to help us?"

Kana nodded. "We decided we can't leave your wolves to suffer."

Ember let out a relived breath. "Good. Let's sit down, and I'll tell you our plan."

Everyone took seats, Mika and Sora on the coffee table and the others on the worn couches.

"Thanks to Kana, there are only three vampires left," Ember began. "I can see two ways of getting rid of them. The first is hitting all three at the same time. If they see an attack coming, like they would if we attack them one by one, Octavius will run, then return when it's most advantageous to him. He'll have the chance to make more vampires, and then we'll be the ones killed when his army attacks us in revenge. If we go after him first instead, there's no telling what the other two will do. This means we need a force ready to take all three at exactly the same time, which we don't have. Even with Kana's help, we just don't have the manpower."

"Are the other two vampires strong like Octavius?" Kana asked.

Although he had never tried it, it was possible to write a spell circle on a piece of treated paper. If he sent Mika and Sora with one paper each after the two weaker vampires, they could light the spell on Kana's behalf. Werewolves would serve as backup to keep them safe until the spell circles were lit.

Except Ember was already shaking his head. "Penelope was Octavius's flavor of the week. He found her already turned just before he moved us here and has been using her for entertainment purposes only. He liked them dumb and simpering, which was why she didn't know to check the reporter's neck before trying to bite. Xavier was old, but he never developed any significant power, which was why Octavius let him stay. I believe Xavier was enamored with Penelope, and her death set him off. Had he been thinking, he could have avoided your circle.

"Lucas and Sophia, the two remaining vampires, are not so weak willed, unfortunately," Ember finished.

"I still like option two better," George said.

"That has its share of problems as well," Ember replied. He looked at Kana. "The other idea we have is to kill Lucas or Sophia before our attack. We should then have enough forces to pin down the two remaining vampires in a coordinated attack."

That sounded good to Kana, but he could tell there was a *but* coming. "Why won't that idea work?" he asked.

Ember sighed. "We need to make it look like it was entirely their fault; like they tried to bite the wrong person, and it ended badly."

"That's really difficult," Ralph said.

"Exactly." Ember ran a hand through his hair. "If they die and fall into dust, we have no proof of how they were killed. Octavius will assume either we did it, or that I didn't take care of the witch like he ordered. He'll punish us. Which means we can't stake them like you did to Xavier with the apple tree, and we can't zap them with Hunter's Bane like you did to Penelope."

"Don't vampires always turn to ash when they die?" Kana asked.

All three wolves shook their heads. "It only happens if their heart is destroyed or they are hit with magic that removes their vampire essence, which is what Bane does."

"Sunlight turns them to ash too," George added.

"Which is another problem," Ember said with a nod to George. "The best way to kill a vampire without them turning to ash is to rip their bodies apart. I mean really rip them apart. If no piece larger than their hand is left, they can't heal the extent of those injuries and will die. As long as whatever rips them apart doesn't touch the heart, no ash. But, if their remains stay outside past sunrise, we lose our evidence."

"And a werewolf can't be implicated," Ralph said, his voice sharp in warning. "If Octavius sees wolf marks on the body, we're all done for."

"Which also brings up the problem of finding a creature strong enough to rip a vampire to shreds, who also has the willpower to remain sentient enough amid a bloodbath not to touch the heart." Ember flexed his fingers as if he were curling his claws in his wolf form and thinking about ripping the vampire apart himself.

Kana sat back in his seat, thinking. If Xavier would have had the ability to evade Kana's hasty circle, had he been in his right mind, then Kana's idea of sending Mika and Sora with a spelled piece of paper was useless. He had no connections to people who could help bolster their numbers, and he had no spells he could use to prevent any of the vampires from escaping. Unless they could get rid of one vampire before the big attack, they would be in trouble.

I want to play, Mika said.

Me too! Sora added. *You know we can do it. All we need is someone to lure one of the vampires into a basement or something where the sun can't reach, and we can do the ripping and shredding.*

"How often do the vampires leave their house?" Kana asked.

"Once a week?" Ember asked George and Ralph.

"About that, yeah," Ralph replied. "They get their fill of werewolf blood most days, but they like the chase. Sophia once told me it warms the human's blood to the perfect temperature."

Which meant they had to travel to the city where there were plenty of pickings, and also plenty of basements.

"If you guys can find someone able to lure one of the vampires into a basement or a windowless room, Mika and Sora volunteered to do the ripping and tearing," Kana said. "Cat claws are shaped differently than a wolf's, so Octavius won't think a werewolf did it."

The three wolves looked at Mika and Sora, who were lounging on the coffee table. They were a little over a foot long, not including their tails, and their claws were sized to match.

Sora stretched, waving his tail in the air as he lowered his shoulders and flexed his front paws, and then he hopped off the table.

You think the floor will hold me? he asked cheekily.

Guess we're about to find out, Kana responded.

Sora's body started to shimmer as magic gathered. Just as his stripes started to be obscured, his body began to expand. He grew bigger and bigger, and Ralph and George both let out shocked gasps when his side brushed against the coffee table. Seconds later, a six-hundred-pound primordial tiger was standing where the small house cat had been.

Sora grinned at the wolves, all of his sharp, inch long teeth on full display. The floor groaned underneath him.

"Shit." George's eyes grew wide and his jaw slack, but that didn't stop him from continuing to swear. Ralph didn't say anything, but his mouth was also hanging open slightly.

Ember's face was blank. However, his eyes were narrowed, and Kana presumed Ember might be evaluating the best way to attempt to take Sora down. Kana didn't think even an alpha wolf would have a chance against Sora in his primordial form, but he was welcome to try. Sora would appreciate the exercise.

The floor groaned again. *I'm changing back before something breaks,* Sora said as he started shimmering again. He shrank to cat size and daintily hopped back onto the coffee table, where he curled up with Mika.

"T-two! There are two of them!" George gasped out.

Ember's half smile was back, and his eyes burned with excitement. "They'll do," he said in a voice that was soft, yet full of deadly promise. "Who do we know that can act as bait?"

*

KANA'S HEAD WAS spinning from the discussion by the time Ember's watch started beeping. Ember stood and pressed the button to silence it.

"Time to go make nice with the vampires," he growled.

Ralph and George both groaned, but they stood as well. Kana followed suit, and he opened his bag so Mika and Sora could climb inside.

"You have a cell phone?" Ember asked Kana as they moved to the door. "We don't know exactly when Sophia or Lucas will go hunting. I'll call you when one of them goes out so you and your—" He paused and glanced down at Kana's backpack. "—cats can get into position."

They walked into the hallway, then waited while George locked the door and Kana dug his cell phone out of an outer pocket of his bag. He unlocked the phone and opened contacts, then handed it to Ember.

"Put your information in here. I block calls that aren't in my contacts list."

Ember started tapping at the touch screen as they headed downstairs. When they reached the main door, he swiped to a different app on Kana's phone and used the keypad to type in a number. A second later Kana heard something vibrating, and Ember pulled a cell phone out of his jacket pocket. He handed Kana's phone back, then unlocked his own phone and input Kana's name into his own contacts list.

"We're good," Ember said. He locked his phone and stuffed it back in his pocket. They walked outside and the black car pulled forward and slid to a stop in front of them. Ember opened the rear passenger door for Kana.

"Thanks for your help," Ember said softly. He leaned against the open door, his eyes soft and that half smile in place making Kana's heart beat faster. "You're going to save us."

"No pressure," Kana said as he buckled in. He was trying to joke, except his voice came out as more of a wishful purr. What would it be like, Kana wondered, if they could meet up just to meet up. No vampires or planning a coup, just the two of them. Except, Ember probably didn't have any interest in Kana beyond what Kana's magic could provide. Ember was an alpha wolf; he likely had dozens of pretty wolves at his beck and call. Kana probably couldn't compare to what Ember already had and Kana needed to keep his head on straight and stay focused on the task ahead.

"I'll make sure my phone is on and charged, so call the second you have word," Kana said, attempting to keep his voice professional.

Ember's smile faded, but he nodded firmly and stepped back. "You know I will." He shut the car door and turned to jog down the sidewalk. The car pulled away in the opposite direction, and Kana lost sight of Ember.

Did I say something wrong? Kana asked.

So many mixed signals, Mika replied.

From both of you, Sora added with a snort. *I don't think either of you know what to think of each other, and Ember's understandably distracted right now. Maybe after this vampire thing is done, you guys can sit down and figure things out.*

That would be nice. Kana sighed softly and turned to watch the city roll by outside the car window. The sun was set, but the last rays were still visible in bright pinks and glowing yellows on the horizon. The streetlights were beginning to come on when the car pulled to a stop in front of Kana's apartment. Kana climbed out and headed inside.

When the door was locked behind them, Mika and Sora changed to their human form. Kana headed into the kitchen to start figuring out dinner, but he turned to lean on the counter when Sora started speaking.

"When was the last time I changed to my big shape?" Sora asked. He stretched his arms over his head until his shoulders cracked, flaunting his flat stomach and firm chest for Kana to greedily devour.

"Before Kana started at his job," Mika replied. When Sora lowered his arms, Mika draped himself against Sora's back with his arms hanging over Sora's shoulders. Both cuddled close, their opposing skin colors a painting of beauty.

"Right! When we went out to that forest to play." Sora leaned back into Mika's body. Mika licked his lips, a slow sensual swipe. His eyes darkened as he stared directly at Kana. He dipped his head slightly to lick a line up the side of Sora's neck, and Kana was lost.

Chapter Eight

FIVE DAYS PASSED, each one inching along like a glacier. Kana woke with his alarm, went to work where he did his best to chat with Beth and act like everything was normal, and then went home to sit by the phone and wait with his familiars.

Even over the weekend, when he at least had freedom from work, Kana was jumpy and twitchy, and simply too hyped up to settle on any one task. Every time his phone chirped to provide a weather report or something else innocuous, adrenaline rushed. Kana's heart thudded frantically, and his fingers and toes would tingle.

Kana told himself over and over to calm down. There was no reason to be worried about a phone call during the daytime; the vampires were sleeping so if Ember called, it would only be to add something to their plans. After dark, he at least had the spell books he was studying and Mika and Sora to distract him.

And then Monday rolled around again, as if a week full of vampires and werewolves and crazy plans was inconsequential to the passing of time. Which it technically was, Kana reminded himself as he packed up his things after yet another long day at work. Overtime wasn't fun, particularly when he wouldn't be paid for the extra hours, yet his boss kept piling on the work.

"You'd think they would have wanted to air the vampire story already, since we had so many big meetings about it"—Beth grumbled as she stacked papers into multiple piles all over her desk—"instead of stalling with research and more rewrites."

Kana hadn't thought about it, but Beth was right. They had that big meeting last week to decide exactly what they wanted to air, and Beth and Kana had submitted a final draft of the article for the newspaper and website. It wasn't like the station to sit on a big story like that.

"Maybe they're afraid the vampires will want retribution for airing something negative about them?" Kana asked.

Beth shook her head. "I don't think so. I think they're waiting until they have more proof the vampires are up to no good. That clip of the vampire trying to bite Stephen was partially obscured by the magic flaring. My guess is they're worried someone will claim it was doctored."

"But if they've got another story of someone totally unrelated to the studio who was also attacked..." Kana trailed off.

"Exactly," Beth finished with a firm nod. "More interested in covering their asses than getting out a public awareness story. Besides, none of our local competitors seem at all interested."

Probably because they actually cared about the safety of their employees and knew better than to go near vampires, but Kana wasn't about to say that aloud while in the office.

"Well, whatever," Beth sighed. She shut down her computer and turned to wait for Kana to help Mika and Sora into his bag. "I hope I never become that soulless, but given I'm working here..." She sighed again. "I guess it's just a matter of time."

"As long as we continue to worry about stuff like that, I think our souls are fine," Kana replied. He pulled his bag on and waved toward the door. "Shall we go?"

Beth gave one last look at all the piles of work on her and Kana's desk, and then scurried to the door before someone else could come to give them more work. Kana followed and caught up with her at the elevator. They walked outside together, the setting sun already touching the horizon and casting long shadows on the sidewalk in front of their building. Beth sighed at the sight, disgust clear in the twist of her lips. They should have been able to leave work hours ago, but of course at four o'clock—just a half hour before they were supposed to leave— Amanda had emailed them with a massive project that had to be completed before close of business.

Beth let out another heavy sigh. "See you tomorrow," she said.

"Yeah, see you." Kana waved when Beth turned to go to the parking garage. He continued onward to the bus stop.

He was just stepping inside the bus shelter when his phone blared. Kana jumped and fumbled the phone out of his pocket. *Ember*, the caller ID read, and Kana quickly swiped across the screen to answer.

"Hello?" he said.

"Kana? Good," Ember answered. "Lucas has decided to feed outside tonight. Where are you? I'll send a car to get you."

"The bus stop outside my office." Kana's voice was calm, but he had no idea why. His hands were shaking and his heart thudding, yet his knees were as steady as his voice as he left the stop and headed back to the curb.

"Okay. A car should be pulling up any second. I'll see you in a few."

Ember hung up.

Kana stared at his phone for a long moment, then put it to sleep and stuffed it back in his pocket.

Abrupt, Kana said.

He's probably busy, Sora replied easily.

True, but Kana couldn't help wishing Ember had a desire to linger with Kana a bit longer. Before he could dwell on ridiculous hurt feelings, a familiar black SUV pulled up in front of him. Kana yanked the back door open and hopped inside. The door was barely closed when the car turned back into traffic. The driver took the car farther into the city, where a popular outdoor shopping center attracted all sorts of customers. People waited in lines outside restaurants, went door to door with their arms full of shopping bags, or hung out on park benches eating ice cream or drinking coffee. Prime pickings for a hungry vampire.

The car double-parked and Kana quickly opened his door and climbed out. The car drove away a second later, and Ember stepped into view on the sidewalk. He waved Kana over, and when Kana reached him, he backed into a nearby alley.

"I just got word Lucas left the compound. Are you ready?"

Kana swung his bag around and unzipped the top. Two grinning cats popped their heads free, and first Mika and then Sora jumped out and vanished into the darkened alley.

"They'll know where they're supposed to be. Where do you need me?" Kana asked.

"This way," Ember said. He pulled a key from his pocket and unlocked the side door of a closed shop. The room was dark, but enough illumination from streetlights outside filtered through the windows to light the way as Ember guided him through the back of the shop to a stairway leading to an attached upstairs apartment.

The stairs let out into a living room as empty as the shop below, but two wooden chairs were pulled up to the window overlooking the street.

"How does your pack own so many properties around here? I thought you just moved here?" Kana asked.

Ember sat in one of the chairs and let out a heavy breath. "This is our home territory. I don't know if Octavius forgot after twenty years of being away, or whether he's taunting us, but he decided to move us back here. The house in the country is our pack house. This building is still owned by one of our families. Back in the day, it was a successful restaurant, and they couldn't let it go."

Kana took the other chair. "Hopefully, the new restaurant will be even better."

Ember snorted and leaned his head against the back of the chair. "Another reason why we need to be free. Tonight's going to bring us just a bit closer."

He looked out the window and smiled, so Kana turned to look as well. Despite all the people, Kana's attention was immediately snagged by a woman innocently walking down the sidewalk. She appeared completely innocuous. Black hair, simple green shirt, and black pants, and absolutely nothing unique and remarkable about her, except Kana couldn't look away.

"What is she?" Kana asked. He dragged his gaze back to Ember, who had his half smile firmly in place as he watched Kana watch her.

"Magic," Ember said. "Most people think new wolves are always bitten, just like vampires, and for the most part they're not wrong. The majority of new wolves are bitten, but there are two types of wolves that are born: really strong ones, and really, really weak ones. In the strong ones, the wolf comes out in the DNA. For the weak ones, we think it's a defense mechanism, something to protect them, but that's just a guess. The rest of our children are born human and can choose to be bitten when they reach adulthood. Except, in rare cases, one of our children is born like her."

Kana glanced out the window again and saw she had crossed the street and was walking down the sidewalk adjacent to their building. Kana breathed in and out, then released just a touch of his power to brush across her. She felt like a familiar, as if she were made of the magic of the other side, but she was much more rooted in the real world than Mika and Sora. She probably couldn't access the other side to pull more magic into her, but Kana would be willing to bet he could make a pact with her and use her magic like he did with his familiars.

But you've got us, Mika said, his voice stern, yet joking at the same time. He knew Kana better than to believe Kana would take advantage of her like that. However, someone unscrupulous—like the vampires— would.

Why would I take a second look at her magic when I've got both of you? Kana sent back to Mika and Sora. He received contented purrs in reply. He turned to Ember instead. "The vampires don't know about her, I bet."

Ember shook his head. "We've been very, very careful. Children like her won't change to wolves no matter how many times we bite them, but you're right that a vampire would take them in a heartbeat. She volunteered when she heard about tonight."

Lucas wouldn't be able to resist. More than enough time had passed since Lucas was supposed to have left to go hunting, so Kana looked out over the shopping center hoping to see a glimpse of him. The girl stopped to look in a shop window just past where Kana was hiding, and when she resumed walking, she turned to come back toward them.

A dark shape suddenly dropped down next to her and looped an arm over her shoulder. She didn't have a chance to let out even a squeak before he yanked her into the alley, but it was a masculine scream that echoed out a second later. Ember jumped to his feet as people immediately turned to look. One or two even started moving toward the alley.

Kana quickly drew in the dust of the windowsill with his pinky, a fast circle and pentagon with two runes tucked into each side: silence and avoidance. He pushed a bit of magic into the circle, which then glowed for a second before it faded away. A second scream cut off midway, and the watchers relaxed and continued about their business as if they hadn't heard anything. Kana blew into the dust to obscure what was left of his circle. When he looked up, Ember was staring at him.

"You're damn fast with those things," Ember said, a touch of awe in his voice.

Kana's checks went hot in a blush. "Thanks," he mumbled as he focused back down at the disturbed dust. "I figured it was important to keep anyone from noticing."

"Definitely. We want the scene completely undisturbed when Octavius demands we locate Lucas for him tomorrow."

Kana looked back out the window, hoping his blush would die down soon. The woman walked out into the sidewalk, turned to look up at the second-floor windows where Ember and Kana were watching, grinned, and flashed the okay sign. A second later a familiar black car pulled up next to her and she climbed inside. The car drove off, and only once it was gone from sight did Kana feel safe to look at Ember again.

Ember was texting on his phone, his lower lip pulled between his teeth as he focused on the touch screen—and now Kana was blushing for a different reason. Did Ember have any idea how sexy he looked biting his lip like that? Probably not, since Kana was pretty sure the move was completely unintentional.

"Is she okay?" Kana asked, forcing his brain to focus on the task at hand.

Ember nodded. "Just before the vamp tried to sink his teeth in, she said a giant shape jumped on him. Shoved him down the open bilco doors, just as we planned." He looked up at Kana. While his lip was free from his teeth, his grin was back and that didn't do anything to quiet Kana's libido. "How are your cats doing? Any problems on their end?"

Kana concentrated down the links he shared with Mika and Sora, opening them a touch wider so he could share some of what they were doing. Sora's glee was plainly evident as he raked his claws down one of Lucas's arms from shoulder to elbow, then hooked his claws in to yank. Kana heard the pop as the shoulder was pulled out of the socket and hurried to check on Mika instead. Mika was having fun pouncing. He dashed across the room, leaped high, and landed hard, and ribs cracked under his weight.

Mika! Careful of the heart! Kana admonished down their link.

His heart's just fine, Mika replied smugly. *His lungs aren't, though.*

Fine, Kana sent back, before shutting the link down again. "My two cats are playing with a helpless mouse," he told Ember. "They're cats, so they can't help having a little fun first, but they'll have it done soon."

Ember rolled his eyes, but his smile didn't dim. "Octavius will demand to know why Lucas hasn't returned. If he makes the request before dawn, I'll bring him to see the scene."

He was repeating what they had already discussed at the meeting in the safe house, but Kana appreciated hearing it again. "But you think he won't want to see it until tomorrow?"

Ember snorted. "He's lazy. With dawn approaching, he won't want to chance having to rush home. Means he'll want to go first thing tomorrow night, though."

Which was when one of Ember's wolves would sneak Kana into the mansion. Ember was certain Octavius wouldn't allow Sophia to go out at the same time, so she would be in the mansion. They had to wait for Octavius to return before they could attack Sophia, just in case she was able to get some sort of message out to him and he was able to escape the trap. One group would be lying in wait for her, and Kana and a second group would be waiting for Octavius. Then, both groups would attack at the same time.

"I'll make sure I leave work on time," Kana said. "I assume another car will pick me up?"

Ember nodded. "They'll idle in the neighborhood until they get word Octavius has left."

And that was all their plans hashed out yet again. Kana didn't have anything else to say, and they lapsed into awkward silence. He had zero idea what to say. Should he ask more questions about tomorrow? But they had already gone through the plans twice now, so that seemed silly. Kana definitely didn't want to ask Ember about his family, since the vampires had taken care of that. Did he dare say something about how hot Kana thought Ember was? No, this didn't seem like an appropriate time or place for that.

Why not? Sora asked. *He's cute, you're horny, and I know Mika and I would enjoy a bit of that too.*

Because we're about to go into battle. I'm sure he's focusing on that and doesn't want to be distracted.

Riiiight. Sora sank as much disbelief into that one, drawn-out word as Kana had ever heard. *Well, whatever. Mika and I are done.*

Come down and pick us up.

"They're done," Kana said.

Ember stood, then paused to press his hands against his spine until his back cracked. Kana couldn't tear his eyes away as that deliciously flat stomach and firm chest were pushed in his direction. Ember didn't appear to notice, as he simply dropped his hands and turned toward the door. Kana scrambled to follow.

They exited the building from the same side door. Ember locked it, then turned to walk deeper into the alley. Mika and Sora were waiting there in their small forms, and they were both completely covered in blood, their fur matted with it. Ember heaved the metal bilco doors closed, then slid a chain through the handles and clicked a padlock closed.

A car pulled up as they were walking back to the street. A wolf jumped out and opened the back door for Kana, who climbed inside. Mika and Sora dashed in after him, moving fast so they wouldn't be seen.

Ember waved as the car pulled away, so Kana waved back.

I need a bath, Mika grumbled, his voice disgusted.

Definitely, Sora agreed. *And then maybe we can help Kana out with his horniness problem.*

Mika laughed. *Sounds good to me!*

Kana's cheeks were warm again, and he was glad he was the only one who could hear Mika and Sora. Still, a bit of fun would help keep his mind off tomorrow night so Kana welcomed the distraction.

Chapter Nine

THE VAMPIRE'S MANSION was even more ridiculous farther inside. Kana was now in a sitting room clearly used by the vampire residents. The couch he was sitting on was completely covered in embroidery. Flowers in multiple colors crossed every inch of the fabric. The ceiling was gold, and Kana couldn't tell if it was painted or gilded, but it was bright and clashed horribly with the couches. Those were only the two most egregious issues, but the entire room screamed snooty.

George and another beta, introduced as Emily, stood against the wall by the door to the hallway. Emily had her arms crossed and looked bored, and George was picking at a fingernail. The opposite wall held a second door; they hadn't told Kana what was on the other side, but he guessed it was a closet, and no one seemed concerned about it.

"I still don't understand why we couldn't just attack them while they're sleeping during the day!" Emily said with a huff.

George rolled his eyes. "Because they sleep inside a fricking fortress. By the time we breached the first door, they'd be awake and ready to kill us. Better to catch them out in the open like this where we have a chance of survival, and they won't have any time to prepare."

"If you say so." Emily's tone was sarcastic and said she didn't believe George, but the question had been brought up at the meeting Emily had missed. George's answer to Emily was the short version of what Ember had explained at the time.

Emily opened her mouth to say something else, but George suddenly held up his hand. His head was cocked so his ear was close to the door.

"They're coming," George said, both to Emily and Kana, and into the mike hooked inside his collar.

Kana tensed, his hands clamping around the cushion he was sitting on, and then he let out a heavy breath and forced his shoulders and fingers to relax. His hands left chalky residue behind on the ridiculous fabric, so Kana tried to brush it off while they waited.

"Why am I being brought to a sitting room?" Octavius's voice sounded clearly, even through the closed door.

"You requested information on the witch responsible for killing Mistress Penelope and Master Xavier, Master Octavius," Ember said as he turned the handle and pushed the door open. "We have identified the witch and brought him to you."

Octavius walked into the room, looked at Kana briefly, then circled the couches until he was standing across the room from Ember.

"I told you to take care of the witch problem, not to bring him here," Octavius said, his voice sharp and haughty as he looked down his nose at the three werewolves and Kana. "Never mind," he continued quickly with an offhand wave. "I already know why you've brought him here: you think your little coup attempt will be marginally more successful with a witch on your side.”

Kana immediately tensed, but so did George and Emily so he didn't feel bad about giving away their plot. Ember didn't move, although his lips might have compressed slightly.

“You think this is my first coup attempt?” Octavius continued. “You are not the first pack of werewolves I'll enjoy putting down like the rabid dogs you are. Now, let's talk about your surrender.” He reached behind him to grip the doorknob and pushed the door open. “Come out,” he snapped, although he didn't take his eyes off Ember as he spoke.

Shuffling noises sounded from inside the closet, and a second later three kids stepped into view. They couldn't have been more than ten, and all of them were covered in brilliant violet bruises and dried blood. Silver shackles encircled their wrists, which were burnt and meant the shackles were real silver. Werewolves were deathly allergic, so the kids must have been born as wolves. If what Ember had said was right, they were either really strong wolves, or more likely, really weak ones who needed protection.

Ember, George, and Emily's faces were pale white and Emily was vibrating in place as if she weren't sure whether to start screaming or crying.

“You have kidnapped our innocents,” Ember said, his voice flat.

“And if you don't want them to die, you'll offer your own neck in sacrifice.” Octavius smiled widely, his fangs visible in a blatant threat.

Ember looked at the kids for a long moment, and Kana looked too. One of them was crying softly, but trying to stifle it in his shoulder as if afraid to draw attention to himself. The other two were standing bravely, their chins set and their spines straight, but Kana could see defeat in the way their eyes downcast. They still had some spirit left, but it had been beaten as severely as their bodies.

Ember next moved his eyes to look at Kana, and Kana saw a fire burning behind them. Fury, not just that Octavius would stoop so low, but also at himself for allowing the children to become a target. Kana also read Ember's plan, even though he didn't use more than his jaw flexing as he ground his teeth to convey it. He would draw Octavius away from the children, so Kana could throw a protection circle around them.

Kana dipped his chin in the barest of nods. Ember returned his attention to Octavius and slowly raised his head until his neck was exposed.

"How lovely," Octavius said. His voice was jovial, as if they were all engaged in a mutual pastime, yet he somehow still sounded dark and ominous. "After I'm through with you, I expect whomever replaces you will deliver the delightful morsel of magic you used to entice Lucas to his death. I will take that as payment for having to rebuild my coven."

He walked forward, but stopped with still a few feet between himself and Ember. He reached out with one finger and tapped the pulse point on Ember's neck, right where Kana had drawn a pentagram in his homemade Hunter's Bane.

"Up to your nasty tricks again, I see," Octavius said, and he grinned his threatening smirk again. He pressed his fingertip against that spot, holding it in place. "Perhaps had I not seen it kill poor Penelope, I might have fallen for such a crude trick, but to try it on me again shows your lack of imagination."

A scent of burnt meat filled the air. Was Octavius willingly burning his finger just to prove he wouldn't be felled by Kana's spell? Except Octavius's smile only grew as the smell increased, and Ember's jaw flexed as if he was clenching it. Octavius was burning the symbol off Ember's neck! And Ember was letting him.

Octavius was definitely distracted. Kana luckily didn't have to move to set his spell circle. He would be stronger if he could take the time to draw the circle in chalk, but as a short-term preventative, a quick-set circle would suffice. He widened the channels between himself and Mika and Sora.

Sora's massive paw swatted Sophia like he was swatting a gnat. She flew across the room and hit the wall with a bone-cracking thud. *Looks like you're in trouble,* Sora said, sharing Kana's eyes for a moment. *We'll finish here and head your way.* Ralph stepped up next to Sora and two more wolves joined him, but by then enough magic had flooded from Sora, so Kana narrowed the channels and lost sight of their battle.

The circle bloomed to life underneath the kids, the pentagram crossing below their feet. Kana wrote in runes for protection and added the symbols for garlic and mistletoe. He also tossed in the rune for healing, although spell circles weren't capable of mending the level of injuries the kids had sustained.

"I can see you'll be a powerful asset once I've broken you to my will, witch," Octavius said. He had turned away from Ember to watch Kana's spell form, although his finger was still pressed to Ember's neck.

Quick as a flash, Ember's hands darted forward and clamped down on Octavius's neck. Octavius let out a little gasp, and his body shuddered as Ember's hands seemed to glow. Ember had a bottle of Kana's Hunter's Bane, Kana remembered. He must have coated his hands with it. George and Emily leaped, and they each grabbed one of Octavius's arms. Their hands immediately started to glow too. Together the three of them pushed Octavius forward, and when his foot brushed one of the chalk lines Kana had hidden underneath the ostentatious purple carpet, Octavius convulsed as the spell flared to life.

Octavius shouted something unintelligible. He raked his claws across George's chest, who howled in pain but grimly hung on.

"Kana!" Ember yelled just before a weight slammed into Kana's back.

Kana hit the ground with a thud that left his lungs aching and him gasping for air. Someone landed on his back and hands pressed on his shoulders to hold him down. A warm, wet breath touched his neck. Kana threw open all his magic channels, drawing power recklessly, and felt it explode out of his body. The weight holding him down vanished. Kana rolled over, then struggled to his feet.

One vampire was leaning against one of the far walls, half his body starting to flake away in gray ash. More were rushing out of the closet.

Kana threw magic outwards and every single chalk circle he had drawn flared to life. Vampires screamed. One was fully caught in a circle and dissolved to ash on the spot, others had parts of their bodies flaking away until the air was gray with floating ash dust.

And still more vampires emerged from what must be a large walk-in closet. Kana pointed to the floor directly in front of the closet and drew a circle in the air with his pointed finger. A large circle appeared on the floor. He drew the pentagram next, and a glowing pentagram emerged as well. Every anti-vampire rune Kana could think of went into the spaces between the lines in the circle. Some vampires stumbled across the circle and immediately flared into ash, but more were coming, and they learned. The next few vampires went around the circle.

He had to stop them. Ember and his wolves were doing absolutely everything they could to battle Octavius; more vampires coming to Octavius's aid would turn the tide against them. Kana was the only person available until the other group finished defeating Sophia and arrived to help.

Kana drew another circle, this one hovering in the air about a foot above the first. When that also wasn't enough, he drew a third and then a fourth, until he had a tower of circles. Magic pulsed in the air, filling the room until Kana felt as if the walls were vibrating with it. More vampires were caught in the new circles, but not enough. The circles wanted—needed—something more.

Not more magic, Kana thought as he closed his eyes so he could listen to the circles better. Kana saw the pattern of magic comprising the circles behind his closed eyelids and heard the dissonant tone associated with the current array. The circles wanted to fulfil their full potential, that tone insisted, and they weren't doing that by staying in their current configuration.

If Kana offset the second circle just a bit, then turned the third and the fourth each a little more... Kana opened his eyes.

All four circles were shining with a brilliant golden light. The vampires who had been able to evade it were shrieking, their arms held up to cover their eyes.

"You can't!" Octavius screamed. There were scuffling noises behind Kana, but he couldn't turn to look; the magic had his full attention.

The fourth circle dropped, hitting the third with a shower of sparks. They then dropped together, hitting the second with more sparks. All three combined circles dropped again, hitting the first with a boom that shook the room. This time the sparks were more like fireworks.

A twenty-pointed star sat on the floor, and its glow was so bright it turned from bright yellow to blinding white.

The magic ached inside Kana, filling him just as the light filled the room. It needed—demanded—release.

"So mote it be," Kana whispered through lips numb from the magic inside him.

The star went dark, leaving Kana blinking spots before his eyes, and then, like a bomb going off, it exploded.

Kana's feet left the ground as he was thrown backward. He slammed into something hard, and then everything went black.

Chapter Ten

KANA WAS PROPPED against something hard and firm. That something was also rising and falling as if breathing. A band wrapped around Kana's chest, holding him securely. No, not a band. An arm, Kana realized as his brain started to engage.

"Kana!"

"Kana!"

Why did Mika and Sora sound so worried? Kana tried to reach out to them through the magic channels they shared to reassure them and… Nothing. Kana tried again, desperate to find his most important ties, and let out a soft breath of relief when he found them. The channels were severely constricted, and they felt tender and burnt, as if he had fried them with too much magic.

Which was exactly what he had done! Kana's eyes popped open, and he immediately looked around, hoping he wasn't about to see another vampire attacking. Instead, he found Mika and Sora, both in human form and looking worried.

Kana looked at Mika and Sora, and then realized if they were sitting in front of him they weren't the person holding him. Kana craned his neck backward, and Ember's face swam into view.

"Wha—" Kana coughed.

"It's okay, Kana," Mika said. "Take a few minutes. You used a lot of magic, and your body took a beating."

"Octa—" Kana tried to ask, but his throat closed again, and he resumed coughing.

Ember smiled that beautiful half smile of his, and this time there was real joy in the way his eyes also lit up.

"George, Emily, and I had him pinned when you started your lightshow," Ember explained. "When you stacked your circles, he got really scared and instead of trying to fight, he tried to run instead." Ember's smile took on a hard, yet still gleeful edge. "His distraction is what really killed him. George got his claws into Octavius's jugular, and the blood loss slowed him down. When your spell exploded, he was caught in the worst of it. Turned him to ash immediately, along with every other vampire in the room."

"And we rushed in just in time to see Ember sprint across the room to catch you," Sora added, and the tilt to his cheeky grin was saying something that Kana's rattled brain just wasn't up to processing at the moment.

"You've only been out maybe ten minutes," Mika added.

"No! I wanna see him!" Kana heard from outside. A second later one of the children from before dashed into the room. Ralph ran in after him but stopped at the door. The boy's shackles were gone, and the worst of his open wounds had been smeared with some sort of ointment. His eyes were wild as they took in the room.

There had to be at least an inch of gray ash covering every single surface. The boy sent up plumes of it as he rushed around, looking at every inch of the space.

"Shannon!" He yelled and then ran into the closet. "Shannon." This time the boy sounded relieved, as if he had found whomever he was looking for.

Ember shifted forward so he could get his legs underneath him, then stood with Kana still cradled in his arms.

"Marc, what's going on?" Ember called after the boy.

Marc emerged from the closet slowly. "You can't hurt him," Marc said, his chin set in a stubborn line. "You have to promise not to hurt him."

"I won't hurt anyone who hasn't attacked me first," Ember replied. "Now show me."

Marc reached back and tugged on something, drawing first an arm, and then the rest of a man into the room.

"This is Shannon," Marc said. "He helped us."

Shannon had been looking down at Marc, but he lifted his head to take in Ember and Kana. His eyes were very blue, his hair pale blond almost to the point of looking white, and he was definitely a vampire.

"Explain," Ember snapped. He didn't sound like he was feeling any strain from holding Kana.

"The one who called himself Octavius was turning just about every homeless person he encountered into a vampire. To create an army, I believe he said," Shannon explained. His voice was soft and unthreatening, with a soft Gaelic lilt. "He encountered me and decided I would join his army."

"So you joined," Ember said, sounding flat and unimpressed.

Shannon shook his head. "I could feel the sun approaching. I followed him home for a place to spend the day."

"And then he saw what Master Octavius was doing to me and he helped!" Marc cut in.

Kana focused on Shannon while everyone else spoke. The ash seemed to avoid him, so he was clean unlike everyone else. His clothing was well worn, darned neatly at the knees and elbows. His hair was long on the collar and looked like he had cut it with a knife. He also, Kana noticed, was completely uninjured.

"My spell—" Kana forced out and felt Ember's arms tighten around him in surprise.

"That spell tore Octavius apart like he was tissue paper," Ember growled. Ralph straightened up from where he had been leaning on the wall by the door and Emily walked into the room.

"The spell was beautiful," Shannon said. "I haven't seen it's like in a thousand years. I hadn't thought witches still remembered the master spells. A lot of knowledge was lost during the witch burnings."

"But it didn't touch you," Ember stated, rather than asking like Kana wanted to.

Shannon just smiled in answer. "I was glad to see someone was capable of stopping him. I don't like to kill my kind if I can avoid it." He looked at Ember a moment longer, his smile not dimming. "I would like to petition you, alpha, for permission to remain in your territory."

"Oh, can he? Please?" Marc begged.

Ember growled, the vibration in his chest moving pleasantly through Kana's body. Marc immediately lifted his chin into the air, exposing his neck to his alpha.

"Please, alpha," Marc asked again, although this time he sounded subdued and penitent.

Ember looked at Shannon for a very long time. Kana had no idea what was going through Ember's mind, but he could guess it had to do with fear that he had just escaped one terrible vampire. The last thing Ember would want for himself or his pack was to end up under the thumb of another one.

"Just remember it's my territory," Ember finally said.

Marc cheered, wrapping his arms around Shannon's right arm. "Let me show you where you can stay!" He dragged Shannon across the room and out the door, although it was clear from Shannon's indulgent smile, he was allowing Marc his fun.

"Damn," Ember said in a low tone. "Ralph?"

Ralph nodded. "Although I don't know how successful I'll be keeping a vamp like that in check. I think he's probably double the age Octavius was." He turned and left the room.

Ember looked down at Kana, still in his arms. "You need to rest." He glanced at Mika and Sora, who were in human form and therefore naked, but Ember didn't even blink at them. "This way."

His stride was as effortless as his unmoving arms as Ember carried Kana out of the ash covered room and through the house. They turned down a number of hallways, and the overly decorated halls began to get simpler and simpler until they were in an area almost completely bereft of any decoration.

"Where are we?" Kana managed to get out. Ember's stride was smooth, and Kana's body was aching. His head was starting to spin as exhaustion threatened to drag him under.

"The servant's wing. I figured you'd be more comfortable somewhere normal," Ember answered. He stopped at a door and looked at Mika and Sora. "Could one of you open the door for me?"

Mika hurried forward and pushed open the door, then stepped

aside so Ember could go first. Ember set Kana down in the center of a simple double bed and then gently pulled the covers back, yanking them out from beneath him. Mika hopped into the bed on one side, but Sora stood next to Ember as if waiting for something.

"You getting in too?" Sora asked Ember.

Kana was surprised when Ember's face immediately went pink. Could Sora be right and Ember did want to join them in bed, or maybe Ember was simply not used to being propositioned, even if it was only for sleep.

"I can't," Ember finally said, and he did sound regretful. "I have to help my pack adjust to our new normal, so I can't vanish for a few hours."

"You're a good alpha," Kana said. He wanted to add something about how Kana would still be here when Ember's work was done, but the words were lost in a yawn. Sora climbed into bed and helped Mika pull the covers over all three of them. Ember waited by the door until they were settled, then shut off the light and closed the door.

Kana snuggled underneath the warm blankets, content between the comforting bodies of his familiars. He wished Ember was also beside him. Maybe someday he would be, but for now Kana was content to enjoy what he had. He happily let sleep take him away.

Epilogue

"YOU LOOK HORRIBLE!" Beth gasped when Kana walked into work. "You sure you're well enough to be here?"

A week had passed since the battle against the vampires, and Kana had called in sick to work. He had returned to his apartment a day after the fight, but today was the first time he had felt steady enough to ride the bus all the way to the office.

"I'm feeling a lot better," Kana replied. A touch of hoarseness in his voice still made him croak, but his magic channels were starting to flow again.

"If you say so," Beth said, but she was studying him as if she didn't believe him.

Kana ignored her and hit the button to power on his computer. "Did I miss anything while I was gone?"

"Oh boy. Did you ever! They finally released the article about the vampires. You won't believe what they did to it!" Beth dug through the piles of stuff covering her desk and handed him a printout of the written article.

Kana's computer was still booting, so he took the paper from her to read.

Vampire Danger Solved, the headline read. The subheading continued: *Hunter-Witch Deals with Scourge Before City is Attacked.*

"Hunter-witch?" Kana asked, although he wasn't certain how the newspaper had also learned the vampires were gone.

Beth shrugged. "Don't ask me. Stephen came in one day last week with it."

Kana skimmed the article, wondering if Ember knew about it. The article started with Stephen's visit to the vampires and the subsequent, foiled attack, but instead of going into what regular civilians needed to know to protect themselves—which was the article Kana and Beth had spent so much time working on—it talked about an interview. Apparently, Stephen had called the vampire house again. Kana couldn't think of why, so he asked Beth.

Beth snorted. "Because he was worried we had that lead vampire's name wrong. Who's called Octavius anymore these days? Although, I'm more shocked Stephen made the call himself. Usually it's you or me doing the grunt work."

And, according to the article, whoever answered the phone said: "Don't worry about the vampires anymore. We had a super witch come in and our vampire problem is gone."

"Glad that project's done with, at least," Kana said as he handed the article back to Beth. "Guess I should check my email and see what my next job is."

He went through his email for a few minutes, deleting the stuff he knew was crap—the all-employee emails usually went straight to the trash bin—and skimmed the ones he wasn't sure about to double-check. Once he was sure Beth was engrossed in her own work, Kana grabbed his cell phone and headed out to the nearest stairwell where he could have a private conversation.

Guess freedom's gone to the wolves' heads a bit, Sora commented. He had followed Kana, but Mika was content to nap on his pillow under Kana's desk, so had remained behind.

Kana pulled up Ember's number and hit Call. Ember had checked in on Kana regularly when Kana had been staying in their spare room and had reached out once a day after Kana had returned to his apartment. Usually they spoke in the evenings, so calling first thing in the morning might throw Ember off.

I hope no one reads that article and decides to travel here to take a look at the super witch, Kana replied while he listened to the phone ring. *I do not need that sort of attention.*

I doubt the wolves want that attention either, Sora admitted.

"Kana, how's work? Is everything okay?" Ember asked the second he answered

"Work's fine. I'm getting back into the swing of things. But my coworker showed me an article from last week saying someone with you talked about a superwitch?" Kana asked.

Ember let out a short growl. "One of our younger members was assigned to monitor the phones. He's not allowed near even his own cell phone after that stunt. There's no way to retract what he said. I'm sorry, Kana. Is it going to cause you problems at work?"

"No, not at work," Kana replied. "They have no idea what I am."

"But you're worried problems might come from elsewhere," Ember said, and his understanding tone indicated he was worried about that too. "I have some more mature wolves than the fool who spilled the beans already working on finding a way to monitor the city so our territory stays safe. I'll make sure to let you know if we spot anything worrying."

"I appreciate that," Kana replied. While it helped to know he might have forewarning if anyone came looking for a super witch, he would have preferred to stay off the radar entirely. Kana wouldn't take back his actions though. He did not regret stopping Octavius or helping the werewolves, and he definitely wasn't upset about having met Ember.

"Hey, you want to swing by the city house sometime this week?" Ember asked suddenly. Kana's heart started beating faster in anticipation as he helplessly hoped Ember might be asking him out on a date, but that hope died when Ember continued. "We're planning to sell a bunch of the glitzy stuff Octavius left behind so we can get some equity and start rebuilding the pack. It would be great if you were here just in case there's something you'd like to have."

Seeing Ember even for some spring cleaning was better than not seeing him at all. "Let me know when, and I'll be there," Kana said.

"Will do. I'll let you get back to work now. Sorry about my wolf." Ember sounded distracted, and Kana could faintly hear someone calling Ember's name.

"See you then," Kana replied, then they hung up.

He's just busy. Give him time, Sora said. He walked a figure eight around Kana's feet, brushing his soft fur against Kana's ankles in comfort. *And until he does, and even after, you'll always have Mika and me.*

Kana picked Sora up to give him a hug and then headed back to his desk. Whatever was potentially building with Ember would or wouldn't happen, but Sora was right. With Mika and Sora at Kana's side, he couldn't help feeling happy.

HUNTER

Prologue

THE LIBRARY WAS quiet at two in the morning. Kana didn't understand why the librarian bothered to lock any of the doors, given most of the community could pop the locks with just a breath of magic. He certainly had never been stopped by something as measly as a physical lock. He walked past shelves of fiction and nonfiction, straight to the largest section of the library: magical studies. Illumination came from one security light in the corner and from moonlight and streetlights filtering in through the windows. Combined, Kana had more than enough light to see his path to the back of the magical studies area and into the separate room where the advanced books were kept.

These were the books the library considered too important or too rare to be checked out. Anyone could read them, but the books could not be taken outside. For most witches, this wasn't a problem. Getting access was first-come, first-served, but an informal list had been generated so "everyone" could sign up to read the books in turn—except for Kana, the only male witch in the coven, who had repeatedly been "overlooked" when the informal list reached his name.

If he wanted the same chance as all the other witches to read the books that would allow him to develop his magic, he had to do so when no one else was around.

Kana found the book where he had left off, flipped to the correct page, and settled in one of the chairs close enough to the window so he had enough light to read by.

The coven's circle of power and his fellow witches might not see any benefit in ensuring Kana was properly trained, but he was going to prove them all wrong. He would read every single book in the advanced section and become the strongest witch in the coven.

As the next few years went by, Kana spent most nights in the library, providing it wasn't cloudy outside or during a new moon, of course. His knowledge of magic was growing in leaps and bounds, and he was also starting to understand that having magic and power would never be enough for his coven. He had been born male, which meant he would always be considered less than his female counterparts. Regardless of how strong his circle work was, in their opinion, he was only good for helping the coven produce the next generation of strong female witches.

The final straw had come at the start of the second half of his senior year of high school. The announcement had been posted for all interested individuals to sign up for a timeslot to attempt the spell to call their familiar. Kana knew his place so had waited for all his classmates to choose their times and then signed up for an empty slot.

"All students who are not planning to cast the spell to call your familiar, you are free to leave class today. Please go to the library for some self-study," his magical studies teacher said to the class the day they had returned to school after winter solstice break.

About a third of the students got up and shuffled out of the room.

The teacher looked over the remaining students, and her gaze froze when she reached Kana.

"Kana, you're free to leave as well," she said, despite the fact that the sign-up sheet was sitting on her desk with Kana's name on it.

"I would like to try the spell as well," Kana said, attempting to sound insistent.

The rest of the students in the class all sniggered around him. Kana heard some of them whispering gleefully about the "pathetic man." Even the teacher had an indulgent, patronizing smile.

"You might be able to do some magic, Kana, but this is a high-level spell," she told him, as if her mere words would dissuade him. When Kana didn't move, she sighed. "Very well. You may sit through this lesson."

Kana sat through that lesson and every lesson thereafter for high-level spells. He was never called on, never asked to demonstrate, and constantly got side-eyed looks and heard snide gossip about him. But he set a precedent. Even though no one thought he ought to be present, they stopped trying to dissuade him from attending. When the timeslots for attempting to call a familiar were finalized, no one bothered trying to stop Kana.

Of course, Kana knew what they were thinking. He was male, so he would fail, and they could afford to indulge him. Also, it was less work for them to let him try and fail than to fight with him about it.

However, what was important were the lessons Kana had learned. He could come out of the calling circle with the strongest, most powerful familiar the coven had ever seen, and he knew it wouldn't matter in the least. He wouldn't prove to them that men could be as magically strong as women. He wouldn't suddenly become acceptable or be allowed to take a spot in the coven circle like a female witch who did the same. No,

Kana had a very strong feeling the exact opposite would happen to him.

Kana didn't want to continue living his life like this. It didn't matter how his familiar calling went; Kana knew he couldn't stay. He would never be happy or able to create some sort of life for himself if he remained here. Leaving would take planning, but it wasn't as if he had anything else to do with his free time.

The library was dark and silent as it always was, but for the last month of his time in the village before he could try calling his familiar, Kana had a different goal. There were spell books in the advanced sections his classmates wouldn't have access to for quite a few more years; only those admitted to the circle were put on the informal list to study them. Kana spent hours scanning them into the computer and emailing them to himself, using a free email service that accepted fake information to join. He was also careful to wipe the computers after he finished to prevent anyone from discovering what he had done. When he wasn't stealing spells, Kana pored over maps, trying to decide on the best possible destination.

By the time his day arrived to cast the calling spell, Kana was as prepared as possible. No matter how the spell went, he was looking forward to finally starting his life somewhere new.

*

Three Years Later

THE LOCAL PUBLIC library had computers available for free use by all members, and Kana had shamelessly taken advantage of the opportunity. He might be living in another nameless city that was almost identical to the last place he had stopped in his ongoing attempt to lay a false trail, but this time he had gotten a job as a secretary at a dentist's office.

He had helped the process along by casting a spell that changed his name and the graduation year on his high school transcript, and he had been hired at more than minimum wage. After a few months of work, he had been able to afford a proper apartment, rather than his original place, which was only still standing thanks to luck and a lack of strong wind gusts.

Kana had an opportunity here that he wasn't about to waste. Not only was he building a proper resume, but he was actually saving money. If he could get more education, his next job would be at a higher rate of pay, and he wouldn't be borrowing internet time at the library because he would be able to afford his own Wi-Fi and maybe even a computer too.

He had about five potential local schools picked out, a ton of scholarships to apply for, and now only had to write his application essays.

Mika squirmed in Kana's lap so he could sit up and look at the computer screen too.

This could be good for us, Mika said, his voice sounding only inside Kana's head. He and Kana's other familiar, Sora, were connected to Kana via magical channels that allowed them to feed Kana magic for his spells and for him to hear them.

Three years ago, when Kana had cast the spell to call his familiar and gotten both Mika and Sora, they had appeared as kittens. Now they looked like adolescent cats, long in the elbows and whiskers, but still filling out the rest of their bodies. As Kana worked stronger and stronger spells, their bond improved, which in turn allowed their bodies to age. Their minds had been adult from day one, but their physical bodies wouldn't match until Kana improved his magic. He was holding them back.

If I do this, I'll have less time to work with you on our magic, Kana said. The last thing he wanted was to take a step to better his own prospects but hurt his familiars. His working and going to school full-time would definitely put a strain on their ability to keep growing their bond.

It won't. We'll find the time to work on our magic, but half of the process is simply being together, Mika replied. *You'll see.*

Besides, if you finish your degree and get a job that pays more, you'll be able to feed us more, Sora piped in. He was roaming the stacks and enjoying being a busybody, and had apparently also been listening in on the conversation.

Kana laughed. He rolled his shoulders to get rid of any last tension and placed his fingers on the keyboard.

Now, what should I write?

Chapter One

YOU SURE THIS is a good idea? Mika asked, sounding worried. His question unfortunately echoed Kana's own thoughts.

Kana looked at the library building and swallowed hard. The place was only brown cement and glass, and it had fanciful pictures in most of the windows, thanks to the proximity of the children's section inside. Kana had walked into the building dozens of times before without issue, yet somehow this time the building seemed to loom over him like an ominous cloud.

Ember asked us for a favor, Kana replied to both Mika and Sora. Mika was in his housecat form, tucked into Kana's backpack where he would still be close while staying hidden. Sora was also in housecat form but had wandered off after they'd gotten off the bus. He would stay close in case of an emergency.

Ember was the alpha of the Tri-Cities werewolf pack. Kana had worked with him a few weeks ago to fight off a terrible vampire who had enslaved the pack for twenty years. Kana had no idea how anyone could recover from twenty years of hell like that. Ember had protected as many members of his pack as he could, and most of the children hadn't even known there was a problem, but the vampires hadn't cared who they hurt in their attempts to retain dominance. A couple members of Ember's pack had been kept captive as blood slaves, their entire existence dependent on providing fresh blood to the vampires at all times. Ember had freed them, but even with the physical bonds gone, Ember had told Kana their minds and souls weren't going to magically recover.

The worst cases weren't able to sleep, their bodies constantly running on adrenaline the second night fell as the ingrained fear a vampire was coming prevented them from relaxing. They needed sleep or their bodies would start shutting down. Ember was in the process of hiring a therapist, but finding someone who could be trusted with pack secrets, and who also wouldn't interfere with the pack dynamics, was proving difficult.

That was where Ember hoped Kana might be able to help. Ember thought Kana might know of a potion that wasn't addictive, but would calm the worst-affected wolves enough that they could sleep. Unfortunately, Kana didn't have any recipes for something like that in the spell books he had access to, and he didn't feel comfortable making up a potion that could potentially cause harm. Herbs and spells that called for sleep were usually poisonous, and sleep sometimes was a permanent side effect that only ended in death. Without a proper, tested spell, Kana didn't think it was safe to give anything to wolves who had already suffered enough. That meant he had to go searching for a book, and what better place to look than in a library?

The coven library from his childhood had serviced a town whose only occupants had been witches. They purchased books for their clientele, and therefore had a ton of spell books. The Schenectady County Library served a much larger city with a considerably more diverse populace. Kana regularly checked out fiction books, which the library carried a lot of, but hadn't dared go near the magical section for fear someone might take an interest in finding out why he was there. He didn't know if the library even stocked spell books, but he had no idea where else to turn. Kana only hoped the library had some books that might help.

Are you going to go inside? Sora asked, teasing him slightly.

Yeah, yeah, Kana replied. He always stayed under the radar, so being seen in public reading advanced spell books was definitely outside his comfort zone. Still, Kana had to do something to help those wolves. He took a deep breath, let it out, then gathered his courage and walked forward through the doors into the building.

The library was completely ordinary, as it always was. Kana didn't know why he felt like there ought to be a fire-breathing dragon crawling along the tops of the stacks today, but all he saw were normal people going about normal library business. He kept walking, looking at the overhead signs until he found one in the nonfiction section labeled "Magic Studies." However, as Kana started looking through the section, he realized it wasn't what he was looking for at all.

He didn't see a single spell book or even an herbalist. Every book appeared to be on simple, broad topics geared toward the everyday person. *A Compendium of Eastern European Water Creatures*, one title read. Another read *How to Know if a Vampire Has Bitten You.* People with no magic who wanted to learn the basics about the different types of magic out there used this section, not someone looking to expand their own magical abilities.

Maybe public libraries in normal cities didn't have what he was looking for? Kana bit his lip as he reached the end of one row and turned down another, only to find the same types of books again. He still walked down the aisle, hoping he might eventually find what he wanted, but it dead-ended at a brick wall with no sign of anything useful.

Kana almost missed seeing a small plaque on the wall, off to the left near the shelves, until he started to turn around with a sigh. He leaned closer to read it.

Magic Users Only Beyond This Point

Proceed with Caution

Magic users only? What the heck did that mean? A wall stood in front of him, so with nowhere to go, what "point" could the sign be referencing?

Kana bent closer to the sign as if proximity might somehow provide an answer. And it did! A small circle no bigger than a doorbell was carved into the lower right corner. Inside the circle was a rune Kana didn't recognize, and there wasn't a pentagram, something Kana had never heard of.

Spell circles at their most basic were simple: a circle surrounding a five-pointed star. The circle bound the spell, ensuring no magic escaped. That allowed for protection of the surroundings and kept as much power as possible concentrated within the spell. The pentagram guided the spell, keeping the magic flowing evenly throughout every component. Once that base was established, Kana could add additional pieces to his spells, like runes, candles, and herbs in smudge bowls.

He had even cast spells without using a circle—the unlocking spell he was so good at was a perfect example—where he shaped the power to his will. However, he was only able to use very little power in such cases.

Kana had never seen a circle that only bound a rune.

The intellectual side of Kana, which had relentlessly studied magic for so many years, begged him to find out more, and Kana really wanted to, but he was on a mission at the moment.

Kana pressed his finger to the rune as if it were a doorbell, then pushed through just a touch of magic. The rune shivered under his finger for a brief second as it activated, and then an archway appeared in the brick wall just in front of him. Kana walked inside before the magic faded away and the archway vanished, and found himself in an annex that looked exactly like the rest of the library.

"Hello, dearie. You're a new face," a wizened old...person...said.

Kana couldn't tell if they were female or male, or whether they were even human. A crooked back and deep wrinkles hid any potentially identifying features, and some sort of otherness about them had Kana doubting gender even mattered to them. He could practically feel the person's magic buzzing against his skin.

"I am the librarian," they continued. "My sole task is to aid seekers in finding the books they want. How can I help you today?"

"Um," Kana began. "I'm looking for books on spells or potions that can aid with sleep?"

The librarian nodded. "It is unfortunately not a common subject, but we do have a few books. Come and sit at this table. I will bring what we have to you in a few minutes."

Kana obeyed, sitting at the small table the librarian gestured toward. He placed his bag with Mika in it on the chair next to him.

Weird place, Kana said to Mika and Sora.

It feels a bit like the other side, Mika replied. *I don't think we're in the library anymore.*

You're not, and thanks for leaving me behind, Sora grumbled. He sounded as if he were talking to Kana from the other side of a tunnel. *Any chance you can grab me? I want to see the pocket too.*

The pocket? Kana asked, but he gathered his magic and opened the channel between him and Sora. A quick yank and Sora slid through the magic and landed in Kana's lap. Sora was hidden beneath the table, but Kana still cast a quick obfuscation spell so no one would notice him.

Someone created a stable bit of humanity on the magical plane called a pocket. The denizens of the plane can't access it, but I bet it's connected to hundreds, if not thousands, of libraries all around the world, Sora explained.

Which doesn't mean they'll have the books you need, Mika added.

Kana chuckled under his breath. Of course, even a library available for the entire world wouldn't therefore have almost every book on magic available. If his past coven was any indication, magic, particularly magic books, was hoarded like it was something precious. This library would only have the books magic users were willing to share. Still, it was more than Kana currently had.

The librarian returned, carrying three books. "This is what we have on sleep magic, dearie," they said. They put the books down on the table. "Call if you need anything else." They toddled off before Kana could say thanks.

Kana pulled the first book in the stack toward him. *Herblore,* Kana read off the cover. *I think I read this book when I was in high school,* he added.

Seems pretty basic, but maybe there's something? Mika said.

Mika was right. Kana opened the back of the book to the index and ran his fingers down the rows of print until he found the section on promoting sleep. Chamomile was the first herb listed, which had Kana rolling his eyes. Chamomile was good for everything, as far as he could tell, and Kana didn't need a refresher on that. Lavender was next, so Kana flipped through the book to the correct page.

For sleep, the book recommended lavender aromatherapy, particularly essential oils, although any sort of aerosol would probably work. Potential side effects included nausea and stomach pain. The book also warned the target patients for this treatment were those with low-level anxiety-induced insomnia, which definitely wasn't strong enough for what Kana needed.

Magnolia root was next, and the book recommended a pill form. It was supposed to be the most effective sleep aid but could negatively interact with other drugs, so it wasn't recommended.

Passionflower was listed, but the book couldn't explain why. It simply said it helped with sleep, but not how or in what form.

The last one listed was valerian root, which was used mostly to help with anxiety. Given that was the main cause of the werewolves' problems, Kana stopped skimming and started reading.

Valerian root is also one of the most commonly used sleep-promoting herbal supplements in the United States and Europe. However, study results remain inconsistent. Short-term intake of valerian root appears to be safe for adults, with minor, infrequent side effects. However, safety remains uncertain for use long-term. Side effects include diarrhea, headache, nausea, and heart palpitations.

The article didn't say anything about how to administer valerian, nor how poisonous it might be. It also didn't warn about how it affected magical creatures like werewolves.

I'm not trying to create my own spell, Kana said with a sigh as he set the book aside. *This definitely confirms that would be too dangerous.*

Agreed, Sora replied. *What's next?*

The title of the next book was simply *Sorcery*. Kana didn't have high hopes, but he popped open the table of contents. In the section labeled "Curses," Kana found "Eternal Sleep." He shut the book and set it aside.

The last book didn't have a title, only the rune for study, which was the one typically used in reference to the study of runes, or runology. Kana already knew the rune that meant sleep, and if he wanted to put someone to sleep by force that was the rune he'd use in the circle he'd draw, but that wasn't what would help the wolves. Still, he followed the index and turned the book to the correct rune, just in case.

The rune was pictured at the center of the page, and around it were arrows indicating the direction the rune was required to be drawn. The description said exactly what Kana was just thinking: used to forcibly put someone to sleep for an indefinite period of time. To reverse the spell, a separate circle with the rune for awake or alertness was needed.

Kana sighed and scrubbed his hands through his hair. He was in a massive library, likely accessible to thousands of people, and there were only three books on the subject!

He stared down at the pages in front of him, hoping something about the shape of the rune would jog an idea in his brain. Sleep runes obviously weren't the answer; there had to be another way to figure out how to help Ember's wolves. Lack of sleep was a big issue, and not sleeping only exacerbated their problems, but the root of the difficulty was anxiety. Their fear was what was keeping the wolves awake.

There wasn't a rune for anxiety, but there was one for calm. If Kana needed a spell to defuse a fraught situation, he would absolutely use the calm rune in his spell circle. That would definitely include calming individuals overwhelmed with anxiety. He flipped through the book until he reached the correct page.

The rune was at the top, with the little arrows that explained how to draw it properly. Below that was a simple description of what the rune did. Except, unlike the previous page, this one had a footnote.

Kana bent closer to the page to read the smaller print at the bottom.

"For use in healing spells, see *The Compendium of Healing for Witches* by Inofah Anderson."

That was it! A book on healing spells for use in witches' magic was exactly what Kana needed!

"Librarian," Kana called, trying to keep his voice low and respectful for a library, but hoping the librarian heard him anyway.

"Yes, dearie?" the librarian asked as they suddenly appeared at Kana's side.

Kana jumped, and Sora hissed softly, but the librarian didn't notice.

"Do you have this book available?" Kana asked. He held out the runology book and ran his fingernail under the title for the librarian to read.

The librarian immediately shook their head, and Kana's hope dropped. "I'm sorry, dearie. We do not have that book in the library. However, I can add it to our ordering list."

A hand vanished into their shapeless robes, and a second later the librarian pulled out a large round scroll. They unrolled it almost to the bottom, and Kana saw a very long list of titles. The librarian pulled out a quill and at the very end wrote the book Kana needed.

"Might take a bit to come in, dearie," they said as they rolled up the scroll and tucked it away again.

A bit? Kana laughed to himself. He would guess years might be a better description, given how long that list was.

"Do you know if that book might be available anywhere else, so I can get it faster?" Kana asked.

The librarian reached into their robes again, and this time they pulled out a small tablet computer. They pressed some buttons and typed on the screen for a few moments, and then turned the tablet so Kana could see.

The Compendium was for sale on Amazon for... Kana sucked in a breath.

"Six hundred dollars?" he gasped.

The librarian nodded. "I'm sorry to say that is likely the best way to get the book if you're in a hurry."

Kana didn't have six hundred dollars he could throw down to buy a spell book. But Ember had asked Kana to find an answer. Maybe he would let Kana borrow the money and pay him back later.

"Can you print that page out for me?" Kana asked.

The librarian nodded and pressed on the touchscreen. A few minutes later, a piece of paper came zipping through the air. The librarian grabbed it and then handed the paper to Kana.

"Can I help you with anything else, dearie?"

Kana looked around the library at the hundreds of books on shelves in every direction. There had to be a book here with the information he was looking for, but Kana had no idea what to ask the librarian to pull. At least he had a lead with *The Compendium*, and he could always come back here later on.

"Just how to get to the exit, please," Kana said.

The librarian smiled, and when Kana blinked, next thing he knew, he was staring at the familiar brick wall in the library in Schenectady. Sora was sitting at his feet next to his backpack, where Mika was hiding, and Kana was holding the printout.

That was weird. Sora shook his head and then washed a front paw.

When we go back, I want to see everything! Mika insisted.

Yes, yes, Kana said, cutting in before they could start arguing. He bent to pick up his bag and started walking back to the doors, hopeful that this strange adventure would lead to something helpful for the wolves.

Chapter Two

KANA WASN'T PRESENT for the discussions, but after what he heard was a lengthy meeting, the werewolf pack had decided to keep the vampire's house in the city. Some wanted to sell it to help with eliminating the bad memories, but it was impossible to find a fortified mansion with land this close to the Tri-Cities. Those arguing to keep the house to take advantage of its prime location won.

No changes were made to the outside of the property, which was protected by a ten-foot stone wall and a massive set of iron gates across the driveway. The guard house overlooked the gates and had a small door inset into the wall just to the right. As Kana approached, the door popped open, and a wolf stepped outside.

"Hey, Kana," he said with a wave of his hand.

"Hey, Greg," Kana replied with a friendly wave of his own. "Is Ember around?"

Greg nodded. "He's organizing the dining hall, I think. I'll show you the way."

Greg held the door open for Kana and Sora to walk inside, then waited patiently while Kana let Mika out of his backpack, before continuing to lead the way. Every time Kana had been brought into the house when the vampires were in control, he had been taken in circles through the halls of the guard house first. Greg didn't bother with the subterfuge now, quickly guiding Kana through the two hallways that led to the underground tunnel.

The tunnel had previously let out into a sitting room that the vampires had used to keep regular peons separated from their personal living spaces. However, now the couches and coffee table were gone, replaced with three long tables and benches for seating. Another large doorway had been knocked through one of the walls where a second big room was being converted into a massive cafeteria-style kitchen. Ember wanted a mess hall where all his wolves could congregate, and apparently the actual dining room and kitchen in the mansion weren't situated in a way that would accommodate that. Kana heard the dining room was being turned into a weight room, but he hadn't seen it yet.

Ember stood in the middle of the kitchen, supervising the installation of a range hood that spanned the entire back wall. He faced away from Kana, but Kana wasn't about to complain about that. The fitted T-shirt Ember wore showed off every single perfectly defined muscle in his back and emphasized the breadth of Ember's shoulders.

Yum, yum, Sora said, echoing Kana's own thoughts.

Ember's head tilted slightly upward as if he was scenting the air, and then he abruptly turned to face Kana.

The sight of Ember's front was even better than his back. A trim waist and firm chest, made all the better because his T-shirt really hid nothing from Kana's greedy eyes. His light-blond hair was shaved tight to the sides and longer on top in a very military style, and his beautiful deep-brown eyes were utterly captivating—especially when Ember focused his full attention solely on Kana like he was doing right now.

Kana swallowed and told himself to concentrate on acting like a normal person rather than a besotted fool. Ember patted the wolf he was talking to on the shoulder and then walked over to Kana.

"How'd it go?" he asked.

Kana sighed. "The library didn't have the book I needed. But," he continued quickly when Ember's shoulders slumped a touch, "I think I was able to find the title of a book the library didn't have that might have the answer." He pulled the printout from his pocket and unfolded it before handing it to Ember. "Can I borrow some money to buy this book?" Kana asked, hoping he sounded bold and certain of himself, but afraid he sounded a touch ashamed that he had to beg.

The corners of Ember's lips tilted upward as he took the page from Kana in the half smile Kana figured he used whenever he thought Kana was doing something adorable. Of course, Kana could very easily be reading into it too much or projecting his own hopes over whatever Ember was really feeling. That didn't stop Kana from hoping though.

Ember crooked one finger over his shoulder, and the wolf he had just been talking to hurried over.

"Buy this," Ember said. He handed the paper to the wolf, who nodded and trotted off.

Kana shut his mouth, futilely wishing Ember hadn't noticed his jaw dropping. The increased tilt to Ember's smile said otherwise.

"But it's so expensive," Kana breathed out.

Ember snorted. "Just one of the hundreds of ridiculous candelabras we sold was worth double what that book costs. The pack can afford to buy a book for you, especially since you need it for a spell intended to help us. Speaking of which, do you have some time? I want to show you something."

Kana's only plan aside from the visit to the library for his Saturday was to cook enough food to have dinners for the next week. Anyway, he certainly wasn't going to say no to spending more time with Ember.

"Sure. Where to?"

"This way." Ember walked through the new kitchen to a wide opening leading into a hallway. Kana followed, then stopped abruptly when he caught sight of the hall.

"Wow," he said, looking both ways. The ridiculous and ostentatious decoration, which had included hand-painted wallpaper, ornately carved furniture, and tchotchkes dripping in gilt and glitter on every surface—including all the candelabras Ember had mentioned earlier—was completely gone. The walls were now a light cream and the floors dark hardwood—simple, understated, and elegant. A faint smell of paint and glue was in the air, but aside from that, Kana saw no signs the space had ever been designed differently.

"Thanks," Ember said. His cheeks were faintly pink, and he scrubbed one palm on his hip.

Kana caught up to him and walked at Ember's side as they continued through the halls.

"Did you design this?" Kana asked. "It's beautiful."

"It's durable," Ember replied, but his blush had returned. "It's a lot easier to paint over scuffs in the walls or to sand down claw marks when the floor is like this."

Kana laughed. "My apartment is still the durable, builder basic the agency put in. It doesn't look anything like this!"

They stopped outside a closed door before Ember had the chance to respond. Rather than opening the door, Ember looked at Kana for a long moment, during which Kana tried not to fidget. Kana had zero idea what Ember wanted or what was going through his head, but it had to do with whatever was on the other side of the door.

"Werewolves have always been self-sufficient. We have our pack and our territory, and that is usually enough for us. Occasionally we work with another creature, most often vampires because of our history of having a symbiotic relationship, but I think my pack is done with that for now."

Kana let out a giggle, then covered his mouth with one hand because it really wasn't funny. After what the vampires had done to the pack, it was a shock that they had allowed the one vampire remaining in the city, a man named Shannon, to stay. But Ember was smiling, too, so Kana didn't feel bad about laughing.

"We were thinking," Ember continued. "I know you didn't want to accept a reward for helping us against the vampires."

"That was a favor," Kana cut in as firmly now as he had when Ember had first made the offer a few weeks ago. "I didn't help because I wanted praise or glory."

Ember nodded. "We understand that, but the pack was wondering if we might be able to hire you on a case-by-case basis. We were wondering if you might be interested in doing spells like the one you're trying to help my wolves sleep whenever we need you. So, we built this."

Ember turned the handle and pushed open the door, then stepped back so Kana could see.

White gauze curtains hung over a wide double window in the opposite wall, but that was the only bright spot in the entire room. The floor and all the walls were painted black. There were full-length bookshelves along the right-hand wall with a few books and a couple of brand-new boxes of chalk.

"It's chalkboard paint," Ember explained. "We wanted you to have a space all to yourself."

Kana's mouth hung open, but he didn't care. He stepped into the room with shaking knees, trying to take it all in. He had never had his own workshop before—he had been making do with a cleared space in his living room for as long as he could remember. This was... Kana took in a shuddering breath.

"Plus—" Ember said in a happy chirp as he strode past Kana to the left-hand wall. He slid his fingers into a slot and pushed a black-painted pocket door open. "—it connects to the old kitchen, so you can brew potions too. You still have to share the kitchen with anyone else who wants to cook something, but all my wolves have been warned not to touch your stuff. Come see!"

Kana walked into the kitchen, which looked like it had also been renovated. The counters were white quartz shot through with black streaks, the cabinets light-brown shaker-style, and all the appliances were stainless steel. There was a tall, double cabinet right next to the pocket door. An oval sign was hanging from one of the handles. Kana bent closer to read it, and in what looked like hand-painted letters, all of which were a different size and color, it read:

KANA'S CLOSET

"Marc and the rest of the kids made that for you," Ember explained.

Kana ran the cuff of his sleeve over his eyes before any tears could escape. He couldn't find words to convey to Ember how amazing this all was, and he probably looked like a fish with how his mouth was gaping.

There's a gigantic cat tree! Mika gasped. *With a hammock bed!*

"A cat tree?" Kana said. He meant to say it just to Mika, but it came out of his mouth instead.

"With a scratching post," Ember added. "We, ah, also reinforced the floor. Just in case." In case Mika or Sora needed to be in their large forms, which were six hundred pounds of primordial cat. Ember had thought of absolutely everything when he had built this room for Kana.

"Thank you," Kana finally forced out, his voice broken and halting. That wasn't nearly adequate, but even swallowing didn't clear his throat enough to get more words out.

Except, Ember was smiling his beautiful half smile as he looked at Kana, and Kana thought Ember understood him completely anyway.

Ember opened his mouth, his eyes soft as if he was about to say something meaningful.

"Alpha!" someone yelled from the hallway. "Alpha." The wolf ran into the kitchen. "Nat and Sejane are fighting again!"

Ember's eyes pinched closed as if he was trying to find patience. When he reopened them, his expression had lost any traces of whatever emotion he had held when staring at Kana.

"Kana, I have to take care of this. Stay and explore as long as you like, and if there's anything you need to make the space work better for you, please let me know. I'll have a wolf ready to drive you home whenever." He nodded to Kana in goodbye before following the wolf out the door.

Kana watched him go, wondering what Ember had been about to say. His heart wished it was something meaningful, but Kana's head knew better. Ember was the alpha. He had no reason to want someone like Kana, no matter how soft his eyes got or how pretty Kana thought his smile.

Kana shook his head, trying to get his thoughts realigned with reality. That didn't really work, but he let out a breath and went to explore his new space, hoping the discovery of very nice smudge bowls would distract him from what could never be.

Chapter Three

THE FEATHERY FEELING of lips brushing up the side of his length, followed by fingers stroking him hard, had Kana moaning. He opened his eyes to see who was giving him a blowjob first thing in the morning, only to have Sora's bright-white hair obscure his vision as he swooped in for a kiss. Wet and filthy, tongues battling, they only broke apart when Mika swallowed Kana deep, and Kana's head flew back as he gasped. Sora didn't let that deter him, instead moving down to press his lips against Kana's neck, and then down to his collarbone.

Slick fingers circled his entrance, and one slowly slipped inside. Kana spread his legs wider to give Mika more room, hoping Mika wouldn't tease him with only one finger for too long. Mika didn't. One finger quickly became two, then three, and Kana welcomed the familiar initial burn and stretch until his body quickly became used to the sensation.

Mika's mouth let go with a filthy popping sound as his fingers slid free. Sora settled onto the pillow behind Kana, his length at the perfect spot for Kana to lick, while Mika gently pushed Kana's legs toward Kana's chest.

Sora's fingers touched Kana's cheek, urging him to look away from Mika, who was lining himself up. He was met with Sora insistently pushing his cock against Kana's lips. Kana opened, sucking Sora deep even as Mika slowly pushed inside.

They rocked together, all three entwined and gasping, until Mika let out a yowl and came, his hard thrusts sending Kana over the edge into his own oblivion. Sora moaned a second later and collapsed half on Kana and half on Mika, who was sprawled next to Kana on the bed.

Kana panted for breath but was ready to go back to sleep comfortably curled up with his lovely familiars for a while longer.

Beep. Beep. Beep.

Kana whimpered, and Sora hissed as he flung one hand out to tap the alarm on Kana's phone. The beeping stopped, but the phone went flying off the nightstand.

"Why does work have to start so early?" Kana groaned. He lay still for a while longer, trying to soak in the peace of the moment before succumbing to the inevitable and sitting up. They all needed to shower, and time was short.

"Come on. Don't want to miss the bus," Kana finally said as he levered himself out of bed.

"Fine," Mika and Sora said in tandem.

Kana left them to get ambulatory and headed off to get his day moving. Although, given how well the day had started so far, he couldn't complain too much.

*

BETH WAS PRACTICALLY vibrating in her seat when Kana walked up to their shared cubicle space. She and Kana had been coworkers from the moment Kana was hired at the Herald, a local TV and newspaper station that was also part of a larger conglomerate. They had quickly become best friends. Beth's eyes were wide with excitement as Kana joined her at their desks.

"You are not going to believe this!" she said as soon as Kana got within earshot.

"Believe what?" Kana asked. He unzipped the top of his bag to let Mika and Sora out and then stashed it in a drawer in his desk.

Kana was reaching for the button to boot up his computer when she said, "A hunter is coming here!" His finger missed the button, and he flailed as he overbalanced and almost smacked his face into the edge of his desk.

"A what?" he gasped, computer forgotten as he turned to look at Beth.

She nodded. "A hunter. He said he wants to do an interview!"

Kana turned back to his desk to hide his expression from Beth. The last thing he wanted her to notice was him cringing in fear.

"What kind of hunter?" he asked.

"I have no idea, but isn't it the coolest thing? First, we interview vampires and werewolves, and now we're interviewing a hunter?"

Kana didn't know how Beth could blithely ignore that she, and most of the staff at the station, had almost died interviewing said vampires, but he wasn't about to remind her. Presumably hunters were marginally more civilized than the vampires, and therefore wouldn't attack humans like Beth, but Kana couldn't say for sure.

What he did know was a hunter coming here was definitely not good news.

Hunters were the closest equivalent to a police force the supernatural world had. They usually specialized in one particular creature, so a vampire hunter hunted vampires, a werewolf hunter hunted werewolves, and a witch hunter hunted witches. Without knowing what kind of hunter was coming, Kana couldn't say who was actually in danger.

There was also the fact that he didn't know why a hunter was coming now. Maybe it was a belated visit by a vampire hunter to double-check the vampires were actually gone, but it could just as easily be one of the dozens of other types of hunters. It could be a witch hunter coming to eradicate the witch helping the werewolves, or someone planning to eliminate the werewolves. Or it could be a simple visit by a hunter to remind magical creatures they should behave because hunters were around.

"Hurry up and open your email," Beth continued. "The researchers sent over what they found about hunting, and now production wants us to start coming up with potential interview questions."

Beth was looking at Kana expectantly, so he hurried to turn on his computer. While it was booting, Kana pulled his cell phone out of his pocket.

Will one of you call Ember to warn him? he asked Mika and Sora.

Mika uncurled from the pillow he was sharing with Sora and padded over to Kana. *I've got it.* He carefully gripped the phone in his mouth and hurried off to find a spot where he could safely shift into his human form and call.

"When is the interview?" Kana asked. His computer finally finished loading, and he hit the button to open his email.

"First thing tomorrow, I think," Beth replied.

"So we have today to come up with the questions for the interview," Kana replied, trying to grouse with Beth, although his voice came out a touch too flat. If the interview was tomorrow, then the hunter was very likely already in the area, and there was no telling what he might be doing.

Beth didn't notice his reticence. She still sounded chipper, but faintly exasperated when she replied, "That's more time than we got for that jewelry theft ring story last month. At least this time the researchers have something for us ahead of time."

Kana forced out a laugh. "True. Let me read through the research really quick, and we can put our heads together and start coming up with questions." He settled in his desk chair and pulled up the email to start reading.

The researchers didn't have anything more to add to what Kana already knew. There wasn't any identification regarding the kind of hunter, nor about why he was here. Kana was just finishing reading the summary when Mika returned.

Ember says thank you for the warning, Mika said as he dropped the phone in Kana's hand. *He's calling all his wolves right now and insisting if they're outside a pack house they have to travel in pairs. One of the pair is supposed to call him or a beta for help if they encounter a hunter, and they're prohibited from engaging in any way. He said it would be good if you did the same.*

Makes sense, Kana replied. *Last thing we want is a hunter poking around.*

I also told him you're helping write the interview questions, Mika continued. *Ember said, if you can, you should try and get all the details about why the hunter is here.*

I was going to try that anyway, but it's good to know Ember had the same idea. Kana scrubbed one hand through his hair and leaned back in his seat. "I don't understand why the hunter decided to come here," he said to Beth.

Her chair creaked as she turned to look at him. "I'm assuming he wants to know more about the vampires and werewolves, since we're the news station that broke that story."

Kana was worried that was only the tip of the hunter's plans, but he couldn't tell Beth exactly why. Still, there was another way to get her interested in asking the question. He also turned his chair so they could talk face-to-face.

"I think there might be a larger story there," he said. "He could have called to ask us that, but instead, he traveled here and offered himself up for an interview?"

"You think he's after something else?" Beth asked, her voice rising with excitement. "Maybe the witch that werewolf mentioned when Stephen called?"

Kana hoped not. A wolf who didn't understand he needed to keep his mouth shut had answered the phone when Stephen, the lead reporter for their station, called, and he told Stephen a witch had helped kill the vampires. Ember immediately removed the wolf from that job, but the damage was done. Stephen happily shared that tidbit on every media source their station used. The hunters could have easily learned a witch was involved, if that was what they were interested in.

"Or maybe he's looking to set up a hunter compound in the city?" Kana asked, hoping to divert Beth's attention from the witch issue. Besides, if they kept the question more open-ended, they might get a better answer from the hunter.

Beth nodded. "It would be best to simply ask the hunter what brings him to our city and let him fill in the blanks."

Kana grabbed a pen and a pad of paper and wrote that first question.

"A follow-up could be how long he thinks he'll be staying?" Kana asked, hoping Beth would agree, but she started shaking her head before he finished.

"That's pushing it. Maybe if the conversation naturally goes that way, but I don't think we should ask that. How about we ask him what he does for a living?"

Kana did like that question. "Phrase it as: tell us about the job of a hunter?"

Beth nodded. "And if he tells us what type of hunter, our follow-up should be something about how he's able to hunt whatever it is he hunts."

Kana scribbled both questions before Beth changed her mind. "We could title the article, 'A Day in the Life of a Hunter.'"

"Yes!" Beth said, and she was back to vibrating happily in her seat. "Stephen's gonna love this!"

"We could ask how the hunter was recruited into whatever organization he's part of," Kana continued, "and what training he went through and such." The hunter would only provide generalities to answer those questions, but they would help conceal what Kana was really after.

"Oh! We should flip the order around. Start by asking him how he became a hunter and how he was trained, then ask him what brought him here. Build out the full story of his life and how that culminated in his traveling to Albany."

As long as Kana's questions were answered, he didn't care in what order Beth thought they should be asked. He started drawing arrows on his paper to move the questions around.

"If he tells us why he's here, we should follow up with how he's going to go about accomplishing his mission," Kana added. When Beth nodded, Kana wrote that question on the list.

"And we can end with something simple like if there are any tourist attractions or restaurants he's planning to visit while he's here," Beth finished. She waited for Kana to write the question, then yanked the pad from underneath Kana's hand. "I'll get this into an email. You've still got those edits for the bakery competition story to finish, right?"

"Ah, damn. I do! Thanks for reminding me!" Kana turned back to his computer and pulled up the document in question, glad when a few seconds later he heard Beth typing on her own keyboard, because it gave him a few private moments to stare, unblinking, down at his hands.

A hunter, here. Kana ought to call in sick or something. He could feign feeling a touch under the weather this afternoon, so no one would be surprised when he claimed to have a fever tomorrow. If he hid, though, there was no telling what he might miss. Yes, he would be safer if he wasn't around for the hunter to notice, but if the hunter was after the wolves, Kana had to be here in order to pass that information on to Ember in time.

Decided, Kana let out a breath and sat up straight again. Besides, maybe he was overreacting. Maybe the hunter was just passing through, and his job was to remind the world hunters were around and ready to respond. He could be using the local news stations as his method of getting the word out.

No matter how much he wished this was all just a simple coincidence, worry still churned in Kana's gut. Even as he finally got to work parsing through misplaced commas and sourcing structure, half of Kana's mind continued to swirl with what-ifs.

Chapter Four

A BLACK SUV waited at the curb by the bus stop when Kana left work that afternoon. As he walked across the street, the wolf sitting in the front passenger seat jumped out and pulled the back door open. Kana slid inside, the door closed, and the car smoothly pulled into traffic. They had done this maneuver multiple times before, but Kana didn't think it had ever gone so swiftly, as if the wolves sitting in the front seats had been warned not to make any sort of scene today. Given a hunter might be watching their every move, that made sense, although Kana hoped they hadn't figured out Kana was involved.

Admittedly, it would probably be better if Kana stayed as far away from the wolves as possible right now. If the hunter was after him, his being associated with the wolves wouldn't be good for Ember or the rest of the pack. Still, any chance to see Ember again had Kana's heart beating faster in anticipation, and short-circuited more rational thinking.

Regardless of what might be best, Kana had already gotten into the car and was on his way to what looked like the city pack house. It was too late to hide now.

Two wolves were standing guard just inside the massive, black iron gate, which swung open as the car approached. The car continued down the drive, and Kana saw more wolves walking the grounds in pairs, all of them in human form although Kana suspected there were some in wolf form around as well. The car stopped in front of the main doors, which opened a moment later, and Ember walked out.

"Do you think it's safe for me to be here?" Kana asked as he climbed out of the car. "Shouldn't we stay apart instead?"

Ember frowned. "It's better to stay close so we can watch each other's backs. I'm sorry if I'm being presumptuous, but I think it would be better if you stayed with us until the hunter problem is solved."

He was definitely being presumptuous, but Kana agreed with his logic.

And you'll get to play with your new witch's room! Mika added, happy with any sort of silver lining.

I definitely need to do something to hide you two tomorrow, Kana told Mika and Sora. *Guess I'll have to open that brand-new box of chalk.*

"I'll need clothes for tomorrow," Kana said to Ember. They walked inside together, and Kana automatically turned toward his new room.

"If you give me your keys, I'll have a couple of my wolves go over and grab your things." When Ember held out his hand, Kana dug into his pocket and passed over his apartment key.

"I'll need an outfit similar to what I'm wearing now for tomorrow," Kana explained with a wave toward his dress slacks and button-down. "And all three toothbrushes."

Ember eyed Mika and Sora, then nodded without commenting. A number of wolves in Ember's pack knew Mika and Sora could transform into six-hundred-pound primordial cats, but only a select number knew Mika and Sora could also take on human form and would therefore want to brush their teeth. Ember knew far more about Kana than anyone else in the pack, although he didn't know Kana's real reason for being nervous about a hunter.

True, most supernatural beings were wary of hunters, particularly since some hunters weren't overly discriminating regarding whether whomever they were hunting had actually committed a crime. Kana was more worried about being exposed than about being hunted, and he was also worried he had brought his own problems down on the wolves.

All of which was presuming his old coven even cared about him, which Kana doubted. They would absolutely want him back if they knew how strong he was, but he hadn't left behind any evidence of that when he left. They wouldn't want him to become a member of their coven anyway. No, they would want to enslave him to take advantage of his powers, and to use him to create strong female children who would become the future of the coven. Kana had fled that life and would fight with everything he had to keep that from ever happening.

"Is there anything else I can get you?" Ember asked.

Kana shook his head. "There's a spell on Mika and Sora that keeps people from noticing that they're out of place. I want to renew that spell and add an obfuscation rune to ensure the hunter doesn't notice them at all tomorrow. Aside from that, I don't have to do anything else tonight."

Ember's beautiful half smile was firmly in place as he listened to Kana. "Can I watch?" he asked.

Kana blinked, surprised Ember was interested, but nodded anyway. "Sure. Just don't muss my chalk lines."

Ember followed Kana to his room. Kana had to pause just inside the door to admire the space again, awed that he had such a perfect place for his magic all to himself. When Ember closed the door, Sora shifted to his human form. Sora walked over to the shelf where a wicker basket held three brand-new boxes of white chalk. He opened one and pulled out a stick, then put the box away and walked over to Kana.

"Maybe you should add a concealment rune, too, to help hide the fact that magic was used around us?" Sora asked.

"Good idea." Kana took the chalk and knelt in the center of the room. He ran his fingers over the floor and had to swallow down a lump forming in his throat. His fingers couldn't find a single blemish, not a dip in the floor or a ridge from the paint. He could draw his circle without worrying anything would cause a break in the lines that would ruin his spell, and Ember and his wolves had gone to all that extra effort for him.

Kana gripped the chalk and bent his elbow to the exact angle, then pressed the chalk to the ground. He spun in a perfect circle and made sure the circle closed by overlapping the line slightly. He changed his grip to stiffen his wrist and loosen his elbow, then drew five straight lines in the center of the circle, each angled to make a perfect pentagram.

Sora was waiting with five white candles in his hands, which Kana exchanged for the chalk. White symbolized protection, and when he placed each one at the junction where the points of the star intersected with the circle, they stood unaided. Sora handed back the chalk, and Kana quickly marked in each separate rune to complete the spell. He studied the finished circle for a few long seconds, looking at every single line and curve to ensure it was perfect before carefully stepping out of the circle.

Kana knelt again and drew a second, smaller circle and pentagram exactly six inches from the top of the first circle. In those six inches Kana wrote the runes to direct the power generated from the big circle into the smaller circle, condensing the spell to exclusively cover Mika and Sora, who would be sitting in the center of the smaller circle when Kana cast the spell.

Sora put the now much-reduced piece of chalk away while Kana looked over the circle again, searching for any breaks in his lines. He nodded and let out a relieved breath when he was satisfied both circles were perfect.

"Why chalk?" Ember asked, his voice soft as if he was afraid of interrupting Kana's concentration. "I know you drew some circles when we were fighting Octavius, but most of your spell work ended up not using chalk."

"Chalk is more precise, and I was always taught precision increases the efficacy of spells. The circles I cast without chalk..." He paused, trying to figure out how to say it without sounding boastful. "Not everyone can draw circles with magic, and even of those who can, few of those circles actually work. They're faster, but often not as strong, and it's a lot easier to make mistakes."

"Yours are strong though?" Ember asked.

Kana ducked his head. "For about three years I didn't exactly have...erm." Kana didn't know how to say it without sounding bad, but it was easiest to just rip the Band-Aid off. "I was homeless, so just getting chalk, let alone a smooth surface to write on, was impossible. The only way I could do magic was with an improvised circle."

Ember glanced at Mika and Sora, who were lounging next to their circle, Sora having returned to cat form while they waited for Kana to be ready. Kana guessed what was going through Ember's mind: two cat familiars and Kana was male. Kana had received magic training from somewhere, meaning he had been part of a coven at one point but clearly wasn't now.

"You're in hiding," Ember stated as if Kana's explanation had only confirmed that fact for him. "That's why you're so worried about the hunter. If he exposes you, whoever you're hiding from will find you."

Kana nodded. "I left my old coven before they realized just what I had bonded to during the familiar calling spell. I'm hoping they have no idea that I have some power, and because I'm male, I'm hoping they have no interest in finding out why I left. I've been very careful to try to keep it that way, but having a hunter parading me around would make hiding impossible."

Ember's chin flexed. "Then we double your protection," he said, and his firm voice didn't allow for any arguments, not that Kana had any inclination to argue if it meant spending more time with Ember.

"Thanks," Kana replied.

Ember opened his mouth to say something, but then snapped it closed as he spun to look at the side door that led to the kitchen Kana had shared access to. Ember strode over to the door, but instead of yanking it open like Kana expected, he froze in place. Kana heard why a second later.

"Move your big head! I can't see!" a young voice hissed, as if the child was trying to be quiet but hadn't yet mastered that skill.

"My head isn't big! And maybe if you did something with your crazy hair, you'd be able to see just fine!" a second voice growled back, his skill in whispering just as poor as the first.

"Come on!" a third voice said, and this one didn't even bother to try being quiet. "I wanna see too!"

Ember's severe expression didn't soften, but he rolled his eyes briefly before shoving the pocket door open. Two kids, a boy and a girl, maybe eight years old, tumbled into the room. Marc, the only kid Kana recognized, was left standing in the doorway, gaping in surprise at Ember. Shannon was leaning against the kitchen counter a few feet behind Marc. His blond hair was still ragged and long on his shoulders, but with new clothes, Shannon looked a lot more put together.

Octavius, the vampire leader Kana had helped Ember defeat, had decided kidnapping the pack's children to coerce Ember into behaving was also the only way to punish Ember for his insubordination. One of the kids had been Marc. Octavius had also gone on a spree, killing humans and changing them into vampires, and hundreds of newly turned vampires completely under Octavius's control had attacked the second Ember had been distracted by the kids. At some point, Octavius had discovered Shannon, who was already a vampire, and brought him along too. Octavius had been arrogant enough to believe he could control Shannon the same as he controlled the newly changed vampires, but Shannon hadn't engaged in the fighting. According to Marc, he had instead protected the kids from the blood-hungry vampires.

After the battle, Ember had allowed Shannon to stay, and Marc had adopted him. Apparently, that included eavesdropping on Kana and Ember when Ember was about to cast a spell. Although, Shannon looked mildly amused at Marc's antics rather than interested in what Kana was doing.

Kana suspected, and he thought Ember agreed with the supposition, even though they had never spoken about it, that Shannon was far older and incredibly more powerful than Octavius. Having him on their side, and keeping Shannon somewhere they could keep an eye on him, was all Kana really cared about. Besides, Shannon seemed to like Marc, and Marc certainly dragged Shannon along pretty much everywhere.

"What do you think you're doing?" Ember growled, his voice firm and angry, but not threatening.

"We wanted to see the magic," Marc answered. His tone didn't waver under Ember's growl, but he did bare his neck in submission. The other two kids were shaking on the floor, unable to stand with Ember glaring down at them.

"Then you should have asked, rather than sneaking around at the door," Kana said in admonishment, trying to support Ember's dominance while also attempting to defuse the situation. "It's not very nice to me or to your alpha."

"Sorry," one of the kids on the floor squeaked out.

Ember continued glaring, and then let out another short growl when no one else said anything.

"I'm sorry too," the other kid on the floor babbled, her words tripping over each other as she rushed to get them out.

Ember turned his glare on Marc, who resisted for a second before dropping his eyes.

"Sorry for eavesdropping," he said.

"And?" Ember asked in a sharp bark.

Marc's shoulders slumped. "And for sneaking."

Ember didn't quite glare at Shannon when he looked up, but Shannon nodded his head once in acknowledgment of the slight he had watched occur. Formalities done, Ember's glare vanished, and he stepped back.

"Well?" he asked them in his normal voice.

Marc glanced up at Ember, saw Ember wasn't angry at them anymore, and smiled. He turned to Kana, his eyes shining and eager.

"Can we watch you do your spell?" Marc asked.

Kana smiled back. "Sit against the wall, where you won't disturb the chalk."

The kids rushed to obey, scrambling to find spots where they could see the circle and not be in the way. Shannon stepped up to the doorway and leaned on the jamb, but he didn't enter the room. Ember stepped back to the wall, standing next to where Marc was sitting.

All eyes turned toward Kana, who turned away, ostensibly to study the spell lines again.

Have I ever cast a spell with an audience before? Kana asked.

Mika laughed. *Not like this. Last time, you were in the middle of a fight and didn't have time to worry about them watching you.*

Don't worry about it, Sora added. *You've cast this spell before; you know what you're doing, and their watching you doesn't change your abilities.*

The growing tightness in Kana's gut loosened at Sora's words. He let out a breath and actually focused on the chalk rather than staring at it blindly. None of the lines were disturbed.

Kana carefully stepped over the lines and sat in the center of the big circle. Mika and Sora curled up together in the middle of the smaller one. Kana pressed his palms flat to the ground on either side of his body and called up his magic. His circle started glowing, and then the lines of the pentagram in the order he had drawn them. The smaller circle lit up too.

Kana faintly heard *oohs* from behind him, but the hum of the magic kept him focused. He poured more magic into the circle, and the candles abruptly lit themselves, the protective illumination from the flames joining with the glowing circle until both lights combined into a solid circle surrounding Kana. He pushed magic into the runes next, and the circles thrummed as if Kana had hit them like a drum. The chalk lines on the floor slowly lifted into the air until they reached the height of Kana's chest and the circle became a sphere.

The spell took with a rushing feeling as magic flew from Kana's circle to the smaller one, the runes vanishing and then reappearing surrounding Mika and Sora. The runes flowed again, losing their form and melding together to drop like a blanket over Mika and Sora to complete the spell.

Kana immediately cut off the magic, and the light vanished, along with all the chalk and the candles. The floor was back to being smooth and unblemished as Kana stood. Mika and Sora both shook themselves, and Kana sensed a slight tightness around their bodies through the bond they shared. The spell took a few more seconds to settle in, and then the tightness faded.

When the kids cheered, Kana turned to smile at them.

"It's hard to believe you're self-taught," Shannon said, his soft Irish lilt easily audible despite the kids. "That was masterful spell work." He turned his head to look down at Marc. "Marc, do you remember those two strange books you asked me about when you were helping me unpack the items I had shipped here?" Marc nodded. "Will you retrieve them for me?"

Marc hopped to his feet and dashed past Shannon in the doorway. "Be right back!" he shouted over his shoulder as he went.

"So your cats are protected now," Ember said after the room was silent for a few long moments.

"Yeah." Kana nodded. "I think it might take even you, with your alpha abilities, a few tries to spot them."

Ember glanced around the room, his eyes skipping over Mika and Sora, who hadn't bothered moving after the spell. He closed his eyes and sniffed, then grimaced.

"I can tell they're in the room, but I would probably have to shift to pinpoint them," he said.

Kana looked up at Shannon, but he just smiled, which wasn't an answer. Kana didn't feel like pushing the issue, so he turned back to Ember.

"I'll reduce the spell once the hunter is gone."

Ember nodded. "Probably would be best. I don't want my wolves going on a hunt to find the cat smell. We have more important things to focus on right now. Speaking of which…" He looked down at the two remaining kids. "It's close to dinnertime and I bet your parents are looking for you," he said pointedly. Both kids groaned but obediently stood and headed off.

Sora stood, stretched, and then shifted to his human form. Mika grumbled and followed suit. Kana's spell was designed to only work on their small form, so he wasn't surprised when Ember immediately looked over at them. Sora opened his mouth to say something, but snapped it shut again when Marc skidded back into the room.

Marc was holding two tomes—books as old as those appeared to be could only be called that. Made of parchment rather than paper, the books had a gravity to them modern equivalents would never match. Magic also emanated from them.

Kana picked out preservation and protection spells immediately, but he also thought they might be locked. Only the owner would be able to open them. Shannon carefully took the books from Marc without even admonishing him for running around recklessly with something that might crumble into dust if it was dropped. Kana would have thrown a fit—or a spell—if those were his books.

"I am loaning these books to you, Kana," Shannon said formally, and Kana felt the brief bite of the locking spell as it enveloped and then accepted him. "I would appreciate you returning them when you have finished." He held the books out for Kana to take.

The books were heavy in Kana's hands, but the spells inside had to be ancient and powerful magic. And Shannon was allowing him to read them!

"Thank you," Kana said, despite knowing mere thanks weren't nearly enough.

"The layered spell you used when we first met, the one you built on instinct and thanks to the call of the magic in your soul?" Shannon began. "I believe you will find more information on how to conduct those spells purposefully in one of those books. It saddens me to know how much magic was lost when humans feared our kind and sought to destroy us rather than welcome us. Some of that lost magic can only be regained by trial and error, much as you rediscovered layered spell circles; however. I am happy to help fill what gaps I can in the meantime."

Kana opened his mouth to say thank you again, but Shannon turned away to look at Marc before Kana could get any words out.

"I believe it is time for your meal as well. Shall we?"

Marc sighed, but nodded. "Yeah, I'm hungry. Cool spell, Kana. Can I come see magic again?"

"Of course. Just let me know ahead of time, okay?"

Marc waved and ran out the door. Shannon sedately followed, leaving Kana alone with Ember again.

"Dinner is being served if you three would like to join us," Ember said.

Kana glanced over at Mika and Sora. Sora nodded while Mika walked to Kana's backpack. He dug into the largest pocket and pulled out two pairs of loose black pajama pants. Mika tossed one pair to Sora, then pulled on the other one.

"Food sounds good," Mika said while they waited for Sora to settle the waistband around his hips. Kana tracked the movement of the cloth, snug over hip bones and a flat stomach, but yanked his eyes away before he did something inappropriate. He looked over at Ember just in time to see Ember looking away from Kana.

Kana didn't know what to make of that. Instead of trying to figure it out, he went over to one of the shelves. The small piece of chalk sat loose in the basket. Kana snagged it and drew a quick circle on the shelf, then put the books down on top of it. They faded from sight the second Kana's fingers let them go.

Ember went to the locked main door, opened it, and waited for Kana to reach him before leading the way toward the dining hall for dinner.

Chapter Five

KANA BEAT BETH into work, but he had only logged in and opened his email when she hustled into their shared cubicle space.

"You will never guess who I saw downstairs!" she gasped as she dramatically collapsed into her chair.

"Who?" Kana asked obediently.

"The hunter! And he's a looker, let me tell you." She fanned herself with one hand while grinning at him. "He and his very buxom secretary were in the lobby when I came up."

"How do you know it was the hunter?" Kana asked.

"He was carrying a glittering spear. I didn't know who else he might be. If the higher-ups can convince him to go on camera with that spear, our ratings will be through the roof." Beth giggled. "Anyway, we should go get the interview room ready now."

Kana nodded. He hit the buttons to put his computer to sleep and followed Beth down the hall to the studio with the couches and desk setup for interviews. Kana headed directly to the computer that was connected to the teleprompter so he could load the questions onto it, while Beth pulled out the novelty station mugs and pads of paper to decorate the desk and small table adjacent to the couch.

They were almost done ten minutes later when Stephen's voice sounded from the hall. Kana was crouched down behind the computer, reading through the teleprompter one last time to double-check for mistakes while Beth was working in the middle of the room with the tech guys organizing microphones.

"Let's get you set up in here first," Stephen said as he walked into the room. The hunter walked in behind him.

The hunter was wearing a dark-gray suit and a darker-gray tie. His shoulders filled the suit jacket very nicely, and the color offset his dark skin perfectly. His hair was tied in braids tight to his scalp, and in his hand was a spear that emitted magic so strongly Kana felt it from the other side of the room. What Beth described as glitter, Kana knew was actually magical residue dripping from the metal point.

Are his shoulders as nice as your wolf's? Sora asked, his voice cheeky, yet curious at the same time.

Kana took another glance, and while the shoulders were certainly very nice, Ember's were definitely better.

No, but I can see why Beth was so enamored, Kana replied.

A third person walked into the room next. Kana caught a glimpse of carefully bleached blonde hair and the buxom chest Beth had described, pushing against the front of her lavender suit jacket, but then he saw her face and immediately ducked lower so the computer could hide him better.

Samantha Bix was a name and a face Kana would never forget, and she was definitely no secretary, for all that she was carrying a stack of papers for the hunter.

From childish taunts, to backhanded comments, to outright, in-his-face verbal sneers, Samantha had been his staunchest detractor. She'd hated the idea that a man was even allowed in the same classroom as her, and the fact that man also claimed to have a bit of magic? She was a very strong witch, and Kana knew her time training with the coven's inner circle had greatly influenced her negative attitude toward him.

Kana had no idea why she was here though. His coven—and hers—was the second largest in the nation and located in Seattle. The largest was located in Eastern Massachusetts, which was only about a three-hour drive from here. Technically, this territory fell under the jurisdiction of the Salem coven, although that three-hour difference did make it possible for witches like Kana to remain under the radar. Perhaps Samantha was taking advantage of that distance too?

She's got to be a member of the coven circle by now, Kana said to Sora and Mika. *Why is she here with a hunter?*

Good question, Mika replied.

She had better not notice you, Sora added. *That wouldn't end well, I think.*

Sora was right. If Samantha noticed him, the least she would do was hurl some terrible verbal abuse. Kana needed this job, and he needed to stay on good terms with his coworkers, and Samantha could easily ruin that with a few sharp words. Worst case, she would try to put him in his place with magic, and he would have to defend himself, which would then draw the attention of the hunter and likely have even more dire consequences.

Beth finished with the microphones and wandered over. "Man, that hunter is really something, huh?" She grinned at him as if she were barely preventing herself from licking her lips or drooling.

"Do you—" Kana let out a stuttering breath to attempt to force his mouth to form coherent words. He took in a smoother breath and tried again. "Would you like to stay out here and work the teleprompter? I'll go to the reviewing room in the back."

"Oh, would I!" Beth said, her smile growing. "I could look at him for the entire interview!"

Kana quickly finished with the teleprompter and stepped back. "All yours," he told Beth. She eagerly took his place, and Kana hurried off to the back room where all the techs worked, and where a wall separated him from Samantha.

I didn't see her familiar, Kana said.

Could be spelled like you did to us, Mika replied. *Or she left her familiar at home.*

Samantha hadn't been nice to him, but she was a good witch. Kana didn't think she would abandon her familiar like that, but then again what he really knew about her now was limited. The coven had certainly looked down on people who cooperated with other species and generally would never work together with someone like a hunter, yet Samantha was pretending to be the hunter's secretary.

Kana pulled out his phone and opened a text message to Ember. *The hunter brought a witch,* he wrote. *She's from my old coven. I don't know why she's here since I don't think she has permission from the coven in Salem. I'm being careful.*

Stay low, Ember texted back almost immediately. *I have a car on standby near your office if you need to make a run for it.*

Hopefully it won't come to that, Kana replied, *but thank you.*

Watch your back, Ember finished.

The techs had apparently completed whatever they were doing

with the microphones because the hunter and Stephen were settling into their respective spots on the set, and people were moving to get out of the camera shot.

Oliver stood in front of the main camera with the clapperboard, and at Stephen's nod, he clapped it and then hustled out of the way.

"Welcome back to the Daily Biz on Channel Seven News!" Stephen said, his plastic-reporter smile firmly in place. "Today we have a special guest with us, Ary Smith, a hunter tasked with keeping us safe from all the things that go bump in the night. Ary, thank you so much for coming on the show!"

"Thanks for having me," Ary replied with a smile. His voice was smooth and unassuming, the sort of tone that made people want to open up and talk to him. He had probably been trained to sound like that. Ary's name was likely also an alias.

"For our viewers at home who might not know, can you tell us about the job of a hunter?"

Ary laughed softly as if he was pleased Stephen had asked. "It's much like you already said, Stephen. I hunt the creatures that refuse to obey the rules of society. Those that are a threat to humans."

Stephen waited a beat to see if Ary would elaborate before jumping into the next question to force the matter. "Is there a specific creature you hunt?"

Ary shrugged. "I don't specialize. If a creature needs to be hunted, I'm prepared. I heard you had a vampire problem not too long ago?"

"We did," Stephen said, eagerly jumping into the story he had broken. "A whole coven had moved to the city, but there was some sort of internal strife, and the vampires vanished. Do you have any insight on why that might have happened?"

"Werewolves and vampires don't always get along, so it's entirely possible the werewolves won that fight. If I remember your coverage of that event correctly, wasn't there a witch involved?"

Kana sucked in a breath. He could have asked about the number of wolves or vampires, or about Stephen's time inside the vampire compound, but had instead asked about the witch. Ary was definitely interested in finding Kana.

"We haven't been able to confirm that report," Stephen replied, much to Kana's relief.

"I'll have to visit the werewolves while I'm here to ask them," Ary said.

Kana unlocked his phone and quickly typed: *The hunter is planning to visit the werewolves to ask about the witch who helped fight the vampires.*

Got it. We'll take precautions, Ember replied immediately.

"Tell us about a day in the life of a hunter. What do you usually do when you're on the job?" Stephen asked.

"Depends on the job," Ary said with a laugh. "When I'm called in because a creature has gone mad, it can be violent. I'm highly trained, of course, but engaging with a bloodthirsty or murderous creature can be dangerous. Sometimes, though, it's simple. For example, I traveled to Albany only to remind any creatures in your city that hunters are here and will hold them accountable. Sometimes that is enough deterrent to keep the creatures playing by the rules."

Something in Ary's smooth tone didn't feel right to Kana. Ary might be lying. He wasn't here as a deterrent; rather, he was here to investigate the death of the vampires and identify the witch involved. Why else would Samantha be with him?

"That is very good to hear. I'm sure all our viewers are relieved to know they have nothing to fear. Can you tell us about your remarkable weapon?" Stephen asked.

Ary lifted his spear from where he had rested it against the side of the couch. "Absolutely. I prefer the spear because it gives me the tactical advantage of enforcing distance between me and my target. The tip is pure silver, hardened using a special method secret to the hunter's association. Silver is effective against werewolves and a large number of other creatures. The wood of the shaft has also been specially treated to withstand what can be incredible forces during a fight, and the bottom"—he lifted the spear so the cameras could see the bottom of the spear where the wood was tapered to a point—"is sharp enough to use to stake a vampire."

"That's incredible!" Stephen gushed. "How do I get one of my own?"

Ary laughed. "Undergo a few hundred hours of training, and they'll give you one when you graduate."

"I see…" Stephen trailed off awkwardly, but luckily for him the editing department would take care of that before the interview aired in the morning. He glanced back at the teleprompter as he regrouped. "You're doing a lot of good work while you're here, but do you have anything fun planned?"

"I was hoping to go jogging on the Mohawk-Hudson Trail while I'm here. I've heard the locks are quite pretty."

"Oh, they are!" Stephen, who had probably never been on those trails in his life, replied. Kana tried to go at least once a summer, if only to get out of his apartment, but he had a feeling Ary's "jogging" was a little more intense than Kana's usual stroll.

"Thank you so much for joining us today, Hunter Ary Smith!" Stephen said to close out the interview. "We hope you have a pleasant stay in Albany."

"I'm sure I will. Thank you for having me."

Stephen and Ary smiled at each other for a long moment before the director yelled, "And cut!"

Ary and Stephen both relaxed, and a flurry of activity started as makeup and tech people descended on the set.

"That was really good, guys," Oliver, the head of production, said as he reached the desk. "Mr. Smith, do you have a few moments to redo a couple segments so we can get some additional camera shots?"

"Absolutely. Do you mind if I take a five-minute break to walk around and stretch my legs first?" Ary asked.

Oliver nodded. "Take whatever time you need."

Ary nodded and grinned his thanks. He stood, grabbed his spear, and vanished from view of the tech room a second later. Samantha didn't follow, which meant Kana didn't move either. Instead, he watched her, looking for anything that might explain why she was here in the company of a hunter.

She looked around the room, her gaze stopping to take in every person for a moment, particularly the women. To most people, Samantha probably appeared to be bored and studying the room to find some entertainment. But Kana knew she was actually scanning each person for magical potential.

Check this out, Mika said suddenly. He opened the channel between them so Kana looked out of Mika's eyes. Mika was crouched low underneath Kana's desk back in the cubicle space, and the wooden shaft of a familiar spear was right in front of him.

Careful! Kana gasped.

Your spell is working perfectly, Mika replied, his voice dismissive. *He's looking for something.*

The spear shaft moved away, and Kana now viewed Ary's gray

slacks as he left Kana's space and moved into Beth's.

"Aha," Ary said under his breath as he bent low over something on Beth's desk. He studied whatever it was for a long moment, before glancing up to find the name tag that hung at the entrance to everyone's cubicles. He noted Beth's name and then strode from the space.

What was he looking at? Kana asked.

Give me a second, Mika replied. *He's still in earshot, and I'll rustle papers when I jump up there.*

Kana tried to wait patiently, but it took far too long before Mika walked out from under Kana's desk and hopped up first into Beth's chair and from there onto Beth's desk. He went to the area where Ary had been standing and found the pad of paper covered in Kana's scrawl where they had first outlined the questions for today's interview.

Why would he be interested in that? Kana wondered.

The questions were rather pointed, Sora said. *I bet he wanted to know who came up with them.*

Damn. *Is Beth in trouble?*

Nah, Sora replied easily, and Kana could feel him shake his head through their bond. *He'll spend three seconds talking to her and realize she's not the one he's looking for.*

Beth is refreshingly ordinary, Mika added. He jumped down and headed back to the pillow under Kana's desk. A pillow that was empty.

Where are you? Kana asked Sora. *You're supposed to stay hidden!*

Oh, it's fine. I went to sniff out that witch's familiar, and I think I found it, Sora said. *Come see.*

Kana allowed himself to be pulled from Mika's mind to Sora's. When the familiar blinked, the main lobby of the building came into view. Sora was tucked behind one of the support pillars, his gaze focused out the glass front doors. A dog sat just to the right of the doors where it would be out of the way.

At first glance, the dog appeared normal. At about fifty pounds, it had short, well-groomed fur and short, pointed ears. A second look said otherwise. It was a dog in the same way Mika and Sora looked like house cats. The fur was more like a seal's than a dog's coat, and the shades of gray and brown were far richer than on any dogs Kana had ever seen. However, they were normal colors from creatures born on the other side. Also, despite the sidewalk outside being full of people at the start of the lunch rush, not a single one looked down or otherwise noticed a stray dog.

You think he has multiple forms like you? Kana asked.

Sora shook his head. *There's no way to tell just by looking at him. I'd have to taste his magic, and I don't really want to get that close. The dog is full grown, though, so her bond with it is complete.*

Kana returned to his own body with a sigh. *Which means she's strong.*

Yes and no, Mika said. *Having a completed bond means she is able to fully tap into the magic her familiar offers, but it's still a dog.* The derision in Mika's voice was so stereotypically catlike, Kana had to stifle a laugh.

Mika did have a point though. There was a hierarchy of familiars, and even within familiar types there were stronger and lesser powers. A wild cat like a panther was higher than a housecat within the cat hierarchy, but a housecat was always stronger than a dog because cats as a whole were at the pinnacle of the overall scale. That said, smarter animals like dogs were a close second to cats, which meant Samantha was no magical slouch.

Kana looked at the studio again just in time to see Ary leave the person he had stopped to speak with by the door and head directly toward Beth. It took Beth a moment to notice who was talking to her—she was likely engrossed in updating the teleprompter, which Kana was supposed to be helping her with and would have to apologize for missing later—but once she did notice, Beth immediately went starry-eyed.

Kana couldn't make out what they were saying. Beth blushed and reached up with one hand to tuck her hair behind one ear. Ary grinned at her after she said something, and her eyes went wide and dreamy again.

"Ready to start?" Oliver asked, his voice loud enough to be heard over everything else.

"I am ready," Ary replied in the sudden silence in the wake of Oliver's question. He nodded politely to Beth as he turned away and started walking to the set. Except, as he passed Samantha, Kana was pretty certain he shook his head slightly as if to say, "not her." Kana let out a relieved breath at knowing Beth was safe.

Kana relaxed against the piece of wall he was holding up and watched as the crew got everything set up for a second take. Samantha didn't talk to anyone or watch anything other than Ary, but Kana didn't relax until microphones were removed from collars, hands were shaken, and Sora reported from where he watched from his hiding spot in the lobby that Ary, Samantha, and the dog familiar had left the building.

Chapter Six

FRAGRANT STEAM REDOLENT with chamomile, rose, and honey bathed Kana's face as he blew on his mug to cool his tea. Ember leaned back in the chair next to Kana, his mug of coffee in one hand. He took a gulp and swallowed, the heat from the freshly poured cup irrelevant. All Kana saw was Ember's Adam's apple bob and the smooth lines of his neck. Kana forced his attention away, back to his tea, which was still too hot for him to drink. He blew on it some more.

"Where did Mika and Sora go?" Ember asked.

Kana concentrated down his bond for a moment to check. "They're curled up in the hammock you got them, sleeping off eating way too much food."

Ember laughed. "Sounds like some of my wolves." He looked around the dining hall, which was emptying out as people finished eating. The entire pack didn't live here—some lived in the larger pack house about a forty-minute drive away, where there was more land and fewer humans, and some had purchased houses of their own to live with their families—but Ember had instituted a protection order so more were at the pack house than normal.

Kana was in the process of gingerly testing his tea when Ember's phone rang. Ember yanked it out of his pocket, tapped the screen to accept the call, and held it up to his ear. The volume was loud enough for Kana to hear although he didn't think anyone else could.

"We just sighted the hunter's car pulling into the neighborhood. He'll be at the gate in a few minutes," the caller said.

"Conduct a basic security sweep and make sure it's only him and the witch in the car; then let them drive up to the front door. I want a perimeter around the car at all times; some visible, but keep them well back. We don't want our visitors to feel threatened."

"Yes, sir," the caller replied, and then the phone screen went dark as he hung up.

Kana abandoned his tea as he followed Ember out of the dining room and through the hallways to the front door.

"Stay out of sight," Ember warned and waited for Kana to walk over to one of the windows where he could stand at an angle and look out but not be seen by someone outside. Ember pulled open the door and stepped out onto the stoop to wait for the car.

The sun was setting behind the house, casting long shadows across the drive and front lawn. The car was therefore harder to see, but the lighting also helped conceal the wolves on guard. Headlights flashed as the car came into view and slowly pulled to a stop right in front of the door. Ary was driving. He and Samantha got out, and Samantha waited for Ary to walk around the car before they both approached Ember.

"Alpha," Ary said. "We have come to ask you a few questions about the recent incident you had with the vampires. May we come inside?"

Kana studied them both, but they were still wearing the same outfits they had worn to the studio: Ary his sleek gray-on-gray suit, Samantha in her chest-enhancing secretary outfit.

Ember was also studying them, and he waited a few extra moments—probably to assert his dominance over them, Kana assumed—before replying, "You are welcome to visit, Hunter, but the witch must stay outside."

Ary's face didn't change, but Samantha's eyes narrowed, and her lips pursed as if she found Ember knowing about her an inconvenience. She stepped around Ary and stopped right in front of Ember.

"I'll be fine," she said. "Dogs love me."

Kana gasped and looked around the car, trying to spot her canine familiar.

We're already out hunting for it, Sora said before Kana could even ask. *You focus on her.*

"Only the hunter is welcome," Ember repeated.

Samantha smiled as if Ember's words didn't mean anything to her. "It will be fine," she repeated. "Dogs love me."

There was something strange and sibilant about her voice. Kana concentrated, trying to pick out any strands of magic in the air, and saw the coercion spell gently blanket Ember a second too late. Kana reached for the chalk in his pocket to draw a counter, but stopped when Ember only glared at her.

"I prefer cats," he said simply, and the coercion spell shattered.

Samantha frowned as if trying to hide her surprise. Kana practically saw the wheels turning in her head as she tried to figure out another method to force her way inside. If she had been so certain her coercion spell would work on Ember, an alpha-level wolf... Kana stifled a gasp at the realization and turned his attention to Ary.

Layers upon layers of magic coated Ary. Some emanated from his spear, some from what looked like six daggers scattered around his body, hidden underneath his clothes, and some looked like he had ingested potions. Coating all of it like a slick oil spill on water, Kana could just barely make out the runes of coercion. Unlike the ad-hoc spell Samantha had tried on Ember, this spell had been drawn in chalk.

Kana turned to look behind him and, on a hunch, softly called out, "Marc."

Marc's head immediately popped out from around the corner of the nearest hallway.

"Yes?" he asked.

"Sprint to the kitchen and bring me the big canister of salt," Kana instructed. Marc nodded and dashed off.

Kana turned back to the window. There was no telling when the coercion spell had been put on Ary, or how deep the claws of Samantha's magic went, but as long as that spell remained in place, Ary was essentially her slave. Kana couldn't leave him like that. Unfortunately, there wasn't time to be precise about removing it.

"I don't see any issues with my coming inside too," Samantha said as a second coercion spell flew from her and shattered when it impacted Ember. She frowned, and Ary's fist tightened around his spear.

Marc ran into the front hall, the large cardboard container of salt in his hands. He gave it to Kana, and Kana yanked open the metal pour tab at the top.

"Thanks," he told Marc with a nod of his chin back toward the hallway where Marc had been hiding before. Marc pouted but obediently went.

Kana poured salt into his hand until the mound overflowed and spilled onto the floor. He needed a pick rather than a chisel, something sharp and immediate that would pierce through the spell and force it to dissipate before Samantha could raise any defenses.

Kana moved to stand where he was still hidden by the door, yet closer to Ember, who still stood in the middle of the stoop.

"Get ready," he hissed just loud enough for Ember to hear.

Ember didn't tense although his fingers flexed. Warning given, Kana called on his magic. He needed runes for strength, force, breaking, and dissipating. Then he needed a second circle for protection, to keep Samantha from being able to retaliate.

The salt in his hand stirred, shifting around on his palm to form a rough circle as he pushed magic into the grains. When it started glowing, Kana threw the salt into the air.

The salt shot out of Kana's hand like an arrow from a crossbow, arcing over Ember and Samantha and striking Ary in the chest. Samantha let out a screech as she spun to look at Ary, but she was too late. The spell in the salt sank into Ary's chest, cracking through the coercion spell and most of the rest of the magic on Ary. He collapsed to the ground, gasping for air, and the salt scattered around him, forming another circle as protection runes flared to life inside.

Samantha's magic smacked into that circle and rebounded uselessly into a shower of sparks. She spun again, this time to glare at Ember.

"Give me your witch! Bring her to me now!" Her voice echoed with power, as if she were shouting a spell in the middle of a cave. Her spell washed up against him and Ember staggered back a step, but then it flowed back like an ocean wave, leaving him completely untouched. He straightened and glared at her.

"Leave my property at once," Ember said, and while his voice sounded cordial, like Samantha's, there was an echo of power to it that turned the simple words into a promised threat.

Kana was already drawing the magic before Ember glanced over his shoulder in question. A circle formed under Samantha's feet, the lines of the pentagram blossoming as light filled the driveway. The dimming sun from encroaching dusk was eclipsed as the circle's light grew.

Samantha screamed, the circle rocking as she threw magic at it. Kana clenched his fists and poured more magic into the spell. The rune for movement appeared directly underneath Samantha's feet, and Kana felt the spell settle properly into place. He made a shooing motion with one hand, and the circle started moving, dragging Samantha down the driveway and back toward the front gate. Her screaming was still audible long after she was no longer visible, but Kana kept feeding power into the spell until she was well away from the pack property.

Her familiar? Kana asked.

We found him. Sora sounded smug. *He was skulking around the house, trying to find a side entrance that didn't have a wolf guarding it, but when she flew by, he chased after her. He's gone too.*

Kana stepped outside and stood next to Ember on the front stoop. Mika and Sora sauntered into view, and Mika hopped up into Kana's arms, purring and asking for pets. Kana obligingly dug his fingers into the ruff behind Mika's ears.

"How far are you sending her?" Ember asked.

"The bus stop on the main road. The spell won't go any farther than that," Kana replied. Mika crawled up onto Kana's shoulder, which left space for Sora to jump into his arms. Kana cradled Sora close, drawing on the comfort of Sora's fur and gentle purrs to calm his heart, which was still beating wildly after that fight.

Sora licked one of Kana's fingers. *Ooh. Salty!* he exclaimed, and then proceeded to wash Kana's hand completely clean.

Ember chuckled and shook his head at Sora's antics, but then his laughter faded when he looked down where Ary was still crumpled on the ground, unconscious.

"What do I do with him?" he asked, but he walked down the stairs without waiting for an answer. Kana followed and brushed a toe through the salt circle to break the spell.

"I removed all his magic," Kana explained. "He's dealing with a lot of backlash."

"Well, we can't leave him lying there." Ember lifted one hand, and two wolves trotted over from the other side of the driveway. "Put him in one of the guest bedrooms, please," Ember told them. He turned to Kana while the wolves bent to get their hands under Ary's shoulders and knees. "I need to coordinate our defensive measures in case that witch tries to come back."

Kana nodded, but then he bit his lip, undecided as to what he should be doing. Ember would need his help to lay spells along the perimeter of the property to protect the grounds should Samantha try to force her way in. But Ary had been subjected to a coercion spell for who knew how long, and it was Kana's duty as a witch to ensure he was able to recover.

Ember's going to need to move fast to cover everything. You won't be able to keep up. Mika leaped off Kana's shoulder, landing next to Ember. *I'll go with him and pick out good places for you to spell later. You and Sora go with the hunter.*

"Mika's going with you to see about where to lay protective spells," Kana explained. "He'll be able to keep up with you."

Ember nodded. "Thanks. I'll bring you to whichever sites Mika chooses later?"

Kana nodded. "I'll keep an eye on the hunter for now."

"I appreciate it." Ember glanced up at the remnants of the setting sun. "I'll have Shannon stop by when he's up, so you have some backup."

Ember trotted off, Mika tight on his heels, and Kana turned to head inside. He stopped in his workroom to pick up one of the old spell books to read while he was waiting, and then settled into a chair in the guest room where Ary was laid out on the bed.

Chapter Seven

KANA HAD NO idea what time it was when Ary let out a low groan. The spell book was fascinating, and Kana had been completely engrossed from the first page. Layered spells as a magical tool solved so many issues Kana had run into throughout the years.

The spell on his cats was a perfect example. He wanted to protect them, and that protection required preventing them from being noticed and, if they were spotted, preventing the spotter from caring. Kana had added a concealment rune to the spell this time as well, to keep them extra hidden. However, the format of a spell circle lumped every aspect of the spell together in one circle.

With the layered version, Kana could set a base of just protection and then caveat that protection with further layers of everything else. In the case of this spell, Kana would only need one additional layer, but for something more complex, he could create as many layers as he had magic.

Kana understood why the practice of layering circles had been lost. He had only learned to cast circles without actually drawing them due to sheer necessity. Chalk was expensive, and a dry, flat surface suitable for spells hard to find when he had been homeless. If he wanted to cast magic back then, his choice had been a quick-set circle or nothing.

A layered spell required the ability to cast without needing to physically draw the circle. Kana could write the base layer of the spell in chalk, but to layer the spells, each circle must be exactly on top of each other. Any additional layers could only be drawn with magic.

He had no way of knowing whether all witches could easily learn the quick-set method, or if it was only strong witches like Kana who could do it. Plus, Samantha had cast her coercion spell without a circle at all, so there were definitely other ways to do magic that Kana hadn't yet learned. He really wanted to learn about the spell circle using only the rune and no pentagram, like the one he had seen at the library, but his current book didn't have anything about that. He would probably have to return to the library to learn that magic.

Ary groaned again, and this time lifted one hand to press his fingers against his temples. A second later his hand froze, and then his arm dropped to the bed so he could lean on his elbows and leverage himself up. He looked around wildly and immediately caught sight of Kana, sitting in the light from the reading lamp he had been using.

"Where am I? What did you do to me?"

Kana gently closed his book and set it on the reading table next to the lamp. "You are in a city called Schenectady, which is near Albany, in New York State," he began, unsure of how much Ary would remember or when he had been put under the coercion spell. "You are in the local werewolf pack house, where we brought you after we freed you from a witch's spell."

"A witch's spell," Ary repeated slowly, as if he were parsing out the words so they made sense. Then his eyes went wide, and he gasped, "That secretary!"

Kana nodded. "Yeah. She's a witch from the Seattle coven. Do you know why she wanted to come all the way out here?"

Ary grimaced and levered himself all the way up so he was sitting properly. "The hunter's association keeps tabs on the covens too. We know her coven is dying out. None of the children born in the last ten years have had any powers at all, and our informants say the coven believes the goddess is punishing them for some sin they committed. The last I heard, they were going to cast a massive divination spell to try to find an answer, but then the vampires and werewolves started fighting here, and I was distracted by this mission."

"So, the coven casts a divination, and somehow Samantha ends up here to put you under a coercion spell?" Kana asked, mostly thinking aloud.

"You know her name?" Ary asked, his eyes narrowing as he studied Kana. He quickly glanced to the side, where his spear leaned against the side of his bed, but then he froze and reached out with a shaking hand to pick it up. "What did you do to my spear?"

Kana grimaced. "I didn't have time for finesse. Samantha was about to force you to attack us. When I broke the coercion spell, everything else broke too."

"How? Our weapons are supposed to be unbreakable!"

"I used salt," Kana said with a shrug but then shifted uncomfortably when Ary stared, his mouth hanging open slightly in surprise.

"You imbued magic into salt? Salt is supposed to protect against magic and magical creatures! What are you?" Ary shook his head. "No, don't answer that. I can see you're a witch even though you're male." He paused as some thought made his eyes open wide in surprise again. "Was one of your parents a hunter?"

A hunter? Kana slowly shook his head. His mother had definitely been part of the coven circle, but he didn't know anything about his father. His parents had been killed when Kana was thirteen, which was old enough to know some things, like his mother's role in the coven, but certainly not to know any deeply held secrets.

"I don't think the coven would have accepted a hunter as my mother's husband," Kana finally said. "She was part of the inner circle, so my father must have been carefully chosen for her."

However, Kana didn't think his parents had been part of an arranged marriage. They had certainly seemed to love each other, or at least Kana remembered them that way. Every day, after they had died, Kana had been focused on surviving being a male with powers in a coven that refused to accept him.

"Can you not ask them?"

Kana shook his head. "They're dead."

Ary didn't look surprised. "Hunters are prohibited from having children with witches. When they do, the children are capable of doing strange things with their power, such as imbuing salt with magic. Too many of those children abused their powers and had to be put down, so a union between a witch and a hunter was forbidden."

Kana sucked in a breath. "Do you think my parents were killed?" All he knew about their deaths was that it had been a car accident, but no one had ever told him anything else about it. He had seen their bodies prior to the funeral, but they had been cleaned prior to cremation, so he hadn't been able to identify a cause. Kana had scattered their ashes in the forest near his old home in the hopes their lingering magic would help the trees grow strong.

"I can't say. Perhaps it was natural, perhaps not. I have not heard of a hunter betraying our cause out West within the last few decades, but I mostly focus my efforts on the East Coast, so it is possible I missed it. But that still begs the question of what to do with you."

Kana tensed and Sora stalked out from where he had been napping underneath Kana's chair, an angry growl lifting his lips to show sharp teeth.

Ary looked at Sora and swallowed hard, his fist tightening on his spear. The magic might be gone from the spear, but the silver tip and wooden stake were still formidable weapons, especially in Ary's skilled hands.

"I am not capable of hurting you, not as I am now, and certainly not on my own," Ary said, his mouth twisting into a wry smile.

"I don't suggest even considering it, Hunter," Shannon said, and both Kana and Ary jumped in surprise.

Shannon was standing in the far corner where he was hidden in the shadows cast by Kana's reading lamp. He had been in the room for almost as long as Kana, and had been standing silently while Kana had been reading. To be honest, Kana had forgotten he was there, and Ary apparently hadn't noticed him.

"This witch has been accepted into the werewolf pack. Attacking him would be an act of war," Shannon explained as he stepped forward into the light.

Ary gaped at him. "An ancient," he mouthed, the words more air than substance.

"The werewolf pack has been kind to protect my daytime rest, much as they have protected the witch who fights at their side. I recommend your thanking them for saving you and providing shelter, and then going about your business elsewhere." Shannon walked past Kana to the door, pulled it open, then stepped outside. He didn't close it behind him, and Kana saw a wolf standing in the hallway. She peeked inside, saw Ary was awake, and trotted off in the opposite direction to Shannon.

Ary had stared at the open door, his mouth agape, but had just turned to Kana, when Ember walked into the room.

"I see you're awake, Hunter," Ember said. He looked tired and rumpled, his hair in disarray, but he also looked pleased with the day's work.

"Yes, Alpha. And I am grateful for you and your witch's help freeing me," Ary added quickly with a nod toward Kana.

"Kana's got a good touch with stuff like that," Ember replied easily, with his usual half smile for Kana, who grinned back and hoped the sudden thumping of his heart that smile always caused wasn't noticeable.

"So I've learned," Ary said with a wry look at his spear. "Do you know where my cell phone went? I should call my association so they know what happened with my secretary. You said her name was Samantha, and she was from the Seattle coven?" he asked Kana.

"She had you under a coercion spell," Kana answered. He glanced at Ember, who nodded, so Kana added, "Your phone and wallet are in the bedside drawer."

Ary leaned to the side and pulled open the drawer. His phone and other items from his pockets were sitting in plain sight.

"Thank you," Ary said. "While I am a guest in your house, Alpha, I promise my continued good behavior. Could I have some privacy for this call?"

Ember snorted out a laugh. "Yes, although I will hold you to that promise. Sleep well. Someone will come by in the morning to bring you down to breakfast." Ember waited for Kana to gather his book, then shut the door firmly behind them once they were in the hallway. "Mika said he marked all the spots he thought needed a protection spell," Ember said as they started walking. "Do you think you can cast that tonight, or would it be better for you to wait for morning?"

"Better to do it now so we're prepared," Kana replied.

Ember smiled and his hand reached out as if to take Kana's, except Ember glanced down at Sora, his smile abruptly fading, and his hand dropped back to his side. Kana bit his lip and looked down at Sora as they walked.

Did you or Mika say something to him? Kana asked.

Sora huffed. *I think he's decided something based on only half the information. We will have to fix that, but later. Right now, you need to cast the protection spell and get to sleep. As it is, you're probably going to want to call in sick to work tomorrow.*

I can work my spells to protect this place better if I'm here, rather than at work, Kana agreed. *At least until we figure out what Samantha's really after.*

You know what she's after, Sora disagreed. *Samantha wants the powerful witch that helped the werewolves destroy a vampire coven. She doesn't know it's you, but that won't stop her.*

I know. That's why I left, remember? If they found out how powerful I am, they would have forced me to produce baby girls for the coven, like a stud stallion locked in a cage. And Kana definitely did not want that to happen now.

When they reached Kana's workroom, he led the way inside. Mika was sprawled upside down in the hammock, snoring happily away. Sora rolled his eyes at him. He jumped up into the cat tree, then leaped over to the hammock, landing solidly on top of Mika, who yowled. They both fell to the floor with a thud and a tangle of fur and claws.

Kana left them to it while he went to find the chalk and put his book away. By the time Kana had a basic protection circle drawn, Mika was grumpily lying on top of Sora, licking one of Sora's ears clean.

"Can you show me where you left the markers?" Kana asked Mika aloud for Ember's benefit. Ember was standing in the doorway, out of the way of cat chaos and magic.

Mika climbed off Sora and shifted to human form. He held out his hands as he walked over to Kana's circle, and Kana took them in his own. They stepped into the circle together. Kana closed his eyes and concentrated down the link he shared with Mika. A crude map appeared in his mind's eye, a rough circle with the house in the center.

"That's the wall around the property," Mika said. "I put markers on the overlap points, so if you drop a circle on every point, you'll cover the entire wall."

As Mika spoke, eighteen points of light bloomed, spaced evenly around the rough circle on the map. Kana breathed out; then, as he breathed in, he pulled magic from the links he shared with his familiars. He sent the magic down into his circle beneath his feet first and could see the light of the spell activating even through his closed eyelids. Kana opened his eyes and drew more magic.

Eighteen sparks of light ignited about waist height, evenly spaced around the outside boundary of Kana's circle in the exact same places as on Mika's map. Those sparks grew as Kana fed more magic into the spell, and they slowly morphed from sparks into circles. The circles eventually became more distinct, mirroring the larger protection circle Kana had drawn on the ground. Once they were exact copies—albeit smaller ones—Kana flicked his fingers off Mika's palms and outward, toward the physical location on the wall where Mika had left the markers. The circles vanished, but Kana waited for the tug on his magic that said each had settled where they were supposed to before he relaxed and let the magic channels ease closed again. The circle on the floor vanished as the light faded, leaving behind clean chalkboard.

"Samantha can't do that spell," Ember said, his voice low with awe and with what Kana would have called want, if he hadn't known better. When Kana turned to look at him, Ember's eyes were burning. As soon as Kana noticed, however, Ember banked those flames and looked away.

Mika snickered and stalked forward to drape his naked body on Ember's shoulder. "Don't be shy, little wolfy. I smell your lust."

Sora shifted to human form and draped his body along Kana's back, his arms hanging over Kana's shoulders and down his chest. Sora stared at Ember the whole time and grinned when Ember's eyes flared again at the sight.

"What—?" Ember cut off with a splutter when Mika licked his cheek. "Stop that! I thought you three…?"

"We're familiars," Mika said as if that explained it. Given Ember's blank look, it didn't.

"At their base, familiars are bridges between this world and the plane where magic originates," Kana began, trying not to sound awkward even though there really wasn't a way to explain this that wasn't awkward. "The more…connected…I am to my familiars, the better our magic flow. Anyone I choose to be with needs to understand that being with me also means being with my familiars." Not that Kana had ever slept with anyone aside from Mika and Sora. The need to hide Mika and Sora had kept him single. Ember was the first guy Kana had dared to even have thoughts about, and spending the last few months around him had only made those feelings grow.

Ember looked slowly from Kana to Sora, still draped over Kana's shoulders, to Mika, leaning against Ember's side, and the fire began burning in his eyes again.

"I can live with that," Ember said. He opened his mouth to say more, but someone started banging on the closed door.

Sora let out a sigh, but he and Mika obediently shifted back to their cat forms while Ember went to answer the door.

"Alpha!" the wolf on the other side of the door said as soon as the door was open. "Mary is awake, and she's not doing well. Emily was hoping you might be able to come calm her down?"

Mary was one of the wolves who had been traumatized by the vampires, and for whom Kana was researching that sleeping spell. Emily was one of Ember's beta wolves, and if she was having trouble calming Mary down, Mary had to be having a really tough night.

"Tell Emily I'll be right there," Ember replied immediately. The wolf trotted off, and Ember turned back to Kana. "Things in the pack house won't always be this fraught," he stated. "When they've calmed down again, can we revisit this conversation?"

"Absolutely," Kana said with a firm nod.

Ember's lips lifted in his adorable grin, but he vanished out the doorway a second later, back to the duties of being alpha.

That was unexpected, Kana said to Mika and Sora. *No thanks to you two butting your heads in.*

Mika snorted. *If we hadn't, you and your pretty wolf would never have gotten around to clearing up that little misunderstanding. You should be thanking us.* He let out a yawn. *It's bedtime now, especially since the five minutes of sleep I managed to get after running around all night was so rudely interrupted.* He gave Sora a disgruntled side-eyed look.

Kana shut off the light and closed the door behind them as he led the way to the bedroom they had been allotted for their stay.

I was helping guard the hunter, Sora insisted.

Hah! You were sleeping, and you know it! Mika replied, his voice scathing as he let out an audible, angry yowl.

Don't wake anyone up! Kana admonished. They thankfully reached their room, and Kana held the door for Mika and Sora. They hopped onto the bed, curling up on the opposite sides of Kana's pillow while Kana went to change into pajamas and brush his teeth. By the time he was out of the bathroom, Mika and Sora were both asleep. Kana turned out the light, crawled under the covers, and within moments followed their example into sleep.

Chapter Eight

KANA ONLY SAW Ember in passing all the next day. He had overslept, which, given he hadn't gotten to bed until 3:00 a.m., made sense, and he had immediately called in sick to work. Because Kana had woken late, he had missed the communal breakfast, and therefore time to sit with Ember. Kana then spent most of the day walking the perimeter fence to double-check his spells and to see if there was anything else he could cast to help protect the pack house. By the time dinner rolled around, Kana was ready for bed again.

Ember didn't appear at the dinner table, but Ralph, another of Ember's betas, told Kana he was at the other pack house to work on their security and wouldn't be back until later. Kana climbed into bed with the same questions and worries swirling in his mind as the previous night. This time, though, he set his alarm.

Do you think it's a good idea to go to work right now? Mika asked, concerned.

I already missed a bunch of days when we were fighting the vampires, Kana replied. *I don't have that many days of leave, and what happens if I actually do get sick and, thanks to this fiasco, I've run out of leave?*

We'll just have to be extra careful, Sora insisted. *We managed at work on Wednesday when we knew a hunter was coming; we can do it tomorrow too.*

Sora was right. As long as they were careful, going to work wouldn't be a problem. Samantha hadn't found what she was looking for at the news station, and with Ary free, she had no reason to go back. Kana's only reservation was that by going to work, he would leave the pack house vulnerable, but that was what his protection circles were for. They would hold until Kana could get to the house and provide backup. Kana fell asleep with that hopeful thought in mind.

*

"SOMEONE FROM MY organization will be by this afternoon to pick me up," Ary said as Kana sat down to a quick breakfast. "I probably won't be here when you get back, so this is my opportunity to thank you again for saving me."

"Did you tell your organization you think one of my parents was a hunter?" Kana asked while spreading jelly on a piece of toast. He didn't need to keep as close an eye on the clock as usual since he didn't have to catch the bus, but he still couldn't tarry for too long.

Ary nodded. "I had to, but I told them you were under control and, erm, weren't likely to pass on those genes to any children."

Kana laughed. "I guess I'm that obvious?"

Ary snorted out his own laugh. "The way you and your alpha are dancing around each other is adorable. One of my superiors might request an interview, but they also know you're part of the pack, so they'll be respectful about it."

"Thanks. It was nice to meet you, even under these circumstances," Kana said. "I hope they can fix your spear."

Ary laughed again. "They're bringing me a replacement and will definitely be studying my old one for years to figure out if there's a way to prevent what you did from affecting another weapon. The woman in our research department I spoke to about it sounded really excited."

Kana giggled through his bite of toast. He finished chewing and swallowed. "I'm happy to recreate the spell if they want to see how I cast it."

Ary stared at Kana for a long moment as a grin grew across his face. "They might conscript you into their research unit if you offer that, you realize."

A chance to practice magic with other experts, particularly experts who wouldn't care he was male? Kana wouldn't say no to that! Still, he didn't want to commit to anything, so he just shrugged and took another bite of toast.

You're going to be late, Mika called. He and Sora had vanished to get breakfast elsewhere—apparently one of the kitchen staff had a soft spot for cats and was spoiling them rotten—but they were both now waiting by the doorway to the dining room.

Kana stuffed the last piece of toast into his mouth and guzzled his tea. "I have to go to work," he said when his mouth was empty again. "It was nice to meet you, and I hope next time we meet under better circumstances."

"It was nice to meet you, too, and thank you again for all your help." Ary grinned and waved as Kana jogged off.

The usual car was waiting for Kana by the door. He climbed in with

Mika and Sora. The car took off the second the door was closed behind Kana, which was good because Kana caught sight of the clock on the dashboard and realized he was definitely going to be late.

Traffic on the roads was thankfully light, so they made good time. Kana was only a few minutes late when he hurried to his desk.

"I wasn't sure you were coming in today," Beth said with a happy grin when she saw him. "How are you feeling?"

"I think I got some bad takeout the other night," Kana lied. "Once I was done throwing up, I felt better."

"Geez. That sucks. Glad you're feeling better, although I have to say you chose a really good day to call in sick." Beth shook her head sadly.

"What happened?" Kana sat at his desk, but he turned to look at Beth rather than switching on his computers.

"Every last bit of tape we had for the interview with the hunter is gone. The final tape, the stuff from the editing room, even the backup servers. It's all gone!"

"No!" Kana gasped.

Beth nodded. "All of it. And they only figured that out about five minutes before we were supposed to air the segment. Stephen and everyone were scrambling to find something to fill the slot instead. It was a crazy morning."

"I'm sorry I missed it," Kana said.

"No, you're not," Beth said with a laugh.

"I bet it was less awful than throwing up all night," Kana replied with a shrug. He couldn't tell Beth he had spent the night babysitting the very same hunter whose interview had been lost, just in case Kana's magic had hurt Ary. Although, it was interesting every single bit of that interview had completely vanished. That meant it was either an inside job—that someone in the office had done it—or a spell had been cast on the building to remove the interview. At this point the magic had already dissipated, so there was no reason to waste any magic testing for it. The problem was the bosses at the office wouldn't automatically think magic. They would assume an inside job, and Kana was the only one not at work during the incident.

Kana reached to turn on his computers, but footsteps sounded outside their cubicle, and he looked up to see who was there before his finger hit the button.

Amanda, Kana and Beth's boss, was standing in the entrance to their space. She was frowning slightly as she studied Kana.

"Kana," she said. "Will you come to my office please?"

Damn. Kana nodded and stood so he could follow her down the hall and into her private office.

"Do you know why you're here?" Amanda asked as she sat in her desk chair and Kana took one of the chairs on the other side.

"Beth was just telling me about yesterday," Kana replied, hoping the sinking feeling in his chest wasn't an omen of what was to come.

Amanda nodded. "Yes. Someone broke into our servers early that morning and managed to erase everything." She paused as if waiting for Kana to interject, but Kana didn't have anything to say. He wouldn't be in her office if the spell that wiped the servers hadn't also managed to point to him. "Our tech team traced the intrusion back to your cubicle, specifically your computer. Kana, where were you at five yesterday morning?"

"Sleeping," Kana replied truthfully. "I didn't get to bed until after three that night."

"Can anyone confirm that?"

Every single person living in the pack house could confirm Kana's whereabouts, but Kana couldn't tell her that as it would lead to a whole different set of uncomfortable questions.

Instead, he said, "My boyfriend can," hoping Ember would forgive Kana for calling him that before they actually had a discussion on where their potential relationship would actually go.

Amanda's frown only deepened at that admission, so apparently Kana using his boyfriend as a witness wasn't an acceptable option. Probably because Ember would lie if it meant protecting Kana.

"Kana, I do want to believe you. I promise you, I do. Our techs will keep digging to see if they can find an alternate explanation," she said. "But for right now management is forcing me to put you on administrative leave until the investigation is complete. I'm sorry, Kana. I'll call you when it's over and a final decision has been made." She stood and walked around her desk to open the door. "Get your things and go straight home, please," she added as Kana got up too.

Kana nodded and left, heading back to his desk to grab his bag and his cats. Beth was waiting there, her hands clasped against her chest in worry.

"Well?" she asked immediately, and her face fell when Kana picked up his bag and threw it over his shoulder.

"I'm under investigation. Whoever deleted the interview apparently used my computer." Kana bent down to grab Mika and Sora's pillow to tuck into his bag, but that was the only personal thing he kept at his desk. If they didn't allow him back again, he wouldn't lose anything.

"No!" Beth gasped. "How could they? What if—" She paused as she gasped again. "What if they poisoned your takeout to ensure you wouldn't come into work yesterday so blame would doubly fall on you?"

"Beth—" Kana tried to say, but she cut him off.

"I won't let them get away with this, Kana. Don't you worry! I'll get to the bottom of this, and you'll be back here in no time!"

"Thanks, Beth," Kana replied because he didn't know what else to say. There wasn't anything he could do to stop her, and he couldn't tell her the truth that he had been busy casting spells over the werewolf pack house all night, or that a witch likely covering her tracks had used magic to delete the interview.

"I'll see you soon," he said instead, then awkwardly waved at Beth as he walked out.

Text Ember so he can send the car around, and so he knows Samantha is still nearby, Mika said as they headed to the elevator.

Good idea, Kana replied. He pulled out his phone and typed out everything that had happened.

The car will be there in five, Ember texted back. *Stay low until it arrives.*

Will do, thanks, Kana replied. He agreed with Ember's request to stay low. Wiping the interview from the system was probably just a way for Samantha to protect herself from possibly being filmed, but Kana ought to be careful just in case she was still watching the building. Ary had thought the witch Samantha was searching for worked here, so Kana wouldn't be surprised if Samantha was lying in wait, hoping to spot someone casting magic to restore the erased tape so she could capture them.

The elevator let Kana out in the building lobby. He walked to the doors but stood to one side rather than going out. He could see the traffic of the main road and the bus stop where the car would pick him up from his vantage point. After exactly five minutes, a familiar black SUV drove by and pulled to a stop in the bus lane.

Ready? Kana asked.

Let's move fast, Sora said.

Kana pushed the door open. Mika went out first, ranging ahead and to the right where he could watch the street and the sidewalk. Kana followed with Sora, but while Sora walked out the door with Kana, he walked well behind and to Kana's left.

They were almost to the crosswalk near the bus stop when an odd pulse went through the ground beneath Kana's feet. Magic bloomed in the air, but Kana spun around in a quick circle and didn't see a spell forming anywhere. If he couldn't see it, he couldn't cast anything in defense.

Get to the car! Kana yelled as he started running to the crosswalk. The wolves must have been watching him because when Kana started to run all four car doors popped open and four wolves jumped out.

The magic pulsed again, rippling through Kana's magic senses as it flowed beneath his feet. Kana didn't take the time to look for the spell to try and combat it—it was still hidden from view, so he would be better off getting out of range. Except, this time the pulse didn't stop once it went past Kana. The magic continued under the street, then flared and threw all four wolves off their feet with cracking thuds Kana could hear even over the noise of city traffic. The pulse bounced, coming back toward Kana. He stopped running and braced himself, pulling in magic to try to cast some sort of counter spell—except, the pulse never reached him. A black hole yawned underneath Mika, who let out a yowl just before he dropped out of sight.

Mika! Kana screamed. He reached down their link, ready to pull Mika to him, when a sharp pain erupted in the back of Kana's head and everything went black.

Chapter Nine

KANA'S HEAD THROBBED in time with his heartbeat: *thud, thud, thud* reverberated through his skull, centered on one spot on the back of his head. Kana groaned and reached to touch that spot, and his fingers found a lump that sent a sharp jolt of pain through his head and down his spine when he touched it.

"Finally awake, I see," Samantha said, her voice smug and haughty.

Kana opened his eyes and found he was lying on the hard cement floor of a dimly lit cell. Samantha was standing on the other side of a thick iron door, looking down at him through a barred window.

"Where am I?" Kana groaned out, his head aching even more as he spoke.

"That's not important," Samantha replied immediately. "What is important are the questions you are going to answer. Once you tell me everything, I'll bring you back home to the coven where you can be useful for once in your life."

"How did you find me?" Kana asked. He sat up so he could face her directly, and the room did a slow spin before his vision steadied and he could see her again.

Samantha laughed. "Don't think you're that important," she said, her voice dripping with derision. "We weren't looking for you. The coven's spell indicated we would find the witch who would help us in this area. We sent witches all over the Northeast; I was sent to Albany, and what do I find within a few days? A cat familiar wandering around. I tracked that familiar to you, of all people, but then that whole fiasco with the werewolves and vampires occurred, and I knew I needed stronger backup. Luckily, a hunter decided to come see what happened, and I was able to grab him. But then the witch snatched him from me!"

How long had Samantha been poking around? If she had been in Albany prior to Kana meeting Ember, then she must know all about him. However, she kept saying "the witch" rather than using his name, so maybe she didn't. Samantha was like most of the witches in Kana's old coven who refused to believe Kana would ever amount to anything simply because he was male. There was no way someone so blinded by that mindset would ever believe Kana had bonded to the cat familiar Samantha claimed to have been following.

"But you're going to tell us everything. Who the witch is, where we can find her, and why she refused to join a coven like a good witch should."

Kana gaped at Samantha, shocked both by her audacity and her blind ignorance. She really didn't know about Kana.

"How do you know the witch hasn't already run away from you?" Kana asked.

Samantha laughed, a cold, cruel sound Kana remembered from

every time she had belittled him in high school. "We captured her familiar. She won't run until she gets it back." She vanished from the window, and Kana heard a metallic tapping sound. "Come see the special cage we made, just for the familiar, if you don't believe me. The cage is a thing of beauty. Keeps the familiar asleep and blocks the witch from communicating with it."

Kana had to see. Mika had vanished into a black hole, but maybe he was in that cage. Kana levered himself to his feet, glad when the room only tilted a little as his vision swam, and stumbled his way to the door.

Mika lay in the center of the cage, curled into a tight ball and completely asleep. He looked unharmed, and Kana let out a breath of relief. There was no sign of Sora.

Kana reached for his connections to Mika and Sora, hoping to wake Mika and tell Sora where to find them, and his magic slammed into a wall. His cell lit up with an eerie blue light, causing Samantha to cackle in glee.

"Tried some magic to free it, did you? Take a look around you, fool, before you try anything else stupid."

Kana turned to look, leaning on the door for support, and his jaw dropped at what he saw. Samantha cackled some more.

"Impressive, huh? Once I figured out the witch we wanted was in this city, I had to come up with a way to keep her confined until she agreed to work with us. You're just the test run."

The blue light was shaped in a pattern, Kana realized as he followed each line carved into the cement walls. Runes and circles were illuminated, not by the spell, but because they were absorbing the magic Kana had tried to use and dumping it down into the earth. The room was ingenious. Kana could use the strongest power at his disposal, and the circles carved into the cement would simply funnel it away. Kana followed each line, searching for a weakness, but couldn't spot one at first glance. The light started to fade, so Kana turned back to Samantha, who was grinning at him, teeth bared and eyes bright with spiteful glee.

She waved a heavy iron key, as if to mock him with it. "All we want is the name and location of the witch," she said as she placed the key on top of Mika's cage. "Giving us that information is the only way you're getting out of that cell. I'll leave you to think about it," she finished and patted the key to mock him with it again before turning and walking away.

Kana stared at the key, wishing it would grow a set of wings and fly over to unlock the door. If he could access his magic, he wouldn't even need the key, yet his freedom sat, unmoving, right where Samantha knew she could leave it to twist the knife of his captivity.

The whoosh of a door opening and closing sounded. Kana waited a few extra seconds to be certain Samantha was actually gone before hissing, "Mika. Mika," hoping in vain Mika might somehow break the spell of his own cage and come rescue Kana. Mika didn't even twitch.

Kana could only hope Ember was searching for him. The wolves Ember had sent to escort Kana back to the pack house had been attacked—and Kana hoped they were okay—but at least Ember would know things had gone very wrong. There was no telling whether Ember would actually be able to find Kana, especially with Samantha and who knew who else casting spells to hide him.

No, Kana would have to figure out a way to get out of the cell on his own. Once he was outside the influence of the cage, he would have his magic again, and Samantha certainly wouldn't be able to stop him. There was no telling how long that would take, though.

"Mika," he called, hoping this time Mika might hear.

The door whooshed again, and Kana clamped his mouth shut. Was

Samantha still watching him, waiting for him to give himself away by calling out Mika's name? Had she come up with some new torture to try to make him talk? Kana waited, tensed and ready, but no one walked into view.

Kana thought he saw a shadow moving outside the narrow window of the cell door, but he still didn't see anyone. Maybe someone had heard him calling but hadn't been able to hear what he was saying, so they were lying in wait for him to speak again? Kana moved to the right, trying to expand what he could see to his left out the window, but even the shadow had vanished.

A muffled *mew* sounded from below Kana. He gasped and looked down. Sora was standing outside the door in his cat form, a cell phone clamped in his mouth.

"Sora?" Kana gasped, and his voice choked at the end as his eyes welled up with tears of relief.

"Kana, is that you?" Ember's voice sounded from the phone speaker.

Kana swallowed to clear his throat before answering. "Yes. Sora found me."

Ember let out a breath loud enough to be picked up by the phone. "Good. We weren't sure whether they were keeping you at the house they're renting, but Sora seemed pretty certain. What do you need from us for your rescue?"

"I'm locked in a cell that's covered in spells to keep me from casting magic," Kana began.

"So, you need us to come get you out?" Ember cut in.

Kana shook his head, but then remembered Ember couldn't see him and said, "No. They left the key behind to taunt me."

Sora turned to look and shimmered for a second as he called on his human form. He slid the phone through the bars of the cell window, which Kana gratefully clutched, and then went to get the key.

"They didn't even trap it," Sora said, his hand hovering over the key for a brief moment as he felt for any spells. He grabbed the key and hurried back to the door, slotting it into the hole and turning the lock with a clunk. The door swung open and Kana hurried out.

Sora's presence immediately bloomed in Kana's mind as the block between them vanished. Mika's was more muted, but Kana hammered through it and yanked Mika to him.

Mika vanished from inside the cage and reappeared in Kana's arms. He yawned and blinked at them both, then gasped and jumped onto Kana's shoulder so he could get his bearings.

What happened? he asked. His voice still sounded groggy, but he was steady on his feet.

"You got caught in a trap," Sora replied, his tone light, although Kana could hear relief there too.

Mika huffed in disgust. He jumped from Kana's shoulder and landed on the ground in human form.

"What now?" he asked.

Kana looked behind himself, at the cell designed to keep witches helpless. He looked at the cage designed to cruelly imprison a familiar, torturing their witch in the process.

"I have some things I want to destroy," Kana replied. "It's going to make a lot of noise and fuss."

Ember laughed. "Sounds fun. Want us to knock on their front door at the same time?"

Kana didn't know what Ember meant by "knocking," but he had a feeling it wasn't as benign as Ember's simple words made it seem. Still, Ember did sound as if he had a plan, and Kana could use that to cover his escape.

"You causing a distraction would definitely help," Kana said.

Ember laughed, and then his voice rang out as if he had pulled the phone away from his ear so he could shout to others around him. "Kana said we should have a bit of fun!"

Loud, echoing howls sounded as Ember's wolves answered.

"They're ready to hunt," Ember said into the phone again. "And I'm sure your captors heard that, since we're currently surrounding their house. Smash away, Kana, and then come find me so I can assure myself you're safe." His voice went low and growly at the end in a possessive way that had things tightening low in Kana's body.

Kana sternly told his body to behave. "Will do," he said, and his own voice was low with suggestion even after his attempts to corral his libido. "Stay safe."

"You too."

The phone line went dead as Ember hung up. Kana tucked it into his pocket and turned to Mika and Sora.

"Ready?" he asked.

They both grinned at him and their bodies shimmered. A second later they had shifted into their massive six-hundred-pound primordial forms.

Ready, they replied in tandem.

Chapter Ten

KANA THREW OPEN the magic channels between himself and Mika and Sora, drawing in as much magic as he could hold. Spell circles grew in his wake, blossoming across every inch of Kana's cell and Mika's cage. The runes for destruction seemed to glow red as Kana added them. Kana backed up to the door and then sent a final flare of magic into his circles.

The thud of the circles erupting hit Kana in the chest before the roar and crash as concrete exploded and rained down. Kana coughed as dust filled the air, but he waited for it to clear so he could double-check those terrible cages were completely gone.

No one came running despite the noise he had made, so apparently Ember's distraction was working. Kana hoped Ember had some sort of protection against spells—Kana remembered the awful sounds the bodies of the wolves who had come to pick him up had made when they were hit—but Ember had sounded so confident on the phone. Kana trusted him to do what was best for his wolves, and Ember wouldn't blindly attack a witch.

The dust finally settled. Kana picked his way through the debris to check his cell, and smiled at the sight of all four walls collapsed into small bits of rubble. Kana had apparently hit foundation as dirt and roots from outside had made a nice pile along one wall. Kana could no longer see any trace of Mika's cage.

"Upstairs?" he asked but didn't wait for Mika and Sora to give their big-toothed grins. He hurried to the door, which opened into a set of stairs. Kana climbed upward quickly, the stairs groaning under Mika and Sora's weight, but he paused to listen for any telltale noises or other signs that said someone was lying in wait on the other side of the door at the top.

I don't smell anyone, Mika said.

Kana gathered more magic, ready to shape it into a shield spell, and thrust the door open. He needn't have bothered. The kitchen he stepped into was completely empty, the seventies-green appliances rusted and the cabinets hanging at an angle. He could hear howling and a strange sort of chanting, and the awful screech as chalk was pressed too hard on a chalkboard.

The sun had set sometime recently, the barest red flare visible on the horizon out the windows overlooking the backyard. Two wolves were standing at the ready in the yard, and Kana knew if he rushed out the back door they would whisk him away to safety in moments. But that wouldn't end the matter, nor could Kana provide Ember magical support if he was busy running away. Instead, Kana turned to the inside door, which was an old wooden swing-style door. He pushed through into what he assumed was a dining room, although without any furniture he couldn't be sure. No one was in sight, so he continued through an arched door into a long hallway. To the left, Kana finally found the foyer and the front door, which was wide open and let Kana see the walk-way and everyone standing outside. He hurried forward.

Ember was standing in the grass just beyond the doorway, an array of wolves in wolf form around him. The wolves dashed to and fro, growling and snarling, but not jumping forward. Ary and a man Kana didn't recognize stood to Ember's right. They were both twirling their spears in the air, and the stranger was chanting loudly in a language Kana didn't know. Every so often one of their spears would suddenly flare with a burst of light that simply faded away after a second.

Chalk squealed, and Kana yanked his eyes away from Ember to look at the rest of the scene. Samantha was standing on the front porch, a handheld chalkboard in her left hand as she drew feverishly on it with her right. A second woman, who looked barely eighteen, drew on her own chalkboard, but she was slower than Samantha, and when she activated her spells, the flare of them impacting the hunters' spears wasn't as bright. A third woman lay facedown a few feet ahead, bleeding sluggishly from shallow slash marks on her arms. Her chalkboard was broken in three pieces and lay on the ground by her hand.

Samantha was the problem, and neutralizing her would stop everything. Ember could do it, Kana knew, but was no doubt waiting to hear Kana was safe before jumping in. Ary probably could too, but he seemed content to follow Ember's lead. Which meant Kana was best placed to stop this before someone really got hurt.

"You think your paltry weapons will stop us for long?" Samantha shrieked as another spell flared and died against the hunters' spears.

Kana could blast her with magic, knock her out just like she must have done to him, but when she woke she would just go back to her awful ways. There wouldn't be anything to stop her from returning and trying to capture Kana again. No, Kana needed to do something much more permanent, like stopping her ability to cast magic entirely. But doing that would hurt her familiar too, and her dog didn't deserve to be hurt just because its master was a terrible person. Still, if he did not cut off the magic completely, certainly Kana could craft a spell that would constrict her magic channels so only the barest trickle of power could slip through. She would maybe have just enough magic to light a candle, but not enough to kindle a full circle.

If he could complete the spell, that is.

Kana drew more magic from Mika and Sora, spooling it inside himself until Kana's body was quaking from the pressure building inside. Five circles, Kana thought. One for each point on the pentagram. There wasn't a rune for constriction, but there was one to bind. The binding rune was usually used in the ceremony to call a familiar, and it had been one of the runes carved into the walls around his cell. In fact, that gave Kana an idea. Samantha would still be connected to her familiar, so if she was patient, she could very slowly draw enough magic to cast a large spell. However, Kana adding a rune to drain any excess magic she gathered into the ground like the spell in the cell had done to Kana would prevent that.

There were also ways to write runes and circles that limited the power of the spell by adding certain flourishes. Instead of adding those flourishes to the runes, Kana added them to the actual circle. The circle was usually the boundary that kept spells from dangerously escaping a witch's control, but Kana turned it into the actual rope to bind the spell to Samantha.

Only seconds had passed while Kana was building his circles. Samantha was frantically scribing another spell onto her chalkboard, but Ember was smirking at her. He looked up for the briefest second, past her to where Kana was standing, and he winked before throwing back his head and howling a wolf's howl out of his human mouth. The wolves around him, in human and wolf form, howled too. Samantha let out a scream of rage and slashed her chalk across her board. Ary grinned as her spell shattered against his spear in a flare of light.

As the howls faded, Kana heard police sirens quickly growing closer. One of the neighbors apparently wasn't happy with what was going on, which meant Kana needed to stop it now before the police tried to step in.

Kana pulled as much magic as he could hold and focused on the spell in his mind. He raised his hands, which were shaking from the power still vibrating inside his body, and flicked his wrists at Samantha.

The magic rushed from his body as if the dam holding it back had suddenly shattered. Five identical circles formed over Samantha's head, the light flaring even brighter than her spells against Ary's spear. She looked up, shrieked again, and started adding new runes to her chalkboard.

Kana couldn't let her complete that spell. He slowly lowered his hands, and the bottommost circle began to descend. Samantha's body went right through the center of the pentagram, and as the circle passed, her body started to glow. After a few inches, the second circle followed, but it was a little different as Kana twisted one wrist and the circle spun until it was at an angle to the first. The third circle spun a little more as it, too, began to descend, and the fourth and fifth followed suit. The first circle stopped moving at Samantha's knees, the second at her hips, the third at her waist, the fourth at her shoulders, and the fifth at her head. They pulsed with magic, their light blindingly bright. Kana turned his hands so his right was held palm down at head height and his left palm up at chest height. He clapped them together, and a boom like a cannon going off exploded from him, shaking the trees and forcing everyone near Samantha to take a staggering step back.

The five circles converged, slamming together into one single twenty-five-point star hovering at Samantha's waist. The star flared brighter and brighter. Samantha's chalk and chalkboard fell to the ground as she shuddered. Her mouth was open and her eyes clenched shut as if she were screaming, but no noise came out.

The magic built and built, until Kana was shaking with it too. He was leaning against Mika because the sheer force of the magic weakened his knees and made it impossible for his legs to hold him up. Finally, Kana felt the instinctual tingle that said the spell was perfect.

"So mote it be," he forced out through numb lips.

The magic vanished the second Kana's mouth closed on the final syllable, snuffed out like a candle in a tornado. Kana collapsed onto Mika, shuddering at how empty he felt inside with the spell completed. He carefully closed the channels between himself and Mika and Sora and had to shut his eyes when the floor below him swam side to side.

"What...what?" a woman babbled. Kana judiciously turned his head and opened one eye. The young witch had dropped to her knees next to Samantha, who had flopped bonelessly on the ground, unconscious. The young witch wasn't looking at Samantha though; she was staring at Kana, her mouth hanging open.

Kana's vision swam again, and he shut his eye and tried to breathe slowly. He really didn't want to throw up as the roiling in his stomach from the way the world was rotating around his head got worse.

"Kana?" Ember said, sounding worried.

A hand rested on Kana's back and someone knelt at his side. "It's his head," Sora said, which meant he had shifted to human form. "They walloped it pretty good, and all the magic he just used didn't help."

"Possible concussion," Ary said from somewhere to Kana's right.

"Can we move him to the ground so his cat can get smaller again? The police are arriving, and I don't think they'd appreciate seeing a tiger roaming around."

Gentle hands slid under his back and his knees, and Sora's familiar palms cradled his head and neck. Kana barely felt the change as he was lifted from where he had been hanging over Mika's back and laid on the grass. When Sora slowly placed his head down, it was onto a pillow of the soft fur of Mika's stomach in his small form.

"This is a hunter matter!" someone yelled. "We logged a report with your office first!"

Kana wanted to know what was going on, but he didn't dare open his eyes to look. He was also afraid if he opened his mouth he might throw up on himself.

"My wolves have cleared out," Ember said softly, as if he could read Kana's mind. His hand was resting on top of Kana's, so Kana turned his over so their palms were aligned and then curled his fingers around Ember's. "Shannon is on the house's roof, keeping an eye on the situation. Turns out, the hunter's association has a coordination system in place for when they have to apprehend someone within the police's jurisdiction. Ary's boss showed up at the same time as I got the call that you had been kidnapped. He apparently wanted to have a word with you—something about salt?—but when he heard what had happened, he decided to work with us to get you back."

"House is clear, Alpha. What should we do with the witches?" someone asked Ember.

"They violated multiple national magical treaties," Ary said. "They're coming with me and will be subject to the will of a tribunal. Although..." He paused as if he were looking at something. "It would be good to know what Kana did to Samantha."

"No magic," Kana forced out, and when speaking didn't exacerbate his stomach, he continued. "I blocked her ability to access all of her magic. She might be able to light a candle now, but she definitely won't be drawing a full spell circle ever again."

"She was part of the coven's inner circle!" a youthful-sounding woman exclaimed. "How dare you!"

"She's not the kind of person you want in an inner circle. Too cruel and mean," Kana interjected. "The coven will be better off with her gone."

"EMTs are here," another voice said. "Alpha, with your permission, I would like to search the house for evidence for the tribunal. Is there anything you would like to have if we find it?"

More voices approached, getting louder as they got closer to Kana. They must be the EMTs.

"I'm going with Kana to the hospital," Ember replied. "Shannon will stay here, so if you find anything you're not sure about, ask him." Ember's thumb stroked the back of Kana's hand. "I'm sure Kana would appreciate getting any spell books you might find," he added.

"Will do," the stranger, who Kana guessed might be Ary's boss, said. "I have a car coming with backup to take the witches into custody. Once they're gone, Shannon can stop being lookout."

Ember's hand loosened, and he pulled away. "It's his head," he said.

A thud sounded where Ember had been sitting and then a creak as if someone's pants were too tight at the knee when they kneeled.

"We're going to have to get a neck brace on you, son," the EMT said. He placed a hand on Kana's shoulder, then choked and yanked it off. "Is that a cat?"

Mika meowed pointedly. Sora meowed as well, which meant he

had switched forms again, and snickered when the EMT let out a surprised gasp.

"Both cats will be coming with us in the ambulance," Ember said. "Can you work around the one under his head?" When the EMT didn't answer right away, Ember continued. "We know he doesn't have a neck or back injury, just a nasty hit to the head. Can we skip the brace?"

"No. We don't want his head rolling around on the ride over. Besides, the cat will have to move for the CT scan anyway."

"Mika," Kana said. Mika grumbled, but bobbed his head in a nod.

Someone held Kana's head to stabilize him while Mika crawled out, and then contraptions were tied around him. He was tilted so they could slide a board underneath him, which was then also tied to him.

Ember's hand found Kana's again after he was in the ambulance, two cats curled against his body. Kana held on as tightly as he could, and Ember squeezed back.

Kana had no doubt Ember had dozens of other things he ought to be doing right now, especially after attacking the witch's house. His wolves needed him, but Kana also needing him was more important to Ember right now. At least, that was how Kana was interpreting the situation, and somehow he didn't think he was wrong.

Instead of doubting himself, Kana held on to Ember and, despite everything else going on around them, let himself relax in the warmth Ember's presence and his love imparted.

Epilogue

KANA CANCELED THE lease on his apartment two months after he got out of the hospital. There was no point in paying for something he wasn't using.

"The final inspection looks good," his landlord said as she walked out of the completely empty bedroom and back into the living room where Kana and Sora were waiting. "Your security deposit will be returned to you at the forwarding address you put on file. Expect it in about six weeks."

She shook Kana's hand and waved for him to precede her to the door. Kana took one last look around the apartment, surprised he wasn't sad about leaving it behind. This was the first truly habitable place he, Mika, and Sora had lived in since running away from Kana's old coven—the first place they had actually been able to call home, and Kana had zero regrets about leaving.

The gigantic piece of slate raised some eyebrows when the wolves

Ember provided to help Kana move had first seen it. Ember snickered and Kana suspected Ember planned to install it somewhere in one of the two pack houses for Kana to use. A touch of magic put the wood planks of the floor back in place without any evidence they had ever been moved, hence why Kana was actually getting his security deposit back.

He sold his beat-up couch and coffee table to a neighbor, but his bedroom furniture replaced the furniture in the room Kana was provided at the city pack house. Not that he used that room all that much anymore either...

Kana and Sora walked out the door, and the *thunk* as the landlord firmly shut and locked it behind them had a good finality to it. Kana's life as it had been while living in that apartment was over; it was time for his new life to begin.

He and Sora walked down the stairs and outside to where Ember and Mika were waiting by the car. Mika was draped over Ember's shoulders like a purring cat scarf. Ember's lips lifted in his perfect half smile when he saw Kana.

"How's your head?" he asked.

Kana grimaced, tired of people asking, even when it was Ember. He still got headaches occasionally, but the blurry vision and nausea were healed. The hospital had conducted a myriad of tests and scans, and he luckily only had a concussion. It wasn't a bad one, but a concussion was still a concussion and had resolved itself in its own time.

For the first few weeks after the hospital, Kana hadn't been capable of leaving his bed. He survived that ordeal thanks to Mika, Sora, and Ember's help and slowly got better. Step by step as the dizziness eased and the pain faded, Kana fought his way back to health. Now, after two months, he was almost completely healed. A short outing to finish up with his apartment definitely wasn't taxing enough to send him into a relapse.

"All right, sorry," Ember said with a laugh as he held his hands up in front of him in apology. "You'll tell me if you get tired. Ready to go to your next stop?" he asked.

Kana grinned in return. "Let's do it."

Ember waited for Kana to climb into the front passenger seat of the car, then got in the driver's seat. The car started with a rumbling growl that said Kana ought to know the brand name and be impressed, but all he cared was that they didn't crash. The drive to Kana's office building was quick, far quicker than taking the bus, and Ember idled the car at the curb so Kana could climb out.

"I'm hoping this should be quick," Kana said as he waited for Sora to jump to the sidewalk.

Ember nodded. "I'll find a spot to pull over. Text when you're on your way down."

Kana shut the door and waved, then hurried inside. He went directly to Amanda's office and knocked on the partially open door.

"Kana!" she gasped. "It's so good to see you."

Kana doubted that. Since she had put him on administrative leave, neither she nor anyone else in the company had tried to contact him. There hadn't been even one word about how the investigation into the deleted footage was going or whether he was allowed back to work. Only Beth had texted him, but their conversations had been friendly rather than work-related. Kana could read the writing on the wall.

He reached into his backpack and pulled out a sealed manila envelope.

"This is probably only a formality at this point, but here's my letter of resignation," Kana said. "I refuse to work for a company unwilling to care about their employees." He placed the envelope on her desk and left the room without waiting for her response. She didn't come after him, which didn't surprise him at all. Instead, he walked to his old cubicle.

Beth immediately stood when he walked in and gasped happily. "Kana!" she said. "Are you back now?"

Kana shook his head. "No. I turned in my letter of resignation."

"Oh, Kana!" Beth gasped, but as he turned to look at his old desk, her indignation immediately turned to guilt.

A young woman was sitting in Kana's chair, looking completely at home. Her back was to them both, and she didn't even turn to acknowledge that Kana had entered her workspace. His name was gone from the nameplate, replaced with hers, and everything he had left on the desk was gone.

"Looks like they've already replaced me anyway," Kana said, his voice wry.

Beth gave the woman a sour look. "I had hoped it was temporary. Still, I'm happy for you. Do you have a new job lined up yet?"

"I have a part-time one right now, but hopefully it will lead to something full time," Kana explained. He didn't go into detail about the part-time job working magic for the werewolf pack, and that since he was living with them, he technically didn't need to have a full-time job.

"I hope it works out for you," Beth said. She threw her arms around him in a hug. "I'll miss you though."

"I'm just a text away. We can always do lunch," Kana replied as he hugged her back.

"Definitely." Beth stepped away. "Now get out of here. You've escaped this cesspit. Don't come back."

"Thanks, Beth." Kana obeyed, turning and walking away without looking back, another chapter of his life closed with no regrets.

He texted Ember on the elevator ride down, and the car was just pulling up when Kana and Sora went outside. This time, Kana made it to the car safely, and he sank into his seat, grateful to get off his feet. He was tired, but it was mentally rather than physically, and his head still felt fine.

"Let's go home," Kana said.

Ember smiled at him and then turned to focus on pulling the car away from the curb. This time of the day, there wasn't much traffic, so it wasn't long before they were heading down the side streets leading to the city house. But as they drove past the next-door neighbor's, they saw three massive moving vans pulled in their driveway.

"Is someone moving in?" Kana asked. "I didn't even know it was for sale."

"Neither did I." Ember slowed the car to a crawl so they could rubberneck. In addition to the moving vans, a number of cars were also parked in the driveway. Someone was leaning against one of the cars, and when he saw Ember and Kana, he jumped up and waved. Ember snorted and rolled his eyes as he put the car in park.

"Who—?" Kana broke off when Ary got close enough for Kana to make out his features. Kana popped open his car door and stepped outside. "Ary?" Kana asked loudly.

"Hey, guess who your new neighbors are?" Ary called back, his voice cheerful. He joined Kana next to Ember's car.

"Why are hunters moving next door to the pack house?" Ember said with a growl as he walked around the hood of his car.

Ary grinned. "It's our new research and development site, with a side bonus of keeping an eye on a werewolf pack powerful enough to take out vampires and witches."

Ember didn't glance over at Kana at Ary's words, but Kana had a feeling Ary had already guessed how much Kana had helped with the vampire removal. He didn't need to guess about the witches since he had been there. Apparently both incidents were enough to convince the hunters to set up a headquarters in Albany.

"How is Samantha holding up?" Kana asked, partially because he was curious and partially to change the subject.

Ary gave Kana a sharp look that said he knew what Kana was doing, but he answered anyway. "The tribunal for all three witches who kidnapped you was last month. I told you that on the phone."

He had. The witches were found guilty of kidnapping and incitement against fellow magical creatures, and of doing so in a way that could have brought harm to innocent nonmagical humans.

"We ended up sending a letter of censure to the entire Seattle coven, by the way. Not that it will keep them away from the East Coast forever, but letters of censure are logged by most group-minded creatures. I believe you received a copy?" he asked, turning to look at Ember, who nodded. "The big coven in Salem got the letter, too, and I'm sure they aren't happy Seattle tried to encroach on their territory. Seattle is going to have to calm Salem down before they can even think about traveling farther east than the Rockies. Samantha was sentenced to ten years in our prison; I think the judge was lenient because of what you did to her. She's barely able to do any magic, just like you said. The other two were fined heavily and returned to Seattle with warnings about how we won't be so gentle with them if they step out of line again."

Ary grinned at Kana and Ember and then waved his hand toward the driveway filled with cars.

"I have a proposition to make to both of you," Ary finished.

Ember frowned at him, but Kana was interested to know what Ary wanted. "What kind of proposition?" Kana asked.

"The association has done our research on your pack, Alpha, and aside from your unfortunate tiff with the vampires, you do have a stable situation going on. Given we're neighbors, my superiors were hoping to hire the pack to extend your security perimeter to include our property as well. We have a contract we would like you to read that outlines what we're asking from you and the compensation we're offering."

Ember's frown didn't waver as he listened to Ary speak. "You also mentioned Kana?"

Ary nodded. "I did mention this is mostly a research and development facility? We're hoping to hire Kana as one of our researchers, working on spells and potions to make hunters more effective in the field."

That sounded amazing. Using his magic for his job, all while building his own abilities to help the hunters was an incredibly interesting proposition.

"Will Kana be doing the research, or will you be researching him?" Ember cut in before Kana could reply.

Ember asked a valid question. The hunter association believed Kana's parents were a witch and a hunter. Ary had mentioned before that the hunters would be interested in seeing why Kana's powers hadn't overtaken his reason. Why he hadn't lost his sanity and started attacking everything, and how to not only prevent other children like Kana from losing it, but also how to better stop those children when they did go off the rails were their major concerns.

"Look," Ary said with a sigh as he ran one hand through his hair. "I won't deny my superiors are interested in seeing what makes Kana tick, but they are more interested in watching Kana actually use salt to cast a spell and then discovering how we can incorporate that into our protective measures when we confront bad creatures."

The latter part was exactly what Kana was hoping, and to be

honest, he wouldn't mind the former if it meant helping other people like him. He didn't want to be turned into a guinea pig or a pin cushion, but allowing some research about his own quirky magic wouldn't be too bad.

Still, that wasn't a decision he could make right now, standing in the middle of the road barely twenty minutes after quitting his job.

"When do we have to tell you by?" Kana asked.

Ary laughed and waved one hand toward the moving vans, which had at least a dozen people working on unloading them. "It's going to take us a week just to get unpacked, let alone situated. Once our lawyer has some semblance of an office ready to go, how about I have her draft a contract for each of you, and we can go from there?"

"Sounds good to me," Kana replied. "Welcome to the neighborhood."

Ary headed back to the moving vans while Kana and Ember got back in the car. Ember drove the last few yards to the front gate of the city house, which opened after a few seconds of the car idling in front.

"I think I'd like working as a research magician," Kana said. "But my degree in journalism won't be much help, and my magic is all self-taught. Do you think it's a job that will actually work out for me?"

Ember chuckled at Kana's words. "You have spent how many hours researching the potion currently bubbling in your kitchen?" he asked. "Magical research and implementation is definitely right up your alley."

A potion Kana needed to get back to, but it wouldn't hurt to let it simmer for a few more minutes. The spell book Ember had bought for him had come in while Kana was bedridden. Once the dizziness passed, Kana found he was actually able to read—the doctors hadn't been certain whether he would be capable of reading until he was fully healed—and that was the first book he had grabbed. He would test his latest attempt at a calming potion once he got back to his witch's room, and hopefully this time it would be ready to help the wolves who needed it so badly.

Ember parked the car in the massive garage and shut off the engine. They climbed out and started walking to the door, but Ember stopped walking suddenly and spun to face Kana.

"Don't feel like you have to take this job to repay the pack for taking you in," he said, his voice slow and awkward as if he wasn't sure it was something he ought to be saying.

"You know I don't think that," Kana replied, although he could see why Ember might be worried about just that.

Tell him, Mika added when Kana hesitated.

Yes, tell him, Sora echoed with a mental shove down their link.

"I love you," Kana said. "It's not everything you gave me, like the witch's room or a place to live here. I'm staying because of you."

Ember's eyes were soft as he looked at Kana, and his grin was gentle. He reached out and pulled Kana into his arms. Kana rested his cheek on Ember's chest, listening to Ember's heart thump rapidly.

"I love you too, my mate," Ember rumbled back, his voice a low growl as he hugged Kana tight.

They stood together like that for a long while, Ember's chin resting on top of Kana's head while Kana breathed in his scent and felt the weight of being in Ember's arms. And Kana knew, no matter what had happened in his past, and whatever might come next, this was exactly where he was supposed to be.

WITCH

Prologue

"MAGIC IS ABOUT precision, Kana," Dad said, his voice firm, but understanding. He gently repositioned Kana's hand around the chalk. "Now, hold it steady, but not too tight. Pivot with your feet and keep a stiff elbow. Now place the chalk to the floor and spin."

Kana spun, the chalk scraping along the smooth floor as he tried to keep his arm completely still and allow his momentum to direct the chalk. When he finished a complete turn and the two lines of the circle intersected exactly, Kana pulled the chalk back and grinned up at Dad.

"Very good!" Dad crowed. "Look how exact this circle is compared to the one you drew before."

Kana stood to look. Where the previous circle was a wiggling wave that suddenly arced to force the two ends to meet, his new circle was almost perfect. A few bits were still slightly skewed, but overall, it was a circle whereas the old one was more of an awkward oval.

"Practice makes perfect, though," Dad continued. "You need to draw at least ten circles a day, until it becomes second nature. An imperfect circle will lead to an imperfect spell, and an imperfect spell can be very dangerous."

Kana nodded. Dad was right. Kana's wobbly circles were harder to call magic into, and the results didn't always match what he wanted the spell to do. If Dad said Kana needed to write ten circles a day, Kana knew he ought to instead do twenty. He had to perfect his spell circles so the coven and his mother would accept him as a witch.

"Dad?" Kana asked, reminded of a question that had been bothering him since Dad began this lesson. "Momma's the witch in the family. You don't have any magic, so how come you know so much?"

Dad's smile was a little sad as he patted Kana on the shoulder. "It's a long story. I'll tell it to you when you're older. Now, why don't you draw your ten circles for today, and then we can go out for ice cream?"

Ice cream? Kana grinned and hurried to a clean spot on the floor. Ten good circles in return for some ice cream was a great bargain! He put chalk to the floor and got to work.

*

FOUR YEARS LATER, when Kana was thirteen, Atlantea, one of the head witches on the coven council, pulled him out of class. His parents' car had been found at the bottom of a ravine, their bodies still inside. Her arms were warm and comforting as Kana cried, but it was also the only time he could remember her ever being nice to him. Certainly after the funeral her cold attitude toward him returned.

Kana quickly learned the magic lessons his dad had been giving him were lessons he should have been receiving from the coven, but they had refused to include him. He was a male witch and therefore not worth the coven's time, according to them. Why and how his dad had been able to provide those lessons instead, Kana never learned, but he was grateful for every one as he fought his way into the high school's magic classes.

Thoughts of his dad soon faded, however, beaten down under the onslaught of the coven's vitriol, but Kana knew someday he would be free of the coven. Someday, all the magic lessons he had been hoarding would be of use, and until then he would continue to perfect his spells through constant practice and repetition.

And then, once he was eighteen, Kana had forced them to allow him to cast the spell to call his familiars. He had run away right after that, tired of the coven's mistreatment and knowing it would only increase after he walked out of the testing room with two cat familiars—cats being the strongest familiars, and Kana had received two of them. His only choice was to leave, so Kana had run as far and as fast as he could.

*

THE FIRST RAINDROP hit Kana in the head, and he curled into a tighter ball, desperately wishing he were anywhere else. He was shivering cold in just a T-shirt and jeans in mid-autumn, and rain was definitely not going to help.

After two years of constant running, his money was gone. Kana had nowhere to sleep, aside from the dirty back alley where he was currently squatting, and certainly nowhere to get out of the rain. He needed a job so he could get some money, but Kana couldn't remember the last time he had showered, let alone had clothes clean enough a hiring manager would even let him in the door. If Kana had chalk, he could spell himself for long enough to get hired, but these days whenever he scraped together a few dollars, he had to use the money for food and maybe a trip to the laundromat. Money never lasted long enough for Kana to splurge on something like chalk.

Wet! Sora, one of Kana's cat familiars, howled in disgust through their mental bond as the rain started falling in earnest. *Put up a blocking spell!*

Kana uncurled just enough to glance down at the ground, where before the sun started setting he had been idly drawing circles and pentagrams into the muck. Those circles were already deformed, the muck not stable enough to hold the shape for more than a few seconds. He certainly wouldn't be able to draw a complex rune, especially as the rain washed away what was left of his circles.

How? Kana asked. *Even if I had something to write with, there's nowhere flat or clean enough to put it.*

Draw it with magic, then, Mika, Kana's other familiar, said with his own whine as a rumble of thunder sounded overhead.

With magic? Was that even possible?

Another rumble of thunder sounded overhead, and the rain began pounding down on Kana's head, the drops cold and painful as they hit any exposed skin. Kana pulled magic down his bond with Mika and let it gather on the tip of one finger. He drew a circle in the air, trying to push the magic to follow his finger and remain behind. The circle faded before he got all the way around.

Hold it with your mind as well as your magic, Mika said.

Kana tried to still his shivering so his hand would stay steady as he moved it in another circle. This time, as he drew with his magic, he held the image of the circle in his mind as well. The circle stayed, glowing in the air.

Kana grinned, but tried not to wreck his concentration as he let his heart jump in excitement at it actually working. He drew the star next, all five lines intersecting at exact angles. When the pentagram hung in the air, as perfectly connected to the circle as if he had drawn it on a flat surface with chalk, Kana allowed himself to let out a breath of relief. He drew the runes in quickly, before the shivering and the rain made it impossible to concentrate, and the spell took hold with a rush of warmth as if Kana were sitting at the beach in the sun on a warm summer day. Raindrops skidded around him, repelled from his body as if he and they were opposing sides of a magnet.

Kana finally uncurled and sighed as warmth settled into his bones for the first time in days. Mika and Sora uncurled too, both of them purring happily in Kana's lap.

Magic circles without chalk... What a crazy concept, but it had worked! Kana had no idea why he hadn't heard of that before. There were so many opportunities that opened up for him if he didn't have to spend money on chalk or time to find a suitable surface to draw his circle. A spell to make him appear less dirty, a spell to help keep Mika and Sora hidden so he could go out and about with them without worry about their getting spotted—or even so he could get into a shelter for the night without his "pets" being a problem—and— Kana sucked in a breath at the thought. He could draw a spell on a resume that would prevent anyone from looking too closely at his name or high school, both of which he had to lie about in order to stay hidden. With that, he might be able to get a real job, something not under the table and therefore grossly underpaid for the work involved.

But first, he had to practice. A complex spell like what he wanted to do for his resume wasn't a couple of simple runes; no, that would require multiple combined runes with very specific flourishes, and he would have to be competent enough at holding such a complex spell in his mind all while increasing the amount of magic he pushed into the circle to compensate for not being able to smudge any herbs or light candles to boost the spell. His wobbly, barely there circle that was mostly keeping the rain off said he wasn't ready for that just yet.

But he would be ready soon, Kana swore to himself. He just had to practice.

A cleanliness spell was easy, only a couple of runes. Kana fixed what he wanted in his mind, then slowly and carefully pointed one finger and moved it through the air to draw it out.

One day he wouldn't need to actually draw the circle, Kana realized as he completed the last rune and the lingering sour smell of unwashed human and cat faded from inside their magical cocoon. He ought to be able to push the circle held in his mind directly into action without the extra steps of drawing it out, and Kana knew he would one day. For now, though, he needed to stop thinking such lofty thoughts and focus on getting the most basic aspects of this new magic down exactly. He could only build up to the stronger versions he was envisioning if he had a solid base to work from, which meant lots and lots of practice was in his future.

More thunder rumbled overhead, and a flash of lightning obscured the next circle Kana was writing. This one was just for practice—and to see if he could dissipate the circle without casting it as easily as wiping his hand through a chalk-made one.

Kana grinned when the spell vanished, the magic dissipating exactly as it should.

With this magic, Kana had a future again, and his grin didn't fade until he drifted off to sleep, images of circles dancing through his mind.

Chapter One

"HEY, KANA?" JOHANNA called as she walked into Kana's workroom. Kana quickly held up a finger to stop her, focusing intently on the potion gently bubbling in the center of a spell circle hovering about six inches above his worktable.

The spell circle itself was taking most of Kana's concentration. He had invented it only recently, after both electric and gas stoves as well as a real fire had all proved to have too many inconsistencies with their heating, thereby leaving some of his potions lacking in power or simply not working at all. After six months of research, failed attempts, and a good bit of grumbling, Kana had worked out his mobius strip-style circle.

Normal spell circles vanished once they completed the tasks written into them via runes and Kana's intent. His mobius strip made the spell incapable of completing itself, constantly spinning back to the beginning without end. The only problem was how much concentration and magic the spell required. Kana's channels between himself and Mika and Sora were wide open and starting to ache as he continuously pulled magic from his familiars for the spell.

Thankfully, the potion was just about at the right consistency. He only needed another minute for it to be perfect. Kana watched carefully, and the second it looked exactly right, he reached out with a gloved hand to take the hot potion away and cut off the magic powering the spell. Mika and Sora both let out relieved sighs when Kana tightened the channels between them again.

Kana set the potion aside to cool, and finally turned to Johanna, pulling the glove off to drop on his worktable while he waited for her to stop staring at him and collect her thoughts again.

Johanna was Kana's research partner and boss at the hunter's compound. She was over six feet tall, and every inch of her body was toned muscle. She might spend most of her time sitting at a desk doing research for the hunters, but she was as capable of wading into a battle as anyone. Her skin was deep black, and her thick braids were dyed red. She was beautiful, but she definitely appreciated that Kana wasn't interested in her.

"That spell—" She cut herself off and shook her head.

"I don't recommend it, and I don't think I'll be using it again any time soon," Kana replied, and his voice sounded as tired as his magic felt. "It's not practical, even though it solves the heat source issue. I'll keep looking for a new solution for that, instead."

Johanna shook her head, her grin wry. "If it's too difficult for you, it's an impossible spell for the rest of us," she replied with an easy shrug. "You'll find it eventually. Anyway, didn't you once work as a journalist or something? Before you started here?"

Kana nodded, wondering where she was going with this. He had worked for one of the local news stations, which had TV, online, and newspaper, and was part of a national conglomerate as well. About a year ago, the station had interviewed a hunter for their morning news segment, but a vindictive witch had magically erased the footage and ensured all fingers would point at Kana as the culprit. Kana hadn't been upset to lose the job, despite how hard he had fought to get it in the first place, because his life had completely changed at that point. He had gone from being alone, and in hiding, to living openly as a witch with the local werewolf pack. The job that had helped spring him out of poverty had served its purpose, and Kana was ready to move on. Luckily, his current position as a researcher with the hunter's association had come around not long after, and using his magic in addition to his research skills—finding research interesting had led him to a journalism degree in college—had been too exciting to pass up.

"Oh, good," Johanna continued with a smile. "Looks like one of the local news stations finally figured out we're here. They're sending somebody over first thing tomorrow to inquire about doing an interview, and we need someone who speaks the lingo to tell them to shove off."

Kana frowned, having flashbacks to how he had gotten involved with the werewolves in the first place. His previous job had callously sent him on a very similar fact-finding trip to the local vampire coven, starting the journey that had eventually led him to where he was now. He wouldn't take any of it back, but he wasn't about to put someone else through a similar situation.

Also, there was only one station that seemed interested in regularly interviewing the magical community, and Kana wasn't certain he was ready to face his old coworkers again. Nor was he willing to do them any favors, considering how his old boss had written him off so completely when he was forced to quit. Although it was gratifying to hear

Johanna wasn't interested in moving forward with any sort of interview.

Kana sighed. "I don't know if my being there will only encourage them. Especially if they're the people I used to work with."

Johanna shrugged. "You at least know the lingo. If it was me, I would think I was telling them to pound sand, and next thing I knew we would be front page news."

Kana giggled and Johanna laughed with him. "All right," Kana replied. "I'll do it, but you'd better be ready to jump in and save me if they get aggressive."

"Please," Johanna said with a snort. "You could shove them out of the house and back into their cars before they blinked, and you know it. Now, finish whatever you were doing with that potion and head on home. Your wolf is probably waiting for you."

Kana laughed again. He reached out and gingerly touched the side of the flask, and when it was cool to the touch, he picked it up and handed it to Johanna.

"It's a strengthening spell for your weapons. I followed your recipe, but I changed the main herb combination."

"Oh?" Johanna asked as she took the flask from Kana. She carefully sniffed the mouth. Her nose wrinkled, and she frowned as she thought. "I can still smell the ginseng and peppermint oil, but what is that horsey smell?"

"Ashwagandha," Kana answered.

"Indian ginseng?" Johanna mused. "Interesting idea. You mind if I run some tests on this combination to see if it's more effective?"

"That's why I gave it to you." Kana smiled at her, but Johanna didn't notice, her eyes focused on the viscous liquid in the flask.

She glanced up at Kana briefly, blinked in surprise to see him still there, and waved toward the door with her free hand. "Go home. I'll see you tomorrow before the news people come, and I'll let you know how the tests go if we finish them before you're able to join us."

Kana put a few of his tools away and cleaned his workspace but obeyed Johanna's orders. The lab he worked in wasn't a private space, but there were so many labs in the hunters' building Kana often had the room to himself. The hunters' association had converted an old McMansion into a research space as well as living quarters for most of the researchers on staff. Construction had taken nine months, and the building still smelled of new paint and construction dust.

Kana was one of the exceptions because he didn't live on-site, however he didn't live far. The association had chosen their house because it was next door to the werewolves' city pack house, and Kana lived there with his boyfriend, the pack's alpha, Ember Maxwell. The association could keep an eye on the pack, and Kana benefited because of his incredibly short commute.

Ready? Kana asked.

Sora let out a wide yawn and flexed his front paws so his claws flashed in and out. *Yeah, after that much magic use, I want to go home and take a nap.*

Mika was hanging out with Ember for the day, but he was listening in to the conversation through their shared link. *Food first, please,* he said.

You always want food, Sora grumbled as he hopped from his perch on a nearby shelf and landed on Kana's shoulder. A few days after Kana had started working in the lab, the shelf—which had been intended to store supplies—had somehow been upholstered like a couch cushion with padding covered in simple blue cloth. Kana didn't know who had done it, but he—and definitely Mika and Sora—appreciated it a lot.

And you don't? Mika shot back with a derisive snort.

Kana left them to it, enjoying their banter as he abandoned the lab and walked through the halls to the front door. He let himself outside and followed the long driveway to the black iron gate at the end. The gate was inset into a ten-foot wall, which had taken the longest to build out of all the construction. The hunters had copied the wall around the pack house, so it at least created continuity in the neighborhood. A small guardhouse stood adjacent to the gate, and a hunter popped outside when she saw Kana coming.

"Done for the day?" she asked as she tapped the code into the keypad to open the pedestrian door adjacent to the massive gate.

"Yep," Kana answered with a smile for her.

The security inside the walls was manned by hunters, but the association had contracted with the pack to guard the perimeter and patrol the surrounding neighborhoods. Kana therefore wasn't the least bit surprised to find a wolf in wolf form sitting on the side of the street, his tongue hanging out as he panted in the afternoon heat.

"You're my escort today?" Kana asked and the wolf nodded his massive head.

Werewolf biology was an interesting subject. A hundred and fifty pound human turned into a hundred and fifty pound wolf, which meant the werewolf strolling at Kana's side was as tall as Kana's waist. Their muscles, claws, and teeth were all sized to match their large form. Their hair color as a human became their fur color. While this wolf looked ordinary brown, Kana had seen blond wolves too. In fact, the only thing they really shared with a real wolf was the basic overall shape to their form.

Werewolves were completely different than Kana's familiars, who appeared to be regular nine pound house cats, but in their human form were about a hundred and forty pounds, and in their primordial shape—

which was a mix between a tiger, a lion, and something wild only magic could dream up—they were approximately six hundred pounds. Kana hadn't ever found a scale to measure their weight with, but they made floors creak when they walked on them and had torn apart two powerful vampires without getting hurt themselves.

The werewolf at Kana's side wouldn't stand a chance against Sora should Sora decide to stop lazing on Kana's shoulder and change forms; the wolf knew that, and, more importantly, Ember knew that, but Ember had assigned Kana the escort anyway. Partially, the escort was a show of force—to prove the wolves protected what they considered theirs at all times—but it was also to help Kana because only a select few actually knew his familiars had their primordial forms or even how strong Kana's magic was. Besides, as mate to the alpha, Kana was afforded certain extra entitlements, including a guard whenever he stepped outside the protected fence.

The pack house—and the hunter's association—was located down a quiet side street in the suburbs of Schenectady. The houses were huge, on equally big parcels of land, but the neighborhood still managed to come across as quaint, if a bit snooty. The two adjacent properties with their massive walls surrounding them didn't quite fit in, yet at the same time, Kana had a feeling the rest of the houses might as well have a wall around them too. Certainly the neighbors hadn't been particularly welcoming so far.

"Yoo-hoo," someone tootled from across the way, putting a lie to Kana's thoughts. The wolf tensed and Kana turned to look, only to find a lady wiggling her fingers at them from the end of the driveway across the street. She was sitting under her mailbox, digging in the dirt to bury the flowers lying at her side in cheap plastic tubs. Her hair was once brown but was now heavily graying and her eyes were covered by a pair of dark-rimmed glasses. Farther up the drive a moving van was parked, the contents being busily unloaded.

"Hello," she chirped, her voice sounding cheery like a stereotypical grandmother's from the best kids' movies. It was so sickly sweet Kana's teeth ached in sympathetic reaction. "We're new to the neighborhood. It's so nice to see you out walking your dog. Where do you live, dearie?"

"Are you moving in today?" Kana asked instead of answering her question. If she had been outside for longer than five minutes, she had to have seen Kana leave the hunter's association, so at the very least she knew he was associated with them.

Mika, can you ask Ember if he knew about this? Kana asked.

I already did. He doesn't, Mika replied immediately. *Like when the hunters moved in, he didn't even know the house was for sale. He says he's assigning someone to figure out how these house purchases are happening without our knowing. He also wants to know if you have any idea if it's just a regular human, or if it's someone we should be concerned about.*

Good question. I'm leaning toward being concerned at this point. Kana sighed mentally. *I'm sure we'll learn really soon.*

"Oh, yes, dearie," she continued in her far too chipper voice. "It's a lovely day to move in. My daughters are overseeing the furniture and unpacking, but I thought it might be nice to cheer up the place with some flowers. As she spoke, she gently placed another flower into the ground and pushed the dirt to fill in around it until it was firmly in place. Her fingers brushed the small petals of the purple flower bud.

Had Kana blinked, he would have missed it. Magic flared, but so subtly it took him a minute to pinpoint how. The flowers, he realized, were planted in a circle, and the one she had just placed completed a star. The mailbox might be in the center, but that was irrelevant to the spell. The flowers weren't touching to make perfect, unbroken lines, but magic connected them anyway, similar to how Kana's quick-set circles worked when he drew them with only magic in the air. The flowers helped anchor the magic, much like chalk, but Kana realized in the half-second before the spell formed, the combination between anchor and magic to set the circle gave the circle an extra boost. It was similar to using candles in a circle, and yet Kana had never heard of using plants.

The spell arrowed, not at Kana, but at the wolf at his side. Kana didn't have time to do anything more than gasp and futilely grab for his own magic before the spell hit. The wolf grunted but otherwise seemed okay.

"Go on, now," the woman—the witch—said, her voice still genial, but it had lost that sugary syrup tone. "This young man and I need to have a private conversation." She made a shooing motion with one hand.

The wolf locked his knees, but Kana could see them trembling as he fought the spell. He let out a low growl as his body started to shake under the strain.

Kana couldn't let him continue to suffer. "It's okay," he said. "Go on."

The wolf whimpered, but he obeyed, reluctance clear in every movement as he slowly walked off in the direction of the pack house.

Kana turned to the witch, angry. "What do you want?" he snapped.

Chapter Two

THE OLDER WOMAN smiled serenely at Kana, apparently completely unconcerned with his anger.

"Just to chat, dearie. It's not every day I see a young man with a cat sitting on his shoulder."

"And that made you think it was okay to attack someone?" Kana growled out, sounding almost like a werewolf himself.

She waved her hand through the air as if physically brushing aside his words. "Oh, that little wolf wasn't hurt. I don't know what you're so concerned about, dearie."

Kana really wished she would stop calling him that, but he wasn't about to give her his name. Instead, he just gritted his teeth and tried to contain his anger.

"If I hadn't sent him away, he could have torn muscles and tendons fighting against that spell, and you know it. Stop pretending your nonchalance."

She suddenly frowned, and the ground lit up where her fingers were still buried in the dirt. Except this time Kana was ready for her. He let the spell hit him, but he drew a quick circle—carefully hidden underneath his clothes where she wouldn't see it—that funneled the power through him and directly into the ground below his feet where it harmlessly dissipated.

"Now then," she said, and her smile had a sharp edge to it now that the fake sugar syrup tone was gone. "Perhaps you'll be a little more amenable. Tell me who you are and why you're working for the hunters and werewolves."

Sora let out a wide yawn from where he was draped over Kana's shoulders. Kana just glared at her.

"I said"—she emphasized with another flare of magic that Kana let run into the ground without touching him—"who are you?"

Ember says to blast her, Mika stated, his voice a touch too eager.

This isn't a dominance fight, Kana replied in disagreement. He wasn't trying to prove he was top dog—or top wolf, in this case. He just wanted to get her to stop.

She won't stop until you force her to, Mika said, no doubt echoing Ember's words to Kana. *Her spells will only become more and more powerful until she starts bothering the neighbors.*

Kana let out a breath. He could see the logic in that, and the sooner he made her stop the sooner he could go home.

The ground flared again under her hand, but this time Kana changed his spell. Instead of redirecting the magic, Kana reflected it, sending the spell arrowing back at the caster. She waved her free hand in front of her body, and the spell vanished. Her eyes narrowed when she looked back at Kana.

"So you do have some power, boy," she said, her voice sharp. "But do you think you can keep up with one of the Three?"

Kana had no idea what she was talking about, although—if she was throwing out a title like that—he thought it pretty safe to assume she believed she was powerful. Luckily, Kana was powerful too. He threw open the channels between himself and Mika and Sora, drawing in magic through them until his fingers and toes were vibrating with power.

He had to stop her before she did something that would hurt the neighbors. The hunters and the wolves could take care of themselves, but the rest of the street was comprised of regular humans who wouldn't be able to defend themselves against whatever she was about to throw at Kana.

Magic built around her, so Kana built his own circle around her magic. He suppressed his power so only the barest hint of it was visible as he used it to draw his circle. The light he generated was easily concealed by hers as her magic continued to build. Pressure punched Kana in the chest as her magic hit a crescendo, and a split second before she released it into a completed spell, Kana flooded the miniscule lines he had drawn with as much power as he could.

Her magic slammed against the walls of Kana's circle, both spells lighting up the street like miniature supernovas. Kana had drawn his circle and star, with runes for containment and protection, with her in the center. She still had her fingers buried in the dirt, her plants forming the base of whatever spell she had tried to send at Kana. Her runes were obscured by the dirt and the light from the spells.

She poured magic into her spell, and it battered against Kana's circle, sometimes chiseling at it as if to force an opening and other times bashing against it as if sheer force could blow Kana's circle apart. Kana met every surge with his own power, gritting his teeth as he pulled magic from Mika and Sora and thrust it into his circle to match her.

His Mobius circle had at least been designed to sustain a circle indefinitely. This containment circle was one spell and forcing it to keep working against every onslaught was draining Kana's magic almost faster than he could pull it from Mika and Sora. His already taxed magic channels between them were starting to ache. Kana lifted one hand and twisted his wrist sharply. His circle twisted as well, forming into the shape for his mobius. The magic pull instantly reduced by a third, but Kana was still panting for breath. His locked knees were all that was keeping him standing, and Sora was lying limp on his shoulder rather than sitting up. His only consolation was the woman was now laying on the ground rather than sitting, her face bright red as she gasped for air with every blast of magic she sent.

As long as she kept sending magic, Kana had to keep up his own circle, which kept them locked together in this strange dance.

"That is enough!" Ember roared, his voice so powerful some of the people still unloading the vans, oblivious to the battle, finally looked over. Two women dropped what they were holding and rushed over. "Stop right now before you kill yourselves," Ember added, his voice alpha-firm in a tone that brooked no arguments. Kana wanted to obey, but he couldn't risk the neighborhood.

"Mother Diana!" one of the women gasped in alarm when they reached the older woman's side.

Diana grimaced. She looked at Kana and lowered her chin slightly as if she were acknowledging him. She didn't send out another blast of magic, and the light from her spell faded away. Kana gratefully dropped his own spell. He staggered, his knees finally giving way, and fell into Ember's warm, strong arms. Ember slid one arm around Kana's waist, effortlessly holding most of Kana's weight. Kana was happy to curl up against Ember—he was ready for a nap and napping with Ember was a rare pleasure—but Diana letting out a low groan reminded Kana he had to figure this mess out first.

Kana didn't know when he had closed his eyes, and it took work to fight the weight holding his lids down, but he finally opened them. The other two women were helping Diana sit up. Diana looked as tired as Kana felt, her shoulders stooped as she continued to lean on one of the women for support. The flowers she had planted were brown, the leaves flaking off in brittle pieces as a breeze wafted past.

"You're no Horned Lord," Diana said, her voice scratchy, but still strong.

Kana didn't know what that meant either, so apparently another trip to the library was in his future, but Diana was still scrutinizing him, her eyes focused on Kana and Sora so Kana pushed that thought aside to focus on the present.

"A male witch with a feline familiar. And you were able to push me to a standstill..." she trailed off as she paused to study him some more. Her gaze moved to Kana's right to study Ember briefly, then to Kana's left, past him to the hunter compound. "You are mated to a werewolf, yet you work for the hunters. Are you a hunter's get?"

Apparently, it was that easy to figure out the origin of Kana's powers. Diana wasn't the first one to peg Kana's magic after seeing him use it, and Kana doubted she would be the last. However, aside from the hunters, a witch had probably the most reason to hate what Kana was.

Kana's mother had been a witch, and a powerful one, as she had been part of the Seattle coven's inner circle at a fairly young age, but his father had been a hunter. Kana didn't know much more than that about them, but he had learned their relationship was considered taboo. Children born from the union of a witch and a hunter usually ended up with screwy magic, and that instability usually drove them insane. The hunters had originally come to Albany to deal with Kana, but when Kana had proven he was an exception to the rule, they had hired him instead. Kana had no illusions that part of their reason for hiring him was to keep an eye on him, but they had abandoned their plan to kill him for the moment, so he couldn't complain.

The question now was: Would Diana decide Kana didn't have a right to exist, or would she wait on her judgment? Of course, that was assuming she was willing to acknowledge a male with strong witch powers existed. Kana's old coven certainly hadn't, which was why he had been able to hide what he was from them for his entire childhood.

"Why are you here?" Ember asked when the silence dragged on a little too long.

Diana sighed. "Thanks to your little escapade with Seattle's coven last year, we identified a hole in the coverage of our territory. We are here to establish a circle and ensure neither Seattle nor any other coven thinks about encroaching again."

"This city is already claimed as my territory," Ember growled, his voice low and full of menace. "My people defended the city from attack, and we don't need some witches coming in thinking they're top dog. You're not, and you're not welcome here if this is how you greet us."

Diana let out a snort as if she wasn't sure whether she should be laughing or disgusted. "Too bad. We're here and we're not leaving."

"And if you continue to cause problems, we'll have to insist you change that decision," Ary said from behind Kana and Ember. He stepped into view a second later, his thickly braided hair in disarray as if he had been yanked out of bed to respond to Kana's and Diana's lightshow.

Ary had originally been sent to Albany to investigate what had happened when Ember's werewolves had fought and defeated the vampires keeping them captive, however at some point a witch named Samantha from the Seattle coven had caught him in a coercion spell. Samantha had wanted to use Ary to identify the witch who had helped the werewolves, but Kana had managed to free Ary instead. Samantha had then kidnapped Kana to force Kana to reveal who the witch was—her bias against him not allowing her to understand Kana was the witch in question—and Ary had rallied the hunters to come save Kana along with Ember and the werewolves. He was now second in command of the protection half of the hunter compound and helped patrol the tri-cities and surrounding area to keep any bad magical creatures from hurting people.

"Given you couldn't last five minutes without attacking someone, I am going to have to input Alpha Ember's complaint into our system of record. You, and your parent coven in Salem, will receive a letter of warning, and any further aggression will force the hunter's organization to act to suppress the entire coven."

Diana's face had been pale from exhaustion, but it went even whiter at Ary's words. One of the women hovering protectively over her let out a soft gasp.

"I suggest you rethink your position in this city immediately," Ary finished, his expression flat and stern in a way that said he was being completely serious. He turned his back on the women to look at Kana and Ember. "Kana, Johanna wanted me to tell you she rescheduled that meeting until tomorrow afternoon, so you should come into work late." He glanced at Ember and nodded his chin in the direction of the pack house. "I'll finish up here," he added pointedly.

Ember nodded back, then bent to scoop Kana into his arms. He walked to the pack house, and Kana watched over his shoulder as the two women helped Diana to her feet, then supported her as they walked up the drive of their own house. Ary waited, hands on his hips, until the women were inside before he turned to head to the hunters' house.

The large iron gate at the end of the pack house's driveway was open a few inches. Ember stepped through and it slid shut with a clang.

"Guess we now have witches for neighbors," Ralph, one of Ember's betas, said with a disgusted sniff.

"Better than more vampires," Ember replied. They walked together up the drive, Ember's steps even and his arms not wavering in the slightest under Kana's weight.

"I like our vampire," Marc piped up, somehow exactly where he wasn't supposed to be. Again.

Werewolf children came in three different types. The majority were born as a regular human, and when they grew up, they could decide whether they wanted to be bitten and turned into a wolf or continue their lives as a human. The second were children born with the ability to shapeshift into weak wolves. Ember theorized because the children were so weak, the wolf genes were activated at birth as a protective measure. Kana hadn't seen any evidence to dispute that. However, a very small percentage were the third type of werewolves, Marc being a perfect example. Those with alpha or beta potential who would become the future leaders in the pack were born as incredibly strong wolves. Ember had also been born a strong wolf, for example, and he said it was because the wolf genes were so powerful they manifested naturally. Marc was going to grow into a very powerful wolf, but for the moment he was simply one of the odder children in Ember's pack.

The vampire Marc was referencing was his friend, a man named Shannon who had protected Marc and a number of other kids against the bad vampires Kana had helped Ember dispose of. Marc had an interesting habit of being exactly where he wasn't supposed to be, without seeming to care that he kept putting himself in danger.

"How was school today?" Ember asked Marc, his voice even and unsurprised by Marc joining them at the gate, where he wasn't supposed to be when there was a battle happening right outside.

Marc groaned. "Do I have to go to school? Why can't I stay with the homeschooling, like we used to do?" Ember gave Marc a sharp look, and Marc let out a heavy sigh, but the tone was less whiny and accusatory. "I know, I know," Marc said with a sigh. "The schools are better than homeschooling, and I need to meet more kids my own age. It's just there are so many humans, and they're all so...human. Can I see your wolf? Can I pet you? Blah, blah, blah. Like I'm a dog or the class pet."

"There are other nonhumans in your class, Marc," Ralph said. "Why don't you make friends with them?"

Marc sighed again, his shoulders slumping. "They're all scared of me."

"I didn't have any friends at school either," Kana said, hoping to reassure Marc. "It took me a while, but I did find someone for me." He glanced up at Ember, who was already looking down at Kana. They shared a smile.

Marc hopped up the front steps and spun around at the top to wait for them to catch up. "I already have my someone. I've got Shannon! And he's a much better teacher than the one I've got at school. So, it doesn't matter that I sleep through class and only want to play outside, because Shannon makes sure I'm going to pass all my classes."

"At least Shannon is a responsible adult," Ralph muttered under his breath. "Sounds like one of us is going to have to go to his next parent-teacher conference to do some teacher educating."

Ember snorted in laughter, but quietly, so he wouldn't offend

Marc. "Try to make friends and behave in class," he said to Marc, his voice firm, but still full of levity from the situation.

"I'll do my best," Marc replied with a pout, but then he brightened. "I have to go get my schoolbooks and homework ready, so Shannon can teach me when he wakes up! Glad to see you're doing okay, Kana," he added over his shoulder as he spun around and darted into the house. By the time Ember and Kana got inside, Marc was gone.

Can we curl up for a nap now? Sora grumbled. *Mika's already sleeping.*

Kana's answer was interrupted by a wide yawn.

"All right, enough chitchatting. We can figure out what we're doing about the witches when you're more awake," Ember said.

Kana tried to answer, but with Mika already sleeping and Sora quickly following, Kana, wrapped in the comfort of Ember's arms, couldn't help succumbing to exhaustion as well.

Chapter Three

LIGHT WAS FILTERING in through the cracks in the room-darkening shades over the bedroom window, so Kana knew it was much later than he normally woke. His body felt refreshed, which was nice, but his magic channels were still sore. He could cast magic if he needed to, but it would be better if he rested for a few days.

"Finally," Mika groused. He sat on the side of the bed with a thump. "It's already ten o'clock. I was starting to worry you'd sleep forever!"

"Hah! As if you didn't just wake up not even an hour ago," Sora cut in. He walked into the room from the direction of the bathroom, completely naked except for the towel he was using to dry his hair.

Mika stuck his tongue out at Sora but turned back to Kana instead of retaliating. "Hurry up and shower so we can go get something to eat."

Kana's stomach immediately rumbled at Mika's words. He had missed dinner and breakfast, all after expending a ton of magic, so it was no wonder he was hungry.

"Where's Ember?" Kana asked as he pushed off the covers and swung his legs over the side of the bed.

"He got up with the alarm you slept through," Mika answered. He collapsed into the warm spot Kana had left behind on the mattress and flapped one hand at Kana. "Hurry up."

Kana obeyed, hurrying through his shower and getting dressed as quickly as possible. Ten minutes later, his hair still a touch too damp, Kana left the bedroom and ventured into the halls of the werewolf house. Mika and Sora had changed into their cat form—it meant they didn't have to wear clothing, which they were forced to whenever they walked around in human form—and they vanished down the hall ahead of Kana, toward the kitchen where someone would take pity on them and give them food. Kana had two options: he could make something himself in the small kitchen adjacent to his witch's room, or he could go to the mess hall where he would have to eat whatever happened to be available at the moment. The latter option was faster, and Kana wouldn't have to clean up after himself, so he turned in that direction.

Once there, he made a cup of tea and grabbed some toast. Only a few people were still in the room, most of them chatting over coffee. The city pack house served a number of purposes, but in times of peace most wolves only used the dining facilities if they worked or lived in the building. Over the last few months, most of the wolves who could afford it had purchased their own homes. A lot of the ones who couldn't, instead lived in the second pack house out in the suburbs north of the city, which was bigger, nicer, and a lot more private. Ember split his time between the two houses, but because Kana worked with the hunters next door, Kana mostly lived in the city house. The majority of the wolves who still lived here too were guards for the building or worked in the city.

Kana's tea was finally cool enough to drink, so he took a sip. He looked up just in time to see one of the kitchen staff walk over with a plate in hand.

"You need some protein," he grunted as he placed the plate next to Kana's plate of toast. He walked away before Kana could say anything, leaving behind two perfectly fried over-easy eggs.

Kana happily dug in, quickly assuaging the rumbling in his stomach. By the time he was done, Mika and Sora had reappeared.

I guess I should go to work, Kana said to them.

Ember wanted to walk you there, Mika replied. *I'll go find him, and we'll meet you at the door.* He hopped off the table and dashed out of the room.

Kana returned his dishes to the cleaning station and waved his thanks to the kitchen staff before heading back to his room to get his wallet and phone. After retrieving his items, Kana walked to the front door, where he found Ember and Mika waiting for him. Ember smiled when he caught sight of Kana.

"Sleep well?" he asked when Kana reached his side. He bent his neck and tilted his head in obvious invitation, so Kana obliged with a quick peck on the lips. Kana would have preferred more, but as alpha, Ember had to obey certain proprieties, including not making out like rabbits with his boyfriend in the foyer of the shared pack house.

"I'm feeling better, thanks," Kana answered with a smile. "My magic is still a little sore, but I can use it if I have to."

"But it would be better if you didn't have to for a few days," Ember added, immediately understanding what Kana was saying. "Maybe we should add a gate in-between the pack's property and the hunter's," he added. That would certainly make it so Kana didn't have to leave the protected grounds to travel to and from work, but it would open the wolves to a potential vulnerability if the hunters ever decided they didn't want to work with the wolves anymore.

Kana shook his head. "I think we put the witches in their place yesterday, and our outside defensive procedures worked. If we hide away, we'll seem like we're scared of them."

Ember sighed. "Fine, but you have to call when you're leaving work so I can come pick you up."

"Will do."

They walked outside together, and down the long driveway. A wolf nodded to them from the window of the guard building when they reached the gate, and a second later the gate slid open just enough for Ember and Kana to walk through. Sora remained inside, where he wouldn't be seen by the witches, and so he could stay with Ember for the day in case Kana had to pass messages to him like he needed to yesterday. Either Mika or Sora usually stayed with Ember; they liked him, and Kana appreciated having one of them near Ember in case Kana had to cast a spell through them to protect Ember. Today was Mika's turn to join Kana at work.

The gate immediately shut behind them and they continued down the road to the hunter's gate. Kana could feel eyes following them from within the witches' house, like hot spots on his back, but he never sensed even the slightest spark of magic. The gate at the driveway for the hunter's compound slid open when Kana approached.

"Call," Ember repeated. He bent and Kana happily kissed him again, then stepped back to watch Kana walk onto the property and the gate close safely behind him. Kana stayed by the gate, watching as Ember walked back alone, until Ember was also safe in pack territory again. Kana hurried inside, heading to Johanna's office first to check in.

"How are you feeling?" she asked the second she saw him. "That was crazy yesterday."

Kana shrugged, awkward under the onslaught of her praise. "Diana demanded answers I had no interest in giving to her. Ember said I should stop her, and I didn't want her to hurt the rest of the neighborhood."

"Why are you calling her Diana?" Johanna asked, her voice strangely choked.

"When the other two women came running up to her, they called her Mother Diana. I figured Mother was her title and Diana her name. Am I wrong?"

Johanna nodded slowly, but her gaze wasn't focused on Kana. Instead, she appeared to be ruminating on an internal thought.

"Sometimes I forget how many gaps there are in your education," she finally said as she returned her attention to Kana. "What do you know about the Three?"

Kana blinked, surprised to hear that term from Johanna as well. "Diana said she was one of the Three. That's the first time I heard that term."

"Did she say anything else?" Johanna asked, rather than explaining.

Kana had only been confused before, but now he was worried. Diana had seemed like a witch—an incredibly powerful one, but still a witch. What if she was something more, and Kana had mortally offended her because of his ignorance? Kana didn't need more to worry about.

"Witches have different belief systems," Johanna finally explained. "Each coven follows a slightly different theology, based on the lore and mythology from which they believe their power derives. A coven is as much a religious order as it is a spell circle; you understand?" She waited for Kana to nod before continuing. "The Seattle coven's beliefs were broader: that a great mother granted power to all her daughters, and through casting spells in the time-honored tradition, her daughters continued to honor her gifts. The Salem coven also believes in a greater, unknown, but all-knowing power, however they believe that power is manifested in the goddess's aspects here on earth. They believe in a powerful trinity of women: the crone, who represents wisdom, the mother, who represents stability and power, and the maiden, who represents youth and promise. Some say they represent past, present, and future. Their titles are Crone Hecate, Mother Diana, and Maiden Lucina, and we apparently have Mother Diana at our doorstep." She paused and stared at Kana as if another crazy thought had just entered her head. "You held Mother Diana to a standstill," she breathed out, her voice shocked.

"She, um, she said I wasn't a horned lord, whatever that means?" Kana added, his voice tentative because he didn't know whether he ought to be happy at what he had done, or scared.

Johanna shook her head. "The Horned Lord is the male equivalent to the triple goddess belief. The Seattle coven doesn't believe he exists, while the Salem coven do believe in him, but he would never appear as a regular witch with a cat familiar. The hunters would define the Horned Lord's powers as those of a sorcerer, someone who pulls magic from within themselves, while witches pull power from the other side. The witches only see a male born from the coven who embodies the powers the goddess gave to men as a balance to women."

"I'm definitely not a sorcerer," Kana said in agreement. He didn't know what he was, but his powers were pure witch, and his unusual strength came from his hunter father. Kana had no idea what power was imbued in hunters, just that they had the ability to fight all kinds of magical creatures, and some of that strength had been passed to Kana.

Johanna laughed. "You are a witch, through and through. I wouldn't worry about it. Today, we need to toss the news station out on their ears and then go test that potion you made yesterday."

"Yeah. Thanks for moving the interview to this afternoon."

Johanna laughed. "After what I saw yesterday, I'm surprised you made it in today at all. Your wolf must be taking very good care of you." She winked at him.

Kana ducked his head and hoped the warmth in his cheeks wasn't too obvious. Not that Ember had done anything except carry him to bed yesterday, but it was a bed they shared in all the ways a couple could.

"Anyway," Johanna continued once she finished laughing at him. "I'm going to set you up in Stan's office, since he's never here, and it's the most generic office we have without being completely unused."

Stan was Ary's boss, but he was in charge of the hunters for multiple offices so was constantly traveling between them. His office had the usual pens, pads of paper, and old coffee rings, but he took all his paperwork with him so there wouldn't be anything for the reporters to snoop.

"They should be here within the hour," Johanna finished. "Why don't you go get settled in, and I'll bring them over when they get here?" Kana nodded and waved goodbye as he headed in the other direction, away from the lab space where Johanna was headed. He hoped the interview would go quickly since all Kana had to say was the hunters weren't interested. If the reporter, or whoever was coming for the pre-interview, didn't try to wheedle and push to make Kana change his mind, he ought to be able to at least spend a few hours testing his potion.

Stan's office was nicely sized, with a big wooden desk in the center. On one side were two plush visitor's chairs, and Stan's chair was an ergonomic monstrosity that Kana sank into and never wanted to get up again. He leaned back in the far too comfortable chair. Mika hopped into

Kana's lap, and Kana ran his fingers down Mika's spine, scritching his fingers through Mika's fur, as they settled in to wait.

Chapter Four

"KANA?" BETH GASPED when she walked into the office. Beth was Kana's old coworker from when he had worked for one of the local news stations. Channel 7 was the local network; however, they were part of a larger conglomerate that included the newspaper and national level press. Kana and Beth had been in charge of all the grunt work. One of their responsibilities was finding potential stories and conducting the initial interview to see whether the piece was worth the time and effort of the bigwigs at the station. When Kana had worked at Channel 7, being sent on one of those preinterviews had brought Kana to the attention of the vampires and werewolves.

"Hello, Beth," Kana replied. He ought to have guessed she would be the one he was meeting with. Channel 7 had a strange fixation on reporting stories about the supernatural community, and it was actually surprising they hadn't reached out to the hunters before now. Certainly, they regularly called the wolves to ask for an interview, and Ember's phone receptionists had gotten really good at fending them off.

Beth's brown hair had been cut in a pixie bob the last time he had seen her, but it had grown down to her shoulders recently. Still, her friendly smile and happy demeanor seemed unchanged. She was followed into the room by a second woman who Kana vaguely recognized.

"This is Lyra," Beth said as they both walked into the room, and Lyra closed the door behind them. "You met her the day you quit. She's the one they hired to fill your position."

Lyra nodded to him but didn't smile or say anything. For someone who was supposed to want to entice and convince Kana to work with her on behalf of the network, she was being very dour. Her face was the pale white of someone who didn't know how to match their foundation makeup to their skin tone, and her dark blue eyes were thickly lined with black. Her hair had also been dyed black, but Kana didn't think she was going for a goth look.

Something's weird in the air, Mika said, sniffing in Beth and Lyra's direction from where he was hidden in Kana's lap by the bulk of the table.

Something's definitely weird, Kana agreed. He didn't want to use magic today, but it was better to be safe than sorry. Kana's magic channels ached and were sluggish as he widened them between himself and Mika and Sora, but he would need the boost of magic from them.

Beth was her usual bubbly and exuberant self, eager to do her job and genuinely happy to see Kana. Lyra's demeanor, on the other hand, conveyed the exact opposite: she didn't want to be here, she didn't care about the story, and she had better things to do with her time. Kana had never been as effective as Beth at turning on the charm to get the ball rolling on a story, but he had tried a hell of a lot more than Lyra, which made him wonder why she was doing the job at all. Kana felt safe assuming the something weird he and Mika were sensing was coming from Lyra, although he couldn't tell if it was a bad something, or just odd.

Kana waved toward the two visitor's chairs and, while Beth and Lyra were busy taking their seats, he used magic, rather than chalk, to draw a couple of circles. The first was a basic containment circle under Lyra's chair, which ought to hold her in place for at least a few seconds should she try anything. The second circle was much bigger—and layered. He drew on the walls of the room itself, first a base of a protection circle. The second layer was a combination of containment and concealment. Kana dithered over whether to add a third layer—he wasn't sure whether it was worth wasting the energy to do it when there might not be an actual problem brewing—but he concluded it was still better to be safe than sorry. Kana drew a third layer with the runes for power and strength, to bolster the two previous layers.

The spells lay dark and dormant—invisible to the naked eye—and would remain that way until Kana activated them.

Beth was just pulling a pen out of the spiral spine of her notebook when Kana refocused on his guests.

"What are you doing here, Kana?" Beth asked as she flipped her notebook to an empty page.

Kana shrugged. "Lucky coincidence," he lied, giving her the canned story he had prepared in case anyone from his old job discovered where he now worked. Beth didn't know he was a witch, and Kana saw no reason to tell her. "The hunters found out I was fired because they had deleted the interview footage at the same time they were looking for a media consultant for their new office. They hired me."

Beth grinned happily at him. "I'm glad you found a new job so quickly. Also, I'm glad I don't have to explain why we're here. When can we set up the interview?"

"The Hunters Association does not conduct interviews," Kana said formally. "Sorry, Beth, but we have to decline."

"I know that's what they said on the phone, but I'm sure we can work something out," Beth insisted. She smiled her patented "I'm cute and you want to listen to me" smile.

Battle lines drawn, Beth wasn't going to back down, and neither was Kana.

"Beth, I promise you, any footage or interview material you try to generate about hunters or their association will mysteriously vanish before you have a chance to release it. We are not willing to agree to an interview."

"I'm sure there's someone here who would be happy to be interviewed," Beth tried again.

Kana just shook his head. Beth's chin was set and her eyes blazing as she tried to think of some way to convince Kana to change his mind. Lyra, on the other hand, was leaning back in her chair with her cheek resting on one fist as if she were incredibly bored by the entire process. Except her eyes were blazing too as she watched Beth and Kana speak.

Something bad is happening, Mika said, his voice a mere whisper as if even in mind to mind he didn't want to be loud enough to be noticed.

Kana reached out with his magic, tentatively feeling through the air for whatever Mika was sensing. He found it almost immediately—what could only be described as a black miasma dripping from Lyra. It was hidden from physical sight, but his magic could detect it pooled on the floor underneath her where her feet were planted on the ground. Two lines going in two different directions stretched from that pool.

One line had a loop around Beth's ankle, and as Beth exclaimed,

"Kana, work with me here!" the line flared as if it was backlit by a blue light. The second line was creeping its way under the desk, heading toward Kana.

"Why are you really here?" Kana asked, his voice sharp as he cut Beth off. He was looking at Lyra as he spoke.

What is she? he added to Mika.

Mika shuddered in Kana's lap. *A summoned creature of some kind. Something from the demonic realm, I think, although it's not a demon. Either way, it's bad news.*

Beth gasped and the line around her ankle flared again. "What do you mean? We're here to set up an interview!"

Kana had to stop this before it escalated. Lyra was controlling Beth, and there was no telling what she might have Beth do if Kana kept denying her. He reached out with his magic, past the room to the hunter's alarm system. The system could be tripped by hand and by magic, and Kana zapped it. The silent alarm immediately went off, letting everyone know there was a problem in the building. That done, Kana focused on forming his magic into a sharp knife, one that would cut the line controlling Beth. At the same time, he connected to the spell circles he had already drawn.

Kana slashed the knife through the black miasma, slicing it neatly. Beth let out a soft gasp. Her eyes rolled back and her body slid to the floor. Kana's circles lit up with blinding flares, and Lyra let out an ear-piercing screech.

"Why are you really here?" Kana asked again, but this time his voice echoed with the power he was using to keep both circles running.

Lyra screeched again and flailed her arms, beating at the simple containment circle holding her captive in her chair. The circle was cracking under just the pressure of her fists. Kana needed to reinforce it, but even then, he wasn't sure it would hold. He ought to let it drop and catch her in another, more complex circle instead.

Kana built the more complex circle just outside of the first, but this time he made it a layered protection circle, much like the one blazing on the walls of the room. He set the runes for the three levels, then spun the two upper circles so they were slightly offset from each other before activating the spell. The upper levels dropped into the base layer, and together they formed a fifteen-pointed star. Each point of the star where it intersected with the circle glowed in another pinprick of light.

The initial circle collapsed and Lyra let out a shriek of triumph that made Kana's ears ring. She let out another shriek when she immediately ran into Kana's new circle.

"Please, please, Mother Diana," Sora said, his voice somehow breaking through the ringing in Kana's ears. It took Kana a moment to realize he was hearing Sora through their shared channel.

"Kana's locked himself in and none of us are strong enough to breach it to help him. His familiar can't even reach him," Ary's voice said next.

"But you were powerful enough to go toe-to-toe with Kana yesterday," Ember continued.

A feminine snort sounded next. "I hate seeing cats and dogs cry, and being owed a favor from the hunter who threatened to censure us is a boon I particularly like. Show me the way."

The voices faded as Lyra let out another piercing screech. She pounded her fists into Kana's circle, her knuckles bloody, and the miasma around her flailed, trying to pound the circle as well, yet backing away as if the light pained it every time it dared to come close.

"Why are you here?" Kana asked again. Lyra only shrieked again in reply. Perhaps she wasn't capable of speech? She had been using her miasma earlier to force Beth to speak for her, and Kana suspected the second line of miasma heading in his direction was meant to force him to do her bidding as well. She wouldn't have had to say anything aloud with that sort of power at her disposal.

The circle he had erected to protect the entire room suddenly rang, like someone had hit a mallet to the side of a bell. The vibrations ran through him, shaking his concentration enough Lyra's next hit fractured the first circle around her. Kana fed more magic into that circle, shoring it up so Lyra wouldn't break free, which didn't leave any concentration for whatever was going on with the room's circle.

Kana, we're coming in! Sora's voice called down their link.

This time Kana sensed the pressure building against his outer circle; however, when it went off, the bell was more of a gentle knock. The first tolling had been to force him to pay attention. The knock was to remind him they were still waiting. Kana dropped that circle with a gasp of relief, glad he didn't have to split his magic in half anymore.

The office door flew open and Ary strode inside. He looked around, assessing Kana and Lyra quickly, before stepping back outside.

"We've got an imp!" Ary yelled. "Someone get me a gallon of holy water, now!"

Ember and Diana walked into the room while Ary continued to yell orders outside. Diana's gaze was more calculating than Ary's, and she was studying Kana's circle rather than the situation as a whole.

"Another well-built compound circle," she murmured. She walked behind Kana and around to the part of the circle Lyra was still pounding at. The crack wasn't growing, but it was still an obvious weak point. "You are currently using your magic to sustain the spell," she said, this time to Kana. "Continue doing that, but at the same time I want you to think of the circle as newly drawn. Send your power through it as if kindling it for the first time."

Kana could see where she was going with her instructions. He split his magic so the majority was still powering the spell, but let just enough go to the base circles. He couldn't drop the three separate parts together again, but he could flash the circle with magic as he would to activate a single-circle spell. Kana did it and watched as the crack vanished as if it had never been there. Lyra let out another shriek.

"Good." Diana harrumphed once the shriek stopped, but she looked pleased. "You may not be the Horned Lord, but you have some promise."

Ary hurried back into the room, a gallon-sized milk jug in each hand. The tops were off and they were both filled with what looked like water. Ary calmly walked to Kana's circle. He set one jug on the ground and gripped the other in both hands, before flinging the contents at Lyra.

The water went straight through Kana's circle, splashing all over Lyra's body and the miasma surrounding her on the floor. This time her shriek was so piercing Kana had to clap his hands over his ears. Ary splashed water at her again and again, until the first jug was empty.

Lyra's screaming continued, and her body began to smoke slightly as if the water were lighting her on fire. The smoke stopped at the boundaries of Kana's circle, filling the space and concealing Lyra completely from view.

Ary grimly held the second jug, still glaring at the smoky circle while he waited. The screeching had stopped, as had the pounding on Kana's circle, but Kana kept the magic flowing just in case.

Slowly, ever so slowly as Kana began to pant for breath as his already strained magical reserves began to tap out, the smoke began to clear. Lyra was gone, as was the miasma, but a strange, glowing slash had appeared on the floor where she had been standing.

Ary grinned. "Kana, drop the circle. We know how to handle this." He lifted his jug in preparation as another two hunters, each armed with their own jug, rushed into the room. They took up positions around the circle, and Kana gratefully dropped the spell.

Thankfully, Kana was already sitting, because as he cut off the magic it was as if he also cut a string holding him up. Kana collapsed into the padded seat, his arms hanging uselessly off the armrests like weights were attached to his wrists, and the room did a one eighty around his head. Utter exhaustion made it impossible to keep his eyes open. The last thing Kana saw was Ary and the two hunters pouring their jugs directly into the slash, more smoke billowing before sleep took him away.

Chapter Five

KANA'S HEAD ROSE and fell slowly and rhythmically. The feeling was soothing, although it was weird too, and he enjoyed the sensation for a few long moments as his body and brain took their time waking up. His head was resting on someone's chest, he realized as neurons started firing again. He opened his eyes to see the familiar ceiling of the bedroom he shared with Ember, darkened, as the lights were off and it was apparently nighttime. He was probably lying on Ember, as Mika and Sora—who also shared the bed with them—still liked their space.

How long was I asleep? he asked, and then winced when the magic channels between himself and Mika and Sora proved to be raw and aching.

Two days, Sora replied, and Kana winced again. Even receiving their mental communication hurt. He was completely tapped out magically, and he would not be able to draw out more magic from his familiars until those channels healed.

There was a soft thump as either Mika or Sora jumped on the bed. A second later, Mika sauntered by Kana's head in his small cat form. Kana carefully turned to look, and winced when Mika stopped by Ember's face, lifted one paw, and bopped Ember right on the nose.

Ember's eyes flew open, and he gasped, which made Kana's head slide off his chest and onto the mattress below.

"What—" Ember quickly choked off, his voice loud in the quiet room. He glared at Mika before turning his head to check on Kana.

"Hi," Kana croaked out, his voice rusty from disuse, when Ember looked at him.

"Kana!" Ember said as he sat up. He gently reached out to brush his fingers along Kana's cheek. "You're awake."

Kana nodded, the movement awkward from a prone position. "Sora said I was asleep for two days. What did I miss?"

Kana's neck started to ache from looking up at Ember, so he gingerly shifted around. When moving his head didn't make anything hurt—apparently only his magic channels were injured—Kana sat up so he could face Ember.

Ember was frowning at Kana, but when Kana didn't yelp in pain, the frown faded. "According to the hunters, you caught an imp, which they say means we have a warlock floating around somewhere."

An imp was a creature summoned from the demon plane, Kana knew. Technically it was a type of demon, but it was so low on the power scale many magic users classified it as a separate species, as a sort of lesser creature. Certainly, the creature Kana had fought hadn't seemed particularly demonic. That said, summoning creatures from the other plane to use as servants or power sources was the purview of a warlock; that was the only way they obtained power to cast spells. The stronger the warlock, the stronger creatures they could summon, and the stronger the creatures they could summon made the warlock stronger in turn, in an endlessly escalating scale. Allegedly there was an upper limit, but Kana hadn't researched enough about them to know more than that. Summoning an imp could mean a couple of things: one, that the warlock was weak and an imp was the current limit to their power, or two, that the warlock hadn't seen a need to send a more powerful creature for whatever task Lyra had been set. Unfortunately, the only way to know was to find the warlock, which meant preparing for both possibilities.

"The hunters told me they were going to focus all their local resources on finding the warlock, and, surprisingly, the witches agreed to help too."

"Probably to get that citation Ary threatened them with erased," Kana said, hoping he didn't sound sarcastic because he was honestly pleased Diana was helping. Someone with her power and knowledge would be invaluable.

"Yeah, that's probably it, but Ary's leaning on them pretty heavily until you're back up to speed. Anyway, apparently one of the anchors for Channel 7 news fainted live on-air at about the same time Ary tossed holy water on the imp. Our sources in the station said about half the staff suddenly passed out too. They're calling it a gas leak, and the station's been shut down while the gas company investigates."

"What about Beth?" Kana gasped.

Ember gave Kana his beautiful half grin. "Don't worry. Ary said an imp will steal energy from their victims, but once that connection is broken, the victim just needs to sleep it off. Once we were certain Beth would be okay, we drove her to the hospital, claiming we found her passed out on the side of the road, and we made sure the hospital staff found her work ID so they could connect the dots. Last I heard, she was awake, and her doctors were running a few more tests to make sure she's okay. She'll probably be released soon, and Ary said he'll make sure her medical bills are covered. Apparently, it's the hunter's association's responsibility to do that whenever one of their investigations impacts a member of the innocent public. Word is the people at Channel 7 who were also impacted by the imp have all also woken. You're the only one we've been waiting on," he added cheekily, although his hand reached out to gently brush Kana's cheek again in a way that said he had honestly been worried.

Kana leaned into Ember's hand, wondering how he had managed to win Ember's heart. For Kana, it had definitely been lust at first sight, but his feelings for Ember had swiftly grown from there. Ember clearly had those same feelings; his eyes were soft and concerned as he gazed at Kana in a way no man had ever looked at Kana before—like he wanted to coat Kana in a protective wrap and tuck him safely away like Kana was Ember's most-prized possession. And yet, at the same time Ember was an overprotective alpha wolf whose chief drive was to keep his people safe and happy, but he was still willing to step aside and let Kana live his own life. Kana knew all he had to do was reach out a hand and Ember would be there to support him the whole way. A heady feeling, yes, but also a wonderful one.

Mika had shifted to his human form sometime while Kana was lost in Ember's gaze. He leaned against Ember's back, his arms draped over Ember's shoulders so his hands could drift downward, caressing along the lovely defined muscles of Ember's chest and stomach. His fingers stopped at Ember's nipples, tweaking them gently, before continuing down to circle Ember's belly button for a moment, ruffling through the short hairs until he reached Ember's pajama pants. Ember's deep-brown eyes darkened as his pupils blew open. Mika licked his lips and grinned.

Sora, ever the bolder of Kana's two familiars, didn't bother with foreplay. He climbed onto the bed behind Kana, and his hands immediately dipped below Kana's waistband, gripping Kana exactly right and stroking until Kana was panting for breath. His other hand shoved Kana's pajamas down to his knees, and then slick fingers pushed inside. Kana was tighter than usual—too many nights of sleeping off magical exhaustion—but Sora was gentle and thorough, hitting just the right spot over and over as he slowly added fingers and kept stroking Kana from the front.

Kana tried to keep his eyes open so he could watch what Mika and Ember were doing, but every time Sora got him just right, Kana's eyelids fluttered closed. He vaguely felt Sora turning him around, but did notice when breathing suddenly got harder thanks to Sora's tongue in his mouth. And then Ember's familiar heat pressed against his entrance, and slowly pushed inside. They rocked together as Sora helped Kana turn his body to drop to all fours, and then Sora's length pressed against Kana's mouth, sliding past his lips to stroke his tongue, and all Kana could do was ride on the overwhelming sensations.

Ember's fingers were rough in just the right way as he stroked Kana along with every thrust, but he knew better than to bring Kana off with him. Ember's moan as he came was loud in Kana's ear, and just the sound almost set Kana off too. Ember pulled out a moment later, but when he moved away, Mika filled his space, quickly thrusting inside and pounding into Kana's now loose hole. Sora let out a yowling moan a moment later, as he spilled down Kana's throat, Kana swallowing as Mika slowed to give Kana a chance to catch his breath. When Kana was ready, Mika slid his hands underneath Kana's chest and pulled him up so his back was pressed to Mika's chest. He resumed thrusting, and Ember and Sora each took a side of Kana's now-revealed length and started licking, and only seconds later it was Kana's turn to moan and come. After a few more thrusts, Mika let out his own yowl.

The four of them collapsed on the bed in a tangle of limbs, panting for breath. Ember managed to get his arms around Kana, although Kana was pretty sure Mika's arm was caught between them. Sora was draped over them all, purring softly.

Kana relaxed into their embrace, enjoying the fading aftershocks and the comfort of warm arms holding him close. Ember's soothing breath tickled Kana's ear, Mika's warmth surrounded them, and Sora's body covered them like a gentle blanket. Kana could lay like this forever.

Ember let out a soft growl full of disappointment just seconds before someone knocked loudly on the door, and the peace was immediately shattered. Kana sighed, but untangled his limbs from them all, freeing Ember to get up, locate his pajamas—which had somehow landed across the room—and answer the door.

"Hey, Alpha," Marc said, apparently unperturbed by the fact that he had woken Ember in the middle of the night.

"Why are you awake, Marc?" Ember asked with a heavy sigh full of resignation.

Marc was...Kana couldn't think of a better way to describe him other than eccentric. He was twelve years old, his best friend was the extremely powerful and very old vampire Ember had allowed to live with the wolves, and he had issues with listening to directions or common sense.

"I was playing with Shannon," Marc replied, his voice completely unconcerned that his alpha sounded disapproving. "But then I saw all sorts of headlights going down the street and turning in at the hunter compound. I thought you might want to give them a call and ask what's up."

"Thank you for letting me know," Ember replied simply.

Kana wanted to know just what sort of game Marc was playing with Shannon—and just where they were playing—that had allowed him to see that, and Kana was sure Ember would have words with Shannon about that later, but Ember knew better than to ask Marc.

"Now, go to bed. You still have to go to school in the morning."

"Aww," Marc began, but then Ember must have given him a look because he stopped whining and instead said, "Yes, Alpha," before leaving.

Ember shut the door and walked back to the bed. Rather than climb under the covers, he sat so the pillows were behind him. His legs pressed up against the tangle that was still Kana, Sora, and Mika though. He grabbed his phone off the side table—the light as the screen lit up in the dark room making Kana squint—tapped it for a few moments, and then the sound of a phone ringing through his speakerphone filled the room.

"You keeping tabs on us?" Ary said in lieu of hello, his voice only half joking. "I figured we had at least a few more minutes before someone on your end noticed."

Ember laughed. "Lucky coincidence. A wolf out of bed, wandering around where he shouldn't be."

Ary snickered too. "That sounds like Marc. One day you're going to have to put a leash on that kid."

"I'm not sure even that would work," Ember replied. "Anyway, what's going on?"

"A warlock is serious business," Ary said with a heavy sigh. "I reported the incident and our concerns up my chain of command, and they mobilized the troops. So far, we've gotten three strike forces and one surveillance team, all of whom I have to figure out how to bed down tonight. First thing in the morning I'm going to brief them about you and the witches being our neighbors and allies, and then I'm going to want to brief them about everything we know so far about the warlock."

"You might want to mention Shannon to them as well, just in case," Ember added when Ary paused. "The last thing we need is having a hunter accidentally start a conflict with him."

"Oh, man. We so don't want that to happen." Ary let out a breath. "Okay, I'll mention you, the witches, and that crazy vampire who is hanging around for some unknown reason, but that probably has something to do with a child alpha-level wolf. I can already tell that's going to go over well." He groaned. "Right. I was going to ask you to come over around eleven for the warlock bit, but I have a feeling we might not get to that part on our end until later instead. Why don't you come over around one, and I'll ring the witches first thing in the morning to ask them too. Oh, is Kana around?" he added suddenly.

"I'm here," Kana called.

"Great. Kana, you've got the week off work, same as we'd do for anyone who tangled with an imp. We want you to recover and be healthy for the next battle. No more magic, okay?"

Kana nodded, then remembered Ary couldn't see him and called, "Agreed. I'm tapped out right now anyway."

"That's what I thought. First fighting Diana and then fighting that imp, I'm surprised you're awake right now, to be honest. You're welcome to come over with Ember tomorrow if you're up to it, but no magic."

"I'll be there," Kana replied. He had already been quite literally up for other activity; there was no reason why he wouldn't be able to go over to the hunter's compound for a meeting as long as he didn't have to do any magic.

"Good. I have to get back to figuring out sleeping arrangements. Have a good rest of your night, and I'll see you tomorrow."

"See you," Ember replied before hitting the button to end the call. The room went dark again, but Kana could still see Ember putting the phone back on his side table. The covers shifted as Ember lifted them, and Kana welcomed his warmth as he slid back into the tangle that was Kana, Mika, and Sora.

The afterglow might be gone, but the comfort of having Ember there was more than enough for Kana. He yawned, settled his head against Ember's arm, and happily fell back asleep.

Chapter Six

THE HUNTERS HAD turned their house's massive formal dining room into a meeting room. A conference table filled the center of the room, and Diana immediately took one of the few empty chairs around it when she walked in. More chairs were placed along the wall, but those were already filled, so Kana stood, holding up a patch of wall instead. Ember could have taken a chair at the table but had chosen to stay back with Kana.

All three were getting a lot of side-eye. Diana appeared to be blithely ignoring them, but the hair on the back of Kana's neck was standing up. He could call on his magic to defend himself if it came to that, but it would hurt. Even a full night's sleep on top of the two days he had already gotten hasn't been enough to heal. Just talking to Mika, who was draped in his small cat form across Kana's shoulders, and Sora, who had wandered off somewhere once they had entered the building, was still unpleasant. His magic channels felt bruised, but they would heal as long as Kana didn't use any magic for at least the rest of the week.

Ary and his boss, Stan, finally walked into the room, a pair of hunters Kana didn't recognize trailing behind. Johanna walked in just behind them, but while the hunters went to find seats at the table, she joined Kana along the wall.

"You should be so glad you didn't have to come to the first meeting," she muttered under her breath to Kana. "I had no idea we had so many hunters with sticks up their butts until they started arguing."

"Let me guess," Ember replied, his own voice soft. "They hunt wolves; they don't work with them."

Johanna snorted. "And witches. Can't forget all those evil witches we've hunted down, and now you're saying you've hired one to work in our research and development sector? Ary left out the rest of your history, of course," she added.

Kana let out a relieved breath, glad the hunters who didn't know him well weren't about to attack him because of his admittedly worrying parentage.

"Which brings us to this meeting. We've told them we're working with you, they bitched about it, we held firm, and now we're going to lay out a plan that includes your participation." Johanna sighed. "I'm expecting more fireworks."

"Thanks for the warning," Ember replied.

Stan knocked his fist on the table, then waited for the noise to die down. "Thank you for coming today," he said with a glance at Diana and then Ember. "I said this earlier, but I want to reiterate it for our partners: warlocks are not good news. To obtain power, they have to summon creatures whom they then enslave. Even the nicest person eventually becomes twisted. I've had a couple of historians combing our archives for the last few days to gather all the information we have about warlocks.

There are plenty of documented instances where hunters have worked together with the local magical population, werewolves and witches included," he added pointedly, "but not one report of a good warlock. In fact, our historians only identified three types of warlocks: those who don't use their power to summon anything and live a magic-free life, those who have summoned creatures and are using their magic for evil purposes, and those who are dead.

"We know the imp was using black arts to influence and control people around it based on what happened at the news agency and on what happened here."

"You said someone here was able to contain it until you arrived with the holy water," a woman standing along the wall on the other side of the room called. "Were they able to find out why an imp dared come into a hunter's compound in the first place?"

Ary turned in his chair to face Kana. "Kana?" he asked.

Kana let out a breath to try to still his nerves. He had never spoken in front of a crowd like this before, and jittery butterflies filled his stomach, but Ember standing next to him and Mika on his shoulders gave Kana enough confidence.

"The imp wasn't capable of speech," he said loud enough for the entire room to hear him. "Instead, it was putting hooks of power into people to force them to do its bidding. The woman who came here with the imp was completely under its control, and she was doing everything she could to convince me to allow the news station to come here to conduct an interview. The impression I got was she wasn't willing to take no for an answer."

"Why the heck would an imp want a news station to come here?" someone asked.

"Wrong question," one of the visiting hunters, sitting next to Ary at the table, said. "It sounds to me like the imp needed an excuse to come here, and I'd bet they wanted to use the chaos from having the news crew here to go poke around unsupervised."

"To do what?" the other visiting hunter at the table asked.

Ary shrugged. "Good question. Put poison in the food in the kitchen, steal a weapon from the armory, or put those controlling hooks Kana mentioned into every single hunter in the area? The options are limitless, and we have no real way of knowing."

"The imp didn't say anything else?" Stan asked Kana.

Kana shook his head. "I think it realized I wasn't going to give in and let the news station come, so it sent a hook my way. I had to defend myself, and once I locked the imp in a circle, I broke its connection to everyone. It couldn't speak any longer."

"Out of curiosity," the first hunter said, "why were you the one conducting that interview?"

"He used to work for that news station," Johanna cut in. "Since he's familiar with how they operate, I asked him to be the one to rebuff them. Turned out to be a good decision for a different reason. I'm not sure I would have noticed the imp sending a hook my way."

"Then how do we defend against that?" someone else asked, her voice sharp with worry.

"Holy water, like we always do against demonic creatures," Ary replied as he took back control of the meeting. "We will be issuing protective amulets to everyone who steps foot outside this building, and everyone who comes in will have to dip their hand in a bowl of holy water. The shipment will be here this afternoon, so starting tonight we will follow that policy for the foreseeable future. You might not have noticed, but everyone was sprinkled with a drop of it as they walked into the building."

Kana hadn't noticed, but he had been distracted by the glares and general mistrust of all the people he didn't recognize.

"We are protected," Ary said, "however we must find and neutralize the warlock as quickly as possible. Here's the plan Stan and I have come up with. Charlie"—he turned to the first visiting hunter at the table—"I want you to split your surveillance team in half, so we have two teams. I want you to fill in the missing members with some werewolves and at least one witch. Alpha Maxwell and Mother Diana have graciously offered some of their people for that purpose. I want one team canvassing this neighborhood—if the hunter's association was a target for the imp, it's possible the warlock might try again. That team's job is to locate that potential threat. The second team will deploy in the city and suburbs, to look for the warlock.

"Marge," Ary continued quickly before Charlie could voice whatever his furious expression meant. The second hunter at the table turned her head from Charlie to Ary, a resigned expression on her face. "I don't want you to split up your strike teams, but I do want you to find a way to incorporate some wolves and a witch. I have worked with Kana and Alpha Maxwell before in just such a capacity, and I can tell you they were invaluable. I would like one of your teams to remain here on standby, while the other provides support to our surveillance team in the city."

Marge's resigned expression didn't change, but she did nod.

"But..." Charlie spluttered.

"Kana, Diana, and Alpha Maxwell will remain here to help with coordination and local defenses," Stan cut in quickly. "If they ask you for something, feel free to run it by me or Ary, but I promise you they are asking for a good reason, and I trust them."

General grumbling broke out in the room, but no one said anything distinct enough for Kana to make out.

"You're sure about them?" Charlie asked, not bothering to keep his voice quiet.

Stan frowned, at Charlie and at the question, Kana assumed. "To be perfectly honest, it doesn't matter if I'm sure. Kana alone is powerful enough to defeat all of us. He's the one who put a spell on salt, if any of you bothered to read the report Ary released."

Diana's eyes narrowed as she glanced at Kana, and Kana hoped Stan hadn't just opened another can of worms for him.

"If you've been paying attention to the Salem coven, you'll already know who Mother Diana is, and trust me when I say tangling with Alpha Maxwell would not go well for you. Oh, and just as a reminder in case any of you weren't listening before, an ancient vampire has chosen to throw his weight behind Alpha Maxwell. If you see him while patrolling at night, be very polite, and let him go about his business. He will likely have a werewolf child with him. Leave the kid alone too. Any other pertinent questions?"

Stan scanned the room, looking at as many people as he could as if he was able to gauge their willingness to do as he had ordered with just a glance. When no one spoke up, he nodded to them.

"Dismissed."

Kana and Ember waited with Johanna for the space to clear, which didn't take long. Johanna clapped Kana on the shoulder as she turned to leave.

"I'll see you next week. Try to stay out of trouble until then."

"Thanks," Kana replied and waved as she headed back to work.

"Alpha," Charlie said as he and Marge walked over. "Mother Diana," he added quickly when Diana joined them. "I wanted to ask you about how your people will be integrated with mine."

"And mine," Marge said.

Ember nodded. "Of course. Kana, this may take a while. Do you mind waiting?"

Kana wanted to pop downstairs to see what his coworkers were up to, but he knew that was a bad idea. He would get pulled into work, which he wasn't supposed to do until after his magic had recovered.

"I'll wait out front; get some fresh air," he said instead. "Come find me when you're done."

Ember gave Kana one of his beautiful half grins before putting on a more serious face as he turned back to the hunters. Kana headed out, walking through the halls until he reached the front door. Hunters were everywhere. The ones who knew Kana said hello, but there were far more who didn't know him. Kana received cold and suspicious looks from all of them. He was thankful to step outside into the sunlight, where he could get out of the way of the hustle and bustle.

The air was warm with summer heat, but Kana liked it. He tilted his head back to the sky and closed his eyes, breathing in the air and letting the sun bathe his skin.

"How the heck did you convince the hunters here to hire you?" someone said rudely as they approached Kana.

Kana let out a breath, his moment of happiness gone, and tilted his head back down to look at the man standing in front of him, hands on his hips and a scowl on his face.

"You'll have to ask Johanna and Ary that," Kana replied, trying to keep his voice even and unassuming so he didn't antagonize the hunter.

The hunter spat on the ground to his right. "They said you're some sort of magical heavyweight, but you look like a scrawny kid to me. I say no way you held off an imp on your own."

Kana should have known this was coming, and unfortunately, he wasn't able to prove his abilities at the moment. Somehow the number of hunters in the front yard seemed to have doubled over the last few minutes, and Kana didn't recognize any faces.

"Ask me again next week, when I'm off leave," Kana replied, hoping that would work.

"What, and give you time to prepare some secret spell that will trick me into thinking you have a bit of power? I don't think so."

Mika let out a yowl, showing off his fangs, and then turned so he could stare the hunter down.

"You think your trained rat is going to change my mind? I bet your real familiar is a cockroach."

Several snickers sounded nearby. Kana didn't know how to end this, but if Mika was stepping in, then he had told Sora, and Sora would go get help.

As if summoned, Sora came dashing out the door. He planted himself at Kana's feet and let out his own yowl.

"Two?" someone whispered off to Kana's right. "That can't be possible."

Ary strode into view next. "I'm sure Kana would be happy to provide you with a training session," he said as he reached the front lawn. "But it will have to wait until next week when Kana returns to work."

"A training session against a witch would be good for us," Marge added as she, Charlie, Ember, and Diana joined Ary. "Since we're apparently lacking discipline. You lot are lucky Kana's friendly. Try this with the vampire Stan mentioned, and you'll go back home in a body bag." She glared at the assembled hunters. "I'm sure you all have somewhere else you're supposed to be right now."

Hunters vanished even faster than they had appeared, scuttling off to wherever they were actually supposed to be at the moment. The hunter who had confronted Kana glared at him one more time before slinking off as well.

Ary shook his head in disappointment but turned to Ember and Diana a moment later. "Sorry about that. Anyway, shift change is at six today, so if you could have your people here by four? That will give us enough time to make introductions and give them a debriefing. I'll get the rest of the week's schedule to you by this evening as well."

"Will do," Ember replied.

Diana nodded in agreement before turning and walking down the drive.

"Ready to go?" Ember asked Kana as Ary, Charlie, and Marge headed back into the house.

"Yeah. If I stay here, those hunters may come back. Who do you have in mind for the surveillance and strike teams?" They followed Diana down the drive, but at the gate she walked across the street while Kana and Ember turned right to head to the werewolf house.

"I'm going to assign each of my betas to a team and let them choose who they think would fit best. Although, I'm going to work with the surveillance team that stays nearby so I can be on hand for any pack issues, and I'm going to ask Shannon if he's interested in taking at least one shift at night." They reached the gate, which slid open when they approached and then shut immediately after they were inside. "I also have to invest in some holy water, apparently, and I need to ask Shannon if that will bother him."

"Let me know if there's anything I can do to help," Kana said.

Ember grinned his usual grin at Kana. "Since I'm going to be away from the pack house more than usual as I set things up this week, and since you're not working, it would be helpful if you could hang out in the public areas so anyone with any issues can come ask you," he said.

Kana could do that. "I'm going to get a cup of tea in the mess hall, then," he said. "I'll see you tonight at some point?" They walked inside the front doors and stopped in the foyer.

"I'll make sure of that, even if it probably won't be as fun as last night." Ember's grin took on an edge to it that made Kana wish they could sneak off for a few minutes for some privacy, but now definitely wasn't the time. Unfortunately.

Kana took control of himself so he didn't do anything untoward in public. "See you then."

They kissed, a quick peck on the lips that was far less than Kana would have wanted, but was entirely appropriate for being out in public. Then Ember turned right to head deeper into the house to go find his betas, and Kana went left to get himself a cup of tea before going to be the alpha's mate for a few hours.

Chapter Seven

"UGH," MARC GROANED as he collapsed into the seat next to Kana. He slumped and rested his forehead against the table.

"Long day?" Kana asked. A glance at the clock showed it was quarter to five, so Marc had just gotten back from school.

Over the last few days of Kana spending most of his time in the mess hall, one of the public sitting rooms, or walking around the grounds, a number of wolves had gotten up the courage to come speak with him about things they felt were too minor to mention to Ember. Kana had handled more marriage disputes, disagreements, and awkward questions than he could count, but somehow Marc coming to find Kana after school every day never got boring.

"We had to do show and tell today," Marc said into the table, his voice muffled slightly. "When it was my turn, the kids started chanting 'show your tail' instead of 'show and tell.'"

"Didn't your teacher stop them?" Kana asked, appalled.

Marc laughed, but he sounded like his choices were either laugh or cry. "She tried, but it's a class of thirty kids and she couldn't do much. I finally growled and told them to shut up."

Oh dear. Kana could guess where this was going, if Marc had used his alpha-level powers to force the kids to behave.

"One of the kids peed herself. Two fainted and one ran out of the room screaming. I heard a whole bunch of them didn't speak at all for the rest of the day, not that I really know if that happened since as soon as the teacher stopped shaking she sent me to the principal's office, where I spent the rest of the day being stared at by the secretaries."

"The principal never spoke to you?" Kana asked.

"Hah." Marc let out another terrible laugh. "Only after he called my dad about ten times, and my dad didn't pick up."

Despite knowing Marc really well, Kana had never actually met Marc's parents. They had to exist, and they had to have some sort of job with the wolves who lived and worked in the pack house, but they were absentee parents as far as Kana could tell. Certainly, Ember and Shannon spent more time parenting Marc, who didn't sound the least bit surprised that his dad hadn't answered the phone.

"The principal asked me for a better number, so I gave him Shannon's cell." Marc glanced at Kana and his grin was full of mischief. "Of course, no one answered there either." Shannon was not going to be pleased to find a dozen messages from Marc's school on his phone when he woke, but Shannon forgave Marc just about everything so Kana didn't think it would be a problem. "By the time the principal gave up with that number, it was time to go home, and he had to put me on the bus. I had to sit in the spot right behind the bus driver, while the kids behind me made fun of me the whole way. Oh, and I have to give my dad this." He rummaged in the bag at his feet for a few moments before he handed

Kana a piece of paper.

"Notice of Suspension," Kana read from the header. He didn't bother with the rest.

"It wasn't even my fault," Marc continued, his voice choked as he fought back tears.

"No, it wasn't," Kana answered. He put his arm around Marc's shoulders for a hug and Marc immediately turned and buried his face in Kana's shoulder.

I'll go find Ember, Sora said. Kana felt only the slightest twinge from the mental contact, but his magic channels had been steadily healing. Another day or two and Kana would never know he had blasted them so badly. When he returned to work on Monday, he would definitely be back at full power.

He let Marc cry while Sora hunted Ember down. Ember was supposed to be at the pack house today, rather than working with the hunters. As long as he wasn't busy with something important, he would come when Sora called.

Thankfully, Ember arrived only a few minutes later, just as Marc was reaching the hiccupping stage. He sat on Marc's other side and picked up the paper Kana had left there.

"What happened?" Ember asked, his voice soft.

"He was being bullied in class and used a touch too much power to ask them to stop," Kana explained.

"And none of the other kids were reprimanded?" Ember asked with an angry growl.

"One of them peed their pants," Marc replied. He pulled away from Kana with a sniffle and rubbed the back of his hand under his nose.

Ember grinned at Marc. "I never had anyone do that. Nice job!"

Kana shot Ember a look, unsure that he ought to be encouraging

Marc. However, Marc only let out a watery laugh and settled back into his own chair.

"What do I do about school?" Marc asked.

Ember frowned down at Marc's suspension paperwork. "I think I'm going to have a discussion with the pack lawyer before I make a decision, but I do think it's time for that parent/teacher conference I've been putting off."

"Can Shannon go with you?" Marc asked. "He said he'd love to have a 'word with your instructor.'" He lowered his voice and used an Irish accent to mimic Shannon's.

"We'll see," Ember replied. "For now, continue your nighttime studies with Shannon, and I'll let you both know what the lawyer recommends."

Marc made a face, no doubt about the fact that he had to continue school even if it was with Shannon, but obediently nodded.

"Go have a snack," Ember added.

Marc eagerly jumped to his feet. "Thanks, Alpha. Thanks, Kana," he said before rushing off to the serving area of the dining hall.

Ember sighed once Marc was out of earshot. "That kid's going to be something when he grows up. If he grows up," he added with a growl. "I keep finding him wandering around the neighborhood at two in the morning, and one day something not as nice as me will be the one doing the finding. He's powerful, but he's still a kid."

"But he has Shannon and, right now, a dozen hunters prowling around," Kana said, wishing he could sound more certain of what he was saying. Marc was a good kid who always meant well, but he was far too curious and tended to poke his nose in places it didn't belong.

"And if he's not going to school during the day, I'm putting him in a special class with Emily. She can teach him control and how to fight."

Ember shook his head again, but then he turned to look at Kana. He slid over to take Marc's abandoned chair and reached out to caress Kana's cheek with the tips of his fingers. "How are you doing? I'm on the night shift again, so this is probably the last time I'll get to see you until morning."

Ember took the night shift because it was the most difficult one. He was being a good alpha, and Kana loved that about him, but it was lonely at night without him. Luckily Kana had Mika and Sora to keep him company, but it wasn't the same, and half the time one of Kana's familiars went out with Ember anyway so their shared bed was even colder.

"I know," Ember said, his voice soft as he apparently read Kana's disquiet off Kana's face. "Hopefully we'll figure out this warlock issue soon, and life can return to normal. I miss you."

"I miss you too. Have the hunters found anything?"

"Not a thing," Ember replied with a heavy sigh. "In fact, the only evidence a warlock was ever around at any point was the imp. If we don't find some sort of evidence soon, the extra teams are going to stand down and return home, which I would guess is the warlock's plan. Our numbers right now are probably too much for him, so he's hiding until then."

"And probably laughing as we run around like chickens with our heads cut off trying to find him," Kana said, his voice dry with disgust. "I'm hoping I'll be able to help with the magic side of things on Monday."

Ember nodded and grinned at Kana. "I forgot to tell you, Johanna grabbed me yesterday when I went over for my shift to ask me how you were doing. I know she was probably genuinely worried about you, but I think they're also missing having your power at their disposal."

That was both flattering and worrying. Kana liked what he did for the hunters' association, and he particularly liked using his magic and learning new magical techniques, but there had to be a line between him doing a job and the hunters taking advantage of him. Johanna was good about it, but Kana could see that becoming a problem in the future. He could also understand why Diana and other witches hadn't worked together with the hunters before this.

Kana wanted to help, with this imp issue and to combat other magical creatures and people who were harming humans. He supported what the hunters did to protect people, and the best way he could provide support was to use his magic on their behalf—presuming they didn't take advantage of him because of that, of course.

"As long as they understand my power is only at their disposal for as long as I continue to work for them," Kana replied, his voice firm. "I'm not their trained puppet, but at the same time, I enjoy what I do for them."

Ember shrugged. "If it becomes a problem and you need to quit, you and I can move to the rural pack house for a while. Although, not to put any pressure on you, but I'm hoping when you're healed and back at work, you'll be able to come up with something that will help."

Kana laughed. "I'm hoping that too. I'll definitely be back to work on Monday, and then we'll see."

Kana relaxed into the arm Ember slid over his shoulders, cuddling as close as the mess hall chairs allowed without actually climbing into Ember's lap. They stayed like that for a few stolen moments, Kana enjoying the warmth and strength of Ember's body as their scents mingled in a form of marking that told every werewolf Kana encountered that he was paired with Ember.

Quite a few minutes passed like that before Ember stirred and looked over at the door. George stood there, looking apologetic, but when he saw he had Ember's attention, he waved.

"Back to work," Ember said with a sigh. "I'll try to come say goodnight before I head over to the hunters for my shift."

Kana nodded and smiled at Ember. "I'm sure as soon as you're gone someone will approach me to ask about some problem. I'll be too busy to notice you're gone," he finished with a cheeky grin.

Ember laughed as he pulled away and stood up. "Don't pretend you're not enjoying it." He bent down and Kana arched his neck upward, and their lips met in a brief peck.

Then Ember was gone, striding across the room to meet up with George before both of them headed deeper into the pack house. Kana sighed and returned to his cooling tea.

Soon, Kana reminded himself. If he used his magic now, he would only reinjure his magic channels. No matter how much he wanted to follow after Ember and help to find the warlock, he had to be fully healed or he would continue to be a liability. Still, he would be healed on Monday and would hit the ground running, which was at least some consolation. Until then, he would support Ember in other ways, including by helping the young woman shyly approaching him, her hands clasped in front of her as if Kana was the answer to her prayer.

Kana smiled and waved her over, happy to help, though he would be even happier on Monday.

Chapter Eight

"KANA, YOU'RE HERE!" Johanna called the second Kana stepped through the front doors of the hunter building.

Ember had escorted Kana as far as the front gates, and Kana had walked up the driveway with only Mika and Sora for company. Johanna was holding a clipboard, and it looked like she had simply been passing through rather than waiting for him, but she stopped next to a bowl on a stand to wait for Kana to reach her.

"You just have to touch the water," Johanna added.

Kana reached out and trailed his fingers in the water in the bowl. Mika grumbled, but reached down from where he was lying across Kana's shoulders to dip in a paw.

Do I have to? Sora whined, but when Kana bent and picked him up, Sora obediently dipped his own paw in the water.

"Looks like you're demon-free," Johanna said with a smile. "I'm headed to Stan's new office to drop off some paperwork. I'll see you downstairs?"

"Sounds good. I'm sure I have a lot to catch up on," Kana replied with his own smile.

Johanna headed off. Sora apparently didn't want to walk on a wet paw and curled up in Kana's bent elbow, with Mika still lying across Kana's shoulders, as Kana went in the other direction to go to the stairs that led down to his office.

"Wait a minute!"

Kana stopped walking and turned his head to see who had yelled. The hunter who had confronted Kana on the lawn last week was standing near the bowl, scowling at Kana.

"You've proven you're not the warlock, since you could touch the holy water, but I still say you're a fraud!"

"Erich!" Johanna snapped, but Ary walked up behind her and placed his hand on her shoulder.

"Kana, Erich is concerned you're a fraud," Ary said, his glance at Kana pointed.

"I don't care what Erich thinks," Kana replied, his voice easy as if the tense atmosphere in the entry hall wasn't affecting him at all. Hunters were trickling in from all directions, as if they had been called to the room.

Kana threw open his magic channels and power poured into him as smooth and easy as usual. No hint of bruising remained. He didn't need anything big to stop Erich, just something flashy enough to show Erich he was wrong.

"I'll prove it right now!" Erich snarled out. He stomped toward Kana, both hands held out as if he was going to grab Kana around the neck and squeeze.

Kana drew a small circle and star, added in the runes for stop and hold, and wrapped the circle around Erich's left ankle just as he lifted his right foot to take another step forward. He fell, slamming into the ground face-first with a crunch that said his nose hadn't enjoyed the experience. Kana drew another circle with his magic, this time on Erich's back. He added the runes for weight, but carefully added the embellishments to the rune that would limit it so Erich couldn't get up but wouldn't be crushed.

Erich got his hands underneath his body and pushed. His arm muscles strained, and he groaned, but he didn't move even a centimeter off the ground.

"Anyone else?" Kana asked. The two circles hadn't tired him at all, so he was ready if anyone tried to back up Erich. No one else moved. The hunters who knew Kana looked unsurprised, and the newcomers were apparently too busy staring at Kana in shock. Had they never seen a witch cast a circle without chalk before?

"Let me up, damn you!" Erich snarled.

"Not until you promise to stop threatening me," Kana retorted. Mika meowed pointedly as if to underscore Kana's words.

Erich huffed for a moment, and his arm muscles bulged as he tried and failed to free himself again. "Fine, I promise! Now let me up!"

Kana waved his hand for showmanship purposes and the circles vanished. Erich stumbled to his feet, one hand pressed to his bloody nose. He glared at Kana but didn't appear to have any interest in trying to attack him again.

"What are you?" Erich asked, his voice muffled by the blood and the hand squeezing his nose. "You might be a witch, but that's not all you are."

"Lucina," a woman gasped.

Erich jerked in place in surprise, and Johanna let out a soft gasp.

She wasn't alone, as other people also made noises of surprise and disbelief. Kana—and about two thirds of the room—looked over at the woman and saw one of the witches from Diana's coven.

The woman blushed bright red, squeaked, then turned and fled deeper into the hunter's house.

Who or what is Lucina? Kana asked. The name did sound vaguely familiar, as if someone had mentioned it to him sometime recently, but Kana couldn't remember when.

No idea, Mika replied with a mental shrug.

"All right," Ary called. "Hunters don't hunt by spectating. I'm sure there's something more productive all of you could be doing right now."

There were some grumbles, but the room did begin to empty. Johanna thrust her clipboard into Ary's hands before hurrying over to Kana's side. Kana waited for her, and then they walked into a side hall together, heading toward their office.

"What's Lucina?" Kana asked when they reached a deserted hallway not too far from their destination.

Johanna stopped walking and turned to face Kana. "It's one of the power designations in the Salem coven. You've met Mother Diana. Crone Hecate remained in Salem to run the coven, but as far as we know, that coven hasn't identified a person as Maiden Lucina since the last one passed nearly twenty-five years ago. The fourth designation in that coven is Horned Lord, which is a title they begrudgingly give to a male with some power."

Diana had mentioned multiple times in Kana's hearing that he wasn't a horned lord. But Kana had no idea what it meant that one of her coven had called him Lucina instead.

"I'm not from that coven," Kana replied when Johanna's silence seemed to indicate she wanted a response. "My coven had circles of power with the inner circle comprised of the most powerful witches. Each successive circle diminished in power from there. As a male, I wasn't allowed to be part of any circle, so I could never have filled a power role for them like the Salem coven's Maiden Lucina."

Johanna nodded. "I don't know how much you know about the animosity between covens, but they all generally follow their own version of witchcraft. The circles and runes are the same, but each coven adheres different meaning to why you have the ability to use magic and why one witch's magic might be stronger than another's. Your previous coven—the Seattle coven—believes strong witches birth strong witches, so the inner circle is prized as they are the ones who will ensure the future of the coven. The Salem coven follows the rule of Three—with the occasional fourth, the Horned Lord. They believe the Goddess bestows power to her witches regardless of the power of their parents, and She is the one who chooses who rules their coven by bestowing certain attributes to the Three. The Salem coven has never gone decades without actually having three witches in power. That witch calling you Lucina means she thinks you're their absent leader."

"I don't follow their religion, so I can't be one of their three!" Kana gasped, appalled. He didn't have any interest in being a coven leader, and quite frankly he was worried he was being mistitled.

"As long as Mother Diana doesn't confirm it, you're just Kana, mate to Alpha Maxwell, and employee of the Albany Hunter's Coalition. Even if she does confirm it, they won't really have a choice if you refuse to take on the mantle. You're not one of their coven, like you said."

Which means we need to make sure Diana doesn't do something squirrelly to make us one of her coven, Sora added.

We'll be careful, Kana replied in complete agreement with Sora. He could definitely see Diana trying something like that, but now he was forewarned and would hopefully catch her at the trick.

"Anyway, let's focus on why you're actually here," Johanna continued. "You have to come see the two things we've been working on." She led the way down the hall and held the workroom door open for Kana before following him inside.

The room erupted with: "Kana!", "Hey, man!", and "How're you feeling?" when he stepped inside.

Kana grinned and waved at the entirety of the local research department, all of whom had been his coworkers since he started. "I'm all healed. How are you?"

"Check out our protection amulets," Niale called.

Kana obediently went over to that work station, where he saw what appeared to be glass beads in a teardrop shape with blue water inside that glowed even in the bright light of the workroom.

"The holy water inside is just holy water, but we imbued the glass with all sorts of fun things," Niale continued. "First, we made it so the holy water doesn't know there's glass between it and your skin, so if you're infected with demon magic it will burn you and help drive it out." Niale and Nancy, his partner, were both druids. Usually they imbued magic into trees and plants, so using glass must have been a fun experiment for them. Kana was sad he had missed it. "We also spelled the glass to turn opaque as a warning if demon magic is being used near you. We're still working out the spells to make the holy water repel that demonic force before it has a chance to touch you, but at the very least, it functions the same as having that bowl of water out front. We're going to mass produce them so everyone working this threat has one."

Niale held one of the teardrops out for Kana to take. He felt a slight warmth from the magic, but otherwise the teardrop felt like a simple glass ornament. There was a loop at the top to fit a chain through.

As if Kana's thought had conjured it, Nancy held out a chain. "This one's in thanks for stopping that imp," she said. "I don't think any of us were prepared for that. It could have ravaged through us."

"Ary did a pretty good job," Kana said in disagreement, but he took the simple silver link chain from Nancy and slid it through the loop. He hooked the clasp behind his neck and the teardrop landed just below his collarbone, in the vee of the unhooked top button of his collared shirt.

"Only because you gave him enough warning to get some holy water," Johanna cut in. "What do you think of the charm?"

Kana pressed his palm against it, feeling the slight hum of magic. "I like it. Let me know what you're thinking about for the repelling part, and I'll let you know what happens if I run into another imp."

They all laughed at Kana's joke. "Let's hope that never happens again," Johanna said. "Come see the searching spells we've been doing. This is where we can really use your help." She pulled Kana to another table across the room.

The table was covered in runes, spell circles drawn on crumpled paper, and research books. At least one full incantation—a type of spell used by sorcerers—was half written and lying abandoned amid the rest of the detritus.

"What have you tried?" Kana asked. He picked up some of the circles and runes to study. "This is good stuff," he added after a moment of reading. They had already tried spells to search for demons, demonic magic, and residual demonic energy. "Why didn't any of it work?"

Arnold let out a heavy sigh. "Apparently, we need to activate the spells at the exact same time the warlock is using energy, otherwise our spells can't sense anything. We don't have the magical energy to keep the spells running indefinitely, and we tried your new mobius strip idea, but none of us have the control to spin our magic into the correct shape.

Besides, I read your notes where you said even you can't keep it up that long."

"Not indefinitely," Kana said with a frown at himself. If only he could figure out that last little bit of the spell, but creating a magical battery was still beyond him. The mobius spell was primarily a way to recycle his used magic back into the spell, but as Arnold had said, it was far too taxing to use except in the most dire emergency.

"Which means we can't track the warlock unless we get really, really lucky when we activate one of our spells," Arnold finished.

"We can't track the warlock in real time," Kana mused as he flipped through the spells covering the desk. "What about searching for residual magic? Didn't you say you were looking for that?"

Arnold sighed again, and Johanna and everyone else surrounding Kana shook their heads.

"I think we literally have to be standing where the warlock physically cast the spells to find residual magic," Arnold explained. "We're having trouble creating a magical equivalent to a radar for a broader search."

Sora jumped down from Kana's arms and strolled across the table. *How does a warlock cast spells anyway?* he asked.

Kana had no idea. *I know they steal magic from the demons they enslave,* he replied. *But beyond that?*

Sora walked across the spell circles, hopped over the rune dictionary, and then abruptly stopped at the incantation as if he had noticed something. He read the paper, then pushed it with a paw in Kana's direction.

Read this, he said.

Kana obediently picked it up and read through the lines. One stanza stood out in particular.

For lo the summoned demon cries
Enslaved to magic's price
Freedom lost to cruelty's master
Home stolen when greed calls

Summoned, Kana read again. A warlock had to summon the demons from the demon plane, likely in a similar process to what Kana had done to summon Sora and Mika from the magical one.

Kana dropped the paper back on the table as he spun to head to his own workstation and grab his chalkboard and chalk.

He started drawing rapidly and, aware the rest of the room was staring at him, started explaining. "The spell for summoning familiars is a massive one. It's so powerful even the weakest witches leave a residual impact when they cast it. My previous coven created a separate building from which to cast the spell, and the building was warded from the foundation to the roof to prevent that power from spilling out and affecting the rest of the coven lands. Even I, the much hated and ostracized male witch, was given access to use that building when I wanted to attempt calling a familiar. They didn't expect me to succeed, but even what they believed would be a futile and weak attempt needed to be warded."

Kana had to pause to concentrate as he chalked in the more intricate runes. Johanna and Arnold had moved to read over Kana's shoulder as he drew, and Johanna's soft gasp of realization as he finished the rune to open the path to the magical plane told Kana she was following him.

"I doubt our warlock has access to the same sort of facility, but they had to cast a similar level of spell to open a door into the demon plane to pull the imp across. A spell like that will leave something we can track, and if the warlock uses the same location for all their summonings..."

"We might find the warlock's lair," Johanna finished, her voice breathy with anticipation.

"Exactly. If we can figure out to how track this spell to summon a familiar, we can definitely alter it to track the spell to summon a demon." Kana put the last flourishes on his circle and then placed the chalkboard down so everyone could see it.

"Brilliant," Johana said. She turned to the rest of the room. "Niale, Nicole, your teams keep working on those charms. They're our best defense right now, and I want them to start going out to everyone by tonight. Arnold, pull a couple people to help Kana dig into this new idea. I don't want to put all my eggs in one basket, though, so the rest of you keep working on the other projects. You never know what might work!"

Kana went to get another chalkboard, hoping his idea would at least help, but glad they weren't abandoning everything else. That incantation showed promise too. Still, despite how much Kana wanted to learn how incantation writing worked, he needed to focus on his own project. He settled in with the team Johanna had assigned and got to work.

Chapter Nine

KANA WAS NOSE-DEEP in a rune textbook when a strange buzzing interrupted his concentration. Another second passed before Kana realized the buzzing was accompanied by the familiar tune of his ringtone. He looked up, blinking in confusion at the phone, which was lit up and vibrating on the desk in front of him.

The caller ID read Ember, Kana noticed, so he quickly dropped a bookmark into the textbook, set it aside, and reached out to hit the Accept button on the phone.

"Ember?" Kana asked.

"Hey, Kana. Sorry to bug you at work, but Marc's principal got back to me. He wants to meet at six today. Did you want to join us?"

Kana glanced over at the clock, which read three thirty. That would give him another two hours of work before he had to meet Ember, and he could come back after dinner to work some more. They needed to find the warlock, and Kana had missed helping out long enough while he was healing, but getting Marc's issues fixed was also important.

"Sure. I'll be working late anyway, so it'll be good to get away and focus on something else for an hour," he replied.

"Perfect. See you then."

"Bye," Kana said before hanging up. He returned to his research, but Kana didn't get as engrossed this time. He kept glancing up at the clock, worried he would get buried in work and miss when he needed to leave. He wasn't as productive over the next hours as he hoped, but had made some headway into figuring out if there was a rune for demons like there was for familiars, or whether he would have to somehow create a rune himself by combining a few already existing ones, when the clock finally ticked over to five thirty.

"I have to run to the elementary school for a parent teacher conference," Kana told Johanna as he tidied his notes. "I'll be back by seven."

"I was just about to start sending everyone off in staggered shifts to go find dinner," Johanna replied with an easy smile. "You'll be part of the first shift."

"Thanks," Kana said before walking to the door. The trip down the hallways and back to the foyer was thankfully uninterrupted. Kana was worried another hunter would be lying in wait by the front door to confront him, but only the woman manning the bowl of holy water was in the room as Kana went through and out the front door. By the time he walked all the way down the drive, a car was idling in the street, waiting for him. Ember was driving, a wolf in a suit whom Kana didn't recognize was in the front passenger seat, and someone in very dark clothing was sitting in the back passenger side. Kana pulled the rear driver's side door open and slid in. He was still buckling his seat belt when Ember took off.

"This is Meryl, the pack's lawyer," Ember explained. "I'll let

Shannon explain how the heck he's here."

Kana looked over at the dark-swathed person he was sitting next to and gaped. Shannon—if it was Shannon because Kana couldn't actually see who it was—was wearing a black, wide-brimmed hat. Opaque black fabric hung from the brim of the hat down past Shannon's shoulders, completely concealing his face. The rest of him was covered in thick black clothing so no hint of skin was visible.

This time of the early autumn, the sun was already setting by six, but definitely still visible in the sky. Vampires wouldn't be safe until the sun was fully down, and Kana had thought most of them slept during daylight hours anyway.

"I am able to move around during daylight hours, and I can withstand a brief touch of sun to my body, but it will be a few centuries more before I will be capable of prolonged contact. This costume is made of specially treated fabrics that prevent wind from blowing them and protects the clothes from tearing and exposing my skin. I am able to exist in the sunlight for the amount of time it will take to attend this conference only thanks to this outfit."

That was awesome and Kana really wanted to know what magic was involved with creating the fabric, but he knew better than to ask. Something like that had to be a closely guarded secret within the vampire community, and there was no way Shannon was going to share it with Kana.

"Let's talk strategy," Meryl said. "The principal and the teacher will probably be scared of you, Alpha, and of Shannon. I doubt they'll figure out what Kana is, but the goal is for us to be suing them, not them to be trying to charge us for threats of bodily harm. That means we need to tone down any aggression. Let me do your talking as your lawyer, get them afraid of legal jargon rather than the supernatural creatures in the room. We're more likely to get what we want that way."

"Agreed," Ember said. "If they were afraid of Marc, Shannon and I are going to terrify them. Scared people won't do what we want."

Meryl nodded. "And will claim later in a court that you threatened them to get it, which would be counterproductive. Kana, they won't know what you are, so as long as you appear to be fully human you should be fine. Still, let me do the talking unless they ask you a question directly."

"Makes sense," Kana replied with a nod. "I just want this to be over for Marc."

"Our goal is to get them to agree to remove the suspension from Marc's record," Meryl continued. "That way we can enroll him in the local private school, which I've already vetted as being a much better place for supernatural creatures."

Ember pulled into the parking lot of the school, which was just emptying of cars as the work day came to an end. He found a spot close to the door and shut the car off.

"Ready?" he asked as he unhooked his seat belt.

"Let's do this," Meryl agreed.

They all got out of the car and headed inside, where they followed the signs to the main office.

We'll stay out here, Mika said, as he and Sora took seats outside the door.

Probably a good idea, Kana replied. If Shannon and Ember were too scary, being confronted a witch with two familiars wouldn't help.

A secretary jumped to her feet when they walked inside the office, her eyes wide with fear as she looked at them, but she still waved toward the door to the principal's office.

"He's ready for you now," she said, her voice only shaking a little.

Kana smiled at her, trying to be reassuring but not stopping to chat as they walked past her and into the office.

The principal was an ordinary man, with balding brown hair over brown eyes and a body that was showing its age by increasing its girth. He was sitting comfortably behind his desk in a wide leather chair. A woman and a man were standing behind him. The woman was wearing a suit and carrying a portfolio, so Kana didn't think she was Marc's teacher. She could be a lawyer instead. The man was wearing the school security officer's uniform, which meant the principal thought he'd need protection for this meeting. Was he that afraid of the supernatural? Kana knew there were humans who were, but he had never interacted with one before. How had Marc and the other supernatural children in the school really been treated? Kana knew Marc had been having a hard time, but Kana had only thought it was because of school bullies and an incompetent teacher. What if the principal was encouraging the bullying?

"Let's get this over with," the principal said. He didn't invite them to sit or even pretend at niceties, which only cemented Kana's dislike of him. He pushed a manila folder across the desk, which Meryl picked up.

"What is this?" Meryl asked, one eyebrow lifting in surprise as she opened the folder and read the cover page.

"Marc's behavior report from his teacher as documented by incident," the principal replied. He looked smug as Meryl flipped through the pages, and the lawyer woman behind him had her own slight uptilt to her lips that told Kana she was proud of the document too.

"Then we have a problem," Meryl said as she paused on one of the pages. "On this page the teacher writes, 'Marc slammed a boy—'"

"Named Josh, I believe." Ember interrupted.

"—'into the lockers. Marc growled at Josh and forced Josh to give him his lunch money.' But you see, Marc wasn't actually in school on the date of this event, nor was he attending for the next two written here. There was a family issue at home, and he was absent for two weeks."

Meryl closed the folder and gave the principal a sharp look. The principal's smugness was gone, replaced by a hard, blank face.

"You handed us a folder full of lies. To what end?" Meryl asked. "You must have known how easy it would be to discount this, and now we can accuse you of libel as well as slander. I will bring this document to civil court when we sue the school district for gross misconduct, and I find it hard to believe providing us with evidence of your crimes was your aim here."

While the principal's face was still blank, it looked a little paler.

"You come in here with your attack force and threaten us?" the principal forced out, his voice slightly breathy as if trying to hide his fright. He pointed to Shannon. "You've got a ninja and a monster,"—he moved his finger to point at Ember—"and you think suing the school district will work when I have my two witnesses explain how you threatened me into compliance?"

The room was on the eastern side and the window completely in the shadow of the building. Shannon reached up and pulled the long cloth covering his face away, revealing what at first glance was merely a handsome face. As long as Shannon didn't show his fangs, no one could tell he was a vampire.

"You left six messages on my cell phone," Shannon said, "explaining how Marc was going on a rampage, injuring children and teachers. You demanded I come pick him up at once. Yet, when I did not answer, you did not call the police or the hunters, who are trained to handle such issues. Instead, you sent Marc home on the bus."

Meryl looked at the school security officer who, while gray-haired and starting to show the deep wrinkles of age, still had the strong shoulders and sharp eyes that said he had been a police officer in his previous life. "Would you feel comfortable swearing to anything this man has said in a court of law?" Meryl asked him. "We have pointed out two significant lies, and we have the evidence to prove it. Can you stand in a court of law without perjuring yourself?"

The officer looked at the folder Meryl was still holding for a long moment, then shook his head. "I cannot."

Meryl smiled viciously as she turned to the principal and his lawyer. "There you have it. Either I sue the school district on Marc's behalf and expose all your lies—which will definitely get you fired—or you agree to remove the suspension from Marc's record and provide his full—and completely accurate—school records to us so we can enroll him in a school where his talents will be better understood."

The principal glanced behind him at the lawyer, who grimaced but nodded.

"Fine," he snapped. He reached into the top drawer on his desk and pulled out a key, then spun in his chair to access the bank of filing cabinets behind him. A moment of rummaging later, and he spun back with another manila folder in hand. "Here's his records. The suspension paperwork is in the back. Shred it, and it's like it never happened."

"Where are his digital records?" Meryl asked. She took the file from him.

The principal scoffed. "No point in keeping real records for creatures like that brat. They never last long in real school. I keep their activities documented in this cabinet, and happily get rid of the paperwork when they're gone."

"The only record of Marc being suspended is one piece of paper in this folder?" Meryl tucked both Marc's folder and the fraudulent file the principal had given her into her briefcase.

"That's what I said!" he replied with a roll of his eyes. "Are we done here? Some of us have real things to do right now."

Kana walked with their group as they left the office, Mika and Sora rejoining them. Shannon moved the cloth so it covered his face again, but otherwise they were quiet. Kana gritted his teeth on the angry words that wanted to come out, trying to keep his seething silent as long as they were inside the school. His grimace probably didn't help, but if Ember could remain quiet after hearing Marc be called a monster, Kana could too, even if he wanted to form a spell in that office to force that nasty man to only tell the truth.

Besides, they got what they came for. Marc's record would be clean when Ember submitted the application for him to attend the private school instead. Kana tried to be happy with that, but it was so damned hard after meeting with that slime.

"Are we really just walking away?" Kana bit out the second they walked through the doors and into the parking lot.

"Hah," Meryl laughed. "I promised not to sue the school district, and I won't, but I've already scheduled an Uber to take me to the Albany FBI office. They'll be very interested in prosecuting that bastard federally for hate crimes. New York is a one-party consent state, so I recorded our conversation just now. With that, the fake behavior papers, the copies of the voicemail messages on Shannon's phone, and Marc's testimony, I'm literally handing them an open and shut case. He won't see the outside of a jail cell for ten years to life."

A car pulled up as she finished speaking. Meryl checked the license plate against the app on her phone, then nodded to them before getting in the back. The car pulled away, and Ember, Kana, and Shannon continued to where their car was parked.

The lot was almost empty. Only a few stragglers' cars remained, parked by the back fence where the people who had likely gotten to work late were also working late. Ember's car sat alone in the white-lined lot, and it seemed to shimmer in the light of the setting sun. Which was...odd. Kana stopped walking, and he grabbed Ember's arm to stop him too.

"Don't cars only give off heat waves like that in ninety degree weather in August?" he asked.

Ember squinted at the car, then sniffed the air. "I don't sense anything."

"Nor do I," Shannon added, but he had stopped with them.

The necklace! Sora hissed.

Kana clapped a hand on the teardrop, which was warm from Kana's body heat. It didn't feel any different, but Sora wouldn't have said that for no reason. Kana pulled it out from under his shirt and gasped. The gentle blue color of the infusion inside had turned black, and it glowed as if lit by a blue light.

"Damn," Ember said with a snarl. He yanked out his phone and hit a button for speed dial. "Ary," he snapped out when the call connected. "We're still at the school and the necklace your researchers gave Kana is reacting." He listened for a few seconds before hanging up. "The strike team is on its way. Can anyone sense where the demon magic is coming from?"

"The sun won't fully set for another hour," Shannon said. "My powers are severely curtailed until then. Kana?"

Kana closed his eyes and opened his magic channels wide, pulling power to him and then casting it out in a formless searching spell. The school was clean—Kana half wanted the damned principal to ping as the warlock and had to quell a touch of disappointment—and aside from

Ember's car, the parking lot was as well.

"I wouldn't touch the car until after it gets doused in holy water," Kana murmured, mostly focused on sending his magic out farther.

Nothing on the baseball diamond to the left, and nothing on the soccer fields to the right. Kana couldn't find anything on the school grounds at all. He surged his magic in front of him, into the road and across the street, and immediately felt like he had dipped his fingers into a bowl of oily sludge.

Kana opened his eyes and turned to look at the area his magic had found. Heavily wooded, Kana thought the entire space over there was part of a nature preserve. The spot Kana had identified was literally straight ahead of where they were standing.

"He's in the woods, I think," Kana said.

Ember clenched his jaw for a moment, then relaxed as he let out a breath. "We need to keep him there until the hunters arrive. Why don't we go say hello?"

Chapter Ten

THE WOODS WERE absolutely silent, as if the birds, squirrels, and bugs all knew something bad was in their midst and were hiding. Kana led the way with Ember tight on his heels. In the shade of the trees, Shannon removed the cloth covering his face again. Where Kana and Ember's footsteps crunched on dried leaves and sticks, Shannon seemed to glide over it all. They were just past being visible from the road when Kana rounded a tree and found a man leaning against another tree just ahead.

"Ah, Kana. Nice to see you," the man said with a smile. He was fair-haired and pale skinned—although not as blond or pale as Shannon—and his smile was as greasy as the feel of the magic in the air.

"Do we know each other?" Kana asked, remembering Ember's admonition that they needed to stall until the hunters could arrive to really take care of him.

The man's smile widened. "You don't know me, but I certainly know you, dear Lucina. Allow me to introduce myself. I am Abe, First Warlock. Pleased to make your acquaintance."

Kana doubted his name was actually Abe, and the whole "first warlock" thing was probably bullshit, but it wouldn't hurt to play along while he set up some protections.

"Nice to meet you too, Abe," Kana replied as he pushed his magic channels open to their widest. "How do you know me?" Kana started drawing a containment circle, carefully keeping the flare of magic hidden in the ground underneath Abe's feet. Just one circle wouldn't be enough; Kana thought he would need five total, layered in the air above the base. When he combined them, Kana would get a twenty-five-pointed star. The problem was the other four circles had to be visible and he wasn't ready to play his hand just yet.

Abe let out a little sigh. "Being observant is one of the most important qualities of someone with power, Kana. You really must learn to watch your surroundings. You see I noticed you and your two wonderful familiars years ago and decided I needed to meet with you."

Years ago? How long had Abe been living in the area? Although if he was telling the truth, Kana definitely hadn't noticed him.

"Oh, I'm such a chatterbox. Do forgive me? I'm just so excited I get to finally meet you!"

Ember's hand gently brushed against Kana's back, both to provide the comfort of touch and to encourage Kana to keep Abe talking. The longer Abe talked, the more time the hunters had to get here, and the better chance they had of neutralizing him completely.

"Why did you want to meet me?" Kana asked.

Despite admitting he was chattering, Abe didn't show any signs of stopping. "To meet your familiars, of course. I have summoned dozens of creatures from the other side, trying to build my magic. But not even one came close to the power of your familiars. I wanted to ask you to give them to me. So, I convinced the vampires it was time to return, and sent a little nudge to your TV station to get you sent there. The vampires were going to capture you for me in exchange for a few demons to snack on. Octavius became powerful enough to catch you, but then your damned werewolves had to intervene. Next, I found a witch with her pet enslaved hunter. She was desperate to find you and promised to hand over your familiars in exchange. I should have realized like follows like and including that one hunter meant more would show up. This time, I didn't want any mistakes. No intermediaries who could mess things up. So here I am, Kana, and now you will give me your familiars."

Abe held out his hands, as if Kana would immediately scoop up Mika and Sora and drop them into Abe's palms.

"You know that won't happen," Kana replied after staring incredulously at Abe for a long moment.

"Then we have a problem," Abe said. "I want those cats, and you're going to give them to me whether you like it or not!"

The time for niceties had clearly passed.

Kana's base spell bloomed like a flower underneath Abe, and he quickly started drawing the next circles, but then Abe let out a disdainful sniff and flicked his fingers. The circles cracked and then shattered as if they were made of delicate glass.

"You have all this power at your fingertips, and that's all you can do?" Abe asked, his tone incredulous and mocking. "Give them to me. I can do so much more with their strength than you've ever dreamed!"

"They're not toys," Kana snapped out, hoping his angry tone hid his fear. No one had ever broken his circles so easily; not even Diana had been able to break free, and she was probably the most magically powerful person he had ever met. And Abe had barely flexed a finger muscle.

Fine, then. Even if Abe could break through his magic like it was tissue paper, Kana could still use it to stall for time. When the hunters arrived, they would hopefully be better prepared.

Kana's new circle had barely even begun to glow when Abe let out an exasperated sigh, and Kana's magic shattered again.

"Of course, they're not toys. They're magical conduits, just like demons. Familiars come from a different plane of existence than demons, a place with incredible magic, and once I have your cats, I'll be able to tap into that too. Shall we stop with the games, or are you not ready to give into the inevitable just yet? I suppose not," he added when he shattered Kana's third attempt with equal ease and an eye roll.

"You have polluted the very ground you stand on," Shannon suddenly said, his voice echoing through the forest from somewhere off to Kana's right. Kana didn't dare turn away from Abe to find Shannon, but he did glance down at the ground where Abe was standing.

Something twisted and blackened was planted into the ground by Abe's left foot. A second was near his right foot, and a third near his heel. In fact, now that Kana knew what to look for, the strange shapes completely encircled Abe.

"Trust a vampire to notice something dead," Abe said. He nonchalantly looked away from Kana, turning to face Shannon. "How do you like my ward? I only had to chop off the fingers of two demons to get enough to set up a proper bone ward."

No wonder Kana's spells weren't working! Abe wasn't overpowering Kana's magic with his own, the ward was preventing Kana's circles from setting properly. If the circles weren't grounded, a child could shatter them. Kana had absolutely zero idea how to overcome the ward though. Even creating a circle larger in size than the ward to attempt at encapsulating it wouldn't work; the circle itself might set, but the pentagram and any runes would have to overlap the ward and essentially be rendered inert by the contact.

There were circles without pentagrams, which Kana had been studying in his free time after his interest had been piqued the first time he went to the magic section of the local library and saw one in use. At the very least, Kana could set a basic one of those around the bone ward to prevent Abe from having an easy escape route.

The resulting circle looked sad; a simple thin line glowing on the ground about a foot in diameter wider than the bone ward. Abe saw it and immediately dismissed it with a disgusted sniff and an eye roll as he returned his attention to Shannon. Neither Shannon, Ember, nor Kana would have been stopped by such a sad and pathetic circle for more than a half second, and Kana guessed Abe wouldn't have any trouble with it either.

There had to be something Kana could do. Right now, Abe was just toying with them, and Kana had until Abe actually got serious to figure something out.

"I am merely being observant," Shannon replied. "I have set a few bone wards myself, although I never had the luxury of using demon bones."

"The high and mighty vampire has used something so base as a bone ward?" Abe asked, laughing, but Kana stopped listening to them.

Demon bones, he said to Mika and Sora. *To combat a demon, you need holy water.*

But it's not the holy water that actually hurts demons, Mika replied. *It's the belief the person imbuing the water has. If they believe the holy water will stop demons, that influences the spell they're incorporating into the water.*

Not that most of them know they're casting magic, Sora added with a disgusted sniff. Kana agreed with Sora and with Mika. When he was homeless he'd had one too many negative run-ins with religious organizations who preached love and tolerance and then callously threw him out when they learned he wasn't interested in ascribing to their very narrow set of beliefs. The belief whomever making the holy water had in the holy water working was what in turn created the spell that made it hurt demons. If Kana could find a way to recreate that same spell via writing runes in a circle, he might be able to disable the demon-bone ward.

Might, but that was better than nothing.

First, he had to figure out a way to draw a circle at all. The lines of his magic couldn't touch or cross the ward, which meant he had to draw something around the whole thing that could still somehow influence it. Kana counted quickly and saw twenty fingers planted grotesquely into the ground, which meant he needed twenty simultaneous spells.

Kana's simple, single circle was still glowing weakly, and it would work as an anchor and connector. He kept the magic hidden from view by drawing all twenty small circles underground. The top edge of each small circle intersected with the inside edge of the single larger circle until it looked like a beaded bracelet. Inside each small circle Kana drew the usual pentagram, but then he paused to think. The runes he chose had to be perfect. He would only get one chance to break the bone ward.

Protective intent, Mika repeated.

Kana drew the rune for shield and combined it with the one for shelter, creating a dual rune of protection, but then Kana paused as he thought of another idea. He set the protective rune on all twenty circles, then quickly drew a second combination rune, this time focusing on attack by interlocking fight and strength. He set the second rune on the circles and then focused on his crazy idea.

Drawing the rune for demon was hard. The lines and turns were complex, and it wasn't a rune Kana had any experience using before. Except, the last thing he wanted was to summon a demon. Instead of drawing perfectly straight lines, they wobbled and didn't quite connect. When he finished, the demon rune looked like a kindergartner's drawing in comparison to the rest of the circle. While it clearly read demon and would technically work, breaking it would be pathetically easy for anyone with a bit of power, which was the point.

Kana drew an intent line from the attack rune to the demon one, indicating when the spell started the attack rune should immediately destroy the demon. The rune would instantly shatter, but within that instance the demon rune ought to attract the demon bones and the attack spell would continue fighting the bone ward.

Twenty lines like the spokes of a wheel bloomed, one from each circle. Each line pointed directly at one of the finger bones, but Kana carefully stopped each line exactly a half inch from actually touching the ward.

He looked back at the circles and frowned. The protection rune wasn't redundant as is, but its purpose was limited. Kana couldn't leave it like that, even if adding more complexity was making him sweat. He carefully drew lines from each protective rune to tie it to the circle and pentagram, which would hopefully keep the bone ward from dismantling the circles before the attack rune finished its job.

Kana studied his circles one last time, looking for any imperfection or anything else he could add, but he didn't see anything.

Ready? he asked Mika and Sora as he threw open his magic channels to their fullest and started drawing in as much magic as he could. He was going to burn out the channels again, but if it broke the bone ward it would be worth it.

He looked up at the scene in front of him, but only a few seconds had actually passed. Shannon and Abe were still at a cold standoff, Ember hadn't moved from his protective position at Kana's side, and the bone ward still lay in an evil-tainted circle on the ground.

Let's do it! Sora said, his voice firm.

Kana threw his magic into the massive, combined circle. The forest lit up like a flood lantern had been turned on, but before Abe could retaliate, Kana compressed the circle. Twenty perfectly straight lines pierced the bone ward, reaching for the assigned fingers, and Kana activated the runes.

Shrieking echoed between the trees. High pitched, low pitched, full of agony, but the noise wasn't coming from anyone's mouths. Kana's individual circles had popped free of the single larger one and traveled down the line until they surrounded their assigned finger. The demon rune was gone, and in its place was a finger glowing with black fire. The fingers writhed as they burned, and the shrieking only got louder as Kana continued to pour magic into all the circles.

Something popped, like a firecracker going off. Then a second pop resounded, and a third, and suddenly three of the circles were no longer drawing power. A fourth popped, this time where Kana could see the bone finger literally explode into harmless dust within the confines of his circle. The fourth circle went dark, and Kana let it and the previous three go. Sixteen circles left.

"How dare you!" Kana thought he heard Abe yell, but it was hard to make out words when his ears were still resonating with the shrieks. Off to Kana's right, just visible in his peripheral vision, a shadow of some kind appeared, but Ember dashed after it with six more pops punctuating his departure.

Ten fingers left.

Kana's magic channels were throbbing with a fiery heat that said it was going to take much longer than a week to heal this time. He still didn't dare stop.

Pop. Pop. Pop.

Three more gone, and Kana let their circles fade with a groan of relief. *Pop.* Another one gone, and a grateful *pop* as the fifteenth finger vanished.

The shrieking was fading, as was the light. Kana heard his own panting breaths, two creatures growling, and Abe yelling something. Kana couldn't make out Abe's words, but one of the creatures growling had Ember's familiar timbre.

Kana gathered magic for one last push, thrusting it into the spell with a yell of his own. The last fingers exploded simultaneously with a massive bang, and Kana's spell fluttered away to nothing.

He couldn't feel his body, Kana distantly realized as his knees hit the ground. He managed to splay his hands to either side, which kept him from pitching face-first into the forest mulch, and all he could do was try to keep breathing.

Suddenly Shannon stepped into view, like a ghost appearing from thin air. His hands seemed to float autonomously through the air, easily passing through the space once protected by the ward. Abe's eyes barely had a chance to widen and then Shannon's hands landed on Abe's head, one under his jaw, the other behind his skull.

The twenty-first *pop* was somehow the loudest of all, as Shannon's wrists flicked and arms turned, and he broke Abe's neck.

Just like that, it was over.

Kana distantly thought he heard yelling and the cracking sounds as multiple rushing footsteps broke sticks and leaves, and then he blinked and the forest was abruptly full of people. Hunters, Kana's brain eventually supplied.

"Kana?" Ember's voice filtered through the white noise filling Kana's mind. The worried tone said he had called Kana's name multiple times.

Kana slowly turned his head, worried if he moved too fast the careful equilibrium keeping him upright would fail. Ember was on his knees at Kana's side. He was covered in blood, but he seemed to be more concerned with Kana than himself.

"No...magic," Kana forced out, his lips as numb as the rest of him.

"Okay," Ember said, sounding relieved that Kana had answered. "We'll get you some help. Mika and Sora are already asleep, if you want to join them."

That sounded like a wonderful idea, and as if just the thought imbued permission, Kana's eyes slid closed, and his body tipped. He was asleep before he hit the ground.

Chapter Eleven

THE FAMILIAR CEILING of the bedroom Kana shared with Ember swam blurrily into view. He blinked and the bland plaster and simple but elegant ceiling fan and overhead light snapped into focus. His body felt heavy, as if a weight was pressing him down into the bed, and Kana couldn't find the energy to turn his head and look around. Instead, he simply lay where he was.

Someone must have lowered the shades over the windows to darken the room, Kana thought, his brain still muzzy with sleep. *Or it was night?* But usually at night Ember would be in the bed next to Kana. All Kana could hear at the moment was the twin sets of mewling breaths that said Mika and Sora were asleep, curled together in their cat forms in the oversized cat tree over by the window. He couldn't hear any of Ember's familiar sounds.

Maybe it was night and something bad had happened? That thought sent a shot of adrenaline through his body, and suddenly the comfort of lying in one place turned into a light ache that said he had been lying in one spot for too long. Kana let out a soft whimper, but the weight holding his arms in place was too much to overcome, and his brief fight to sit up ended only a half second later.

The bedroom door flew open, and Ember rushed into the room.

"Kana!" he gasped. He stopped at Kana's side of the bed and reached out with one hand, but then snatched it back before he could touch. "How are you feeling?"

"Ember," Kana said, and the adrenaline faded away with the confirmation that Ember was safe.

Ember, liberally coated head to toe in blood as he fell to his knees at Kana's side.

Kana blinked, wondering why for a second that image had superimposed itself over the blood-free Ember standing next to the bed. No, Kana realized, not an image. A memory. A memory from the aftermath of a terrible battle, one in which Kana had overextended his magic past anything he had ever done before.

"You were bleeding," Kana said, wishing he could make his arm obey so he could reach out and touch Ember to ensure he was okay.

Ember grimaced. "Most of the blood wasn't mine. When you activated your spell, the warlock called on a number of summoned demons to stop you. Shannon and I had to fight them, and I got a little bloody."

"Most of the blood?" Kana asked, giving Ember as much of a pointed and worried look as he could while prone.

Ember laughed and started rolling up the sleeve on his right arm. "We could see your spell was working, but we also knew the second you broke the bone ward, the warlock would cast something else. I took on two demons at once while Shannon got into position, and one of the demons got me with its claws." Ember held out his bared arm for Kana to see.

A lurid, bright-red scar ran the length of the back of Ember's arm, from his wrist, up past his elbow, vanishing beneath where the sleeve was rolled around his bicep.

"I'm lucky it got the back of my arm. Doc says I would have bled out if it had been an inch in either direction. I'm a werewolf, so with my enhanced healing abilities it's already mended," he added and flexed his arm so Kana could see the smooth movement of muscle and bone under the marked skin. "But I'll probably always have a scar."

"I'm glad you're okay," Kana said, wishing again he could find the strength to lift his arm and run his fingers down that jagged red line to see for himself that Ember was healed. Still, Ember wouldn't lie to him about something so important. Kana forced his thoughts to refocus. "How long was I asleep?"

"Four days. Mika and Sora woke up briefly yesterday, but they didn't have the power to shift shapes. Since they didn't seem worried about you sleeping longer, I figured you must have really drained your magic."

Kana laughed. He didn't even bother reaching down his magic channels; he couldn't even feel a trickle of power coming through, which meant they were even more burnt than the last time.

"I've got nothing right now," he replied. The magic would return though. He was certain of that. What Kana didn't know was how long it would take him to heal. Probably a few weeks. "I'd prefer not to battle a warlock on my own ever again," he added.

This time, Ember laughed. "I'd prefer that too. Did you want to move out to the sitting room for a change of scenery?"

Kana wanted to move, but his energy was flagging, and he didn't think he could stay awake for the short journey to the other room.

"I—" Kana started but cut himself off when he couldn't think of how to describe the heavy feeling in his limbs and the wish that he could move and also the wish that he stay just like this.

Except Ember smiled his beautiful half grin. He kicked off his shoes and carefully climbed onto the bed and then gently tugged and pulled Kana over so Kana's head was resting on his shoulder and Kana's body was pressed down the length of Ember's. The heavy feeling from being in one spot for too long faded quickly, and the comfort of Ember's warmth and the protective strength in Ember's arms soothed the rest of Kana's battered body. He wanted to enjoy the feeling for a while, but instead, helplessly slipped back to sleep after only a few moments.

*

ANOTHER WEEK PASSED without Kana noticing much. Sometimes he would wake in bed, curled in Ember's arms. Other times Ember had moved him to the overstuffed couch in their sitting room, and he would wake there. A few times he woke alone, except he never really was alone because Mika and Sora were always nearby. Ember moved them around too, always ensuring they were in the same room as Kana and were as comfortable. Their mewling snores kept Kana company when Ember was called away.

Eventually the time Kana spent awake increased, and in those intervals, he began to have the strength to lift his arms to adjust the blanket or to run his fingers down Mika and Sora's backs. By the end of the second week, Ember would help him sit up with his back supported by pillows and the headboard, and Kana would spend an hour or two reading, often waking later with the book on the bedside table and himself tucked back in bed.

By the start of week three, Kana finally felt the first trickle of magic seeping through, pooling in the empty place inside of him from where he drew his power. Mika and Sora finally woke as well, but until Kana's channels recovered, he couldn't talk to them mind to mind and they didn't yet have the energy to change forms. However, with the return of magic also came a return of strength to his body. Kana could totter around the room by himself and switch between the bedroom and sitting room on his own.

Which was why Kana was already in the sitting room one afternoon, reading a spell book that had been on his to-read pile for longer than he wanted to admit, when Ember hurried inside.

"The witches have requested an audience," Ember said in explanation for his abrupt entrance. "They're at the front door now, and there's a really old lady with them. She smells…" he trailed off with a grimace. "She's powerful," he finally finished with a shrug that said he didn't know how to describe the scent he had picked up in words that Kana—with his human nose—would understand.

Kana put a bookmark in the book, closed it, and set it on the small table next to the couch, thinking hard. Why would the witches come here to see him, and why bring a very powerful witch along with them? Kana was healing, and it wouldn't be too much longer before he could return to normal activities. If they were patient, they would have plenty of opportunity to speak with him then. So why ask to see him right now?

"They came here, rather than asking me to go to their house, so even if the older witch is really strong, they know they're at a disadvantage," Kana said, trying to parse out the bigger picture. "Even if I can't cast any spells at the moment, they still won't be able to fight off an entire pack. I think they might have come simply to talk." At least, he hoped they had come only to talk.

"Do you want to see them?" Ember asked. "I can tell them you're sleeping."

And then Diana would either insist on waiting until he woke or would keep coming back every day until she saw him. "No, it's better to get it over with," he replied with a sigh. "Do I look presentable?" Given he was in pajamas and had only bathed the night before with Ember's help, he doubted it, but the witches would have to take him as is. If he went to clean up, he would use all his energy, and then he really would be sleeping.

Ember smiled and bent to press his lips against Kana's. Kana eagerly leaned into the kiss, and the welcome heat of Ember's body.

"You're perfect," Ember murmured as he pulled away, his voice husky in a way that reminded Kana just how long it had been since he was up to any athletics in bed. It would be a while more before he was up to that again, but Kana still reached up to cup the back of Ember's head and pull him back down to resume their kiss.

Kana didn't know how long had passed when Ember pulled away again. He ran his thumb just below Kana's lower lip, and it came away wet.

"I'll walk slowly," Ember said as he stood with a pointed glance down at where Kana's pajama pants tented. After a moment to adjust his own pants so they were more comfortable, he then took a couple of deep breaths before heading to the door.

Ember closed the door softly as he left, and Kana let out a heavy breath. He closed his eyes and leaned his head back against the couch cushion, trying to think unsexy thoughts, which was difficult when all he wanted was to chase after Ember, drag him back to their bedroom, and finish where that kiss had been leading. Instead, he rubbed his sleeve over his mouth to dry it and tried to focus on the witches he would be seeing in a few minutes.

"What do you think they want?" Kana asked. He opened his eyes and looked across the room to the armchair where Mika and Sora had been curled up together, but the chair was empty. An imperious *mew* sounded from near Kana's feet, and a second later Sora, followed by Mika, hopped onto the couch. Sora kept climbing until he could sprawl behind Kana's head on top of the couch's backrest, while Mika contented himself by curling up in Kana's lap.

Can't be too bad, if they're coming here. Mika's voice sounded like he was standing at the other end of a long tunnel, but Kana could actually hear him.

Ember will squash them if they try anything. I'm not worried, Sora added, his own voice just as distorted, yet such a wonderful thing to hear again after so long.

Kana reached behind to give Sora's chin a scritch and ran his other hand down Mika's back.

"I hope you're right," he replied with a sigh. He wished his magic would return to full strength sooner, but he could barely communicate with his familiars. Casting any magic was still beyond him, and the vulnerable feeling in the pit of his stomach was growing with every minute that passed. At least his hard-on had faded, although that definitely wasn't the sort of silver lining Kana usually looked for.

Thankfully he didn't have to wait and worry too much longer. Ember pushed the door open and walked inside but stood there while Diana and another young witch Kana didn't know helped an old woman through the door. They escorted her to the armchair, and once she was seated, the young witch stepped away to stand near the wall and Ember joined Kana at the couch, standing by the armrest. Diana turned to Kana.

"Hello, Kana," she said after scrutinizing him for a long moment.

Kana focused on her because something in the pit of his stomach was telling him to avoid looking at the old lady. "It's good to see you're doing better."

"Looks terrible," the old woman snapped out, and Kana automatically turned his head to look at her. Despite the thick wrinkles and bowed spine, she radiated authority. Her deep-set brown eyes were sharp with intelligence, and Kana didn't think she missed any aspect of how weak and helpless he was at the moment.

"This is Crone Hecate," Diana explained. "She traveled here from Salem to see you."

Hecate? Kana thought with a mental gasp as he fought to keep his face blank so his shock wouldn't show. According to the reading he had been doing about how the Salem coven was structured, Hecate was allegedly the most powerful witch in their circle.

"He's no Horned Lord," Hecate cut in, thankfully before Kana had to decide whether to reply to Diana with any niceties. "I've never heard of a man with power like his." She leaned forward to study him more. "He could very well be our absent Maiden Lucina, but he is male. I do not believe the more stringent members of our circle would accept him in that role."

"I'm not interested in joining your coven," Kana quickly cut in before the conversation could spiral away any faster. Him, Lucina? Ridiculous. He was a male witch with hunter parentage, which was why he was so strong. What would Hecate do, Kana couldn't help wondering, if she went out on a limb and declared him Lucina, and then two minutes later a baby girl was born to fill that spot in the coven.

Hecate laughed, a dry cackle. "You see, Diana? He can't be our Lucina. Perhaps he was meant to be Seattle's, but their blindness was their undoing."

"Kana can be the werewolf pack's instead," Diana added with a smile at Kana and Ember.

Hecate looked from Kana to where Ember was hovering protectively behind him and cackled again. "Yes, yes. Let the werewolves have him." She focused her attention back on Kana, her brown eyes piercing. "But, Kana, you are allowed to join our rights and holidays as a very welcome guest. Diana will be remaining in Albany for the foreseeable future, and she will see to it."

Hecate waited and Kana knew he wasn't going to be allowed to skip the niceties this time.

"I appreciate the offer and will gladly accept," Kana replied. He couldn't remember the last time he had celebrated any of the holidays properly, so it would be a nice change. Especially if he was only a guest at those events, rather than the pariah he had been in Seattle.

"Wonderful. I will be staying in Albany for a few more weeks to ensure the offshoot branch of our coven is settled properly. I hope to see you again before I return home."

Kana nodded. "Let us know when you're leaving, and I'll make sure to come visit before then." Hecate had welcomed him and accepted him for who he was as both a male witch and as Ember's lover. He refused to be rude to her after that.

"We will do that." Hecate turned to look at the young witch. "Help me up, Clara." Clara hurried over, and with Diana's help, they got Hecate to her feet. "Nice to meet you, Kana," Hecate finished with a nod.

Ember gave Kana a brief look before he hurried to get the door. He left, escorted the witches back out of the building, and returned a few minutes later.

"That went well," he said as he sat on the couch at Kana's side. Mika squirmed out from underneath Kana's hand and moved over to lie in Ember's lap.

"I think so," Kana agreed. "Sounds like the witches aren't a threat any longer."

Ember laughed. "More like the coven doesn't want you as their enemy. Lucina or not, you are incredibly powerful. Having you as their ally is more beneficial to them."

Kana sighed. "As long as it means there is peace in the city, I don't care." Kana didn't want to think about the witches any longer. That problem was done with as far as he was concerned. He was much more interested in resuming where their kiss had left off and exploring the limits of Kana's admittedly reduced endurance.

Kana reached out to gently grip Ember's hand, running his thumb along the tender skin of Ember's inner wrist. Ember's worried frown immediately faded, replaced with a heated smirk and fire in his eyes. He turned his hand to slide his fingers between Kana's and bent closer to kiss. Kana gladly met Ember halfway, giving everything of himself into their embrace and taking everything Ember gave in return.

Surrounded by the love of Ember, Mika, and Sora, and the love he felt for them, Kana eagerly went where this one instance would take them, knowing it was one wonderful moment of many more to come.

Epilogue

SORA SCAMPERED AHEAD of Kana, pushing open the door to Kana's witch room and vanishing inside. Mika was in his cat form, content to stay draped across Kana's shoulders. Kana followed Sora into the room but stopped short in the doorway to take it in again: the beautiful black chalkboard paint over every surface, the shelving along one wall for all his materials and books, and the cat tree in one corner—and not one speck of dust anywhere.

Kana hadn't been able to visit his witch room in the many weeks since fighting the warlock. Only in the last week and a half had he actually had the strength to leave the suite of rooms he shared with Ember, and he had only gone to the dining hall a couple of times in order to reassure the pack he was healing. He had also enjoyed the sense of normality going to get his food—rather than having someone deliver it to him—brought. Today, though, Kana felt strong enough to try a bit of magic and had come here instead.

His magic stores weren't back to 100 percent, but his magic channels were healed enough that Sora and Mika could shift into any form they liked, and Kana wanted to feel that final bit of normalcy by being a witch again.

And the room, despite his absence, was immaculate. But then, Ember did like to do little things like this for Kana. From building the room in the first place, to keeping it clean when Kana wasn't able, Ember always found surprisingly intimate ways of showing his love.

Sora brought over a fresh stick of white chalk and gave Mika a sharp look.

Fine, Mika said with a sigh. He hopped down from Kana's shoulders, and when his feet hit the ground, he was in human form. He went over to the shelves to pull down a smudge bowl. Sora vanished into the kitchen where the herbs were stored in Kana's pantry.

Kana left them to it and crouched in the center of the room. He touched the chalk to the floor and spun on the balls of his feet, a perfect circle forming around him. Kana switched his stance, and a few slashes of chalk formed the pentagram with exact angles. He hadn't lost his touch, and he grinned as he studied his work to find any imperfections. The runes for health and prosperity fit in the empty spaces on either side between the lines and the circle.

Witches weren't capable of healing, but this small spell would buoy him. Kana settled cross-legged in the middle of the circle. Mika placed the smudge bowl in front of him, and Sora dropped a small herb bundle into the bowl. They both shifted back into their cat forms and settled on either side of Kana within the circle. Kana placed his hands on their backs, let out a breath, and called on his magic.

The magic flowed a touch sluggishly, but it came, and the circle lit up, glowing softly in the dim room. Kana sent a breath of magic into the bowl, igniting the herbs. The light floral scent of lavender and chamomile filled the circle, mixing with the glow as the runes shone.

Kana kept the magic flowing as the herbs burned, breathing in the scented air and feeling the soft fur of Mika and Sora under his fingers. Once the scent began to fade as the herbs smoldered down to coals, Kana let the spell dissolve. The chalk was gone and the bowl empty, and when Kana let out another breath, he felt as if his lungs had opened up and a weight had lifted off his shoulders.

"Beautiful," Ember called.

Kana was too relaxed to jump in surprise, but he did turn to look and found Ember standing just inside the closed door. He must have come in while Kana was distracted.

"Feeling better?" Ember added, one of his lovely half smiles growing as he looked at Kana.

"Getting there," Kana replied with his own grin. "What's up?"

Ember walked farther into the room and held out a hand to help Kana climb to his feet. Kana took it, glad for the help. He grabbed his smudge bowl and put it away, and when he turned back to Ember, Sora was settling across the back of Ember's shoulders. Mika meowed pointedly at Kana, who laughed and picked Mika up so Mika could emulate Sora as Kana's neck warmer.

"I'm heading out to the other pack house for a few hours. Did you want to join me?" Ember asked.

A chance to get out of the house, even if it was only a short car ride straight to another house, sounded lovely.

"Let's go," Kana answered. He held out his hand again, and Ember took it. Hand in hand, with Mika and Sora purring contentedly, Kana and Ember left Kana's witch room, heading into the house and onward to wherever their lives would take them together.

About Mell Eight

When Mell Eight was in high school, she discovered dragons. Beautiful, wondrous creatures that took her on epic adventures both to faraway lands and on journeys of the heart. Mell wanted to create dragons of her own, so she put pen to paper. Mell Eight is now known for her own soaring dragons, as well as for other wonderful characters dancing across the pages of her books. While she mostly writes paranormal or fantasy stories, she has been seen exploring the real world once or twice.

Facebook

www.facebook.com/MellEightFiction

Twitter

www.twitter.com/MellEight

Website

www.melleightfiction.weebly.com

Threads

www.threads.net/@mell_eight

Tumblr

www.tumblr.com/blog/mell-eight

Instagram

www.instagram.com/mell_eight

Other NineStar books by this author

Witch's Circle Series

Coven

Hunter

Witch

Ge-Mi Series

Ge-Mi, Part One

Ge-Mi, Part Two

Oracle Series

The Oracle's Flame

The Oracle's Hatchling

The Oracle's Golem

The Oracle's Sprite

The Oracle's Prophecy

The Oracle's Current

Supernatural Consultant Series

Dragon Consultant

Dragon Deception

Dragon Dilemma

Dragon Detective

Dragon Soldier

Dragon Adventures

Dragon Lesson

Out of Underhill Series

Kelpie Blue

If a Butterfly Don't Fly

Magnified Series

Magnified

Justified

Dragon's Hoard Series

Finding the Wolf

Breaking the Shackles

Stealing the Dragon

Melting the Ice Witch

Road to... Series

Road to Revenge

Road to Home

Wizard Wars Series

Ground of Insurrection

Ground of Resurrection

Standalone Books

Elemental Ride

A Little Fairy Dust

Wounded Alpha

The Coup and the Prince

Space Stars

Water's Price

Twin Elements

www.ninestarpress.com

www.facebook.com/ninestarpress

www.facebook.com/groups/NineStarNiche

www.twitter.com/ninestarpress

www.instagram.com/ninestarpress